PRAISE FOR
MUD SEASON

"A riotous exploration of ambition, passion and greed, carried by concrete mixers and run through car washes, always with a keen eye on contemporary American folly."

—CHRISTOPHER SMITH, theater critic, *The Orange County Register*

"This hilarious novel within a novel showcases all the wit and brilliance long-time fans will remember from Jeff Kramer's humor columns. From the halls of publishing to small-town entrepreneurship, no one emerges unscathed, not even Woody, the bumbling but well-meaning hero of his own purple prose. A raucous satire of our times that is also an affecting study of family bonds and an acerbic tribute to the flawed, glorious, once-mighty dinosaur that was daily journalism."

—ANA MENENDEZ, critically acclaimed author of *In Cuba I Was a German Shepherd* and *The Apartment*, winner of the Pushcart Prize for short-story writing, award-winning *Miami Herald* columnist, and creative writing professor

"Jeff Kramer is still the funniest writer I know in real life. He somehow makes you root for a man who starts at rock bottom and begins digging. A painfully funny look at the death of newspapers and the birth of one man's midlife crisis."

—CHRISTOPHER FARNSWORTH, bestselling novelist, screenwriter, journalist, author of the *President's Vampire* and *Jesse Stone* series of novels

"With his uproarious novel *Mud Season*, Jeff Kramer delivers a laugh-out-loud satire, one which still manages to have compassion for its protagonist. Woody Hackworth is a writer by trade, but he is all of us by his foibles: vanity, delusion, pettiness, ambition, self-doubt. Anybody who has ever felt overlooked, resentful, or whiplashed by a mix of grandiosity and insecurity will relate to Woody. Kramer's dialogue is pitch perfect, each of his characters gleefully and hilariously delineated. They are the perfect foils and cheerleaders for Woody, most often bursting his bubble, sometimes filling it with hot air. The dialogue is real and sharp, never descending into sentimentality but still arousing the reader's emotion. Kramer uses a striking 'page-turner within a pager-turner' form to illuminate the mind of Woody Hackworth as he toggles back and forth between the drama in Woody's own life and the drama Woody creates on the page. Kramer's voice as Woody and his voice as Woody-as-author are distinct yet clearly belong to the same mind and ego. Brilliantly done. If you want a cathartic laugh at yourself, at others, and at the world, this book is a must."

—ALFREDO BOTELLO, author of the novels *Spin Cycle: Notes from a Reluctant Caregiver,* and *180 Days*

"Jeff Kramer's *Mud Season* is a razor-sharp, fast-talking ride that weaves pulpy crime caper through family drama. A veteran humorist at the top of his game, Kramer delivers laughs, heart, and soul while making you consider the modern twists of the traditional trade-offs between personal ambition and family obligation."

—THOMAS KOHNSTAMM, author of *Supersonic* and *Lake City*

"Jeff Kramer's *Mud Season* is a well-crafted story of a writer's professional and personal frustrations finding their way into his manuscript—with a number of problematic embellishments! The storyline and characters are well developed, allowing the reader to be drawn deeper into the plot step by step until he finds himself on a tightrope with the main character, Woody. *Mud Season* is a light, entertaining, and humorous read, which continues to draw the reader in page by page. Jeff Kramer is a skilled writer that will keep you guessing until the end. A great read!"

—MONIQUE TAYLOR, author of *Suicide Jockeys: The Making of the WWII Glider Pilot*

"Woody Hackworth, *Mud Season*'s endearing protagonist, comes at us in a hall of mirrors, bouncing awkwardly between his luckless reality as an out-of-work reporter and the world inhabited by his grandiose fictional alter ego. The villains in his environmental potboiler lead his readers to confuse them with Woody's real-life in-laws. What could possibly go wrong? Everything! Kramer's deft hand at dialogue turns scene after scene into the kind of hilarity we are promised in other works of satire but rarely get."

—TOM MORONEY, former Bloomberg News managing editor in Boston and radio host

"An immensely entertaining novel within a novel. Atwood (Woody) Hackworth, the antihero, is a hapless unemployed journalist of dubious talent who sets out to write the great American novel. But when Woody's fiction too closely resembles real life, he alienates his wife, his daughter, and every member of his extended family. Woody's obsession with literary acclaim leads him on a hilarious, twisting path where he finds something he cherishes even more than fame—redemption. A wry tale filled with razor-sharp wit and just the right amount of heart."

—BILL BURKLAND, author of *The Misconceived Conception of a Baby Named Jesus*

Mud Season

by Jeff Kramer

ISBN 979-8-88824-649-8

Cover art and design by Lauren Sheldon

Published by

köehlerbooks™

3705 Shore Drive
Virginia Beach, VA 23455
800-435-4811
www.koehlerbooks.com

MUD SEASON

A NOVEL

JEFF KRAMER

VIRGINIA BEACH
CAPE CHARLES

For my wife, Leigh, a lover of fiction whose devotion to this project made it possible

CHAPTER 1
THE NAMING

Atwood "Woody" Hackworth will show them all. His wife. His wife's family. His journalism pal who went global, leaving Woody to twaddle in the polar recesses of their profession.

He'll show the two-faced editors at the dying Icarus *Blaze*—the ones who canned him last year for making up a source, which he absolutely hadn't done, at least not on purpose.

The star reporter who had been leading him on for years? He doesn't need to show her anything. He couldn't care less about her anymore, not since he overheard her and another female reporter in the cafeteria of the 107-year-old daily speculating about his connubial prowess.

"What do you think Mandy sees in him?"

"Maybe he's great between the sheets."

"The Wood Man? Ya think?"

"Naw. I bet he's like his writing—mechanical, short, and quickly forgotten."

On second thought, he'll show her, too.

"We'll see who's forgettable, Celeste," he murmurs as he drives to the hardware store.

What stung most about being let go was knowing he'd never write the stories on his checklist. Blowing the lid off the state's corrupt maple syrup grading program would have been huge. He was also going to expose the financially pressed Icarus Symphony for secretly piping in recorded tuba parts to augment its thin lower brass section. A disgruntled violist had been talking off the record—now all for naught.

He guns the Lexus through the wintry mix, navigates around an oatmeal-colored slush pile, and pulls into the left-turn lane. He avoids eye contact with a grizzled, ponytailed panhandler in the median sawing on a worn fiddle. Yet it's hard to turn away. The man, all angles in his tattered jeans and flannel coat, looks about thirty. He's lanky and light on his feet, the bow flashing into a concrete-gray sky. Woody's thoughts skip from curious to compassionate then back to the matter at hand: his resurrection.

In time, they'll all see how wrong they were. Woody's destiny is literary acclaim, not playing out the string in a gasping industry or taking a token job in the marketing department of his father-in-law's powerhouse company, Dunn-Rite Dig & Demo.

Woody Hackworth will write a novel, a great one, one that is three hundred pages or longer and not padded by oversized print. And it will be commercially successful—perhaps even a Netflix adaptation—yet of undeniable critical merit. It will showcase Woody's distinctive prosaic stylings as well as his penetrating Weltanschauung. Readers may even hear echoes of Proust and Joyce. (He makes a mental note to read some of their works.)

The best part will be shoving it straight up the asses of those gutless agents who passed on his first stab at fiction, *Tick Tock, Check Your Sock.*

Why anyone with a brain would reject a ninety-three-page psychological thriller about a deranged entomologist who weaponizes an army of mutant ticks carrying Ebola makes no sense. *There's no logic in publishing anymore,* Woody thinks. *But what's the point of dwelling on the stupidity of others?*

A scratchy rendition of "Camptown Races" distracts Woody,

prompting him to realize a back window isn't shut tight. He takes care of that, noting a look of smug virtuosity on the fiddler's face, as if he's channeling Jascha Heifetz.

Woody just needs an idea, he assures himself—a plot, some characters, et cetera. It will all come together just as surely as mud season—the season of slop—yields to blossoms and birdsong. Mud season is a time of transition, and transitions are hard but necessary.

"Light's green, asshole!" the fiddler shouts.

Rattled, Woody punches the gas then slams on the brakes to avoid a rear-ender. The car in front of him hasn't moved. The light is still red. Woody turns to see Heifetz howling with glee.

"Get a job!" the out-of-work scribe yells, belatedly aware of the irony.

At the hardware store, the many sizes and shapes of lightbulbs confound Woody. He's looking for one that fits the foyer sconce. Mandy had handed him a sticky note with the correct bulb size, but he'd left it on the kitchen counter. He makes his best guess and heads for home but not before grabbing a pair of emergency window breaker escape tools he spots in a discount bin. Mandy and Ella, their high school junior, should keep one in their cars, just in case. Up here, mud season can also be flood season.

To Woody's amazement, the lightbulb works. An omen. His fortunes are changing already—fortune backed by immense talent. After all, Woody is no stranger to creative writing success.

In third grade, his teacher Mrs. Throckmorton submitted his short story, "The Magic Waffle," to a countywide contest. It won second place, although the judging panel had been fooled. The judges thought "The Magic Waffle" was a precocious satire about a vacillating politician. In fact, Woody's story was an exercise in one dimensionality, detailing the life of a toaster waffle that could do magic tricks.

Later in life, Woody would credit his subconscious for embedding powerful subliminal ideas into "The Magic Waffle," but as a kid he was focused on the $25 consolation prize, which was matched by his proud parents. At age eight, Atwood Hackworth was a professional writer—plus there was ice cream in the deal, no matter that on that early May day in Buffalo it was spitting snow.

"Looks like we have another Shakespeare on our hands," his father pronounced.

"Another Margaret Atwood," his mother, Elsa, corrected.

Canadian by birth and a voracious consumer of fiction, Elsa was a fan of the accomplished novelist from her hometown of Ottawa long before Margaret Atwood hit it big. If Woody had been a girl, his name would have been Margaret, but out popped a caterwauling, brown-haired, seven-pound, seven-ounce boy. So, Atwood it was, an understated tribute to an author of limited renown at the time.

The understated part changed in 1986 as *The Handmaid's Tale* became a thing. A well-meaning English teacher asked Woody in front of the class if he knew he shared a name with a famous author. Woody had said yes, thinking nothing of it. But word got out. The next day, a bully two years older shoved young Atwood against a row of lockers and asserted, not incorrectly, "You're named after a girl!" A bracing nipple tweak emphasized the point.

From that day on, Atwood preferred to be known as "Woody," although that came with its own burden. Buffalo's Millard Fillmore Middle School often resounded with shouts of "Woody's got a woody."

"At least I can get one," Woody learned to reply.

But for all its annoyances, the name was incentive to write.

Now, with his successful hardware venture complete, he draws motivation from his favorite Peloton instructor. As he spins in place, fixating on her neon-green halter top and impressive cleavage, a plot begins forming in his mind: A passionate and courageous local journalist (loosely based on Woody) will investigate an illegal waste dumping operation and discover that his wife's family's business is behind the crime. That will not stop him from pursuing the story. Rather, it will embolden him. Woody's alter ego will possess a journalistic ethic so pure he will keep digging even if the price is loss of domestic harmony and, quite possibly, his life.

Nefarious dumping of body parts, even whole corpses, should be part of the deal. *Readers love that shit,* Woody thinks. Maybe it's not what Proust would do, but a few concessions to modern sensibilities will only broaden the appeal of his deeper truths, whatever they are.

Woody spins into the heart of his workout, but he remains focused on his book. Amidst the giddy rush of artistic genesis, a tickle of apprehension arises. Is his plot edging too close to home? A reporter investigating his relatives' construction business in a small Upstate city isn't exactly a creative reach given Woody's circumstances.

See, he scolds himself. *I'm doing it again—overthinking.*

He just needs to portray the scumbag fictional in-laws in a way that bears no resemblance to his actual in-laws and their stellar excavation/demolition empire. Woody knows he has the skill—at least suspects he does—to build in the necessary distance. It's all part of The Process of being a writer. The best fiction demands a healthy separation from the novelist, or it ceases to be fiction. Those boundaries must be observed and celebrated.

So, whereas Woody's real-life in-laws are widely liked and respected throughout Greater Icarus, a Rust Belt city of 150,000 at the corner of Rundown and Revitalized, the fictionalized in-laws will be grotesque studies in evil. Should he make them Italian? No. That would be a cliché. It's also out of his comfort zone. He doesn't really know that world beyond the *Godfather* movies and the Pacino remake of *Scarface.* He'll be on firmer ground if he makes them some other sinister-sounding Mediterranean ethnicity. Slovenian maybe. Sure. Why not?

Woody is proud of himself. He jumps off the bike before the cooldown ends, stopping to admire the instructor, who is slowly extending her arms over her head. She winks at Woody (and 2,211 other riders) and tells him he's amazing and that she is "honored" to be part of his "journey to greatness!"

"You came and you conquered, and you have only just begun!" she exhorts.

Woody catches his reflection in a hallway mirror. He's no Ryan Gosling, but he'll do. He declares himself a six-footer on his driver's license, but he's five foot eleven and change. The sandy mop has thinned slightly on top but gives no ground on the front lines, even advancing between haircuts toward notable eyebrows, which curdle in concentration and jump in surprise. His "emotibrows," as a girlfriend once dubbed them, lend intensity to an owlish, contemplative visage.

Woody could lose fifteen pounds and still not be confused for an underwear model. But he's handsome in a generic way, and he can pass for a man five years younger. When present, he moves with an athlete's ease and purpose. But when he's in his head, as is often the case, he evinces the befuddled, put-upon posture of a man whose connecting flight was just canceled.

That night, undoing any salutary Peloton class gains over beers with his childhood pal JB, Woody unspools the nascent plot, which by then has evolved. The corrupt business of the fictional in-laws will be a successful Upstate sand and gravel operation with the largest fleet of concrete mixer trucks within one hundred miles.

Woody spent the summer before college assisting an independent cement mason, so he knows a few of their dark secrets. He hated the job, the way the lye burned his clothes and his skin and how the mud—as it was known in the industry—had to be poured quickly into wooden forms before it hardened into a costly mess that could only be undone by a "breaker," a hydraulic jackhammer attached to an excavator.

Once, Woody had knocked a half bucket of roof cement onto a customer's driveway. When he climbed down at the end of the day, he was greeted by a two-foot-long spill that had hardened into the unmistakable shape of a penis.

"Real-world knowledge like that is what elevates the best fiction," Woody explains to JB. "Hemingway understood this."

"The only thing I ever read of Hemingway's is *The Great Gatsby*," JB says.

Woody pretends he didn't hear that and keeps going.

"All those mixer trucks will be illegally dumping not only toxic waste from their company but doing it for other businesses all over town," Woody gushes. "Even the hospital. Shit, maybe even the newspaper."

Whatever his literary blind spots, JB's a tough-minded entrepreneur who spent his first five years out of high school digging graves at Montridge Cemetery to sock away money to fund his dream of opening a bar. He's not some fey intellectual doofus, which makes him ideal as a one-man test market for Woody's concept.

"I'm envious, Wood Man," JB says. "I couldn't write made-up shit like that if my life depended on it."

"It's just how we novelists work," Woody explains. "We take wisps of reality and spin them into parallel worlds."

"Just like you did with 'The Magic Waffle,'" JB says.

Woody, suddenly self-conscious, wonders why he's discussing his book with a noncreative who has a two-year degree in hospitality management from Monohawkwa Community College.

Not that JB hasn't done well for himself. Twenty years ago, he'd acted on his dream and then some, opening a combo laundromat/chicken wing bar called Cluckin' Clean. The concept worked. Upstate now boasts seven Cluckin' Cleans plus a new one across the state line in Erie.

Unmentioned in this meeting is that JB brings home more in quarters every month than Woody's best year as a senior reporter at the *Blaze*. Even that sum was six grand less than what three less-accomplished colleagues were earning, based on a payroll ledger carelessly left in a printer by a section editor.

Woody isn't jealous of his friend. Vexed, yes, but not jealous. Props to JB for identifying a nexus between clean clothes and clogged arteries. But upon reflection, maybe it wasn't a great idea to bring him into The Process this early. What does JB know of Art?

"So let me get this straight," JB says. "You're writing a book that fucks over your in-laws? Only you're making their business cement instead of excavation and demo? You've got stones, dude." He raises his glass and tips it toward Woody.

A clot of pub cheese bobs in Woody's gut. His cheeks burn. He takes a swig of ice water. "It's not about them," he insists, striving for nonchalance but hearing defensive. "If my main character is married, he's going to have in-laws. That doesn't make them *my* in-laws." He bites down on an ice cube and crunches it into nothingness.

"Whatever. I'm just busting your balls," JB says. "You'll figure it out. What's the title?"

"Still deciding. By the way, it's concrete, not cement. Cement is an ingredient in concrete."

A thirtyish redhead approaches. It's Celeste Henry, the *Blaze*'s prolific investigative reporter.

"Hey, Woody," she says, "what brings you to this side of town?"

His grudge wilts in her presence. He hates himself for being thrilled to see her.

"Just drinking away my severance."

"Wait, you're the Cluckin' Clean guy, right?" Celeste brightly inquires, recognizing JB.

"Cluck, yeah," JB replies. "The one and only."

"Your commercials are great. But I have to confess—I've never been to a Cluckin' Clean."

"Our loss," JB says, taking in her curves. "But you're missing quite the experience."

"'Suds, spuds, wings, and buds!'" Celeste quotes.

"It makes my heart happy that you know our slogan. Now you just need to take that next step."

In one smooth gesture, he reaches into his shirt pocket and hands her a drink chip. "Have a cocktail on me. Good at any of our eight locations." He winks.

"Thanks. Okay, I'll go, promise. My boyfriend does the laundry most of the time, but I can bring in a comforter or something unwieldy we can't handle at home."

"Going big out of the gate. I like it. We have six new LG heavy-duty commercial bad boys at our Clifton Avenue location. They're monsters."

"Oh, by the way, I'm Celeste Henry," she says, extending a hand. "I used to work with Woody."

"Charmed." JB takes her hand.

Woody smiles limply.

"And I'm JB Seniac. Nice to meet you, Celeste. I've read your stuff. You're good."

"Thanks. Hey, something I've always wondered—do people ever accidentally get wing sauce on their freshly laundered clothes and have to redo their wash? Or is that the whole point?"

They laugh louder than the inquiry warrants.

"Funny you should ask," JB says, launching into a story, but Woody isn't listening anymore. He watches a bubble of Blue Light rise in his glass and tracks it until it is subsumed into the watery head. How he desperately wants the same for himself, to rise from oblivion and become part of something bigger—the literati. It will happen, he vows. Celeste will be one more name on a long list of people who underestimated him. She usually had great instincts for a story, but in this instance, she was clueless that a much bigger story than the founder of Fuckin' Clean was sitting at the bar.

The next morning, nursing a proper authorial headache as he scrambles a pan of egg whites, Woody finds himself fixating on JB's thumbnail description of his book. He assures himself that JB was full of shit. The book will absolutely not be about Mandy's family. One key distinction is that his real in-laws are generous. His mother-in-law, Bev, for example, just gave him a signed first edition of Seymour Hersh's *Reporter: A Memoir* for his birthday, a lovely gift, although he could have done without the notation scrawled inside the cover: "May this book inspire you to new heights worthy of your own memoir someday!"

On multiple occasions, Woody's father-in-law has invited him with his two sons on fishing junkets paid in full by the distributor of the heavy equipment that is the lifeblood of Dunn-Rite. The trip to Norway had been a blast. Over tumblers of aquavit after a particularly good day of salmon fishing, Joe had bestowed his stamp of approval on Woody's life choices. "You do good work at the *Blaze*," Joe told him. "They pay you peanuts, but you're doing something you enjoy. There's a lot to be said for that. I'm fucking proud of you."

"Just don't ever investigate Dunn-Rite," Cameron, the older boy, had joked. "That could get dicey."

"No shit," Joe Dunn had said. "We have ways of dealing with troublemakers."

"Come on, Dad," Tanner, the younger brother, interjected. "He's married to your daughter. You wouldn't lay a hand on our boy Woody."

"Not a hand," Joe responded, "but maybe a Komatsu bell crank."

It was all in good fun. Joe could talk a tough game. Excavation and demolition, after all, was a tough business. But Dunn-Rite was clean. Taxes were paid on time and in full, and messy entanglements with unsavory contractors were avoided. The company coddled its customers, who, in turn, repaid Dunn-Rite with pangenerational fealty. Dunn-Rite's success had been profiled in glossy trade magazines and even in the *Blaze*'s crimped business section. Beneath Joe's gruff jousting was humility, decency, and calm. He refused to bid on any job connected to the biggest commercial real estate developer in the county, Panther Peak Corporation, due to its owner's sleazy reputation. The decision had cost Joe millions but spared him untold stress and court costs.

"I like to be able to sleep at night," he was fond of saying.

Tanner was the same age as Woody. They shared a love of ZZ Top and AC/DC and the hapless Buffalo Sabres. Tanner had raised his glass of aquavit for a toast.

"You're one of us, like it or not, Woody. If you ever want to put down that notepad and start doing real work, we'll get you trained on the dragline excavator in a week."

"Thanks—I think," Woody had demurred against the backdrop of a darkening fjord.

Alas, all that jolly verbal grab-ass now seems ironic following Newsroom Purge No. 6 of the new millennium. Woody has, indeed, put down his notepad, but not by choice. He left the *Blaze* with fifteen other click-stained wretches eleven months earlier, taking a buyout that consisted of one year's salary plus credit for five unused vacation days. Joe and Bev had been supportive. Not only did his in-laws offer him work on Dunn-Rite's marketing team, but they'd canceled their thirty-two-year home subscription to the *Blaze* in protest. (Joe quietly kept it coming to the office. After all, a businessman needs to stay informed.)

Woody tells everyone that he chose to leave, but no one believes it, not even Woody. His untimely exit has been a blow to the ego and his illusion of self-sufficiency.

"You do good work; you just make too much money," an editor from a rival cost center told Woody in confidence that awful day.

"Did good work," Woody replied.

"Well, at least from how it sounds, you weren't canned for making shit up. Were you?"

"I never made up anything."

Still, Woody is luckier than the other castoffs. A steady influx of money from Mandy's family, no questions asked, continues as always. It isn't just a cushion. It's a gilded daybed. There's money to spare for a bathroom remodel, a vacation home in the Adirondacks, and Ella's East and West Coast college tours. Woody is grateful as hell but also at emotional arm's length from his good fortune. He knows money corrupts. That's what they taught him in journalism school at the University of Connecticut Stamford. He knows it's true because money has corrupted the natural arc of his Woodyness. In unemployment, he feels even more acutely the muddled blessing of his matrimonial jackpot, how it short-circuited what might have been, distorting his dreams and tamping his ambitions. Without Dunn-Rite, does he cultivate a taste for Wagyu tenderloin and hundred-dollar bottles of pinot noir? Does he suffer from gout? Would he have not gone slumming at a third-rate rag like the *Blaze* and instead risen to higher ground with greater income, job security, and prestige?

The whole thing is emasculating, really. After he was let go, Ella, then a sophomore, had asked him, "Would I have to go to a state school if it wasn't for Grandpa?"

But who argues with found money? Besides, he is not the first writer to be subsidized by family wealth. He once did a quick online search for "famous writers" and "family money" and hit on Montesquieu, Tocqueville, Keynes, Schopenhauer, Hegel, Freud, Darwin, Huxley, and Melville. Woody's in good company.

Still, the underlying insecurity persists. It comes up during his travels when he's asked where he went to school and answers "Stamford," saying it fast enough for the casual listener to infer a Palo Alto pedigree.

Woody returns to the present. With coffee and Tylenol clearing his head and the egg whites edging toward doneness, he grates in some Havarti. He believes Havarti is underappreciated, like he is. The cheese melts in quickly, and Woody shuts off the heat. A line cook at a diner once gave him a great tip: Undercook scrambled eggs a little because they continue cooking on their own. That, he thinks, is one of those details that might find itself into his novel somehow. Readers love access to privileged information.

As he eats his breakfast alone, he resolves to commit to writing every day and to drink less. Hemingway rigor, minus the booze. Not minus all of it, but much of it. He wouldn't mind a Bloody Mary about now, but before he can act on that, he hears Mandy approaching the base of the stairs by the front door.

"Bye, hon. Don't forget to start the crockpot at three," she calls out. "The cutlets are in the sauce already, in the bowl with the red lid. Remember to stir it after the first two hours."

"Got it," Woody says, adding, "Ms. Dunn," in an inaudible murmur.

Soon after their engagement, there'd been an ugly fight about her unwillingness to become a Hackworth.

"I just like my name, for God's sake. How's that a threat to your masculinity?"

But these days, quarrels were rare. Money, a source of conflict in so many marriages, wasn't an aggravating factor. The pink window breaker escape tools had been a hit. Mandy had teased Woody about being paranoid but feted him for his thoughtfulness. Ella had half-joked that the seatbelt cutting tool would be perfect for grinding bud at parties. Woody enjoyed the ribbing and encouraged it by playing the stern, safety-conscious patriarch.

"I suspect the two of you would be less cavalier if you were underwater in the Erie Canal hanging upside down," he'd lectured in his father-knows-best voice. "May you never have the misfortune to find out."

Now, he hears the door close behind Mandy as she leaves for her six-figure job as a strategic planning officer at Mid-State Hospital Group.

This is the time of day Woody loves most. Ella's at school, and Career Girl is out there asserting her primacy in hospital finance. He has space to think and eat his egg whites. Later, he plods into the basement fitness studio to prepare his mind and body for the great task ahead. As he rides his $2,000 stationary bike, his mind races. Mid-State has the only Level 1 Trauma Center within a hundred miles. At least one of his characters, possibly the protagonist, should end up there as a patient. *A poisoning victim, perhaps? Also, the hospital needs to be doing some illegal dumping. A hospital of horrors.*

By the end of the thirty-minute Funk & Fat Burn class, Woody is pumped with authorial adrenaline. He jumps off the bike before the cooldown ends, grabs a yellow legal pad from his desk, and scribbles, "Trauma Center. Poison. ER doc in on dumping, too? Important: Make wife's job nonmedical."

Woody spends the next week working on an outline and trying to settle on a name for his main character. He likes Noah—a righteous guardian saving the world from a malevolent deluge seems apt—but he worries its biblical connotations promise more than he can deliver. He moves on to Walt. He loves its stolid, old-time ring. But then he remembers Walt from *Breaking Bad*. Best to leave that alone.

For a good thirty-six hours, he's convinced he's going with Will Pickton, which suggests strength, determination, and mining (with a pick) for truth. But a Google search reveals Robert Williams "Willy" Pickton was a proficient Canadian serial killer. The setback puts Woody into a brief funk, which he self-medicates with Oreos. How dare polite, friendly Canada have serial killers? Writing is hard.

Finally, while sharing a flan with Mandy at Geppetto's Table, the right name comes to him: Custer Stanton. The Process is like that. It kicks in automatically if you trust it. Woody's Process goes as follows: *Flan. Flanman. Stan Flanman. Stan Flanson. Stan Pudding—Puddington. Stan Brûlée? Ken Brûlée? Too cute. What about custard? Stan Custardo. Custardman. Custerson. Custerham. Custer's Last Stand. Custer Stanton.*

"Holy Shit! That's it! Custer Stanton!"

"Great name," Mandy assures Woody, desperate to switch topics. "Maybe now you can actually start writing."

"It's time for me to start writing," Woody says.

"I just said that."

"I know," Woody lies. "I was just agreeing with you."

CHAPTER 2
NOT REALLY AN AFFAIR

At 9:24 the following morning, he begins, sort of. First, he needs to come up with another name, this one for the fictional city that will serve as the backdrop of his novel. He wants to mirror Icarus, so a Greek or Roman moniker is a must. Woody has always been amused by the contrast between the grandiosity of Upstate place names and the downtrodden reality of so many of the towns themselves. The communities were founded during the neoclassical era at a time of great reverence for Greco-Roman culture, but to Woody, they're a postmodern study in irony. He settles on the name Tiberius, the second Roman emperor. He knows nothing about him, but that doesn't matter. He can always round back to him later in the book. For now, he just likes the way it sounds. *Ti-beer-ee-us.* How can subliminally introducing beer into a novel ever be a bad idea? And so, he begins for real:

Fear as Mud

A Novel by Woody Hackworth

It wasn't a particularly stormy night, but it was definitely dark, dark as the ink drying on the latest scoop of the best all-around reporter at the *Tiberius Daily Informer*. Custer Stanton, almost six foot five with the engaging manner of a more handsome Tom

Selleck, minus the mustache, felt good about his story. The next day, readers would learn of a slight but real spike in benzene levels in Lake Ranswill.

That in itself would not send the populace into a panic. Lake Ranswill was already the most polluted urban lake in America, a stew of heavy metals left by defense contractors and other industrial predators. There were also phosphates from fertilizer runoff and oxymoronic "liquefied solid waste," courtesy of the city's ancient wood-piped sewer system. Forget swimming. The city's inhabitants could only ambulate or pedal around the lake and wonder "What if?" Some winters the lake froze over, but increasingly throughout the year it was possible to spot a blue heron swooping down to snare a mercury-deformed perch or sunfish.

Despite the civic ennui toward Lake Ranswill, Cus (he reserved Custer for his byline) was activated, his finely honed instincts aquiver. This benzine story was just the first strand of a far larger ball of evil—he knew it in his bones. It would take some ruffling and plucking of feathers to expose the truth. Nothing wrong with that.

Pissing off people, speaking truth to power, was all part of the job. But what exactly was going on?

One of Cus's favorite Ayn Rand quotes popped into his head: "The truth is not for all men, but only for those who seek it."

And so Cus sought, driven by a powerful, invisible force to hunt the truth. He was a self-made, award-winning investigative journalist, impeccably sourced and tireless.

You could make a solid case that the *Daily Informer* didn't deserve him. Hell, it wasn't even a daily anymore since home delivery had been cut to three days a week. But Cus was no mercenary, never one to cast resumés to the winds in pursuit of more money and status. He had grown up in Tiberius, the son of a foundry worker and a nurse. He was tough, honest, and independent minded. He had worked his way through SUNY

Colton-Ashburgh doing everything from roasting coffee beans to laying carpet. He'd spent two years in Africa with a team digging wells, and he'd traveled to every continent except Antarctica. He'd gotten stabbed in the arm by a drunk in a bar fight in Wales, but the paramedics spent more time working on the assailant, whom Cus had decked with a left cross to the temple. Once things quieted down, he paid the guy's bar tab.

But for all his foreign adventures, Cus, at heart, was a homie. He cared deeply about the faded manufacturing town and its rustic surroundings. He knew its soul, and soul mattered, which is why he minored in philosophy. Yes, Tiberius had more than its share of faults, but to Cus they were character marks. Much like Jenny, his high school sweetheart and now wife of eighteen years, the town could come off as distant and dull. But shift the illumination a few degrees and an inner beauty revealed itself, like when they test you for colorblindness and the number six pops out in a multicolored field.

It was no coincidence that his affection for Tiberius had a green tint. A DNA test had revealed him to be one-sixteenth Mohawk. Cus was one with the land.

And the one man that illegal dumpers should fear most.

Tomorrow, he'd check a few databases to see which manufacturers along an industrialized half mile of Seneca Creek might be dumping or leaking benzines, which he knew to be a frequent component of solvents. It wasn't much of a lead, but it was a start.

Cus had uncovered all manner of local scandals: pay-to-play schemes, bid rigging, medical malpractice, chronic neglect at senior care facilities, and construction kickbacks. But the stories that revved his engine the most contained an environmental angle. Woe to those who befouled the air, the remaining stands of thick woods beyond town, or the fragile watershed. Someone was going to end up paying a serious fine, or worse. Cus would see to that.

He was so deep in thought that he was scarcely aware of his commute home. When he pulled into his driveway, he was thinking of one of his favorite Mohawk proverbs: "From a grain of sand to a great mountain, all is sacred."

He found Jenny in the kitchen. Despite her gathering adipose, Cus still found her beautiful, with her dark-brown hair, compact build, and keen eyes handed down from her late Slovenian grandmother, Zala. Yes, they'd had their share of fights, but Cus loved Jenny. He loved less the buckwheat dumplings she occasionally made from Zala's ancient recipe, but he always asked for seconds.

In contrast to his impassioned workaholism, she worked regular hours, eight to four, at her father's company, the largest sand and gravel operation on the I-81 corridor between Pennsylvania and Canada. Her title was chief financial officer, but she did a little of everything. She even kept her commercial driver's license valid so she could climb behind the wheel of a mixer truck if a regular driver was out sick or suspended following a wreck or DUI. The company, Cold Harbor Concrete, had a decent reputation, and with Jenny overseeing the books, Cus trusted their work was above board. Jenny's dad, Al Holmes, wasn't pristine by any means. What he dismissed as a "youthful indiscretion"—tax evasion—had long ago, before Jenny arrived, earned him a $100,000 fine and ninety days in a low-security prison.

"Whoever that guy was, he fucked up," Al Holmes would occasionally say with a shrug, as if the ex-con bore no connection to the callow offender.

Cold Harbor was a reliable supplier of concrete for the boomlets of growth in and around the city. The company's safety record had improved through the years, although long-timers still remembered when a Cold Harbor mixer truck, fully loaded, lost its brakes on Herring Hill and took out the dining room (miraculously empty) at Parson's Landing. Mud happens.

Al was generous to local causes, including the Boys & Girls Club, The Marco Bruno Children's Hospital—named after another white-collar criminal in need of an image upgrade—and the local homeless shelter.

During dinner that night, Jenny sounded unusually interested in the benzine mystery. That was a good sign. She was no thinker of deep thoughts, but there was a feral sharpness to her. Cus took her interest as evidence that his story was a grabber.

"Maybe it was just an accidental spill," she offered.

"Either way, the culprit needs to be exposed and prosecuted," Cus said.

"Absolutely," Jenny agreed. Cus thought he caught something off in her tone, but he dismissed it as she continued, "Just out of curiosity, how bad are the fines for that kind of thing?"

"Depends," Cus answered. "Anywhere from the cost of the cleanup to hundreds of thousands of dollars."

"That's all?" she said, eyeing the hunk of lasagna on her fork.

The couple had no children. It was more her decision than his. Jenny's mother, Vivian, had self-medicated with pills and booze through much of Jenny's childhood, never in a dramatic or overtly abusive way, but benign neglect hurt, too.

Jenny and her younger sister, Kara, had practically grown up at a friend's house, which was fine with Viv. She had more important people to see than her kids, parties to attend, and delivery boys to seduce. She viewed her dalliances as strictly recreation, not adultery with a capital "A." She was devoted to Al, or as devoted as her icy heart would permit. Her daughters got the frosty remnants. Once, when Jenny was barely five, she had asked her mother who she loved more, Daddy or her and her sister. Vivian, two martinis into a croquet match with a friend, replied, "Daddy. Because without him I wouldn't have you."

It would have been the perfect answer if Vivian's croquet partner had not blurted, "Pending a paternity test."

"Shh," Viv had said, and the two women cackled like witches. Jenny had slunk off not understanding what was said but not liking the sound of it.

Small wonder that growing up as Al and Vivian's daughter would cause Jenny to doubt she was mommy material. She'd never felt maternal twinges like most of her friends, and she was easily annoyed by children in general. In sympathetic company, she referred to them as "pukesters" and "virus volcanoes."

She'd never babysat, not even once, when she was younger. Whatever nurturing side she had, using it to micromanage her dad's company had proven satisfying enough.

Pressed for time as Cold Harbor drivers often were, they occasionally forgot to bring bags of calcium accelerant to cold weather pours, without which the curing process took too long; Jenny delighted in driving the fifty-pound bags to the site herself.

"Pedro, you forgot the fucking calcio!" she had once hollered at a driver, a recent immigrant named Valintin. She'd crumbled the order ticket into a ball and thrown it at the driver's feet, then pantomiming and speaking slowly, as if to a child, informed him, "Usted pay atencion or usted drive Uber instead of camion muy grande, comprende?"

"I'll be more careful next time, Mrs. Stanton," Valintin had replied in perfect English.

In fairness, the family treated all their workers, regardless of race or ethnicity, like shit. There were no second chances for serious mistakes. Clip a parked vehicle or telephone pole with your mixer truck, and you were likely to be unemployed the next day. Spill mud out the back end because you didn't keep your barrel spinning fast going up a hill—so long.

"No dents, no cops, no fines," Al told new drivers. "If you so much as knock a mirror off one of my trucks, you're done. The truck will be back on the road within a day. You won't."

He pounced on opportunities to show he wasn't bluffing. A

few days before Christmas one year, he canned a driver after the strap to his insulated lunch bag snagged on the charge/discharge barrel control lever. The driver had been chewing on a ham and cheese sandwich at a long light, oblivious to the fact that his rig was discharging mud until he looked in his rearview mirror and saw it oozing around his drop axle. It was a bad break for an otherwise good driver who was about to become a new father.

"Teach your kid to pay attention. That's my parenting advice," Al hollered. "I hope you and your wife have a happy, healthy baby. Now, get the hell out of my sight."

Woody is exhausted but happy. He has written almost two thousand words, a whole chapter if he wants to make the chapters short, which he believes is the right approach. At this rate, a first draft will be done in three months.

But it won't be. He does nothing on his novel the next day or the next. The day after that, he writes a few hundred words, but then another ten days of nothing passes. He's not sure what's going on. He isn't blocked creatively, although maybe he is. It's difficult to tell when you're not trying. Maybe it's just that writing a book is lonely and hard. He meets up again with JB at Liam's to watch their beloved basketball team, the Icarus University Magenta, whose former nickname, the Emperors, was disposed of years earlier by critics for its lack of inclusivity. One professor of comparative literature had called it a "grotesque celebration of proto-European colonialism and White male hegemony."

The switch to the Magenta triggered a lawsuit from the Italian Clubs of America, countering that Icarus University was perpetuating anti-Romanesque stereotypes. An amicus curiae brief from Italy's minister of culture and equality gave an international flavor to the cause. Ultimately, a federal appeals court decided the school, as a private institution, had the right to choose its own nickname, so the

Magenta stuck.

Tonight, the Magenta, which rival student sections routinely bastardize as "The Placenta," are on the road against the Wilmington Engineers, two teams heading nowhere.

"After all these years, I still don't feel right saying *Magenta is*," Woody muses. "*Magenta are* sounds better, but technically it's wrong."

"How goes the book?" JB asks.

"Great for about a day," Woody confesses. "I stalled out."

"I see how that could happen."

"I don't even have a publisher. Maybe I should see if anyone's interested in the concept before I waste more time."

"Self-publish it."

"Meh."

"I suppose it's hard to get it published anywhere if it's not written," JB chides.

"I suck," Woody concurs.

"Why don't you just put it online as you go?"

Woody sips his Diet Pepsi. No beer tonight. He needs to drop a few.

"No one's gonna read that."

"You never know. At least it would force you to write."

Slowly, the suggestion starts to resonate with the stalled novelist. "Like, just put it out on Facebook?"

"Why not? Any of that social media crap."

"I could create a *Fear as Mud* website."

"There ya go."

"I'll think about it. It's not the worst idea."

"I want my twenty percent when it takes off."

"Deal."

They clink beverages.

Woody feels a flicker of rebirth. By the end of the following day's session, he has written another half chapter and launched the *Fear as Mud* website. He finds the latter task enjoyable mainly because it's advancing his *Art* without him having to do any real writing. He's especially proud of how the book title encircles an artsy rendering of a mixer truck he plucked off pics4free.com. He also has changed his Peloton handle from *Woodbeast* to *FearAsMudNovel.* He rereads three times what he's written and adds two additional paragraphs:

Unfazed by a savage drizzle, Cus paddled his kayak up the creek, looking for any signs of something untoward. He glided past Jorgy's Lumber, the Big Harvest Produce distribution center, and Anson's Electroplating. A slight spike in cadmium had registered in the lake along with the benzine. Cus knew cadmium was used in the electroplating process but so did environmental regulators. For that reason, it was unlikely that Anson would dump the toxin directly into the creek. Too obvious and too risky.

Then, on the far corner of the property, Cus spotted something familiar, a Cold Harbor mixer truck. It was rumbling through a gate and toward the main road. Cus was accustomed to seeing his father-in-law's trucks all over town. In the moment, he thought nothing of it.

Woody leans back and admires the effort. He likes the cliffhanger quality of the last sentence, how it reveals a trusting innocence of the protagonist while signaling to readers that Al Holmes is a major douche. There's a term for that in theater, when the audience knows something the characters don't. He can't remember it off the top of his head, and he doesn't care enough to look it up, but he's certain it's a sign of excellent writing. Woody takes a deep breath and posts the beginning of his book on the new *Fear as Mud* website. Then he posts links to the site on his Facebook and Twitter pages with a note: "New novel in progress. Here's the start. Should I keep going?"

The question may make him sound desperate. He gets that. But Woody has a flair for self-promotion. The question will prompt responses, and the respondents will have investiture in the work.

Had he not been sidetracked by entering the moribund field of newspapering and now being destined to write a great novel, he might, he believes, have become a mass media manipulation theorist along the lines of Marshall McLuhan and Noam Chomsky. He makes a note to put a Noam Chomsky quote—any quote—somewhere in the book.

For the next seventy-two hours, Woody spends more time checking his social media accounts than working on his novel. The feedback is mostly positive. An old college roommate has commented, "Fun read—Please, sir, I want some more." One of his old sources, an enviro-nudge at Save the Bay, has checked in as well.

"Your book has great potential to inform the public about the dangers of heavy metals and other pollutants. FYI, cadmium concentrations in drinking water supplies are typically less than 1 part per billion (ppb), so I'm guessing your fictional (lol) Seneca Creek is contaminated by industrial wastewater or seepage from a hazardous waste site(s). P.S. You might want to research how gray water from concrete can change the pH of groundwater. Might be useful to your project—Sid."

"Thanks for the tip!" Woody replies, although his gut reaction is dread. Reader interest: Good. Reader collaboration/plot speculation in a public forum: Not good. Writing is tough enough without dozens of wannabe chefs stirring the pot. Still, eyeballs are eyeballs.

"Make it a wooden kayak," someone comments. "That would be consistent with Custer's ancestry and ethos. Good luck! Jerry Debolt, Debolt Wooden Kayaks Inc., Old Homestead, NY."

"I want to fuck Jenny," someone else tweets. "And I want lasagna."

Woody morosely reads through the feedback. It's not firing the engines the way he'd hoped. He never should have listened to JB. But then comes an instant message that lands like a sugar-dusted whip.

"Are you just teasing us, or are you going to keep writing? I freaking love it!" comments Celeste.

Woody is still pounding away on his keyboard when Mandy puts dinner on the table. He's finishing a scene in which Al Holmes emerges from an Asian massage parlor during a police raid. Rather than getting hauled in for questioning, Al bullshits and bribes his way out of it. Turns out he once paid a $3,000 kickback to a city council member who happens to be the uncle of one of the cops. Connections matter.

"I wouldn't let one of those Orientals touch my dick if you paid me," Al told the officer. "I just got a tight shoulder."

That scene follows an establishing passage in which Vivian terrorizes a Porsche salesman because there's a three-month wait for a 911 Carrera in Violet.

"Don't try to sell me Gentian Blue Metallic when I'm asking for Violet," she screamed in the showroom. "It looks like shit."

"Apologies, ma'am," the salesman replied.

"Are you guys dicking me around because I'm paying cash? Is that it? I know how you shysters make your money. Sorry, not interested in your rip-off financing."

Then Vivian softened and sidled up to the salesman. She reached into her purse, pulled out five $100 bills and shoved them into his front pocket, letting her hand linger.

"Next Friday at the latest," she whispered. "The Premium Plus package."

For emphasis, Vivian gave the associate's package a good squeeze.

"No problem," the now red-faced salesman demurred.

Vivian replied, "Always a pleasure doing business with you," and off she tootled in search of her next victim.

"How's the book going?" Mandy asks Woody at the dinner table.

"The book?"

She sends him a look.

"Oh, right—the book. It's going."

"Anything you care to share with us yet?"

Woody takes a piece of baked haddock as Mandy fills his water glass. "Too soon. But I'm getting there."

"So secretive," she says. "You writers! Did Ella tell you she scored two goals in the scrimmage today?"

"That's awesome, sweetie," Woody says, thrilled by the change of subjects. "I didn't even know you had a scrimmage."

"It was last minute," Ella replies. "They were doing repairs at Mohegan's practice field, so their coach asked if they could practice with us. Instant scrimmage."

Yes, it's good the conversation has pivoted from his book. The Process works better when it becomes automatic versus self-conscious. Writers write; they don't sit around talking about their writing with people who don't get it.

On this issue, Woody and his spouse are perfectly aligned. Mandy has no interest in a keystroke-by-keystroke account of his return to non-newspaper writing. Her husband has a history of diving into fiction projects and quietly abandoning them. There have been three aborted novels and one short story collection quietly scrapped at two stories. Then came *Tick Tock, Check Your Sock,* the novella, and the disappointment when it went nowhere. She's happy to see him working on something, just not particularly curious about what it might be.

"Your father won another Press Club award," Mandy says, spooning more shredded brussels sprouts salad onto Ella's plate. His story, about a decline in the area's flying squirrel population, had been submitted by the paper a year earlier, shortly before he was let go.

"That's cool, Dad. Congratulations."

"Thanks, sweetie."

A quiet descends on the table, an awkward question hanging in the air. Mandy knows the answer but keeps it to herself.

"Second place," Woody says finally. "Again. But I'll take it. It was one of the last stories I wrote for that snake pit."

"Serves them right," Mandy says. "That must be so embarrassing to them after they—"

"After I took the buyout? Whatever," Woody says. "I've moved on."

Later, as the two are out for a stroll, Mandy probes out of politeness. "What's this one about?"

Woody isn't ready to share. "Kind of an environmental thriller, but with deeper stuff weaved in. Why don't I finish a draft and then you can read it? The last thing I want is to snuff the firefly by talking it to death."

"I get it," she says, taking his hand. "Man of mystery."

What Woody doesn't say and doesn't need to say because his wife is cool on social media and doesn't use Facebook, is that his nascent masterpiece has already slipped into the public domain. Roughly three hundred readers have found it, a number that has grown in large part because Cluckin' Clean's home page includes a link to fearasmud.com, a quiet favor and vote of confidence from JB.

The chain's website does surprisingly well for itself. Not every Cluckin' Clean customer drinks through the wash cycle. About half just want to do laundry, content to check their phones or flip through a mag to the ka-dump-ka-dump of tumbling dryers. Laundry signs encourage customers to sign up for free membership in the Chicken Coup for coupons, contests, and other promos. To join the club, patrons must visit cluckinclean.com, where they'll now find the link to Woody's book and a brief note from management.

Need something to read as your clothes get clean? We're proud to post a new novel in progress by award-winning local journalist Woody Hackworth. Click on the link and win a chance to get free laundry detergent for a year.

More exposure comes because JB's establishments host live bands Thursday nights. Millennial hipsters and aging rockers alike check cluckinclean.com regularly to see who's playing. It's subtle at first, but something's happening out there. Just three chapters in,

Woody already has the nucleus of what most unpublished fiction writers only dream of—an audience.

As he ponders his good fortune, he understands he needs to loosen up and embrace online, real-time serialization. The Process can wait. Who needs it? *No,* he quickly corrects himself. *That's going too far. Adapt The Process to mesh with digital media imperatives.* He resolves to post new material by early Saturday to tap into the weekend launderette rush. Smart.

Woody's in a good place. Interest in his book is growing. Readers are sharing and clamoring for more. Most cool of all, Celeste has taken to texting him with plot possibilities.

"Should you make Al gay," she postulates, "and have Vivian stealing from a nonprofit even though they don't need the money?"

And now she's inviting him out for a drink—on the immigrant-heavy east side of town, where they both know they're less likely to be recognized. He has been to McGillicutty's, a holdout from when Irish laborers filled the row houses, twice before. He feels guilty sitting there alone with her but not guilty enough.

"Maybe there should be a beautiful and talented redheaded reporter who brings the wrath of journalistic oversight crashing down on Joe Dunn's empire," he blurts.

"Al Holmes's empire!" she corrects. "You better keep those two straight!" She covers her mouth in a feeble attempt to conceal her twinkly laughter.

God, she's adorable. "Oh, jeez, did I really say that?" he says too loudly.

A lone imbiber looks up from his Jack and Coke.

"That's so funny. I love the way you're satirizing your life and your family," she says. "It's so realistic even you're confused. I wish I could be that passionate about something."

Woody feels tightness in his chest. It surges from Celeste's misapprehension of the novel. He wants to mansplain her error but . . . what if she's right? Complicating matters, there's now an alarming tightness in a secondary location. Everything about Celeste—the way she touches his arm when he makes a joke, the gentle sweeping of cinnamon swirls of hair from her cheek, even the way she holds a mozzarella stick. It's obvious. She wants him.

"One more drink?" she purrs.

"Sure."

"So, it's actually a really good idea," she says.

"What's a good idea?"

"Your idea. A female sidekick. Like Scully in *The X-Files*."

"Can I make her an intern?"

"Not if they're going to screw. That's not okay anymore. Make her my age."

"Twenty-three."

He sees a hint of a blush.

"I'm serious, Woody. A little sex never hurts a story. Excuse me, a narrative." She bumps her ankle against his foot, maintaining contact long enough to establish it wasn't an accident.

Woody can hardly breathe. "They make a good whiskey sour here," he says idiotically.

"I'm thinking about breaking it off with Nikko," she says. "I'm ninety percent certain he's cheating on me."

Woody didn't see that coming. "That's good—I mean, that's good you're breaking up with him but bad he cheated on you. I would never cheat."

"Me neither," she says, pausing wistfully. They both know they're lying. "But our characters can."

Celeste's instincts prove sound. She has always known what people want. That's what makes her a good reporter. Woody's next chapter—the book's first hint of romance—will precipitate a fourfold increase in feedback, not all of it positive, but that's to be expected. Woody doesn't have a great feel for writing women, relationships, romance, or sex. But it's time to push through the block, let The Process work. The first order of business? He needs a name for

Celeste's character. Celeste suggests Aurora Connolly. She says it sounds sophisticated yet grounded "and kind of sexy."

"What the hell," he says. "Aurora Connolly it is."

CHAPTER 3

"MAY I ASK WHAT IT'S ABOUT?"

Whoever sent in the tip did it old school—in a plain brown envelope. For all the newfangled electronic communication, the good ol' US Postal Service still preserved anonymity the best. The postmark was Netcong, 200 miles south in Jersey. It might as well have been Paraguay. The note was both specific and vague. And concerning:

"Re: Your illegal dumping story. Check out 866 Old Spruce Road."

"Isn't that near your place?" Cus asked Aurora Connolly, his lone colleague on what remained of the *Daily Informer*'s once-robust Community Watchdog (CW) investigative team.

Ten years ago, CW had been headed by three-time Pulitzer winner Ed Karavich, lured to Tiberius by a six-figure salary and six weeks of vacation per annum. The team's stories shook up Albany, although those were quietly criticized as low-hanging fruit and went largely unread beyond the state capital. Closer to home, there were several legitimate gets. A CW exposé led to an arson conviction for the chief of a local volunteer fire department. Another story spotlighted significantly slower police response times in poorer, primarily African American neighborhoods. It won first place in the state AP contest, although it fell flat with readers who struggled to see why Black people getting screwed over in Tiberius was news.

One step ahead of the cost cutters, Karavich now did PR for the Saudis. He left behind a mixed legacy. While he'd added punch to the *Daily Informer*—or *Daily Misinformer* as the locals often called it—he'd been ridiculed behind his back, especially by non-CW staff, as an overrated, overpaid blowhard.

Woody pauses. He might be shaving too close to the bone here. The Karavich character bears a slight resemblance to Ken Sarachek, a real-life former investigative editor at the *Blaze* who was never one of Woody's favorites. He revisits the passage and decides on a name and gender change. Ed Karavich becomes Nancy Feldman-Kang. Perfect. Disguised identity: check. A Jewish and Asian presence in the newsroom: check and check. Now, back to work:

"I used to let Boris run off Old Spruce Road," Aurora said, "before they fenced it off."

"Didn't Boris—" Cus stopped himself midsentence. The tireless, lovably incorrigible boxer mix had to be euthanized in his prime due to a fast-moving pelvic tumor.

"Yes, cancer," Aurora said, reading her colleague's mind. "He's not the only dog from there to cross the Rainbow Bridge before his time."

"The Rainbow what?"

"Bridge. The Rainbow Bridge. It's a metaphor for when pets die and go to Heaven. How do you not know that?"

"I guess I'm not a metaphor person."

"Then call it the Ethyl Nitrite Bridge, Captain Literal," she sniped.

Cus loved how Aurora's casual inventiveness with spoken language contrasted with her precise writing style. Gazing at her voluptuous-yet-trim physique, undressing her with eyesight sharp enough to have tied the Normal Stillwell High School record for consecutive free throws, he wondered if he would have been better off with someone like her—sharp-witted and dedicated to fighting the good fight.

Oh, sure, Jenny was good people. He loved her almost as much as he did the day her family had sent them on their honeymoon with a symphony of blaring Kenworth mixer truck air horns.

He loved her as much as he had when he turned down a $1,000 escort procured for him, creepily, by his soon-to-be brothers-in-law, who planned his sodden bachelor party at multiple strip clubs.

Had it been some kind of test? If so, he had passed with flying colors.

Cus was no Boy Scout, but he had principles—principles that made no allowances for debauchery.

His soon-to-be father-in-law, Al Holmes, had been both disappointed and impressed when he got word that Cus had not partaken.

"By the time you get to Bali, you're gonna be as hard as a Cold Harbor slab poured in zero percent humidity on a hot day," Al had joshed, throwing in a wink. Weird.

In fact, Cus had struggled to get it up for his new bride on their wedding night. He blamed jet lag and the preceding forty-eight hours of almost uninterrupted drinking, but the truth was that Jenny's family unnerved him. They were in his head even on his wedding night. While they had never been anything but gruffly gracious toward him, there was something menacing beneath it all. Whatever it was had wilted his dick.

No such dysfunction was evident in the newsroom, however, as he tracked to the nadir of Aurora's cleavage. He reminded himself that he was happily married, more or less.

Discreetly covering the front of his all-cotton tactical pants with a notepad, Cus announced, "I'm going to drive out to Old Spruce and look around."

Twitter erupts once the new chapter is posted.

"WTF are tactical pants. LMAO!"

"Do they treat a cleavage nadir with chemo or radiation?😂"

"Aurora based on anyone you know, Woody? Wink."

"Is this a rom-com or a detective story? Choose a lane, dude."

Then, in response to the above: "It's called hybrid genre fiction, moron. Write your own book."

"Must be a small notepad."

"It's so sad Boris died. I'm literally sobbing. Is Aurora going to get a new dog?"

Father's Day breaks Woody's momentum. As usual, it's spent at the Dunns' 25,000-square-foot Greek Revival manse overlooking Lake Mohegan. Woody is biting into a brat when Joe asks him what he's up to these days.

"Just doing a little writing and getting my resumé out there," he says, fibbing the last part.

"Writing anything good?"

"Everything Woody writes is good," Bev interjects. Then to him: "I'd love to see you working on a novel. You have such a way with words."

A cracker fragment catches in Woody's throat.

"He's on it, Mom," Mandy says.

"Fantastic! May I ask what it's about?"

"You most certainly may not!" Mandy scolds.

"I don't want to jinx it," Woody contributes apologetically.

"You can at least give us a general idea," Joe pushes.

"Just environmental stuff."

"Oh," Joe says, losing interest.

Tanner lifts his glass and toasts, "To new directions and big success with your first novel."

"Thanks," Woody says, secretly wondering if Tanner is slyly mocking him for "only" writing a novella the first time.

They knock glasses. Woody silently pleads for a change of subjects. No such luck.

"It's pretty awesome having a writer in the family," Cameron says. "I mean, don't get me wrong, Dad, blowing shit up and playing in the dirt is awesome, but it must be a great feeling to get paid for something you wrote. I can't wait until they make a movie about your book."

"I'd watch that," Ella interjects, throwing a stuffed front-end loader dog toy to Digger, Joe and Bev's golden retriever.

"Let's not get ahead of ourselves," Mandy says, spreading whole grain mustard onto a cracker. "Let the man write."

Joe breaks the tension with a joke. "Hey, maybe after this one hits the bestseller list, they'll publish that little one you wrote. What was it called? *Tick Tock, Check My Cock*?"

"Dad!"

Cameron laughs so hard a dribble of Amstel Light runs out one nostril.

"*Sock*, Dad—it's *sock*."

Even Bev stifles a laugh.

"That would have been a better book," Woody parries. "You wanna be my editor?"

"Nah, I'm just a glorified ditch digger. But seriously, if you ever want to try any of it out on a regular joe, I'll make time."

"That's generous of you. It's not quite there yet."

"Good things take time. Speaking of . . . I got you a little something."

Joe reaches under the table and pulls up a bottle of bourbon still in the box.

"Caterpillar handed these out at the Vegas show to preferred customers. Happy Father's Day."

"Pappy Van Winkle Special Reserve twelve year?" Woody gushes, accepting the gift. Woody knows bourbon enough to know this one wasn't cheap. "Jeez, Joe, thanks. This is nuts. You didn't have to do this."

"I didn't. But what the hell. You're more or less a good husband to my only girl and a good dad to my grandkid. Plus, I figured you could use a little something after getting dumped by those bastards."

"It was a buyout but, yeah, definitely, this should help kill the pain. Wow."

"Besides, aren't you novelist types required to be shit-faced half the time?" Joe teased.

"It's a job requirement." On cue, Woody chugs what's left of his Amstel. Everyone laughs.

"Author, author!" Bev exclaims, clapping with delight.

Woody feels a flush of shame. For the first time since The Process began, he's worried there might not be enough fiction in his fiction. He quickly stifles his doubts. He's being oversensitive. Write what you know—that's the rule. If writers didn't harvest their lives, there'd be no fiction. It's not like anyone's getting killed here except maybe a character or two.

"What's for dessert?" Woody asks.

A few days later, Woody is briefly blocked while writing a scene in which Al Holmes is dressing down his CFO, a convicted tax cheat with excellent political connections, for undercharging a collision repair shop to illegally dump cyanide plating sludge.

"I'm not in this fucking racket risking getting sent back to fucking Danbury, to break fucking even!" Al screamed.

Al's main point is that the sludge must be transported separately from other toxic waste because it's highly reactive, therefore it's a more expensive job.

But where to go from here? Among other plot points, Woody needs to decide whether the CEO, Tom Ricci, is wearing a wire. Maybe Celeste will have some thoughts. Woody's phone rings. He doesn't recognize the area code, but he takes the call anyway.

CHAPTER 4
STAR-CROSSED

"Hello. I'm trying to reach Woody Hackworth," a charming female voice coos.

"This is he," Woody replies, already smitten but trying to sound gruff and harried in a writerly way.

"My name is Annabelle Riley. I'm working on an article for *New Voices*. We're a small magazine that focuses on emergent authors and trends in literature." She pauses. "Most people have never heard of us."

"*New Voices*, sure, I think I've seen your magazine before," Woody lies.

"Oh, great. That always makes it easier. I'm calling because I'm doing a story about novelists serializing their books online. It's a thing, as you know. Someone sent me the link to *Fear as Mud*. Are you still working on it? I noticed you didn't post anything new yet this week."

A hailstorm of emotion rocks Woody. Elation takes the early lead, but pride and a powerful sense of vindication come on strong. His book will soon be getting even more attention.

"I'm flattered," Woody says. "You must be following it pretty closely."

"I am. Do you have a few minutes to talk?"

The interview lasts nearly an hour. Annabelle invested in the novel not just as a journalist but as a fan. "Skip the wiretap for now," she advises.

The only disappointing part is that there are no plans to run the article in the monthly hard copy mag, just online. The upside is that the digital story will appear as early as next week. Woody hangs up and immediately texts the writer a file containing the same four-year-old photo of himself that appears on fearasmud.com, per her request. He cracks open the Pappy and dispenses himself a generous pour. A small celebration is in order.

Miles away, Mandy is in her office after another head-splitting hospital merger meeting. An analyst in accounts payable, a brainy smartass named Aaron, assumes she has been reading along online already and tries to land a joke.

"Just for my own reference, which massage parlor does your dad frequent?" he asks. "I'll make a note to stay out of there."

"What?" Mandy replies.

Aaron directs her to fearasmud.com and ducks out of the office to avoid further awkwardness, leaving her to read.

She has a lot to be pissed about, but the "happily married, more or less" throwaway line pings in her in a particularly bad way.

"Seriously, Woody?" she mutters. "Was that necessary?"

While Mandy is still at work, Woody plugs away on new material. After his second bourbon, he feels loose enough to try out a sex scene between Cus and Aurora. It's free association, just an exercise. He isn't far enough along to have them screw. Still, if the scene works, it will be nice to drop it in later. Woody imagines himself as a Native American hunter/gatherer, using every part of the buffalo. All is meaningful, nothing wasted. He marvels at his efficiency and resolve and attacks the keyboard.

An electric penumbra of sexual tension crackled around the duo as they hiked toward the dump site, taking care to use the trail that was mostly hidden from the gravel access road. They had chosen the route without even discussing it. Both understood this would not be a good time to be spotted by one of Al's goons.

"Do you love her, Cus?" Aurora asked.

"I don't know anymore."

He noted the parabolic curve of Aurora's left breast through her cashmere sweater. "I think she might be in on it," Cus said flatly.

"So do I," she replied. "I'm sorry. I can't imagine how . . . hard that must be."

Something was hard all right.

Woody wasn't sure about that last line. Too glib? He tried again.

The way she enunciated the word hard stirred him. Did she pause for emphasis before she said it, or was he just imagining?

Much better.

Cus's first instinct was to disregard the possibility of a double entendre. This was no time for a misunderstanding, to embarrass his colleague or himself. He wasn't for crude banter anyway, even with the guys. With women he was chivalrous. That was even more true toward Aurora, for whom he had profound professional respect. Just leave it alone, he coached himself.

But sometimes, when the game heats up, players ignore the coach.

"It's hard, indeed," he replied, astonished to hear the words leave his mouth.

She said nothing.

He hoped they were not on the same sexually loaded frequency. Then he hoped they were. He wondered if he was falling in love with her.

By now, they were crossing onto state land, a shortcut to the dump site. A trio of rental cabins stood among a stand of white pines overlooking yet another lake.

"Have you ever been inside one of these?" Aurora asked.

"No. Why?"

But he knew why she was asking. At least he thought he did. His heart quickened anew.

"They're pretty cool—more modern inside than you'd think. Come on, let's take a look."

They ambled onto the porch, and she let Cus peer through a window.

"Cozy," he said, scarcely able to breathe. She reached into her hip pocket and produced a key.

"I know people," she said.

"But I'm married," he said, bending down to kiss her. His raging man hammer pressed into her denim-clad loins.

"Concrete must run in your family." She giggled. "¡Qué duro!"

"What are we doing?" he asked.

"Taking a break," she said.

The door lock had been recently upgraded. It turned too smoothly for a creaky cabin in the woods, renovated or not.

And so Cus became an adulterer, bedding Aurora on a plaid New York state-requisitioned, flame-retardant, insect-resistant sofa—releasing all of his lust, longing, and investigatory angst into a clenched fusillade of ecstasy.

Woody feels confident that the scene rings true, and there's collaborating feedback—the author has aroused himself.

"Okay if I call?" he texts Celeste.

She sends back a thumbs-up emoji. He resolves to first count to one hundred, so as to not appear overeager, but he only gets to fourteen.

"Hey, sweetie," she answers.

Sweetie? "Okay, I just wrote the scene we talked about. It's either really hot or really stupid. Want me to send it to you?"

"Just read to me over the phone."

"You mean now?"

"Sure. Why not?"

"Where are you?"

"In the newsroom," she says sweetly.

"Seriously, Celeste? Isn't this best done in private?"

"It's a modern newsroom. It doesn't get more private."

As Woody reads his sex scene, Celeste offers a few edits—"Don't use the word *clenched*. It sounds like a seizure. Say *enveloped* instead." Still, her overall critique is encouraging. Woody makes the changes and offers a few of his own.

"I'm going to have her sigh instead of wince when he first enters her," he asserts.

"Pro move," she cheerleads. Then, "You really want to fuck me, don't you, Mr. Writer Stud?"

"Damn, you have a sexy voice."

"Just post it now. You've hit a small lull in your book, which is normal, but this will be perfect to crank up interest again. It's fucking hot, Woody."

"Really?"

"Oh yeah, really," she says breathlessly.

"Done," he says, updating his online narrative from his phone. "It's up."

"I bet it is," Celeste murmurs playfully. "Don't you want to know what I'm wearing? Isn't that what guys always ask?"

"What are you wearing?"

"I didn't go too crazy. Just a pencil skirt and a silk blouse. Maybe a push-up bra, if that helps."

"It helps," he rasps. "What color bra?"

"Boring beige."

"My favorite color."

"A concession to being in the office."

"I'm in my office, too."

"Don't you mean your study?"

"Yes, my study."

"I hope your door is locked."

"It's okay. She won't be home for another—"

Woody hears the front door and wilts in terror.

"Woody!" Mandy hollers from the foyer. "Are you fucking kidding me?"

In that already-complicated moment, Woody's phone lights up with a text.

"I just need your wife's name and your daughter's for the story," Annabelle Riley's message reads. "Is your wife a writer, too?"

Any fears Woody has that his novel strays too close to home are now personified in the five-foot-four native of Gloucester, Massachusetts, glaring into his soul, a woman who has given him many things, including the financial freedom to write fiction.

"Should we talk here in my study?" Woody asks.

"Your study? Now it's your fucking study? There's nothing to talk about, Woody. You need to stop writing that book. It's insulting. It's mean. It makes my family—not to mention me, the mother of your goddamn daughter—look like we're a bunch of fucking scumbags. Did it ever occur to you that I need to live in this town?"

"It's fiction, honey. Clearly."

"Don't 'It's fiction, honey' me. It's based on a family-owned business in the construction industry in Upstate Fucking New York. The main character has a hard-on for some bimbo reporter who sounds a lot like Celeste Henry, which makes me wonder: Are you fucking her?"

"No!"

"Celeste. Aurora. Talk about reaching for the fucking stars."

Woody flushes with shame. He had not considered the astral association between the two names. Dumb.

"Oh, by the way, someone at work asked me what massage parlor my dad uses."

Woody tries humor with no more success than Aaron the accounts payable guy had.

"Which one *does* he use?"

Mandy snatches a paperback copy of Stephen King's *On Writing* from a table and hurls it at her husband of eighteen years, grazing his shoulder.

"I'm not fucking around, Woody. You need to stop before my family finds out. What have they ever done to you?"

"You don't understand. I'm getting famous. I can't just stop."

CHAPTER 5
UNCOMFORTABLE QUESTIONS

Woody and Mandy have, until now, worked well through the years. They met at a gym in Boston while he was working at an overachieving small daily that would be purchased by a real estate company in five years and gutted. She was finishing a master's program in health care administration at Boston University. He got a kick out of her not-heavy-but-noticeable North Shore accent. She thought it was awesome that he'd hiked two hundred miles of the Appalachian Trail (a wasp attack truncated the journey) and that he sometimes interviewed actual murderers behind bars. Like a lot of young guys, Woody was prone to talking about himself too much, but with him it was through the lens of stories he was chasing, which often included funny rants against crazed editors (especially one Rich Sheffield) and their ceaseless demands. They were the ones keeping the young lovers from spending more time together, he complained.

"It's bullshit," he told her over a scorpion bowl in Harvard Square. "I had just gotten back from Ludlow after being out there for six hours. They told me to turn around and go back to Ludlow. You know what I told them?"

"To piss off?" she teased.

"I told Rich, 'Maybe you need to open a bureau in Ludlow.'"

"What did he say?"

"'Perfect. You're our new Ludlow bureau chief.' Such a dick."

"So, what did you end up doing?"

"I drove back to Ludlow. I'm a nobody. A cog in an understaffed word factory. I do what I'm told. I have no free will. Why are you even talking to me? You can—you must—do better."

She loved the beaten-down working stiff schtick. Somehow, it was romantic. And there was their shared connection to Icarus. Was it fate?

Woody had grown up two hours away in Buffalo. When he was twelve, his father, a philosophy professor at Calamount College, had been quietly relieved of his position after taking up with one of his students. He accepted a community college gig—and a pay cut—in Icarus before eventually settling in Southern France with another paramour. The long weekends and summer stretches at Woody's dad's townhouse had given Woody a familiarity with Icarus that would outlast his dad's connection to the once-proud manufacturing town. Icarus had reinvented itself with mixed success as a regional center of microchip manufacturing, craft brewing, joint replacement, and green technologies. Pilots praised its airport as a global authority on runway deicing.

After Woody graduated from UConn Stamford and found work near Boston, his mother fled Buffalo for Arizona to grow hemp and make art with found objects. Woody was on good terms with both parents, but detachment came with distance. He called his mom by her first name.

"I don't think I have your right zip code," Elsa had told him in a phone call. "I sent you a turkey made out of soda cans for Thanksgiving, but it was returned."

Mandy's family had moved to Icarus when she was nine. Her father had chucked his job as a regional service manager for Volvo's construction division to help save his brother Ray's small Upstate excavation company after Ray suffered a stroke. Uncle Ray lived long enough to teach Joe the ropes and more. Together, they grew Dunn-

Rite into the second largest excavation contractor within seventy-five miles.

"We *Dunn* good," were Ray's last words.

The extended family still celebrated Uncle Ray's birthday, both as tribute and as an excuse for Joe to prepare his brother's legendary brisket. Indeed, beneath the gruffness, Joe Dunn's humility was never more apparent than when he credited his fallen brother for "making this life of ours possible."

Despite having never known one another while overlapping in Icarus, Mandy and Woody bonded over their familiarity with the town. They compared notes on shops, restaurants, and mutual acquaintances, even realizing they'd been to a few of the same concerts. They made a pinky swear to never tell anyone they'd both seen Nickelback at the casino.

"I went with a guy who was into them but didn't want to go by himself. Kind of a lose-ah. I felt sorry for him. What's your excuse?"

"Bad taste," Woody replied.

They talked about the future, too. Mandy said she would consider returning to Icarus to live but not right away, and Woody said he'd thought about applying to the Icarus *Blaze* as a steppingstone to a real metro.

"We should open a scorpion bowl place in Genesee Square," Woody enthused through a nimbus of rum. "We'll be rich."

"Screw that. I'm already rich," Mandy slurred.

Woody was in love.

Now, twenty years later, Mandy is all but running a major hospital and Woody's steppingstone has turned into quicksand—which is why Woody needs this book. He needs the sense of creating something significant after the indignity of his exit from the *Blaze*. He needs the interest it's starting to generate as a counterweight to kept man status. But most pressing, he needs Mandy to understand that a novelist has the duty—even the obligation—to tap into personal experience.

"Look at all the great works of fiction erected on an autobiographical substructure," Woody pleads. "*Fear and Loathing in Las Vegas,* Joyce's *Portrait of an Artist as a Young Man, Ashley's Ashes.*"

"It's *Angela's Ashes.* And it's nonfiction, dumbass."

"Okay, whatever. My book is way less autobiographical than those. I'm just borrowing a sense of place and a few details. The characters are completely unrecognizable from anyone in my life except for Cus maybe."

"They may be unrecognizable to you, but how is anyone reading your book supposed to know what's autobiographical and what isn't when the premise is my family's business? I thought you're supposed to be a writer. All you're doing is changing a few names and making me and my family suck. Make it stop!"

Censorship is never the answer, Woody thinks. But for the first time, he allows that she may have a point. There's a twinge of guilt.

After a long silence, she says, "I asked my parents if they've been reading your book."

"And?"

"They said they're saving it for when it's published. They want to read the hardcover version. They believe in you, Woody. I'm not trying to snuff out your art, but . . ."

She tears up.

Woody tries to take cover in self-pity. "I guess I'm the asshole."

There's no rebuttal.

"Please fix this," she says.

"I'll figure something out," he says, then adds, "What about your brothers?"

"What about them?"

"Are they reading it?"

"Cameron is."

"What does he think?"

"He says we should sue you for defamation."

Woody feels dizzy. "It's one thing to sue," he replies lamely, "it's another thing to win."

"Is that right? Now you're James Joyce *and* Clarence Fucking Darrow?"

"I took media law at UConn," he says. "I know how this stuff works."

"Woody?" she says calmly.

"What?"

"Go fuck yourself."

As he sees it, Woody has several options, none of them good. He can abandon his book or soften the in-law characters in a way that mollifies Mandy and her family. He flirts with an idea of turning Al Holmes into a victim, forced by shadowy Downstate mob figures to orchestrate the illegal dumping operation. But he's doubtful readers will embrace such a twist, and besides, all that will do is introduce the possibility that his real in-laws have ties to organized crime. Another creative choice similarly risks the unintended consequence of creating more suspicion. He could restart the book making Cus's family the villains, but that would be like telling readers he'd been pressured to change the story—not to mention there'd more than likely be no more readers if he started from scratch.

Of course, his portrayal of the fictional in-laws is not his only domestic concern. There's no undoing Mandy's vexation with the Aurora character. Maybe the damage has already been done, which makes a good case for staying the course.

"It sounds to me like Mandy and her brother are overreacting," Celeste tells Woody over blackberry mojitos. "They'll chill once they see the book really isn't about them, right?"

"Probably," Woody says glumly.

Now comes a call from Woody's successful journalism pal Nicholas Peters, who also wants to help craft the narrative. They've been friends since they met at a press conference at the State House in Boston, where Woody was covering the story for his suburban rag and Nick for the *Boston Provincial*. Woody often evinced disdain for the rapidly downsizing-but-still-arrogant metro, although that was partly a defense against the disappointment that they wouldn't hire him. Resumés blinking "UConn Stamford" didn't get a sniff from the uber editors of Montauk Boulevard, whose outsized offices were quarantined behind large interior windows. They were like fierce marine creatures displayed in separate tanks for everyone's protection. The rank and file called them "glassholes" behind their backs.

But Woody and Nick hit it off immediately. Nick appeared not to have the condescending gene, taking a genuine interest in Woody's job as an environmental reporter in the burbs and going so far as to compliment him on one of his recent stories. Woody was flattered and impressed by the big city scribe's attention to suburban news. As he swooned from the praise, Nick pumped him for information on the first fifteen minutes of a press conference he'd missed. A lasting friendship formed.

Now, all these years later, Nick was a media star, particularly adroit on the nexus of defense spending and the US economy. He had ensconced himself as a superstar reporter and columnist at *The Apocalyptic,* the revered highbrow magazine hatched at the turn of the century by a wealthy nephew of Joseph Pulitzer himself. Nick was the rabbit of accomplishment and external validation that Woody was chasing, although he'd never admit it.

At the same time, Woody's pragmatic mindset regarding workplace politics was of value to Nick, who now and then consulted his friend on how to navigate the spider hole of superiors who seemed hellbent on editing *The Apocalyptic* to dust. This was one of those times; Nick was calling Woody about Woody.

"I don't read a lot of fiction, but I'm reading your book. It's fantastic," Nick gushes. "I just have one suggestion."

"Just one?"

"Can you give Al Holmes a knife scar, just a little one? Maybe on his neck? And leave it unclear how he got it. It would be a cool detail. I'd like to see more evocation, more scene description—that's my only criticism."

"That's fair."

"You've established a muscular narrative, a great flow. So, take advantage of it. Engage all our senses. Slow down a little, and play in the sandbox. We'll go there with you."

Woody texts himself the word sandbox. "Mandy's not as excited about the book as you are," he confides.

"Are you serious? Why the hell not?"

The friends discuss the art-imitating-life dilemma dogging the author. To Woody's horror, Nick is not unsympathetic to Mandy's concerns.

"It did cross my mind that she might be getting pissed," Nick acknowledges, gently walking back the dismay he'd expressed seconds earlier.

But Nick, a career firster whose devotion to mass media in all forms has proved more enduring than two marriages, has answers. First, he advises Woody, success cures all ills. "If the book is a hit—even more so than it already is—Mandy will eventually embrace the association, and her family will fall into line. Just handle it up front in a disclaimer and dedicate the book to your loving wife. Problem solved. Everybody loves a winner."

"You really think it's that simple?"

"No, but it's a good start. I also think you need to somehow make the fictional in-laws redemptive, at least partly so. It will be better for the book. You don't want them turning into cartoons."

"What do you have in mind?"

"That's your job, fiction boy. You've got time to figure it out. Tell Mandy to reserve judgment, and—"

"Let The Process play out."

"Precisely. Trust The Process. Don't assume the characters in your book are bad people. That's how I'd handle it. But above all, keep writing!"

"Thanks, dude. I really appreciate it. I know how busy you are."

"I'm never too busy for you. Hey, I have to take another call."

"No problem," Woody says.

"Wait, hold on a second. I have one more quick thought."

The line goes silent. Woody waits sixty-eight seconds until he hears Nick ask, "Still there?"

"Still here."

"Sorry about that—that was the defense secretary getting back to me. Anyway, I really do need to go, but the other thing I wanted to say is, think about getting some diversity in your book. If I were writing this, I'd throw in at least one person of color or a nonbinary, something to break up the Milky Way. I'm concerned you're going to end up with a book that screams White people problems."

"Hmm," Woody says, sensing constriction in his throat. The criticism makes him feel defensive. All he is doing is following what all the books on writing advise—write what you know. It just so happens that what Woody knows best is rich White people.

"Right now, Cus is one-sixteenth Mohawk. Should I bump him up to one-eighth?"

"One-fourth would be better."

"That's easy enough. I mean, I could even make him half."

"Half is too much. Half makes it too much of a thing—unless you want to do serious research on his tribe."

"I don't. Let's go with one-eighth for now."

"Fine. But even with the Native American enhancement, I'd still consider adding another character or even two who aren't boring, straight White people. That's just me. I'll catch ya later. Good luck."

"Thanks."

Woody texts the word *diversity* to himself. He reaches for the Pappy Van Winkle and drinks straight from the bottle. He doesn't feel like writing today but, after a fitful night on the sofa, he's back at it the next morning. Because at Celeste's urging he prematurely published the cabin liaison, he now has to go back and flesh out the Cus-Aurora relationship. That's helpful in a way. He can seize the opportunity to distance Aurora from Celeste, which should calm down Mandy. He can also use flashbacks to address ethnic diversity omissions spotlighted by Nick. Woody's next installment tackles all that and more.

Cus's and Aurora's workstations were opposite one another, offset slightly so Cus could gaze at Aurora as she worked without noticing (or at least without him thinking she was noticing). Her full name was Aurora Marquez-Connolly. Her father was a New Jersey wine and spirits importer, her mother a phlebotomist who fled Guatemala's civil war with her parents when she was in her teens.

Woody leans back in his chair, fist balled under his chin in thoughtful repose. "Show, don't tell," he reminds himself. Here is a good spot to take Nick's suggestion and do some evoking. His fingers return to the keyboard.

Aurora had heard endless stories of her mother Marisol's escape with her parents through the next-to-impassable gorge known as Imposible across El Rio Paso Hondo and through loamy fields of coffee and cacao alive with the self-satisfied thrum of cicadas. She could feel her latte-colored shins raked by plantain leaves just as the spindly shins of her mother, then just a child of seven, had been. How had they done it? Aurora's grandmother Lupe had been embarazada at the time with Aurora's future Uncle Fausto, her belly gently swelling like a ripening guava. It was a miracle the frightened familia reached the relative safety of Mexico.

"Eres un milagro de Dios," Marisol would later tell little Aurora: You are a miracle of God.

The family settled in Trenton, New Jersey. Aurora had legally hyphenated her name in college, including her mother's maiden name, as a statement of Latina pride. Over time, Aurora Marquez-

Connolly proved a mouthful. For the sake of convenience—and a punchier byline—she went by Aurora Connolly. But she pronounced "Aurora" with a Guatemalan accent [Ow-roar-ah] and flew a small Guatemalan flag on her desk. She spoke excellent Spanish and was openly bisexual. She liked to tease Cus, who was straight as the arrows used by his Mohawk ancestors, that he should expand his sexual parameters.

One of her great joys was catching him off guard with a suggestive comment and watching him blush, albeit only through her left eye. Aurora was legally blind in the right one from birth, hence her ken for adopting one-eyed dogs. That alone made her a dramatically different woman from Jenny, who disliked indoor pets and was known to say, "We've evolved out of living like animals. Why do people bring them into their homes?"

Cus admired his wife's toughness, but at times he wearied of the bitch-on-wheels townie bullshit. Aurora was different and not just because she was not from Tiberius. She could be tough too, of course; the work demanded it. But there was a softness there, a vulnerability. Cus had never been with a person of color, let alone a bisexual with a vision impairment. His imagination would at times wander in that direction, but fantasy was as far as he'd let it go—or so he believed.

"We should get back to work," Cus would admonish Aurora when her flirtations became too direct.

Aurora always obliged her earnest colleague because the work mattered to her, too. Despite her flirtatious side, she demanded to be taken seriously. During her job interview at the *Daily Informer*, she'd made it a point not to volunteer that she was half Latina. She would not be a nod to staff diversity. She wanted to be hired for her talent, and she was. Aurora knew how to follow money and comb databases for wrongdoing. But she was no mere screen queen. She wasn't afraid to knock on doors and turn on the charm to get answers. Plus, the girl could write. No one at the *Daily*

Informer could touch Cus when it came to seamless, impeccably reported narratives. His study overflowed with awards, including a prestigious-yet-obscure Selden Ring for Investigative Reporting. But Aurora was one of a rare breed of journalists who possessed both fluency in technology-assisted reporting techniques and a literary bent. Clear, concise, and never over-reaching, her prose was flecked with clever transitions and masterfully understated evocation. Once, she had made a hardboiled copy editor tear up when she wrote, "Undoubtedly through the tiny cracks in the frame of her bedroom window, the captive, starving preteen could smell burgers grilling at the Wendy's across the street."

Her varied skill set left her vulnerable to occasional stints on the copy desk as cost cutting drained the newsroom of bodies and talent. She didn't hate the editing, and she took pride in writing catchy headlines. There was also a satisfying something each time she hit the typeset icon on her screen and sent a page to the composing room. In those moments, she felt all-powerful, as if the collective energy required to produce the daily miracle known as a newspaper was passing through her fingertips.

That said, Aurora's highest calling was to report, and she wasn't beyond grousing to Cus about the unfairness of the late-night gigs on the desk.

"Prostitutes get home from work before I do, and they make more money."

"And you give better headline," Cus teased, quickly blushing.

She beamed her remarkable smile and winked at him, and he blushed even more. Their workplace flirtation had risks, of course, but it was the ultimate in team building. Cus and Aurora were smart and hard working on their own, but they worked harder and smarter together. The balancing act was to keep things from getting serious.

Then the tightrope broke.

Departing their rustic State of New York love nest, they walked in silence through the stands of white pine and pink sentries of astilbe, pausing for a long, torrid kiss, then pausing again. The implications of their carnal adventurism weighed heavily on them, but more so on Cus, a married man.

Finally, they reached the back side of 866 Old Spruce Road, which Aurora had already identified as belonging to a mysterious Eco Ventures LLC. They peered through the chain link. Nothing seemed out of the ordinary beyond a few discarded tires. The No Trespassing signs were not welcoming or suggestive of transparency, but in this part of the world, they were not unusual. Most owners of forested acreage did what they could to discourage hunting and trapping without permission.

Only a woodpecker hammering in the distance broke the quiet.

"Should we try to go in and look?"

"No," Cus said. "But apparently we're all about breaking rules today. Why not one more?"

The fence was ten feet tall but climbable for two intrepid, still-youngish reporters. Cus had two marathons under his belt, and Aurora belonged to a climbing gym. She effortlessly surmounted the fence, showcasing a comfort with verticality suggestive of her Mayan ancestry. Cus enjoyed the view as she scrambled up and soon joined her on the other side. They followed a poorly maintained trail along the fence for fifty yards and kept going as it cut deeper into the property. Next, they traversed a makeshift footbridge over a brook. A carpet of lavender blossomed on the other side and led to a clearing.

"What the—" Aurora gasped. An open pit six feet deep and fifty yards wide stood before them. Next to the far edge was a small excavator.

Woody pauses on the word excavator. Best to avoid any association with Dunn-Rite Dig & Demo and its fleet of excavators.

He replaces the word with Bobcat—a brand Dunn-Rite doesn't use—and continues.

Next to the far edge was a Bobcat, a large one, outfitted with a forty-two-inch trenching bucket. They walked to the edge and looked down, taking in an unholy sprawl of discarded concrete, chunks in all sizes, dumped as if they were a handful of pebbles cast by an absentminded giant. Some of the boulders and eco-blocks—great bricks of waste concrete, some weighing several tons—were stained off-green, orange, or yellow. The ground looked faintly damp. And that smell, a sweet-sharp metallic tang. If evil had body odor, this would be it. An aluminum ladder rested against the near wall.

Through their three sighted eyes, the pair beheld the rape of ancient land.

"Whoever did this needs to pay," Cus murmured.

"What's in those bags?" Aurora asked.

Cus hadn't seen them, but he followed her gaze and now saw a half-dozen or so bulging contractor bags partially hidden by debris.

"Let's take a look," he said. He scrambled down the ladder then stopped cold ten feet from the bags. He could see one had toppled sideways and spilled open. The multicolored mass rotting into the earth sent a shiver of fear through him, but surely it was just a dead possum or woodchuck. He inched closer, the stench now overpowering. Then he knew. The object before him was no hapless critter. It was a human foot. Next to it lay what Cus recognized as a glenoid bone, the dish-shaped socket of someone's shoulder.

"What is it?" Aurora shouted down.

He tried to reply, "Nothing good," but before the words could come out, he vomited on a rusted hubcap.

They walked a slightly different route back to the car, back and forth over a muddy brook on mossy makeshift footbridges.

"We should get a water sample," Cus said. "I have an empty water bottle in the car. We can use that."

"This whole thing is creeping me out, Cus."

"I know," he said.

"Do you think . . ." She didn't finish her sentence.

"Look, anyone could have dumped that stuff," Cus said with rare pique. "It could be one of Al's competitors or any contractor for that matter."

Aurora stayed silent. She understood that the knot in her gut, uncomfortable though it was, was smaller than the one in his. It was best to let him speculate on Cold Harbor's involvement; she should stay out of it for now and stick to the science.

Finally, she said, "We'll get to the bottom of this. We're a good fit." She said it with a hint of mischief, intending the double meaning to lighten the mood, but if Cus picked up on it, he gave no indication. A whippoorwill trilled merrily from a stand of fir.

"We are, and we will," he said.

They strode into a clearing encircled by wild mint and lemon balm that led to the trailhead a few hundred yards to the east. The birdsong was louder now, and insects hummed. Cus's F-150 was parked where they left it. Only something about the hood, even from a distance, looked off. As they closed in, they saw a swirly design etched into the dust and pollen.

Then, drawing closer, Cus made out that it was in fact a message: "Back Off. Last Warning!"

By now, Woody has almost four thousand readers, or at least page views, among fearasmud.com, the book's dedicated Facebook and Instagram pages, his Twitter and Goodreads accounts, and Cluckin' Clean's home page. The audience is engaged. People offer plot suggestions and speculate where the mystery might be headed. They discuss whether the book's potboiler tone condemns it to mediocrity or lends a gently satirical bent accessible only to more sophisticated readers. There's even a thread of people debating whether it's their place to critique a work in progress.

"Let the man write!" a fan implores.

The literalists, incapable of suspending disbelief, are having their say too, besieging him with catches.

"Imposible is in El Salvador. Get a map, douche."

"So, let me get this straight: Aurora's grandparents and her mother escaped war-torn Guatemala by fleeing east into El Salvador, hiked over a mountain and then went back into Guatemala? Then they headed to the south of Guatemala and crossed the Paso Hondo into Mexico, which is on Guatemala's northern border? You're either writing magical realism in the tradition of Gabriel Garcia Marquez or a drunken pendejo."

It's easy enough for Woody to slough off the pedants. At least they're reading and sufficiently involved in the narrative to send feedback. It's another category of reader response that has him reaching for the Pepto. The most active social media threads involve his wife and in-laws.

"I know the Dunns," the chairwoman of the Icarus Literacy Foundation chimes in on Facebook. "They're warm, kind, generous people—nothing like the garbage Mr. Hackworth portrays in his book."

Others are unconvinced.

"I doubt Mr. Hackworth's wife and family are as venal as Al and Vivian Holmes and their corrupt brood. Those characters are over the top and not believable, if you ask me. But am I wrong to wonder from whence Woody draws his material? He was a solid reporter and writer at the *Blaze*, but his stuff was dull as hell until now. As they say: Write what you know."

"I've been doing excavation work in this town for 30 years," another post goes. "Lots of shitty little people running shitty little companies. I thought Dunn-Rite was different. Guess that's why I'm just a laborer, but at least I can sleep at night."

"Woody's wife must be a total C*&^," IcarusChickarus12 postulates on Twitter. "My guess: She'd not dirty her manicured nails by dumping medical waste in the woods herself, but how far-fetched is it that she'd look the other way if it helps Mid-State Group meet its quarterly profit goals?"

Till now, Woody has not engaged in the online banter, but he knows he can't let that tweet stand. "Mandy is the treasure of my life," he types. "She's an honest, loving, devoted wife to me and mother to our daughter. She bears no resemblance whatsoever to the fictional Jenny."

In seconds, someone else responds. "I lost my job at Mid-State when your honest, loving, devoted wife outsourced lab work to save a few bucks. Got cancer? You'll wait up to three weeks for the new outfit to tell you, assuming they don't get it wrong. Spare us the bullshit, Hackworth. We all know who Jenny is."

Woody vows to never again enter the online fray. The book must speak for itself. Naturally, some lower-functioning readers will struggle to differentiate truth from fiction. It's an occupational hazard any novelist faces.

Yet beneath his bravado, Woody senses things are spinning out of control. Among the wild cards he didn't foresee: rival contractors leveraging the book to trash his in-laws. He wonders what else he overlooked.

His phone rings at 9 a.m. sharp as he's dripping with Peloton sweat from a forty-five-minute ride at pace. This time he's taken the class from a German instructor, Greta. He barely knows a word of German, but it's easy to follow her turquoise leggings as they pound out metronomelike pedal strokes in grim pursuit of corporeal perfection. Greta intrigues him. He believes she is objectively beautiful, but he isn't sure he is attracted to her. During the ride, he factors in that maybe the guttural harshness of the language is the source of his ambivalence, so he turns down the volume, but he still can't find clarity. Would he like her more if she were from Santa Barbara? Such thoughts distract him from his labored breathing and angry hamstrings. Then comes a phone call. It's Annabelle.

"I have good news and bad news."

"Start with the good news."

"My editors like the story so much that they want it in the print edition after all."

"Awesome. Good for us. So, I guess the bad news is I have to wait a month for the story to run? That's no big deal."

"Yes, well, that's part of the bad news."

"There's more bad news?"

"Kind of. Print stories get edited more closely, and I had to report out the story more than I was planning to originally."

"And?"

"And something came up about the circumstances of your departure from the *Blaze*."

Woody's heart sinks. He knows where she's going. "Let me guess," he says. "Whispers of made-up sources?"

"More like murmurs than whispers."

"If you're a good reporter, you know it isn't true."

"Maybe I should hear your side before I draw any conclusions," she says briskly.

He tells her what happened—how he had gotten stuck working a Saturday shift and covering a 10K charity race for Wounded Warriors. How he'd interviewed a teenager along the route. How the teen earnestly said his dad, Sergeant Neal Horst, was unofficially participating in the race, wearing special high-tech shoes because he had no sensation in his feet after being wounded in Kandahar by a roadside bomb. How, after the story ran, an event organizer phoned the paper to say Neal Horst was in the event as an official participant and running in regular shoes. How Woody's attempt to track down the teenager who had provided the information led to the realization that the teenager had given him a false name. That Woody's editors, while seemingly inclined to believe Woody was merely careless and not dishonest, did not completely discard the possibility that Woody, who had been sulky about being called in to work on a Saturday, had been caught making up a source. How his layoff, while probably not directly related to the incident, might have made it easier for his editors to cut him loose.

"So, you truly believed they had magic shoes that let people with catastrophic nerve impairments feel their feet?" Annabelle asks.

"I guess I just accepted it at the time," Woody says. "Look, I fucked up. Okay? Is this really going to be part of your story?"

"I doubt it," Annabelle says. "It's not really relevant to what you're doing now. Besides, now you're writing fiction. I mean, it's based on your family, but it's still fiction. You can make up whatever you want."

"It's not based on my family."

"Got it," Anabelle says brightly. "Anyway, we should be good to go here. The story will post online sometime March 14, and I will send you some hard copies that should arrive around the same time. You might hear from a fact-checker between now and then. Magazines can be a pain, but they're pretty good about getting things right."

He detects some snark in that last sentence. "Yep," Woody says thickly.

"I really appreciate the help. Sorry about the uncomfortable questions. Your book is crushing it. I love that Aurora. What a hot shit."

"Thanks. I better get back to it."

They hang up. Woody checks his text messages.

"You up for a drink tonight?" reads one from Celeste.

"Cam wants to meet with us," reads another, from Mandy. "Will 11:30 work with your busy Fuck-Over-My-Family schedule?"

Woody messages Mandy back: "About the book?"

Mandy: "Yes."

Woody: "Where?"

Mandy: "His office."

Woody: "No."

Mandy: "No you won't meet, or you won't meet at his office?"

Woody: "Not there."

Mandy: "Why not?"

Woody has his reasons. Years of interviewing the powerful and privileged have schooled him on the importance of body language, seating arrangements, and the politics of venue. He knows, for example, that when the person you're interviewing stands, you stand also to neutralize any attempt at positional dominance. Once he enters Cameron's office, he'll be on enemy turf and at a psychological disadvantage. On the other hand, he doesn't want to signal to Mandy that he considers her brother an adversary. Nor does he want Cameron to think he feels intimidated or defensive. Why does everything have to be so complicated? As all these thoughts spin through his head, one asserts primacy: Now is not a good time for Woody to lecture his wife on journalistic protocols. She's heard it all before anyway.

"Okay, fine. I'll be there," Woody texts back. Then to Celeste: "I think so. Let me see how the day goes."

Except that message goes to Mandy. Another moment of inattention.

"Huh?" she replies.

"Sorry, misfired that," he writes.

"To who?"

Woody is perspiring almost as heavily as he was at the end of Greta's class.

"Just JB. He wants to grab a beer later."

"Don't forget Ella's playoff game is at four."

"I know," he lies. He'd blanked on that.

The doorbell rings.

Two twentysomethings are on his stoop. One carries a clipboard and wears a maroon neck bandanna and a ball cap with a frog logo. "Amphibians go both ways," the caption reads.

Woody spies a man bun. The woman next to him wears jeans and a honey-mustard T-shirt.

"Hello," she says. "My name's Megan, and we're with the New York Public Interest Research Group. We're asking people to sign a petition in support of clean waterways. There's a bill pending in the state assembly, A821—"

"I'll sign it," Woody says, not letting her finish. He doesn't want to be trapped in a meaningful conversation with idealists. He scribbles his name.

"Can you print your name also, please?" Amphibian Boy asks.

Woody obliges, then says, "Are we at the part where you ask me for money?"

"That's entirely up to you whether you'd like to donate, but of course . . ."

Woody fishes through his wallet for a twenty and hands it to the woman.

"I appreciate your hard work," he says.

"Thank you sooo much," she says. "You have a wonderful day."

Woody has no way of knowing that someone at the regional NYPIRG office is reading his novel online, loves the environmental angle, and will soon be thoroughly engaged by a chapter that explores the detrimental effects of Portland cement on groundwater pH. Or that he will be invited to speak on the topic at a monthly meeting of Save the Lake, or that his talk will be livestreamed on multiple platforms, and that snippets of his comments will air on two local TV news affiliates. Or that there's an uncomfortable waste disposal overlap issue between his nefarious fictional concrete supplier, Cold Harbor, and the scrupulously law-abiding business run by his in-laws. The overlap: Disposal of waste concrete is a concern not just to concrete suppliers like the one in Woody's book but for demolition contractors such as Joe Dunn.

At Dunn-Rite, Joe deputized Tanner to establish an in-house green committee to explore environmentally friendly ways to recycle and dispose of demolition materials. Tanner delivered. Crushed waste concrete from Dunn-Rite jobs can now be found throughout the county and beyond—in roadbeds, driveways, and other infrastructure. Dunn-Rite donated most of the fill used to landscape a picturesque creekside park in Carltonville, one of the city's poorest neighborhoods.

Moreover, before the company takes down any building, Dunn-Rite sends in crews to remove hardware, wiring, insulation, even glass, all of which is turned over for recycling. Another crew harvests scrap wood. Visitors to the headquarters can't miss the lobby wall dedicated to awards the company has received from various planet-saving associations. Woody glumly mulls them as he waits to be summoned.

CHAPTER 6

J-O-B

"Mr. Dunn will see you now," Alice, the receptionist, informs Woody.

"You mean Cam?" Woody jokes, asserting family privilege. "Since when did Cam become a mister?"

Alice laughs politely and points down the hallway with exaggerated grandiosity. She's busy.

"What's up, guys?" Woody asks falsely as he enters Cam's office, ignoring Mandy's menacing glare. His dark walnut desk, eight feet long and handcrafted by Mennonites, possesses a no-bullshit simplicity that projects power. Behind the desk hangs a grainy color photo from 1983 of Dunn-Rite excavating the foundation for Shopper's Paradise, still the largest mall between Sandusky, Ohio, and Framingham, Massachusetts.

It's clear from the arrangement that Woody will occupy the Seat of Diminution, the one typically filled by eager-beaver sales reps from John Deere and Komatsu and by employees flagged for viewing porn on company Wi-Fi.

Cam rises from his desk and extends his hand, a polite but formal gesture considering they're brothers-in-law. "I really appreciate you coming in on short notice," Cam says.

"Sure," Woody says pleasantly. "How can I help?"

"How can you help?" Cam asks mildly, casting his glance afar. "Hmm. How can you help?" Then his face hardens, and his eyes turn to Woody's. "You can help by shitcanning that book of yours and leaving all of us—your wife, your family, my family, this business, which my father and Uncle Ray spent forty-five years building—with what's left of our reputation."

"Whoa, whoa, whoa! My book has nothing to do with you guys." His eye catches a trace of the framed photo on Cam's desk of Dunn-Rite's fiftieth anniversary party, the one with the cake declaring, "Expert Blow Jobs since 1963"—a relic from happier days, when the country knew how to laugh.

Cam hits the intercom on his desk. "Winnie?"

"Yes, Cam," his administrative assistant replies.

"Can you have Doug come in here?"

"Sure thing."

They sit in silence for thirty seconds. Finally, a wiry man in his early forties wearing a high-vis vest enters the doorway.

"Come on in, Doug," Cam tells him. "You've met my brother-in-law, Woody, before, right?"

"Absolutely," Doug says. "The famous writer. At the company picnic. Two picnics, actually."

"And, of course, you've met my sister, Mandy."

"Yes, sir." Then to Mandy, "Nice to see you again, Mrs. Hackworth."

"Ms. Dunn," she corrects and gives him a don't-worry-about-it wave. "Nice to see you, too."

Cam says, "Okay, Doug, tell us about your current assignment."

"I'm the onsite supervisor at the Piersaw Farm Supply job."

"And can you tell us what their regional manager asked you?"

Doug looks uncomfortable. "He asked if we could make some expired fertilizer and insecticides from the old warehouse disappear once the new warehouse is finished."

"And what did you tell him?"

"I told him the truth—that we're not a hazardous waste disposal company, we're not licensed for that."

"And what did he say?"

"He asked if five hundred bucks would cover it."

Woody's face feels hot.

Cam continues. "Has anyone ever asked you anything like that before?"

"No, sir. Never."

"And do you have any idea why he asked you that?"

Doug looks nervously down at Woody. "I don't want to get anyone in trouble," he says.

"No one's in trouble," Cam says. "We're all family here."

Doug looks at the floor as he speaks. "Well, he did ask me: 'So, that book Joe's son in-law is writing—it's all bullshit?'"

"And what did you tell him?"

"I didn't know what book he was talking about. I felt like a dumbass, to tell you the truth." He looks at Mandy, embarrassed by his profanity. "Sorry, Mrs. Dunn."

"It's all good, Doug," Cam says. "She's heard far fucking worse."

Everyone shares a quick laugh.

"And said far fucking worse," Mandy adds.

Then Cam, the cross-examiner, resumes. "But you're reading the book now?"

"I am, Mr. Dunn."

"And you like it?"

"I do. I'm a little concerned about how it makes us look. I mean, I know we're one hundred percent by the book here, so to speak, but people—"

"People talk, don't they, Doug?" Mandy says.

"They do, Mrs. Dunn."

Cam takes a deep breath. "You've been great, Doug. Thanks for the info. You can get back to work."

"Any time, Mr. Dunn."

After he exits, Mandy and Cam stare at Woody.

"Was that a setup?" Woody asks.

"For Christ's sake, did it sound like a setup?" Cam asks.

"Yes," Mandy says. "It was a setup. We enlisted one of Dunn-Rite's most trusted employees to lie on our behalf because that's what we do for fun. We're pranksters in our spare time. What the hell is wrong with you? Do you need to go back on your meds?"

That was cheap. He'd been on a low dose of Klonopin for anxiety for about five months during the dark days after he left the *Blaze*. "I'm finally starting to make a name for myself outside of this godforsaken shithole and you want me to just stop?" Woody says. "Who's the one being selfish?"

"This shithole's been pretty good to you," Cam replies.

Woody looks out the window, seeing nothing, and says, "I'm not comfortable with this discussion."

"You think we're comfortable?" Cam asks. "You think we're comfortable being the inspiration for the criminal trash your wet dream alter ego gets to bring to justice?"

"You don't even know how the book ends," Woody snipes.

"How does it end?" Mandy asks.

"I honestly don't know," Woody says. "I started writing the thing and putting it up online with no ending in mind. So, unlike your brother here, I don't know how it ends. I wish I did. It would take a lot of pressure off. All I know is people like it."

"We don't," Cam says.

"So, the answer is to intimidate, to censor me? You know something? That sounds like something Al Holmes would do."

"We're not trying to censor you," Cam says. "That's not who we are. Maybe there's some sort of middle ground here, short of—"

"Suing me for libel?" Woody feels the winds shift in his favor. "You know what? That also sounds like something Al Holmes would do. Maybe I should put *that* in the book."

Mandy and Cam look at each other uncomfortably.

"It's a bad idea," Woody says. "If you sue me, the lawsuit goes public. The *Blaze* will write about it. Their story will be riddled with typos and factual errors, but it will be read, and the book will get even more attention."

He's doing them a favor. They're lucky he's a media guy who understands these nuances. If he was really the selfish prick they're making him out to be, he'd let them sue and reap the benefits. To be the author of a banned book, or a book that others are attempting to ban, how cool would that be? He'd be in the same conversation as Orwell, Nabokov, and Rushdie. And talk about a new wrinkle—to have the author's wife and her family doing the banning? It would be a marketing dream. He imagines the cover of the book screaming, "Banned in the author's own home!" Wisely, Woody keeps those thoughts to himself.

"I have a better idea," he says.

"We're all ears," Mandy says.

"What if I make the fictional in-laws redemptive?" he suggests, channeling his friend Nick almost word for word. "It will be good for the book. They'll be more like real people, less like, you know, cartoons."

"It feels late for that," Cam says. "What if you just stop? Just shut 'er down, say you have writer's block or you're on a sabbatical or whatever you writer types say when you're sitting on your asses doing nothing. Want us to do an intervention and put you in rehab?"

"Cam, easy," Mandy interjects. "Woody has a point. If he suddenly stops working on the book, it's going to seem suspicious—like we have something to hide."

"Good point," Woody concurs, wishing he'd thought of it. "It's a writing problem, nothing more serious than that. I wrote my way into it. I can write my way out of it."

The three sit there, spent. Cam breaks the silence.

"I'm willing to let you give it a shot. Just do me a favor and write fast. This needs to be over. Can we agree you'll turn the book into something my parents can be proud of?"

"That's the goal," Woody says.

"Because the way things stand now, you're dragging our reputation through the mud. My mom went to the symphony last night. You wanna know what Mrs. Blankenship said to her in the lobby?"

Of Bev's vast circle of friends, Arlene Blankenship was Woody's least favorite. He'd long ago sized her up as a snoop and an agitator. "What'd she say?"

Cam cedes the floor to Mandy with a wave of his hand.

"She told Mom she's spending a lot of time these days defending me and Dad on this illegal dumping thing."

"Consider the source," Woody huffs.

"The source is you, Woody," Mandy counters coldly.

Far away, perhaps up on the interstate, a jackhammer pounds.

"How's business?" Woody ventures, aggressively seeking a new subject.

"A little off, to be honest. Slowest March since the housing bubble. Care to take a bow?"

"You don't seriously—"

"I'm sure you're just one of several factors. But when I see a loyal customer like Susquehanna Commercial Development suddenly jumping ship and using the competition, it makes me wonder. Wouldn't you?"

"Are we almost done?"

Cam looks at Woody and shakes his head. "I honestly don't get it. You have all this money. You have an awesome family. You're a more than competent writer. Why screw it up like this? How can this be fun for you?"

Woody tries a little flattery. "It's never going to be as fun as blowing up buildings, but it's all I've got."

Surprisingly, Cam runs with the redirection. "No argument there. Did you see we got the contract to take down Civic Stadium?"

Once the seventy-six-year-old relic is demolished, it will be replaced by the Upstate New York Sports Hall of Fame—a logical priority in a city that perennially registers one of the nation's highest poverty rates. Woody is tempted to say, "So much for business being down" but thinks better of it.

"Mandy told me. That's going to be an event!"

"Yeah, it should be something to see that bad boy go down. Kind of sad in a way."

"Sure," Woody agrees. "You've got great memories from Civic." That's a nod to Cam's high school football days as an all-conference tight end. More flattery.

"We'll get through this other crap," Cam says, brightening.

"I'm just trying to write a book," Woody says. "That's all. I need a creative outlet. A purpose. Is that so awful?"

Woody had almost won the meeting, but his candid admission that he was searching for purpose was a blunder.

Cam shrugs. "Maybe it's time to get a real job, ya know? Get out of your head. I'm just sayin'."

As Woody drives home, the well-intentioned advice becomes a refrain that assumes an almost physical presence in his skull: *Maybe it's time to get a real job, ya know? A real job. Get a real job. Maybe it's time to get a real job. Get out of your head. I'm just sayin'. Get out of your head. Get a real job. Ya know?*

So unfair. He'd had a real job. But this grimy, visionless, potholed cow town fucked him. It's not his fault that Icarus values corn mazes and snow blowers more than an award-winning upholder of truth and justice. It's not his fault the town coughed him up like a tubercular clot of sputum. That's what Icarus did. It was forever destroying its greatest attributes, incapable of seeing beyond its pathologically pragmatic Middle American vacuity.

Maybe it's time to get a real job, ya know? Yeah, and maybe it's time to kiss my ass. *But write fast, Woody. Write fast and get a real job. Sure, Cam. No problem. Any other requests? Can I detail your fucking Escalade while I'm at it?*

Woody isn't exactly driving a Kia Forte himself. He wheels his Lexus hybrid SUV down Longhouse Boulevard and sees that the line at Mega-Shine isn't bad. For all his stated commitment to the environment, he has no problem patronizing the ubiquitous automated car wash monopoly, one of the area's major consumers of fresh water and splasher of harmful phosphates into the ecosystem. He heads toward the autopay lane, and there it is, like a message from the Creator: A help wanted sign.

Maybe it's time to get a real job, ya know?

Yes. Maybe it's time.

He redirects from the autopay lane toward a booth filled by a chubby, cute redhead.

"Are you interested in our three-for-one Lux-o-Shine package for $69.99?" she asks with zombie indifference.

"Yes!" Woody says.

The girl registers a faint look of surprise. "Any other services today, sir?"

"Everything," he replies. "I want it all."

"Interior and exterior?"

"All of it."

"Carpet and upholstery shampoo and sixty-minute hand wax?"

"I want to spend a lot of money," he says.

"We can make that happen," she enthuses, suddenly alive. "How long can you leave the car?"

"As long as you need it." He's so consumed by petulance that he forgets Ella's lacrosse game.

"I can put you in for Ultra Showroom Empire Detail, which includes minor dent and scratch removal. But your vehicle won't be ready until closing."

"Perfect."

"That's going to be $676.87," she says.

"Plus tip!" Woody says happily. "I noticed you have a help wanted sign. Just out of curiosity, how much do they pay here?"

"It's $15.50 an hour, but you can make almost twice that with tips most days unless it's raining."

"Or snowing."

"Or snowing. Don't remind me."

The long, cruel winters, more long than cruel with climate change, connect Icarusians of all ages, incomes, and creeds.

"Can I pick up an application inside?"

"Sure. Or you can have your son or daughter submit one electronically, and they'll call them in for an interview."

"That's awesome. Thanks, Monica," says Woody, who prides himself on reading name tags.

He proceeds toward the conveyor for the basic touchless wash. No need for spray-on wax; extensive hand waxing in the neighboring bay will follow. But he's in for Wheel Max-Brite, Tire Dressing, Undercarriage Anti-Corrosion Treatment, Brake Dust Remover, and Ceramic Gloss Boss.

As he waits his turn, he studies a scraggly dude and a college age girl who might be Middle Eastern working the presoak station. They wear rubber raincoats and boots, their expressions studies in concentration. Maybe they're misunderstood writers, too.

"Your window, sir!" the girl shouts.

Woody realizes one of his back windows is down. He waves a thanks and raises it. He wonders if, in the event he gets the job, they'll start him out hosing down cars or hand toweling at the other end. He's good either way. As long as Mandy, Cam, and the rest of them see it as a giant F.U.

Once the typhoon of suds has worked its magic on the exterior of Woody's Lexus, he loops around and parks it in front of one of the detailing bays.

He takes a seat in the lobby and catches a few minutes of *Sports Center* then opens his laptop. He's too agitated from the meeting to write, so he calls up a website on the effects of concrete leaching into water sources. That's what real writers do—they research. *It's called a J-O-B, and it's real. Very, very, real.*

He starts reading a technical paper in the *ACI Materials Journal.*

"When concrete structures, such as pier supports, are placed in water, they can have a detrimental effect on the surrounding environment by causing pH levels to rise," he reads. "This rise in pH can harm and kill animal and plant life. The concentration of hydroxyl ions leached from concrete can be affected by several factors, including cement type, shape and structure, ratio of surface area, and . . . "

Woody's eyes grow heavy. Soon, he's dimly aware of his chin hitting his chest. It's his last conscious thought until a fellow customer taps him on the shoulder and points to a Mega-Shine employee trying to get his attention.

"Do you happen to know what that stain is on the carpet in the back?" the attendant asks. "It looks like blood."

"Yeah, my daughter got spiked in the shin at her—"

Ella! Her lacrosse game. He looks at his phone. There's a text from Mandy from five minutes ago: "Game just started."

CHAPTER 7
ANNABELLE'S STORY

Woody scrolls up and sees three messages from Mandy.

"Plenty of parking behind tennis courts."

"$10 admission because its playoffs. They only accept cash."

"Sect. 11, row L. Saved you a seat."

The attendant intrudes on his reading. "We're not allowed to clean up blood, sir. State law. You'll have to take the car to a place that specializes in biohazard cleanup."

The woman who woke him looks disgusted.

"Just get my rig out of there," Woody implores. "Now. Please."

"Not to worry, sir. We can still finish your vehicle. We're just not allowed to work on that stain, plus there's a $50 biocontainment fee, again thanks to the good ol' state of New York. Sorry about that."

"I need my Lexus," Woody says.

He and the attendant look through the soundproof glass at the motionless conveyor. A Toyota Camry and a Jeep sit still as statues in front of Woody's Lexus with their doors open and three-person teams attending to each. One worker emerges from the Toyota with its floor mats and trundles them toward a sprayer.

"I can't move you until they finish up the cars in front of you."

Woody slumps in his chair. The woman who roused him says, "This is none of my business, but you were really snoring and it sounded like you stopped breathing a few times. Do you have sleep apnea? Because my husband's a big snorer and finally his doctor got him to use one of those machines, and I have to say I've noticed a huge difference."

Woody barely hears her. He's summoning an Uber.

"Your ride will arrive in 16 minutes," a message informs.

"Blow me!" Woody says to his phone.

"I was just trying to be helpful," the woman says. "Next time, I'll let you choke."

Woody gets up and heads into the convenience store, pours himself a cup of coffee, and waits for his ride. It's supposed to be a gray Acura driven by someone named Hamsa. Before he climbs in, he checks his messages one more time. There's another one from Mandy, a six-second video of Ella scoring the Crusader's first goal.

His ride arrives a few minutes early.

"How are you today, sir?" Hamsa asks cheerfully. He's lean and dark, with bright, alert eyes. He must be tall, too. Even with his seat reclined his head nearly touches the Acura's headliner.

He's sick of being asked how he "is" by people who couldn't care less. "Actually, this is not my best day."

"Oh, I am very sorry," Hamsa says. "Your car, it is not good? They have damaged your vehicle?"

"No, it's just being held hostage."

"Yes, I understand," Hamsa says. "I too was held hostage!"

Woody is too absorbed in his angst to ask for details. "The real problem is I'm writing a book, and my wife and her family don't like it."

"They do not like it!" Hamsa loudly affirms.

"No, they do not like it. They think I'm making them look like bad people even though the people in my book are not real. Do you understand?"

"Yes. I understand!"

"I'm a novelist."

"You write books!"

Woody sighs. "Yes. I write books."

"I am sorry you have this problem with your wife and her family. They should support you!"

"Thank you," Woody says.

Longhouse Street has given way to leafier environs, with small pastures coming into view.

"You make lots of money writing books?"

"Not yet. This is my first one unless you count *Tick Tock, Check Your Sock*, which you've no doubt read."

The sarcasm is lost on Hamsa.

"I have not read it! It is about a sock?"

"Not exactly."

"In the country where I am from, we rarely wear socks. When we do, we must first check them for scorpions."

"Where are you from?"

"I am from Sudan! Thursday will be my two-year anniversary of coming to America."

"Congratulations. And your family, all is good?"

"No problems whatsoever! We are excellent. Except one of my uncles in Sudan is being held by the rebels, and we fear that he is dead. And the village I come from has been burned to the ground, and all the people, they now live in a refugee camp. It is very sad. The political situation in my country is not good."

Woody feels small and selfish, which makes him wish he hadn't engaged the driver. He knows his life puts him among Earth's most comfortable 1 or 2 percent, but this isn't the time he wants to be reminded. Not when he just missed Ella scoring a goal.

"Family stuff is hard," Woody says, a feeble attempt at commiseration.

At the stadium, Woody clambers out of the Acura and speed walks toward the stands. Hamsa shouts, "Good luck with your book and your family, my friend! Family is the most important thing. Trust me, you cannot escape it." He punctuates the sentence with a knowing laugh.

Woody waves goodbye. He wonders why he feels so morose while

Hamsa, whose young life has been marked by imponderable horrors, can be so cheerful. Maybe it's an immigrant thing or an African thing. Woody doesn't have much experience in either camp except for Mr. Goff, his high school woodshop teacher, who was born in Nigeria or someplace like that. Woody once got a few giggles from the class when Mr. Goff asked, "What can cause a dowel to fit too loosely in the hole?"

"Too much beer," Woody wisecracked.

Mr. Goff adjusted his glasses to better apprise Woody and said with cool nonchalance, "What the hell does Hackworth know? Everything he touches turns to shit."

The class exploded in laughter with so much force the overhead lights chimed. Woody could only stand at his workbench and blush, bested at his own game.

Now, his mind circles back to Nick's warning: "I'm concerned you're going to end up with a book that screams White people problems."

It strikes Woody that he might want to harvest this exchange with Hamsa to give *Fear as Mud* another much-needed minority character. While bestowing Guatemalan ancestry on Aurora had been a step in the right direction, there was the risk of her character being perceived as tokenism if she were the lone nonwhite. Two persons of color—1.5 technically—would lend multicultural depth to the narrative. Plus, Woody reminds himself, he can always make some of Cus's newsroom colleagues Jewish. He won't count them in his diversity tally; they're too Caucasian for that. But they are minorities. Jews are useful to writers that way, Woody ruminates. Plug-and-play differentness—a sort of ethnic Quikrete.

Such are his preoccupations as he reaches the "cash only" ticket table and finds his wallet barren. "My wife's inside," he tells the high school kid working the counter. "Can I get the money from her and bring it to you?"

"Don't worry about it," the girl says, waving him in. "The first half's almost over anyway."

Mandy is forgiving. She knows that after the meeting at Dunn-

Rite, this is not the time to find fault.

With just the right note of nonjudging curiosity, she accepts his half lie: "My SUV was stuck in the car wash. The belt just stopped moving." She also promises to cover for him on the missed goal.

"We'll let Ella think you were here for it. Our little secret."

Woody was a decent athlete himself, but not in the same league as Ella, who's gunning for a Division 1 lacrosse scholarship. He played some basketball in his younger days. He was a big guard/small forward type with a reliable shot when left open. Results were more mixed when he tried to get creative.

In high school, he exceeded expectations by cracking the varsity starting lineup. But that was the zenith. During garbage time in a holiday tournament, he came down on an opponent's foot and lost two weeks with a high ankle sprain. After that, he came off the bench and pressed too hard. During practice one day, he face-planted into the bleachers diving for a ball he had no hope of saving. The resulting concussion doomed him to scrubdom and earned him a nickname rooted in his fragility: "Sawdust."

Ella hasn't had her dad's bad luck with injuries, thankfully. She makes a nice centering pass to a teammate for what should have been a score, but the shot hits the post, and the clock runs out on the first half. The Crusaders lead 8-6.

"You doing okay?" Mandy asks.

"I think so," Woody says. "I'm a little beat up, but I'll live. I need a snack. You want anything?"

"Red Vines if they have 'em."

Mandy's devotion to Red Vines is difficult for Woody to fathom, but he'd long accepted it. He starts to turn down the bleachers but abruptly turns back toward Mandy. "Do you have any cash?"

"Sure," she says, diving into her purse and extracting a twenty. "Will that suffice?"

He senses her and the other moms assessing his paunch. *Why must writing be so sedentary?*

It's a long queue at the concession stand. Woody notices he's a few people back from Becky Romero, the mother of Ella's Crusader teammate Lyla.

Lyla's a three-sport athlete, but lacrosse is her passport to college. She's in line for a Division 1 scholarship. Her mother, meanwhile, is in line for more mixer. A day drinker—and a night drinker—with boundary issues, Becky never leaves the house without a few airplane bottles of vodka.

Woody pretends not to notice he's behind her.

"Too famous to say hello?" she says, stepping out of line.

He turns around, pretending she must be talking to someone else. Then he points to himself incredulously, as if saying, "Who? Me? Famous?"

She gives up her spot in line to stand with him, hooking her left arm into his right. It's slightly inappropriate, but that's how Becky rolls.

"Hey, Becky," Woody says, "good game so far."

"They're all good games when the Goose is on board," she says with a boozy wink. "Oops! Am I not supposed to say that on school property?"

"I promise not to tell."

"Aurora's in on it, isn't she?"

"You're reading my book!"

"Of course I'm reading it. Everyone in town is reading it. The ones who say they aren't are lying. Am I right about Aurora?"

"I haven't worked that out yet." He orders a hot dog and a Coke and Red Vines and then another Coke for Becky.

"Extra ice in mine, sweetheart," Becky tells the volunteer mom taking orders.

While a high school kid fetches the items, Becky asks Woody, "Just out of curiosity, what does your lovely wife think of *Fear as Mud*?"

The question disarms him, both because it's a topic he'd rather avoid and it's the last thing he wants readers pondering. "Mandy? She loves it. Mainly she's glad I have something to keep me out of trouble, but yeah, she's following it like everyone else. I'd call her a fan."

Becky releases a seismic cackle that coats Woody's exposed forearm in vodka mist. "A fan? You are too funny!" She touches him lightly on the shoulder and drops her voice to a conspiratorial hush. "Make sure to stretch out when you first get up—those sofa beds can do a number on your back." More boozy guffawing.

Desperate to escape, Woody pays for the order and starts back to the stands. "Thanks for reading, Becky," he tells her. "I really appreciate it."

"Are you kiddin'? It's freakin' great. But give some thought to what I said about Aurora. Make her more of a b-i-t-c-h."

"I'll keep it in mind," Woody promises.

"And just between us, I don't need all that Guatemalan pride bullshit pushed in my face. This is America, for God's sake."

A few heads turn. Woody wonders if Becky is a racist. He'd heard thirdhand that she'd once called Obama a mullah. He also wonders if her idea for a plot twist has merit. Back at his seat, he watches the players warm up for the second half as Mandy chews on a Red Vine.

"How's Becky doing?"

"Shit-faced, as usual."

"Does she like your book?"

A hot dog chunk catches in Woody's throat. He washes it down with a slurp of Coke. "Not everyone's reading it, honey. Can we just watch the game?"

The Crusaders, after surrendering their hard-won halftime lead early in the third quarter, mount another comeback. Now, they're ahead by two goals, one assisted by Ella.

Woody's phone pings with a message, and the news is good.

"Story's live!" Annabelle includes a link. Woody casts a discreet look at Mandy to make sure she's immersed in the game before he dives into the story.

No-Restriction Fiction: The Wacky, Wonderful, Utterly Terrifying World of Online Books in Progress

by Annabelle Riley

They have websites, audiences and in some cases advertisers. They range from precocious teens to parking lot attendants to stay-at-home dads. Their common thread: Impatience. This new breed of internet novelists doesn't sit around waiting for an agent to sanction their work or for a publishing house to bequeath legitimacy. They write, they post and they write some more, often without knowing where they're going.

"If anyone has any idea for an ending—or for that matter a middle—please contact me immediately," half-joked Woody Hackworth, an award-winning but now unemployed newspaper reporter in Icarus, NY. His Fear as Mud toxic thriller is cast in concrete—the sand and gravel industry, more precisely—and reinforced with steely portrayals of familial criminality. It has 34,000 page views and counting.

Serialized fiction is not new, of course. Charles Dickens popularized the format with The Pickwick Papers in 1836. Almost 200 years before that, L'Astrée, immense in size and import, explored a romance between a shepherd and a shepherdess. But L'Astrée was a 20-year project, printed in bite-sized fascicles. Different times. Today a speedy writer can have a book up in 20 days.

The roar of the crowd startles Woody. He looks up to see the Crusaders celebrating with Ella in the middle of the mob. He deduces she has scored again—she's having the best game of her career. He stands and applauds wildly as Mandy shoots him a disdainful glance. She knows he was buried in his phone.

"Maybe give the phone a break, Woody," she mutters. "It's your goddamn daughter."

But he cannot resist glancing at it again when Mandy looks away. There's a text from Celeste.

"I just saw the write-up in *New Voices*. OMG. So awesome! What time tonight and where?"

Woody wants something strong and literary-ish. He wants absinthe.

"Trilogy, 8 pm," he replies. "Btw, chapter 9 is live."

"Awesome," she replies. "I can't wait to read it."

CHAPTER 8
THE D-WORD

Al Holmes owned an island, two of them technically. Both sat amid the Thousand Islands archipelago straddling the border with Canada. The larger one, Sarabeth Island, at almost two acres, contained—barely—one of the family's six vacation homes. Ninety minutes from the grit and bustle of Tiberius, Sarabeth was nonetheless a world away. The secluded five-bedroom manse off Heron Point, done in cedar and stone, was fairly restrained for Al's ostentatious tastes, except for the gold turrets. They afforded views of two rivers and a stunning expanse of salt marsh.

A five-minute boat ride from Sarabeth, still on the American side, was land ironically named Jupiter Island, scarcely bigger than its only residence, a one-bedroom cottage with a sunken indoor hot tub and a $50,000 outdoor pizza oven, never used. There was also a small wine cellar.

Al had a particular affinity for the cottage. When philandering is your primary form of recreation, it's hard to top a love nest on a microisle with no cell service. Al called it his "stabbin' cabin," and he often let customers, particularly ones who shared his predilection for adultery, "borrow" it. His generosity earned him a nice tax write-off. Al's crooked accountant, Harvey Geller, didn't miss a trick.

But that wasn't the only way the 3,000-square-foot charmer helped balance the books. It was good business to have some dirt on as many people as possible. The stabbin' cabin was perfect for that. Customers who might be inclined to dispute a charge or town council members who might be inclined to accept a low bid from a competitor for new sidewalks had a way of backing down if they knew that Al could blackmail them. Just like that, the cash-poor contractor would somehow find a way to pay up or the lower bid would get tossed on a technicality. No need for Al to raise his voice or send muscle. He understood that the best blackmail is the unspoken kind. That's not to say he was beyond dropping a hint.

"Hey, Rico," he once told the president and CEO of Galvetti Construction, a small residential contractor that had fallen into arrears. "Why don't you and the missus stop by Saturday night, and the four of us can watch a movie."

"What kind of movie?"

"I was thinking *The Jupiter Island Affair*. It's shot in black and white. One of those local production companies did it. Sentry, I think they're called."

That was a reference to the security company that provided video surveillance of Al's Upstate properties. It was all the collection agency Al needed. The $33,204.06 Galvetti owed was transferred to Cold Harbor the next day.

For all these reasons and more, Cus wasn't big on the idea of spending his fifteenth wedding anniversary at the stabbin' cabin. Or any cabin. Cabins were big trouble, it seemed. He'd already betrayed his marriage vows and professional ethos in one.

Beyond that, his wife and her family were subjects of the newspaper investigation he was leading. Al had to know Cus was hot on their trail. Was the cabin a fatal lure? Was the hunter becoming the hunted?

It was not lost on Cus that he'd be celebrating his wedding anniversary in his father in-law's den of infidelity. The whole thing was sick. Al was toying with him.

Cus had suggested to Jenny that they celebrate in the Catskills instead—"There's more to do there"—but the idea had left Jenny crestfallen. They'd spent their wedding night in the cabin before jetting off to their resort in the Seychelles islands the following night, and Jenny thought a redo would be romantic. "Dad can run you out there on his boat," she said. "It will give him something to do."

"Just me?" Cus asked. "Don't you mean us?"

Jenny looked surprised but then realized, or pretended to realize, that she had neglected to tell Cus the full plan.

"Oh, crap. I thought for sure I told you. I must have spaced."

"Spaced?"

In a tone that struck Cus as a little too casual, Jenny explained she'd be spending the night before their anniversary on Sarabeth with three of her gal pals from her wedding party, and she'd be arriving to Jupiter on a different pleasure craft.

"We can coordinate so we get there at the same time," Jenny assured him. "It will be like it was when you were not allowed to see me until Dad walked me down the aisle."

Cus thought, yeah, except this aisle is a forty-one-foot-deep international waterway with tides capable of dragging a corpse to the Bay of Fundy in a week.

Woody wonders if the Bay of Fundy connects to the St. Lawrence River. He probably should look it up, but he's tired of looking things up. Who's going to notice or care anyway? It's Canada. It's fiction. Fundy stays.

Cus imagined his lifeless body floating past Singer Island. What a bonus that would be for tourists exploring the castle there: "Look, Mommy. Is that a sea turtle?"

Except if his body is floating past Singer Island, won't it be recovered before it gets to the Bay of Fundy, wherever the Bay of Fundy is? And are there even sea turtles in the seaway? Woody reluctantly drops the Singer Island paragraph.

Cus shuddered at the possibilities. In open water alone with Al on his forty-foot *Mixed Blessing* was a recipe for a bad ending. Only his journalistic rigor and sense of decorum—plus his fading hope that Jenny was somehow oblivious to her family's evildoing—kept him from asking, "Honey, are you setting me up to be murdered?"

Then his thoughts turned to Aurora. Would Al kill her, too? Or was Aurora protection from his ruthless father-in-law? Killing Cus alone would not solve Al's problem. Al was smart enough to know that. And killing them both would raise far more questions than even Tiberius and its clubby district-attorney-for-life could sweep under the rug. Cus looked at his wife and for the first time noticed a hard set in her jawline that reminded him of her father's. All that was missing was a matching scar on her neck.

"Sounds great, Jenny," he lied. "Instead of your dad walking you down the A-I-S-L-E, he'll walk you onto the I-S-L-E. It's perfect."

"Thank you for being so understanding, Cus," she said. "I think you're going to like your present."

Aurora was horrified when, in the newspaper's long-abandoned lactation lounge, where the two reporters were now meeting regularly to swap notes in private, Cus told her the details of the anniversary plan. She reacted in Spanish, something she only did when distraught.

"Actúas como si la vida no valiera."

Cus understood her; he had picked up some Spanish in his younger days roping steers and stringing barbed wire on a Venezuelan finca.

"No, kiddo, I value my life," Cus replied stoically. "Deseo solo hacer lo major para el planeta." I wish only to do what's right for the planet.

The lounge was the color of Dijon mustard and apricot. It had a forlorn, stale quality—a maternal milking station soured by obsolescence. No longer did the *Daily Informer*—heinously mismanaged by the greedy third-generation spawn of its vainglorious founder, Mason Hansely—pay enough for staffers of childbearing age to start a family. The lounge made no more sense than a penguin rookery in the Sahara. Maternity was further discouraged by a cluster of cancers and degenerative nerve disorders suffered by employees—five times the amount of those diseases normally expected in a workplace of 200 people.

Rumors abounded of unsafe use and disposal of pressroom chemicals, faulty ventilation, and temporary fixes in advance of government health inspections.

Who would bring a newborn into that chamber of horrors?

An epidemiological study of the building by nearby SUNY Hampstead had been quietly dropped. There was even speculation that the toxic taint was the reason real estate bottom feeders snapping up newspaper properties nationwide had passed on the *Daily Informer*.

"We're Not Going Anywhere!" a sixty-point banner headline shouted when a deal to sell the ninety-four-year-old building fell through.

Still, the lounge remained technically a room where women could nurse their infants. As such, it retained a faint procreative glow, an inextricable association with the natural prerogatives of fecundity. Like ferns and moss springing from the miasma of a volcanic blast zone, reminders of new life in all its possibilities hung in the air, persistent amid the specter of old media collapse, tragic illness, and third-rate journalism.

"He's going to push you overboard, or he'll have one of his goons do it," Aurora fretted, her luminous brown eyes misting. "Or maybe he will let that bitch wife of yours do the honors."

"Easy, Aurora."

"I'm sorry, Cus. I'm scared."

"Just relax. I've gamed it out. The last thing he wants is for me to disappear under suspicious circumstances from his yacht, on his daughter's wedding anniversary, when he was the last one to see me alive. Most likely he just wants to intimidate me so we'll stop looking into Cold Harbor. Let him think he succeeded."

Aurora let the impeccability of his logic sink in then nodded in affirmation. Yes, it made sense. No one was cooler under pressure than Cus.

"You're one brave dude," she said.

"I'm not brave," Cus said. "I just don't know when to quit."

The old, empty refrigerator in the lounge emitted a low rumble, causing Aurora to cock her head.

"You work so hard," she said, getting up from the small conference table to massage his shoulders.

He bolted into a standing position and turned to face her. "For God's sake, Aurora. Here? Now?"

She drew him to her and pressed her lips to his. As if it had a will of its own, his right hand found a taut haunch. They were both undressed in seconds. She splayed out on the conference table before him, a vision of tawny perfection. Her head was turned to the side, her sighted eye toward the tabletop, its 20/20 vision obscured by ringlets of red-brown hair cascading down her cheek.

In the moment, Aurora wasn't just blind with passion. She was literally blind to what might be lurking in the hallway outside. Plus, her view of the doorway was obstructed by the muscled torso of her paramour. Cus readied himself to take her, but this time it was not to be. He felt as much as heard an extended click from behind, the unmistakable sound of a camera shutter. Aurora thought she heard something too, but, lost in a river of her passion, she dismissed it as another complaint of the refrigerator.

Cus wheeled around toward the door, covering himself as best he could, but there was nothing—only the sight of the door moving slowly back toward its frame.

"We fucked up, beautiful," Cus said in a rare invocation of profanity. "Let's get dressed."

"What?" Aurora whispered. "What happened?"

Careless had happened. Cus and Aurora had taken to meeting in the discreetly located lactation lounge precisely because it was private—so private they'd never bothered to latch the door much less lock it while they swapped intel on their investigation. But this visit to the lounge, their first since she'd seduced him at the state park, had taken a carnal turn. Cus knew he should have seen it coming. Maybe he had. The wick of their mutual lust had burned so hot, so fast, that Cus had let down his guard. He was not the panicking type, but he felt something in his chest that was close. By the time he and Aurora were decent, the clandestine photographer was long gone.

"We need to get out of here—now!" Cus said.

"If you're trying to scare me, it's working," Aurora said. "You look like you saw a chupacabra."

"Maybe I did," Cus said, well versed in the mythology of the bloodsucking beast.

"Who was it?"

"If we're lucky, it was just a Peeping Tom with an iPhone getting his rocks off. Some degenerate from telemarketing—or the editorial board."

"And if we're unlucky?"

"If we're unlucky, someone at this newspaper really wants us to stop investigating my father-in-law."

Aurora fastened her bra and stepped into her skirt. "Do you want to come over to my place and figure out where we go from here?"

"I don't think that's a good idea," Cus said.

Aurora fluffed her hair, crossed her arms, and gave him a slight pout.

"Happy anniversary," she said, heading for the door.

"Use un chaleco salvavidas."

"What?"

"Wear a life jacket."

CHAPTER 9
TRILOGY

Woody's looking forward to the fun, flirty Celeste. A different version shows up at Trilogy. She's dressed down in a Bills sweatshirt and high-waisted track pants. She seems moody, distracted.

"The copy desk is trying to dick with my story," she says, not looking up from her phone. "I might have to go back in there."

"What are you drinking?" he asks.

"Can you just order me a tonic with lime?"

Woody sags. He flags the bartender, relays Celeste's order, and orders for himself a Death in the Afternoon—one of Papa's favorite. Absinthe and champagne.

"Assholes," she says, still not looking up.

"What's up?" Woody asks with feigned interest. The last thing he wants is to talk shop with a reporter on deadline. After the day he had, Woody wants to talk about Woody.

Celeste launches into a tedious diatribe about pushback she's getting from the city attorney on her phrasing of the mayor's position on a threatened teachers strike. "Saying you are not taking a position is the equivalent of saying you're not supporting it. I didn't say he's opposing the strike. I just said he's not supporting it. Because he's *not* supporting it. Am I right?"

"Makes sense to me," Woody says, more interested in the surge of absinthe soothing his synapses than a pushmi-pullyu over semantics. He lets her work and occupies himself with his phone, reading the rest of Annabelle Riley's piece. He skims past the parts about the other authors, looking for more about himself. Then a line startles him like a snake slithering underfoot.

Hackworth, a former journalist, is no stranger to creative writing. He left his newspaper job amid murky circumstances after he inadvertently—he asserts—used a fictional source in a story.

"That bitch!" Woody howls loud enough for an older couple to look his way.

"Huh?" Celeste says.

"The part in the story about me leaving the *Blaze* under murky circumstances. Why would she put that in there?"

"Oh yeah, I saw that. Kinda weak, but it's not that big a deal. At least she included your semiexplanation. She's probably just trying to cover her ass in case you're doing the same thing in your book."

Woody takes a prolonged slurp of Death in the Afternoon. "What are you talking about? I'm supposed to use fake characters in a novel."

"You know what I mean. Like if you're plagiarizing or something like that. I wouldn't take it personally. It's a great write-up. If anything, I thought you'd be more pissed about what she said higher up."

Woody's heart quakes. He scans the whole article and finds the part he missed.

"Perhaps as newcomers to the craft, many of the authors stick to the safety of writing what they know. An assistant DA in DeKalb, Illinois, is serializing a story about an angel of death phlebotomist inspired by a true event. An adjunct philosophy professor turned river rafting guide in Truckee, California, takes us on a whitewater journey that elevates into an existential awakening. In Icarus, New

York, scarcely veiled as fictional Tiberius, an out of-work journalist is writing a newspapercentric thriller inspired by his in-laws and their successful construction business."

Woody's face feels as if it's on fire, but he plays it cool with Celeste. Billie Holiday's "All of Me" washes over the bar.

"Let people think whatever they want. As long as they're reading." He looks over at her and adds, "You're cute when you're angry."

Celeste isn't playing. "Save it for Cus and Aurora," she says.

"Now you're mad at me, too?"

"Why'd you have to make her Latina? Were you purposely trying to take the fun out of our little thing? Because it worked."

"It was a creative choice. I didn't want the book to come off as all about White people."

"Whoever Aurora is, she isn't me. Why didn't you at least check with me first? Sorry, but I'm finding your book a lot less interesting now that you've turned my character into Señorita Elena Brockovichadura de Guatemala." She almost spits the Spanish pronunciation.

"She's a great character."

"She's a fucking cliché, Woody."

"We're all clichés, Celeste. That's partly what the book explores—how we all conform to roles based on societal expectations. I'm a cliché, the bartender's a cliché. Those people at that table over there looking at us, they're clichés. We all like to believe in free will, but as the American philosopher Harry Frankfurt said, free will is, you know, bullshit. It's a conceit we use to avoid the uncomfortable truth that our actions are predetermined."

"Then it's predetermined I'm getting the fuck out of here." She gets up to leave.

Woody gestures toward her. "Okay, okay, I get it. My bad. I should have talked to you first about it. I fucked up. I'm sorry."

Celeste sighs.

The bartender slaps a wooden drink chip in front of Woody. "That's from the young ladies at that table," he says, pointing toward a booth of soccer moms. "They say congratulations on your novel. They're reading it in their book club."

Woody waves a thank you to them. All four of the women smile with delight and wave back.

"Look, maybe it's for the best," Celeste says. "We don't need the whole world gossiping about us, thinking we're involved when we're not."

"That's part of why I made her half Guatemalan—to give you some cover."

"Give *me* some cover?"

"Us. Hey, you have to admit—the lactation lounge scene is hot."

"It's bizarre." She waves a hand dismissively. "Back in the real world for a minute, I have some good news." Celeste brightens, the luminescent smile making its first appearance of the evening. Her eyes twinkle, and in an instant she transforms from a woman scorned to a woman irresistible.

"Another Press Club award?" he guesses.

"Nikko and I worked it out," she says happily. "We're getting married."

Woody's vexed. His Celeste fantasy has been the stuff of schoolboy idiocy. He tells himself they won't last, probably won't even make it to the altar. He heads home and throws himself at the mercy of the only temptress he can trust: his Art.

A light chop unsettled Grayson's Bay, the wind from the northwest biting and dying in random gusts. Otherwise, the day was pleasant enough for the thirty-five-minute voyage to Jupiter Island. Cus had not been there for years, not since Al had been on a brief fidelity jag and offered his son-in-law the house as a base to research an award-winning series on the invasive round goby. Otherwise, Cus was a stranger to the Thousand Islands, a labyrinthine marine redoubt of second homes and summer tourists far from the *Daily Informer* circulation area.

Cus had decided to forsake a conventional life vest, after all, lest he tip off Al to his suspicions. He was wearing a concealed micropersonal flotation device under his windbreaker, tight on his lower back. It was cold comfort. If Al intended to kill him, he'd most likely be dead before he hit the water. All the autoinflating PFD promised was he wouldn't sink to the bottom, improving the chances of another boater spotting his corpse bobbing on the surface.

But in all likelihood, Al and his musclebound first mate and director of security operations, "Tommy the Torque Wrench" Nunzio, would have found and removed the vest, wrapped his lifeless body burrito-style into a tarp, and dumped him overboard. Because they were professionals, they would chain buckets of concrete to him—almost certainly a high-density aggregate, the kind used for bomb shelters and counterweights.

Cus's deepest dread was that they would not have the decency to kill him first. While he did not fear death in general, drowning inside a musty drop cloth was not his preferred exit. Funny how his airtight theory that Al would never murder his son-in-law on his wedding anniversary felt porous now that they were on open water.

"That's a pro move, getting my baby flowers," Al said, having made note of the bouquet of lavender roses and spring blooms Cus brought on board. "You've always been a class act, Custer."

"I mean, it is our anniversary," Cus replied.

A decent-sized swell caught the boat, but the *Mixed Blessing* made short work of it with barely a shudder. "I always knew you were a stand-up guy," Al continued. "You know how I knew?"

Cus didn't know where this was going, but the sound of it made him contemplate plunging overboard of his own volition. "No idea," he said.

Al kept his eye on the horizon as he steered. A gull kept pace with the boat and cried with mournful portent. "I bet you know, don't you, Tommy?" Al said, addressing his deckhand. "Remember Custer's bachelor party?"

Cus felt his stomach lurch. Tommy the Torque Wrench hadn't attended that beery crawl through Boston's fading red light district, the Combat Zone. Not that Cus was aware of, anyway.

"You mean when he rejected that whore?" Nunzio said with a dark chuckle. "She was a looker. I bet the only reason he turned her down was because he had whiskey dick. That's the only possible explanation unless he's queeah."

The two navigators laughed the throaty laughs of hard men with sinister intent.

Drunk as he was at the bachelor party, Cus had been mortified that Jenny's brothers, Brock and Dylan, had brought the prostitute into the $1,200-a-night suite Al had booked for the gala. They'd pushed her on the groom-in-waiting almost literally, but Cus had refused because Cus was Cus.

"Thanks, guys, but prostitution exploits women, and this wouldn't be fair to your sister," he'd told his soon-to-be in-laws.

Then he had turned to the buxom sex worker and said, "Don't take this personally, but I take marriage seriously. I don't want to start mine off this way. You're very attractive. I'm sure you're very good at what you do."

"I'm exceptional," she'd cooed, and then with a pout said, "Not even a blow job?"

"No, thank you," he'd insisted, at which she'd turned to Brock and demanded, "Hey, big spender, you still owe me for bringing me up here."

"Get the fuck out of here, bitch," Dylan had spat, but Brock waved him off and peeled a Benjamin from his money clip.

"She's right," he coached his 240-pound "little" brother. "She's a professional. She should be compensated for her time."

He handed the woman the money and admonished Dylan, "The woman deserves some respect."

Then he turned to the prostitute and yelled, "Now get the fuck out of here, cunt," at which the two brothers collapsed in shrieks of drunken laughter and slammed more vodka shots and toasted Cus.

"Here's to the newest addition to our family, our own Eagle Scout," Brock enthused. "Not even married yet and turning down a free piece of ass. You're a better man than I am, Cus. Looks like sis found a good one."

Cus felt the boat dip and rise and tried to recall if Nunzio had been in the hotel suite. It all seemed so long ago. "I don't remember you being there, Tommy," Cus said.

"I was in the room next door."

"He set up a camera in the bedroom so we could have a cinematic tribute to you screwing that whore," Al explained.

"Tommy's an amateur filmmaker. Ain't you, Tommy?"

"It's kind of a passion of mine," Tommy said. "Still photography, too. What do they call it—the visual arts or some shit like that?"

"Yeah, that's right," Al said. "The visual arts."

Two thoughts vied for primacy in Cus's head. One: Tommy, or most likely some lowlife he'd hired for fifty bucks, was the man behind the camera who caught Cus with his pants down in the newspaper's lounge the week before.

Two: How was it that he had married into a bona fide crime family and been too dumb to know it? Blackmail was as much a part of Al Holmes's tool chest as his fleet of concrete mixer trucks. He was trying to get dirt on Cus even before he walked Jenny down the aisle at St. Bartholomew Our Redeemer. Cus ruefully wished he'd had the wherewithal to run screaming from the church.

The engine cut out. Tommy the Torque Wrench, wearing a bored expression that only added to Cus's growing dread, hit a switch and supervised the playing out of the anchor chain.

"What's going on?" Cus asked.

"I figured we'd do a little fishing before I turn you loose on Fantasy Island," Al said. "Give us a chance to talk. We should talk more often, don't you agree?"

Cus envisioned minnows feasting on his rotting corpse—and Aurora on a stage by herself, tearfully accepting their Pulitzer.

They drifted in diminishing chop a quarter mile off Cummings Point. An outcropping of rock hid the Mixed Blessing from any prying eyes on Malloy Island. With 320 year-round residents, it was one of the more populated of the Thousand Islands.

"Looks like a good spot for smallmouths," Tommy offered.

"Something to be said for smallmouths," Al answered. "A big mouth can get you in trouble."

"Sure can," Tommy agreed.

The men cast their alewife jigs into gray-green seaway. A speedboat hauled ass far to the west.

"I've always admired the smallmouths," Al said. "They're predators. They don't just sit there flapping their fish lips waiting for dinner to swim by—they go after it. Kind of like you do in your job, Cus. You're a predator, too. In the best possible way."

"Thanks," Cus said dryly. He tried to normalize the moment. "Is it too early for a beer?"

The men ignored him.

"Funny how Mother Nature can turn the table on a predator, though, ain't it, boss?" Tommy said. "I mean, one moment a smallmouth is poking his big nose in the rocks and the muck, feeding on crayfish, darters, whatever, and thinking he's King Shit. Then just like that, he's in the belly of a turtle."

At that moment, Al's line went taut. He played the fish efficiently, showing no emotion. The patriarch stood a modest five foot nine, but he had the arms, upper torso, and neck of a much larger man. Still, there was nothing outwardly menacing about him unless he was angry. He had kind, blue eyes and a hint of merriment in his default expression. He gave the appearance of a man in control of, and at peace with, himself. Calmly, he pulled the twenty-inch fish out of the water. Not trophy size, but respectable.

"Nice fish, Al," Cus flattered, angling for camaraderie. "You keeping that one?"

"Nah," his father-in-law replied. "I've become a catch-and-release faggot in my dotage. Guess I've gotten soft."

A mucusy sycophantic laugh emanated from Tommy. "You're all about saving Mother Earth these days, aren't you Mr. Holmes?" The deckhand unhooked the bass but then, oddly, left it in the net rather than returning it to the water.

"That's right, Tommy. We only have one planet. Let's take care of it. Hey, do me a favor, Tommy. Let's send that fish back to the Shining Big Sea Water with a little dignity. Maybe something in the Native American tradition."

"Absolutely, boss."

Cus understood all too well they were mocking his Mohawk bloodline. What was next?

Tommy the Torque Wrench left the netted fish flopping on the thick rubber deck mat, walked casually to the stern, and opened the hatch to the lazarette. He dug around and extracted a thirty-six-inch wooden mallet known in the building trade as a "persuader."

Cus noted the handle was adorned with two eagle feathers. Nice touch, he thought. And hugely illegal.

Wordlessly, Tommy returned to the fish. He had work to do—or Al's work, more precisely. With a tomahawk-chop chant he surely knew Cus despised as racist, he rained blow after blow upon the helpless creature until even the involuntary spasms ceased and the gunwale was splattered with blood and fish guts. And still the blows came until the fish was pulverized into something scarcely recognizable.

Al watched with mild interest and took a swig of PBR. He handed one to Cus, who by now had turned from the horror and looked stoically toward the shipping lanes.

"Good idea on the brewskis," Al said.

Cus did not respond.

"Bloody Mary instead?" Al offered.

"That's funny, boss—Bloody Mary," Tommy ass-kissed.

By now, Tommy had finished making smallmouth puree. He leaned on the handle of the mallet. This time his laugh was high pitched and nasal.

"Release the fish, Tommy," Al directed.

Cus turned his head to see Tommy dump the accumulated gore, including the mat, net, and mallet, overboard.

"Be free, little fishy," Tommy rasped and expectorated a glob of gray-green phlegm into the sea.

They cruised in silence for fifteen minutes to Jupiter Island, gliding up to the floating dock.

"Happy anniversary," Al said. "Don't forget your flowers."

Woody has a lot of balls in the air:

—By following his friend Nick's multicultural advice, he has pissed off Celeste, who now wants him to end their vicarious online literary affair. But it's too integral to the plot to be abandoned.

—Woody's real-life wife, Mandy, in ironic symmetry with his unrequited paramour, Celeste, also wants Aurora written out of the book. "Just kill the bitch off or something," Mandy proposes. "You're a fucking writer. Figure it out."

—Under threat of litigation from his wife's family, Woody has agreed to soften the fictional in-laws, but he has no clue how to do that without spoiling the narrative.

If anything, he seems to be going the other way, making the fictional in-laws even more awful. It's where the book wants to go. Woody hasn't forgotten his promise to Cam, but what about his promise to his Art? How to thread the needle?

A speck of humanity in a villain can be helpful in warding off cartoonish one dimensionality, but a bad guy who is too sympathetic, too morally conflicted, too self-aware takes the fun out of rooting for his demise. That must not happen. To allow Al's corruption to be cast, for example, as a byproduct of childhood trauma or some other form of victimization could work, but it will require a deft touch and so much rewriting. For all his wishful association with the literati, Woody lacks the patience, interest, and—he suspects—the skill to pull it off.

Besides, if he makes Al Holmes a victim, people will just believe he's talking about Joe, which will defeat the purpose. Never mind that a clear majority of Woody's ever-growing readership likes Al, Vivian, Brock, and Dylan just as they are—evil to the core—with Jenny still a question mark.

Woody has struck a chord out there.

"These people make my skin crawl," one reader has emailed him. "So much scum in the construction industry. I gleefully await their undoing."

Another: "I've spent my whole life working for pricks like Al Holmes. You have them down!"

There's also an instant message from Roof Runner, one of Woody's new eight thousand or so Facebook friends. While gratifying to the author who craves praise of any sort, it has to be hastily deleted.

"First book that's held my interest since *My Side of the Mountain*. Nothing like an insider's perspective. And to think, all this time people thought Joe Dunn was a saint. LOL."

Someone else writes, "For a body to float from the Thousand Islands to the Bay of Fundy in a week, it would have to drift at an average speed of 7 knots northeast past Montreal and Quebec City, hang a right before Anticosti Island, float around the province of New Brunswick to Cape Breton Island, make another right at Nova Scotia and navigate around that. Then, assuming the tides were right, it would have to bear another right into the Bay of Fundy—a distance of approximately 1,250 nautical miles. Does this body come with a marine engine and GPS navigation?"

An email from a displeased rabbi rounds out the latest batch of feedback.

"Only you know what was in your heart when you described Al's accountant as 'crooked' and assigned him the Jewish surname Geller. But it has cost you many readers in the Jewish community who were enjoying your work until then. On behalf of Temple Beth Israel, I kindly ask that you abstain from antisemitic tropes, especially in an era when hate crimes against Jews and other minorities are on the rise. Shalom."

Woody is shamed at first but quickly shakes it off. Jews have a right to be criminals just like anyone else, he rationalizes. Years ago, he read a book about Jewish gangsters, *Tough Jews*, which profiled Bugsy Siegel, Meyer Lansky, and other seriously bad dudes, including one who buried a rival alive.

The author starts to craft a defiant reply to the rabbi but loses steam. It's not worth the time. Instead, he replaces Harvey Geller with an Icelandic name, Halldor Gunnarsson. It's impossible to offend Iceland, he posits. If Iceland gave a damn what anyone thought, they'd stop hunting whales.

The other complication facing Woody: His spite job at the car wash starts Tuesday.

"Why didn't you tell me you were looking for a shitty job?" JB asks when Woody tells him he'll be working the driver's side prerinse station at Mega-Shine. "I could put you on the deep fryer. It would be perfect since your ass is already in one."

Woody can't help but laugh as they roll north up the interstate to Barton in JB's Silverado long bed. JB's on a mission. There's at least one vintage motorcycle in each of his laundrobars. The moment he saw an ad for a rare 1960 Royal Enfield Chief, he knew he'd be heading up to Barton for a look.

It doesn't hurt to have another body along to help secure the bike in the bed if it checks out, but that's just JB's excuse for asking Woody along. JB didn't become wealthy by being inattentive to people's needs. He knows Woody could use a friend in this complicated stretch. Not surprising to JB, Woody is doing most of the talking.

"I don't want to burn down your place," Woody says of the fryer offer, "although you deserve it after goading me into writing this book online."

"You kidding me? You're almost famous, dude. Put me in the acknowledgments or whatever you call 'em. And put Cluckin' Clean in there, too. One good plug deserves another."

"Fair enough. If Mandy doesn't shoot me in my sofa bed first."

They mull a lone silo crumbling picturesquely in the near distance.

"You always have a place at my place. I mean not my real place. Jill doesn't like deadbeats. But you can live in the spare office above the laundromat if it comes to that."

It could come to that, Woody knows.

"Do some writing in the morning, work a shift in the kitchen or tend bar. Free laundry if I can trust you with the key to the change machine. Why do you want to work at a car wash, anyway?"

"I want people to see me. Lots of people. I want it to be public. If Cam's gonna job-shame me, let's roll. We'll see who's embarrassed when I win the PEN/Faulkner."

"Isn't it William Faulkner?"

"No. The PEN stands for . . . never mind." Woody starts singing the Rose Royce "Car Wash" song. "'You might not ever get rich . . .'"

JB joins in.

"'But let me tell ya it's better than diggin' a ditch.'"

They exchange a laugh and a low-five. Woody swoons with resolve.

"*Fear as Mud* forever, baby. Fear as fucking mud."

Twenty-five minutes later, they're in Barton in a dank barn as the owner talks them through the particulars of the motorcycle.

The seller's a farmer, Brad Wilkens, who grows onions and cannabis on his acreage north of a former nudist colony. He volunteers what JB already knows: The Indian is a faux Indian, an imported British-made Royal Enfield rebadged with the Indian logo after the original company stopped making bikes in 1953 and sold off its name. Muddled history aside, it's a sweet ride and an uncommon artifact.

"I almost screwed the pooch when I tried to adjust the shifter plate," farmer Brad half shouts above the throaty idle. "Luckily, I realized the holes weren't slotted before I got the whole thing apart, so I said screw it. It's a little obstinate going from second to third. If you take it for a spin, you'll feel the shifter firming up at around three thousand rpm—that's when you shift. These old girls have their quirks."

Woody's impressed the farmer has "obstinate" in his working vocabulary. You never can tell with rural people, or any people for that matter, which leads to a gnawing concern he has about his book. In his race to post new installments, is he succumbing to stereotyping? Maybe Tommy the Torque Wrench should have an advanced degree in linguistics or something.

"They sure do," JB says, responding to Brad and interrupting Woody's thoughts. "But that's part of their charm. Why are you selling it?"

"I was afraid you were going to ask that. My daughter just got back from her first year at Smith. She doesn't like that the bike's called an Indian. She says to me, 'Dad, would you own a motorcycle called a Negro or a Jew?'"

"Ouch," JB says. "What'd you say?"

"I said, 'If it looked and ran like my Indian, sure.'"

"Good comeback," Woody acknowledges.

"She didn't find it amusing. Kids today have no tolerance for White male oppression. Either of you have kids?"

"A daughter."

"How old?"

"Sixteen."

"Then you get it. I love the bike, but I love my kid more. If anyone else gave me the same horseshit, I'd tell them to shove it straight up their ass, but she stated her case well, wasn't nasty about it. I figured, let her win this one. Let her gain a sense of agency, even if it's at the expense of her old man."

Agency, Woody thinks. *There he goes again.*

JB is focused on the transaction. "You sound like a motivated seller."

"Somewhat," Brad said. "But not desperate. I'm getting points just for having it on Craigslist. Look, truth is I'm not riding it much anymore, and parts for these fuckers are as rare as rocking-horse shit. This way I clear up a corner of the barn and a corner of my mind, and I look like a hero to my kid. But either way, the sun will still come up in the morning."

"I'll give you 10K and a promise to always call it a Royal Enfield," JB offers. "I'll never call it an Indian. That should make your daughter happy."

"Make it eleven-five and you can call it Custer's Last Stand for all I care."

JB cocks his head. "Sounds like you're reading my boy's book." He gestures toward Woody.

Brad has no idea what JB's talking about, and so the negotiation is interrupted while JB explains that his near-mute sidekick is writing a book whose main character is named Custer.

"I'll have to check it out. What's the book about?"

Woody brightens and serves up the main plot points, including that the protagonist is one-fourth Native American. He had taken Nick's advice after all and thickened Cus's tribal bloodlines.

"You've got a part-Native American character named Custer?" the farmer asks incredulously. "That's funny. Why'd you make that choice?"

Woody's face grows hot. How had he overlooked such an obvious disconnect? How did he botch the name of the main character? He wishes he'd done an outline or even a storyboard, maybe organized the basic biographies of the characters before he plunged in. Maybe penciled out a plot with the beginning, middle, and end.

"Well, he's only one-quarter Mohawk, and he goes by Cus, not Custer," Woody says. "It's meant as an ironic touch, a comment on the loss of cultural, uh, you know, agency, but maybe it's overly subtle."

"Hey, it's your book, cowboy," Brad says. He turns to JB. "Eleven-five. Take it or leave it."

The deal is consummated with Brad reaching into his overalls and handing JB a small tin of cannabis gummies labeled "Flower Patch Kids." "You'll enjoy these," he promises. "We're their primary grower."

As Woody and JB ride home with the Indian lashed down in the back, Woody decides the farmer is right. It is his book. He needs to reclaim it. He has too many wannabe editors trying to dictate its direction—Mandy and her family, Nick, Celeste, Annabelle Riley, and all those readers chipping in their two cents—their comments swarming inside his skull like agency-sucking murder hornets. In violation of his new resolution, he looks over the latest reader comments.

—"They're using alewife lures off a rocky outcrop? No way. Not in the Thousand Islands. If you want your boys to catch fish, they should be drop shotting flatworms or using crankbait. Research matters, bro."

—"What happened to Vivian? (Remember? She's Al's wife.) Did you kill her off and not bother to tell us?"

—"No mas Spanish dialogue. This is America. We speak English here."

Then he scans a more substantial communique.

"My name is Margo Harriman, and I'm a sensitivity coordinator with the Animal Protection League of the Americas. One of our members brought to our attention a recent scene in your online novel regarding the brutal treatment of a captive freshwater fish. Our organization stands against sport fishing as an exercise in needless cruelty. Your portrayal, fictional or not, of the bludgeoning of innocent aquatic life goes beyond the basic cruelty of that endeavor and strays into outright depravity. Your graphic glorification of animal abuse risks provoking real-life attacks on fish and other nonhuman innocents. As such, we ask that you kindly change or remove the offending sequence. We also encourage you to attend one of our Animal Sensitivity Training workshops in the Greater Icarus area. I'm attaching our meeting schedule to this email. Normally the sessions are for those convicted of violating animal cruelty laws, but all are welcome."

"All this over a fictional fish?" Woody mutters.

"Huh?" JB says.

"Nothing."

JB drives too fast past a state police cruiser, but he gets lucky, as is his way. The trooper accepts JB's driver's license and inspects it using a flashlight bright enough to discombobulate even the most composed DUI suspects. He's curious about the bike in the back, which gives JB an opportunity to explain that it's headed for installation in the Jaspertown Cluckin' Clean east of Icarus.

"You work there?" the trooper asks.

"I own it," JB says.

"All of 'em?"

"All of 'em."

The trooper is impressed. "My wife and I are regulars at your Zeus location," he says.

"No kidding?" JB says, seeing opportunity. "I thank you for your patronage. Do you use the laundry, the restaurant/bar, or all of it?"

"Officially, only laundry, but ya know." He winks. "My wife likes to take our dogs' beds there."

"What kind of dogs?"

"Two German shepherds and an Akita mix. We love 'em like they're our kids, but they shed like hell."

"Yeah, pet hair is tough on those machines," JB says casually. "But no big deal."

The trooper stiffens. Both men know there are signs posted at the chain's laundromats practically begging customers not to wash items covered in pet hair.

"She's real good about getting all the hair off with a lint roller before she brings them in," the trooper lies.

"I really appreciate that. I wish all of our customers were as conscientious."

The trooper writes something on his pad then tears off a green sheet and hands it to JB. "I'm letting you off with a warning, Mr. Seniac. Please watch your speed. Pleasure to meet you."

Once they're on the road again and celebrating JB's luck, Woody pops a Flower Patch brat into his mouth and returns to his deliberations. It's time to tune out the noise and take back control—"to man up," in JB's words.

Woody considers killing off Aurora. That would score points with Mandy, but it would injure his Art if done too soon. He remembers Celeste's words: "A little sex never hurts a story."

But there's more than a story at stake. A few nights earlier, Woody had been interrupted from his writerly musings while grilling a flank steak in the backyard.

"Did you really bang Celeste Henry in the lactation lounge, or do you just want my friends and family to think that?" Mandy demanded.

"I did not have sex with that woman in the lactation lounge."

"So, you fucked her somewhere else. I get it: The lounge is the fiction part."

"Why are you doing this to us?"

"Why am I doing this? Seriously. You've got half of Icarus thinking you did her and half of it thinking you just want to. You know what Paige asked Ella the other day?"

Woody hadn't liked the sound of that.

"Who's Paige again?"

"One of your daughter's friends. They've been friends since Ella was in fourth grade. Note: Ella is your daughter."

"Oh, right, Paige was the one who didn't play lacrosse," he guesses. "A math whiz or something?" Woody has trouble distinguishing Ella's friends. To him, they all look and sound alike.

"Bingo!"

"Okay, I'm all ears. What did Ella's friend, whose name is Paige, ask my daughter, whose name is Ella?"

"Are your parents getting divorced?"

That wounds him. Even Mandy seems surprised the D-word was out there. A malignant quiet replaces the shouting.

"Are we?" Woody asks.

"Let's just say it's trending that way."

"Over a stupid book?"

"Over *your* stupid book. Look, I made us an appointment for next week. Her name is Josephine Dravus. She's supposed to be good."

"A marriage counselor?"

"Three p.m. Wednesday, downtown."

"I'll check my calendar," Woody says, reaching for his phone.

"Good idea, Tolstoy. Check your fucking calendar."

CHAPTER 10
MEGA-SHINE

Woody returns to the present when JB calmly swerves to avoid a shredded truck tire. After the near miss, the author fixates on a grazing herd of cows. How he envies the simplicity of their lives. It occurs to him that if Al has Aurora killed—or kills her himself—that risks being interpreted by readers as Joe Dunn killing Celeste. Solving one unwanted association creates another.

On cue, "50 Ways to Leave Your Lover" plays on sat radio. Woody thinks through the elimination possibilities in rough alphabetical order: aneurism, asphyxiation, Botox, croup, Ebola, flesh-eating bacteria, gunshot, Lyme disease, malaria, ovarian-something-or-other, poison, rabies, scarlet fever.

Nothing jumps out as ideal. Whatever he does, he can't make Aurora sympathetic in death. Then Cus would have to mourn her loss. Celeste might see that as a coded message that Woody is pining for her, the last impression he wants to send.

Woody feels manipulated and abandoned by Celeste. She tricked him into developing a character like her, and now she's not even reading anymore. They had an exquisite virtual tryst going, and she threw it all away for Nikko, a guy with a neck tattoo of a bowling ball picking up a 7-10 split. No wonder Woody—and many male novelists—can't write believable female characters, he mopes. Women defy comprehension.

Then a starburst of genius blinds Woody. *Why not make Jenny sympathetic?* That is going to require some heavy lifting, but it's not too late. He can depict Aurora as so obsessed with Cus that she gaslights him to prevent him from saving his marriage and to bog down his investigation.

Celeste's alter ego, Aurora, will be revealed as a selfish homewrecker, unhinged and scary, a fatal attraction bitch-monster. Her Latinaness will be the least of Celeste's worries. It will be the perfect F.U. to Celeste and, assuming he can read, a heads-up to Nikko that he's about to get hitched to a psycho. (You're welcome, dick!) It will also be an olive branch to Mandy before marriage counseling.

Woody helps JB unload the motorcycle at the Jaspertown Cluckin' Clean. JB offers to buy him a beer, but Woody just wants to get home and write.

He feels free.

Al had reason to fear Cus and Aurora, reason to resort to blackmail and intimidation. Cus was a coolheaded, savvy muckraker with a fearless streak. Worse, from Al's standpoint, was that through marriage to Jenny, Cus had a too-close-for-comfort understanding of the sand and gravel industry, which could be shady even on the sunniest days. Al could only guess how much Cus and Aurora already knew about Cold Harbor's toxic waste disposal scheme. But he was certain of this much: One way or another, through subtle hints or more direct means of persuasion, curious Cus and his puta sidekick were done poking around in his affairs.

The stage was set. The speeding bullet trains of Cus's investigation and Al's censorial imperative were on a collision course. In truth, it had always been that way. The two had eyed each other with suspicion long before Cus got wind of the illegal dumping.

Al, after all, was a convicted tax cheat. Not much to trust there. Meanwhile, he had never trusted Cus because Cus was honest, and to Al, honesty was a disease. It made people immune to bribes and, in rare instances, undaunted by threats. Honesty had a big mouth.

This made Cus dangerous, a reality Al had confirmed eleven years ago when he'd leaned on his son-in-law to use his connections at the paper to snuff a story about a Cold Harbor job. It concerned a finisher killed during an ill-fated pour of a slab for a new Caveman Steak and Brew.

The finisher had entered a portable toilet perched too close to the excavation hole. As he did his business, which was voluminous given he was hungover and weighed 330 pounds, the ground, soggy from two nights of rain, gave way.

The toilet tumbled four feet into the hole atop a bed of compacted gravel. Most likely, it would have been a serious but survivable accident if the pump operator hadn't been distracted. He was smoking a fatty behind a dumpster while a No. 6 slump shot through a five-inch line, running sixty-one feet off a boom into the hole at a rate of one cubic yard per minute.

Woody admires his mastery. He isn't sure the accident could happen in exactly that way, but who's going to notice or care? His command of sand and gravel jargon enchants him. It makes him sound like he knows his stuff, much the way Papa wrote expertly and precisely of hunting and fishing. In *The Old Man and the Sea*, Woody recalls, Hemingway threw in all kinds of boring details about coil filaments, gaffs, and different bait fish. Woody tended to skim those parts, but so what? Since when are all readers supposed to understand everything? What matters is that they embrace the authority of the author.

By the time the other finisher came looking for his partner, only one corner of the green crapper's plastic vented roof was visible above the rising tide of mud. It cost Al 50K to have the coroner list the cause of death as a heart attack.

Cus's refusal to keep the incident out of the headlines had irked Al even though Cus had offered a sound reason. "All it would do is arouse suspicion if I asked them to spike the story," he'd told his father-in-law.

"Good point," Al cheerfully agreed. You ungrateful cocksucker, he thought.

Luckily for Al, the newspaper's feckless ineptitude made Cus's lack of assistance moot. The *Daily Informer* accepted the sheriff department's press release unchallenged. Four days after the accident, it published a few paragraphs about a construction worker dying of "an apparent heart attack during construction of the much-awaited Caveman restaurant in Apollonia, which remains on schedule to open Oct. 1, village officials assured."

A twenty-year-old intern pushed to include that the death occurred in a portable toilet, but her editor talked her down.

"Leave the poor guy some dignity," the editor mansplained. "He's got young kids. How would you like to grow up with all your classmates knowing your dad croaked in a portable shitter?"

But it had been a close call for Al. From then on, he worked only with pump operators over whom he had some control, going so far as to create a separate LLC, innocuously named North Central EliteCrete. The spinoff consisted of twenty grizzled, humorless men in mud-gray pickup trucks pulling mud-gray, hydraulic-powered line pumps on mud-gray trailers. A trio of much larger boom trucks, capable of blasting 400 yards of wet three-quarter-inch rock mix up twelve stories to create condo decks, rounded out the fleet. Suffice to say "safety first" was not in the EliteCrete mission statement. After one particularly gruesome man-machine interface that led to an amputation of a leg below the knee, the hard men of the Tiberius construction industry became fond of referring to EliteCrete as DeleteFeet.

But that was mere context for what was most likely criminality on a much bigger scale.

As Cus pored over county wastewater reports, he pondered how the pump operators might figure into an illegal waste disposal scheme. His instincts told him this oft-overlooked link in the construction chain was integral to the story. He'd always had a gift for visualizing complex ideas in simple terms. In this instance, he viewed the coupling of mixer truck and pump truck as sexual metaphor, a union of evil creating a still greater evil.

"The mixer truck barrel is like a giant testicle loaded with semen," he explained to Aurora as they wandered through the lightly visited Museum of Snow Removal Technology, confident they'd go unnoticed. "The chute coming off the back of the mixer truck is the penis, and the hopper connected to the pump is like the vagina. The semen/mud is loaded into the hopper/vagina, and then the substrate is pumped to the target zone through hoses, which are analogous to fallopian tubes."

Woody pauses from his furious typing. It's getting late. The Great Writers wall clock reads twenty minutes past Gertrude Stein. Something bothers him about the concrete discharge/sexual metaphor. It's the penis part. In a typical tip-and-pour setup, a chute is phallic-looking, but it doesn't really do anything. It just lies there, relying on gravity to carry the semen/mud to the vagina/hopper. It doesn't pump like a penis. The pump pumps, but it's downstream of the chute—and the hopper—so how can the chute be a penis? And do sperm even go into fallopian tubes?

The whole metaphor is shit. Maybe he shouldn't have had that ten-milligram gummy. He'll have to rewrite in the morning. Maybe he can reference newer transit mixers with onboard reciprocating piston pumps that shoot concrete directly into designated zones.

He collapses on the sofa in his study and covers himself with a blanket. Then he bolts upright. Tomorrow is Tuesday. Correction: Today is Tuesday. His first shift at the car wash starts in five hours.

Woody gets quality sleep, if not much of it. He's up before Mandy, so he leaves her a note on the kitchen counter.

"Heading to Mega-Shine to start my new job. Taking your brother's advice to heart. $15.50 an hour!!!"

Despite the company's new employee orientation video touting an application process that weeds out all but "first-rate humans with great attitudes and impeccable character," Woody was hired almost on the spot after a five-minute interview with Larry "Packy" Pakulksi, a gum-chomping regional manager.

The interview began on an awkward note as Larry confused Woody for a pissed-off customer whose Beamer was damaged in the automated tunnel the day before.

"You're the guy with the shark fin antenna that got torn off?"

"No, sir. I'm Woody Hackworth," he'd explained. "I'm here for a job interview."

Larry didn't get many White guys in their forties in slacks and a polo shirt applying to wash cars.

"So, what's the deal?" Larry had wondered, chomping away. "You on work release or what?"

"From my wife," Woody deadpanned.

"Gotcha. I used to have one of those. No thanks."

"Yep, just looking to get out of the house and make a few extra bucks. I always wanted to work at a car wash for some reason."

A horn had beeped, signaling a vehicle was emerging from the Interior Revitalization Zone.

"Was it the song?" Larry asked. "As God is my witness, twenty percent of our apps are because of that damn song. Makes working at a car wash sound fun. You think we have fun here?"

"'Better than diggin' a ditch.'" Woody was sharp that morning.

"I like your attitude, Rudy. Are you interested in learning about our free college tuition program?"

"It's Woody. I'm good on college, thanks. Been there, done that."

"Oh yeah? Where?"

"Stamford," Woody replied, rushing the "m" out of habit and instantly regretting it. There's was no need to overimpress here.

"No shit," Larry said. "Farthest west I've been is Wisconsin. Not sure I've ever met anyone who went to Stanford."

Woody froze. He had put UConn Stamford on the resumé he submitted online. He didn't need to launch his new career by giving a false impression.

"No, Stamford, Connecticut," he corrected. "UConn."

"Ah. Big difference."

"Big difference."

"When do you want to start?"

"Yesterday."

Day one is culture shock, but Woody rolls with it. Kaylon Buckingham, twenty-nine, already an assistant manager just eight months into the job, gives Woody a pair of safety glasses and a tour.

"You get some of them chemicals in your eye, it's fuckin' nasty. Whenever you're working on the machines or cleaning out the pits, wear these because if you gotta go to urgent care, that means more work for the rest of us."

"Got it," Woody says. "Wear safety glasses."

Kaylon strides into the interior cleaning area, and Woody assumes he should follow. But instead, Kaylon turns around and tells him to wait. He watches Kaylon talk with two workers steam cleaning a Volvo interior and after waiting awhile, he drifts back to thinking about his book. He has no African American characters. Perhaps he should introduce someone like Kaylon. He reimagines him as a precast yard worker moving eco-blocks with a forklift. He could even be a valued source for Cus. Lotta potential there.

A rush of giddiness catches Woody by surprise. He is feeling good about life despite the rising temperatures in his Mega-Shine rubber coveralls. He has taken a job just like his wife and in-laws suggested and thrown it right back in their faces. Far from distracting him from his craft, as they'd hoped, the revenge gig will be a treasure chest of new material. *Be careful who you mess with, Cam.*

"Lexus, get in here!" Kaylon barks.

Lexus?

Woody makes his way to the tunnel, chagrined that his high-end SUV has already set him apart. Many of his new colleagues, Woody will discover, ride the bus to work.

Kaylon introduces him to Maurice, maybe twenty. He's at least six feet tall and has a black Jesus tattoo on his neck. Maurice gives Woody a primer, instructing him to use the steam wand to loosen dust and grime before applying the cleaner.

"You save a lot of towels that way," Maurice explains. "Steam is your friend in the shed."

"You like working in here?" Woody asks.

Maurice stops cleaning, disarmed by the question. "Like might not be my word choice," he says, "but it's out of the weather, which is good ninety percent of the time."

They send the Volvo down the line and dive into a Camry, then a minivan sullied by juice stains, sticky candy bits, dog hair, and a human toenail.

"People are disgusting," Maurice mumbles as he cleans.

He lets Woody solo on the van's cockpit.

"You missed a spot, Lexus," Maurice says, pointing out a smudge next to a vent.

Ever concerned with his status, even here, Woody wants to know if there's a pecking order of jobs at Mega-Shine.

"They move us around, but they always put the pretty White girls out in the booths because that's where the plastic is."

"Huh?"

"Because people buy extras from pretty White girls. If you want folks to pay thirty bucks for six cents' worth of leather conditioner, you don't give that job to some scary-looking brother."

Woody experiences a splash of shame. It isn't White guilt. It's because he has gotten the Ambassador Leather Conditioner Treatment for years.

He glances in the rearview mirror, hoping his embarrassment isn't registering on his face. "What about the presoak line?"

"That's a nasty job, in my opinion, especially when it's cold, but some people would rather be outside no matter what, battling the elements. No, thank you."

Woody continues to nibble around the periphery of the real question he wants to ask until he finally senses he has enough rapport with Maurice. "Why am I the only White person working in the shed?"

"You are? I didn't even notice."

Woody flushes. Probably Maurice is yanking his chain, but what if he isn't? What if Maurice didn't give any thought to the color of Woody's skin, and it's Woody who's fixated on race? "I appreciate that," Woody says, trying to cover both possibilities.

"You've got some serious observational skills on you, Lexus. Are you a detective or what?"

"I'm a reporter, or used to be. I'm a trained observer."

"No shit. Are you writing about us?"

"Why, is there a story here?"

"There's a whole book in this place. A series."

"I'm working on a book."

"What kind of book?"

Chimes tinkle delicately in the background, an audio cue that tells customers ceramic sealant is being applied.

"A mystery about an investigative reporter."

"So, a historic novel?"

Woody sags. "Yeah, sort of. But with postmodern elements."

"Am I gonna be in it?"

"Why not? Everyone else is."

They move on to a Kia Sportage. While Woody works the front seats, Maurice handles the rear and offers more nuancing on the unwritten race and gender code at Mega-Shine. During busy days, especially nice weekends, attractive, nonthreatening Black people typically work the prewash and towel-dry stations as long as they do not outnumber Whites in those public interface jobs. Large or overweight African Americans and others that White suburbanites might find menacing get funneled into the shed or detail shop, where there's less customer interaction, which, ironically, makes it a better job, Maurice says. A few token Whites get thrown into the shed for good behavior.

"Am I the token White guy?" Woody asks.

"They probably just put you in here so I can keep an eye on you, make sure you're cool, not gonna steal from people's cars or whatever. Don't steal, Lexus. In my experience, no disrespect intended, a lot of rich White folks will steal anything that isn't nailed down. It's like a disease or something."

"I'm not a thief. I'm a novelist."

"NEUTRAL!" a worker bellows from afar. The cry is heard roughly every thirty seconds when it's busy as drivers are instructed to take their vehicles out of drive as they hit the conveyor.

"When do I get to be the 'NEUTRAL' guy?" Woody asks.

Maurice pulls the rear floor mats out of the Sportage and turns a power washer on them. "That's a big job," he shouts over the spray. "Maybe in a month when it's slow."

Woody deflates again. He wants maximum exposure. How can he be an embarrassment to his wife and in-laws if he's hidden in the shed? "Why not during busy times?" he asks. "It's not like I'm . . ." He catches himself too late.

"No, you're not scary, but you are elderly. In this business, that's worse."

"I'm forty-two," Woody protests.

"Which is a problem," Maurice chides. "They don't want customers thinking, *Who's that sad, elderly White man working at a car wash?* We're supposed to be about shiny and new, cars being reborn."

Woody sees Maurice's point. If his working at a car wash stands to embarrass his in-laws, it stands to reason it could have an unsettling effect on the public, too.

"So, you're just here doing research for your book?"

"Sort of," Woody replies. "Not really. Maybe. It's complicated."

Maurice puts down his towel. "That's cool you're writing a book, Lexus. I love to read. I'll read anything."

Woody hadn't expected that.

The owner of the Sportage left his radio on. "Free Fallin'" plays as they finish up the inside.

"Hey, Lexus, you have any book recommendations?"

Woody hesitates. Does he want the whole car wash knowing his online novel is breaking the internet, that he's an emerging literary star? Is he willing to risk a further muddling of his life and his fiction? Does he really want his Mega-Shine colleagues to treat him like a celebrity, for them to know that even a sixty-minute carnauba hand wax cannot outshine the supernova of his prose? Woody peeks through the glass divider separating the detail area from the customer lounge, its three big-screen TVs aglow. On one channel, he sees his friend Nick, identified on screen as "Nicholas Peters, Senior Columnist, *The Apocalyptic*." Anderson Cooper is debriefing him as video of Ramstein Air Base runs in the background. Had Woody Hackworth, newly hired "vehicle luster restoration associate," not in that precise moment observed his famous friend addressing a national television audience, his decision might well have been the same. But now there can be no doubt. Woody's canine yearning to be validated by the masses, to have his authorial tummy rubbed for performing word tricks, leaves him no choice.

"Have you heard of a book called *Fear as Mud*?" he says to Maurice.

CHAPTER 11
DARK AND VIOLENT IMPULSES

The following morning is the couple's first—and final—counseling session with marriage and family therapist Josephine Dravus, LMFT, PhD. Woody finds her gorgeous, with good reason. Tall, blonde, and apprising her new clients with twinkly blue eyes, she looks like a Viking princess with no hint of Aryan reserve. She has a heavy Upstate accent and laughs hard at Woody's first wisecrack. Woody is convinced he owns the room, especially when she references his Art.

"Just so I'm not assuming, you're the novelist, right?"

"Guilty as charged." Woody raises his right hand as Mandy looks out the window with resignation.

"Okay, I figured as much. I started reading it when I saw you were coming in."

"You like it?"

"That isn't relevant for our purposes today," Josephine replies, abruptly clinical. "Is the book part of the reason you're here?"

"You got that right," Mandy answers.

Woody squirms as he realizes his fantasy has morphed into a likely adversary.

They work through some background information and a few other formalities, and Mandy cuts to the heart of her lament.

"He's stealing from our personal and professional lives to write that goddamn book. It's like being married to an identity thief."

Josephine looks sternly at Woody. "Can we verbally agree that nothing that happens in this room will show up in your book?"

Woody ponders his response, finally breaking the silence with a dramatic exhalation. "It's unlikely that would happen. At this point, I don't have any plans for the major characters to get counseling."

Mandy gives the therapist an "I told you so" look.

"That's not what I asked," Josephine says with a brittle smile. "I need a verbal commitment from you that it won't happen. This needs to be a safe space. Client confidentiality laws require it."

Woody feels bullied. Maybe he will want to add a marriage counseling scene between Cus and Jenny. Or between Al and Vivian. Who knows? The book is at a critical juncture. It could go anywhere. "I can't make that promise," Woody says.

"Are you fucking kidding me?" Mandy shouts. "This is pointless." She gathers her purse and coat and walks out, turning first to the therapist to say, "I'm sorry we wasted your time."

The room is silent. Finally, Woody shrugs and says, "I thought that went well."

"Actually, it didn't," Josephine says.

"What do we owe you?"

She looks at her watch. The visit has lasted thirteen minutes. "I'll bill it as a fifty dollar cancelation fee. I'm here for you both if you're ready to try another time."

Cus climbed into the dinghy tethered to the dock to check the fuel level and fired up the old girl in case he needed a quick getaway. Then he cut the engine, pulled himself back onto the dock, and made his way to the glider on the wraparound porch. He took in a magnificent view of forested islets, a lone jet skier, and, farther, a rust-red freighter before turning to a biography of Aldous Huxley. But it was no use. His legendary powers of concentration evaded him as he waited for his bride to arrive on Jupiter. How best to play what just happened? His instinct was to withhold from Jenny the pulverized fish abomination. But what if she already knew about it? Then Cus's silence would be revealing. Jenny would know he was hiding from her what happened, which would suggest to her that Cus suspected she was aware of the illegal dumping conspiracy and that he might think she was involved.

Or did she already know she was a person of interest? And if that was the case, why play games?

Cus had a slight headache. Probably, he should just be straight with his wife, even about Aurora. Now there was a recipe for a wedding anniversary romance:

Honey, your sick-fuck dad stood by and watched as his top goon bludgeoned a smallmouth bass to intimidate me from investigating your family's toxic dumping ring. Oh, and if he hasn't told you yet, I'm having an affair with Aurora Connolly. Sorry about that, but I trust her more than I trust you. I think.

That would set the mood.

A twenty-seven-footer roared into view. As it got close, Cus saw that Ian Blandell, the brother of one of Jenny's former bridesmaids, Tessa, was piloting it. Tessa and Jenny's maid of honor, Maddy, were also on board. Cus, pulling himself up from the glider, saw them laughing and drinking mimosas.

The boat docked. Cus came aboard, and small talk was exchanged. Cus declined a beverage, and the others declined Jenny's invitation to hang out on the island before they headed back. Soon, it was just Jenny and Cus.

"Happy anniversary, baby. How was the ride over with my dad?"

"Happy anniversary. Just a little light chop."

She stepped toward him and offered a kiss, wrapping her arms around his belt line.

"Not the bulge I was expecting," she said, her fingers locking onto the flotation device still strapped on the small of his back. "What's that? My present?"

Cus had forgotten he was still wearing the thing, another sign the stress was getting to him. He was normally too meticulous for such a blunder.

His nimble mind overrode his honest nature, and he spit out a decent lie. "Someone at work gave it to me as a gag gift in case your dad pushed me overboard."

"Why would my dad do that?"

"He wouldn't. That's why it was a joke."

"So why are you wearing it if it was a joke?"

Cus thought of telling her he'd worn it to humor his colleague, but instead he said, "Jenny, we should talk."

Although the marriage counseling attempt failed, the brief exchange has calmed Woody. He held fast to his principles under extreme duress and thus, that evening, the literary gods rewarded him with a magically productive session, one of those rare times when words flow like sap from sugar maples.

Woody switches off his laptop and sleeps the sleep of the creatively spent. He dreams he's about to have sex with Celeste on a waterbed. Observing his dream as he dreams, he realizes that a waterbed is a strange and dated detail. Where in his subconscious did that come from? He counsels himself not to push the issue because he doesn't want anything interfering with the main objective. Aurora knocks on the door and asks if she can join them. He and Celeste assent, but before anything can happen, a pink mixer truck appears, chute extended, and pours several yards of ground beef into the bedroom. Woody is then transported to a tropical beach, where he is reading *Fear as Mud* to emaciated contestants on *Survivor.* Host Jeff Probst explains to the TV audience that the last participant to remain conscious wins the challenge.

The next morning, Woody jumps on his stationary bike and selects an easy spin along a Norwegian fjord. He has reached a critical juncture in his book. Now is a time to think deep, writerly thoughts, not to be bullied by an aerobic extremist. To save Woody and Mandy, he needs to save Jenny and Cus. His next thousand words will set that in motion. But how? He has established Jenny in the nerve center of Cold Harbor, a trusted jackie-of-all-trades who is at home corporate strategizing or backing a mixer truck down a muddy 12 percent grade. Maybe that was a bad decision. If she is that plugged in, how would Jenny's character not know about the dumping?

As Woody pedals through a red-roofed village on his left, bright blue water on his right, he sees a broad outline of a solution. Jenny would be intensely loyal to Al, while Al would be protective of Jenny. He'd want to keep her out of trouble, give her the gift of plausible deniability if she were ever called as a witness. He'd be motivated to keep her in the dark, and she'd be motivated to not ask too many questions. Deference to the patriarch would be in play. After all, it was his company.

Jenny can't be a fool, of course. Woody knows enough about modern sensibilities to realize he needs a "strong female character"—like Pilar in *For Whom the Bell Tolls* or Sigourney Weaver in *Alien.* Jenny must have agency.

Woody is horrified to find the word *agency* again coming to the fore of his thoughts. His ego pushes it down. That word is proprietary to the farmer who sold JB the motorcycle, who struck Woody as nice enough but a little full of himself. Woody will find his own word, a better word. He combs the thesaurus of his mind but finds it barren. Finally, he conjures a possibility— *effectualness.* But is it even a real word? He looks it up online, and to his surprise, it's right there in *Merriam-Webster.*

Jenny must have effectualness.

As an effectual woman, Jenny would understand the dark side of the construction industry, and the dark side of sand and gravel in particular. She'd understand, for example, that a standard ten-yard mixer truck could easily short a customer a half yard. Who'd know? The $12-an-hour framers massaging their hangovers with Red Bull and naproxen? Even if one of them suspected being shorted, what incentive would they have to blow the whistle? None.

True, there would be elevated risk of detection in state-contracted jobs with a greater level of regulation and supervision. Jenny would understand—but not condone—bribing corrupt field inspectors to look the other way. Bribery, tax evasion, kickbacks—all of that would be just business as usual. Illegal dumping, however—that was next-level slime. No self-respecting daddy would want his little girl soiled by that level of evil.

As Woody gently spins on the bike and breaks a light Norwegian sweat, a supporting pillar of Jenny's rehabilitation comes into view. From somewhere near the start of his book, Woody has envisioned the entire Harbor fleet involved in the covert collection and disposal of industrial waste. But he sees now that such a mass deployment is excessive and implausible.

Each of the 32,000-pound standard-sized trucks weighs 72,000 pounds fully loaded. An eleven-yard, 44,000-pound capacity barrel will hold roughly two thousand gallons of liquid waste. One truck could easily handle most or all the medical waste produced daily by, say, a large hospital like the one where Mandy works. If Al Holmes were dedicating just four of his thirty rigs to illegal dumping, running the scheme as a separate operation, he'd still have enough cargo capacity to make a fortune.

How big a fortune? That requires math. Woody has long bristled at the stereotype that journalists struggle with numbers. He resents it because, in his case, it's true. He failed Introduction to Applied Statistics at UConn Stamford, ultimately eking out a B minus after learning he could retake the course at a nearby community college. He always felt, for lack of a better word, itchy, whenever a story required math, especially when the math conspired with its boogeyman cousin: logic.

One of his most serious retractions involved a causation/correlation error. He had written a story about a spike in cycling accidents in Icarus, concluding that the city's expanding network of bike lanes was unsafe. The city responded with data showing that cycling trips per capita had nearly doubled with the onset of dedicated bikeways and that the accident rate had, in fact, dropped by a third.

Woody lobbied frantically for a clarification rather than the public shaming of a correction. A senior editor, Roland Peck, would have none of it. Indeed, Peck had made a lucrative career, by print journalism standards, of holding reporters accountable for their imprecision. It was not missed by the *Blaze* staff that his thirty-foot sailboat moored at his Lake Champlain summer home was christened *The Course Correction.*

The *Blaze*'s abundance of in-house cynics postulated that Peck's rise as the corrector-in-chief was a damage control stunt, suspiciously launched soon after the Secret Service raided a counterfeiting operation in the pressroom that netted five convictions.

Woody had more than done his part to support Peck's lifestyle. The sleepless year Ella was born, he suffered six corrections, two clarifications, and no raise. The bike path story, which came the following year, still gnawed at him. It didn't make him look just careless. It made him look dumb.

Happily, he reasons, readers of fiction will be more forgiving if the math isn't spot-on, but he still wants to be as accurate as possible.

His virtual ride ends at a marina with a friendly wave from a villager. He's in such a good place he waves back at the six-year-old video. He hops off the stationary bike to google hazmat disposal fees. Hospital waste or red bag waste—a term he learned from Mandy—comes up among the most expensive, as much as $6 per pound, or $12,000 per ton.

He guesses that all forms of hazardous waste removal will average out to half that, or $6,000 a ton.

If Al Holmes has four dedicated toxic trucks, each making two dumps per day of a ton of liquid hazardous materials, that's eight tons of illicit crud five days a week, or $6,000 x 8 x 5.

Woody puts on his math cap.

$6,000 times 8 equals $48,000. Multiply that by 5 and you get . . . almost $250,000 a week!

Even if Al was underselling the legal rate by 50 percent, that's still $125,000 a week times fifty weeks a year, which is . . .

He's lost.

The numbers jumble in his head and drift away like tree pollen. He starts again, but the same thing happens. Grudgingly, he acknowledges he needs help and turns to the calculator on his phone. He's unsettled by the number he sees: $6,250,000 per annum in illicit profits. It sounds high for a scam occurring in a small city based in scruffy Icarus. This isn't Jersey.

He starts to punch in a new set of numbers but grows weary.

"Screw it," Woody says. "It's fiction."

Now, he just needs to figure out where that waste would be deposited. All that volume would quickly overwhelm the two-acre illegal dump site in the woods Cus and Aurora discovered earlier. Woody sets that problem aside for the moment. A solution can wait, but his readers can't. He needs to finish the Jupiter Island chapter. It's been a week since he posted any new material, and his fans are not a patient lot.

"Maybe I'll write a mystery about a writer who stops writing in the middle of his book because he'd rather get stoned and jack off all day," RabidRoofMonkey12 commented the other day.

Time to get busy.

"Talk about what, honey?" Jenny replied, looking worried.

"About your dad. And about Cold Harbor."

"Is he okay?"

"Yes. He's fine."

"Did he say something to you on the way out here?"

Cus paused. Maybe it was best to tread lightly on the details. Part of him still could not accept that his wife was front and center in a regionwide illegal dumping operation. What if he and Aurora were wrong about her? What if Jenny didn't know about any of it? What if he spilled his guts to Jenny and instead of her being defensive, she was devastated—ashamed and horrified to learn from her husband that her father was a monster? In that moment, Cus realized he still loved Jenny, and that if she was an innocent in this, he would hate himself for his suspicions, which he had used to justify his infidelity.

"Let's just say there was something fishy out there," he said, wondering if she'd bite.

"Fishy?"

"I got the sense he doesn't want me working on that story."

"What story?"

"The one about the benzenes."

Jenny registered a blank expression so believable Cus had the sensation of drowning in a sea of false assumption. "The elevated levels in the creek and the lake."

Now, Jenny looked mildly embarrassed. "Oh God, Cus, I totally forgot you were working on that. I've been so wrapped up in my own shit lately. I'm really sorry."

"No apology required. It's not like I've been talking about it much."

Jenny finished the last of her mimosa with an indelicate swig. "What made you think that about my dad? He must have said something. Was he an asshole? I think he's having a midlife crisis or something. Do you want me to say something? Because I will, sweetie. You know I will."

They were similar that way, Cus and Jenny, both inclined toward action. There was nothing passive about her. Energy and effectualness oozed from every pore.

"He was fine," Cus lied, unsettled by how easy lying had become. "He just seemed, you know, worried about the story."

Jenny nodded and tucked her tongue into her cheek to indicate she was beginning to understand. It didn't help that she looked adorable, even more beautiful than the day he married her.

That line pleases Woody. He takes a short break to congratulate himself and devour an apple fritter. Mandy will be touched. The line is also a nice F.U. to Celeste, if she is still reading, which he hopes she is.

Brimming with self-approval, he gets back to work.

"He's worried about you," Jenny said with certitude.

"Worried about me?"

"And probably worried about me too, frankly."

"How so?"

"My guess is Dad knows something or has some suspicions about what's going on and who's behind it. People play rough when they feel threatened. He's so proud of you and the work you do, but he doesn't want you to get hurt." She attempted a joke, but her eyes were dewy. "He certainly doesn't want me to get hurt."

Cus went to the fridge and cracked a long-deferred morning beer. "Are you asking me to stop working on the story?"

"You know me better than that," she said.

Cus nodded and apologized. They hugged, but he wasn't sure about her anymore. He had yet to discover the full extent of Cold Harbor's illicit side business, but he knew the company was neck deep in wrongdoing. Did Jenny know, or was her father hiding it from her? In this moment, it appeared to be the latter. Cus again noodled the idea of telling her all he knew, that Cold Harbor had an illegal dump site a half mile east of Brightbrook State Park. That he was gathering string on a story that might result in her father going to prison.

Instead, he said to her, "It's our anniversary. Let's go in the hot tub."

As they screwed with mechanical efficiency, Cus thought fleetingly of Aurora but not in a sexual way. Aurora had a reputation of using her wiles on sources. What if she was in on this somehow? What if Al Holmes was using her to seduce him for blackmail to keep him off the story? What if, Cus thought as he achieved fruition, his own newspaper was one of Al Holmes's toxic clients?

Later, Cus looked at his phone. A text message from Aurora had penetrated the cellular dead zone.

"Don't let her trick u," it said. "She's dangerous. PS: I love u."

That Sunday, Woody and Mandy drive to Joe and Bev's Lake Mohegan compound, Mandy at the wheel. It's an unseasonably warm early spring Saturday, although what defines seasonable can't be pinned down anymore. Mandy's sister, Tara, is visiting with her son, Sterling, to celebrate his second birthday.

"What are you thinking about?" Mandy asks.

"You mean in the book?"

"Is there anything else anymore?"

Silence ensues as they crest a hill and the lake unfolds before them. A water skier slaloms against a backdrop of forested drumlins.

Mandy starts over. "It's sweet of you to begin decriminalizing me."

"I'm not decriminalizing *you*. Jenny is a fictional character. But I'm glad you approve of the new direction. I don't think it will hurt the narrative."

"When do you plan to start working on my dad?"

"I'm always working on it, okay? It's all I think about twenty-four/seven. How do I make Al Holmes look like a great guy so Joe Dunn and his family won't be offended? It's my life's passion—that and spraying down cars at Mega-Shine."

Another pause.

"Look, I'm not a magician. I'm involved in a process that needs time to play out. It's possible that Al might have to get worse before he gets better."

"Whatever," she says, looking at her phone. "You're the *artiste*."

"Are they reading it?" he asks.

"They're reading it. They're not fucking morons."

"I asked because they told me in the beginning they were going to wait until—"

"I know what they said. I was there, remember? But that was before you and your bullshit Process turned them into thugs. You know what would be wicked awesome, Woody? Throw in a drug angle. Have my dad trafficking cocaine, maybe throw in some fentanyl. How awesome would that be—a giant mixer truck full of fentanyl? My dad could drive it to schools for show and tell and then hand out the drugs to kids in gift bags to grow his business."

"I understand that you're upset," Woody tries. "Like I told your brother, I'm going to fix this. How do you want me to handle this tonight?"

"With mechanical efficiency," she hisses.

"Oh, come on, honey. It's hard enough to write a good sex scene without you personalizing every word."

Mandy laughs. "Oh, is that what they are? Sex scenes? They read like the owner's manual for a cordless drill."

"Why is that a bad thing?"

"Let's just leave it alone for now, sweetheart. Tonight is about Sterling. Let my sociopathic, environmental-criminal parents enjoy their grandchild's birthday."

Woody has an unsettling thought: What if his book is becoming a self-fulfilling prophecy, triggering dark and violent impulses in Joe Dunn that otherwise would lay dormant. As they pull up to the circular driveway, Joe is on the manicured front lawn teaching Sterling how to play croquet.

Tara ducks her head out of a side door, waving at Mandy. Woody senses he's not included in the gesture. Anticipating Sterling will be losing his croquet tutor, his mother brings him a placating Popsicle.

Joe strides to the Lexus and waits for the two of them to hop out. The fifty-minute drive is just long enough for Woody to emerge slightly achy and stiff. Mandy retrieves from the back seat a soft-sided cooler containing spinach, artichoke, and jalapeno dip, a family favorite, and hands it to Tara.

"I'll warm this up in the oven," Tara says, taking the cooler from Mandy and giving Woody a look. "What up, Wood Man? All good with you and your raging man hammer?"

"Tara!" Mandy scolds and cracks up. The sisters stroll into the house, trailed by Sterling slurping on his orange Popsicle. Woody and Joe find themselves alone on the vast driveway except for Digger, the golden retriever.

"How goes it, Joe?" Woody asks with strained nonchalance.

"I can't complain too much. How's life at the car wash?"

"We're replacing all the spaghetti brushes. Everyone's excited about that."

Joe laughs. "I don't blame you. That is exciting. Hey, Woody, I have a request."

Woody braces. "Anything," he says.

"Would you mind going out on the boat with me for a half hour? I'd like us to have a little talk, man to man."

"The boat?" Woody's voice cracks slightly.

"We need privacy. I already told Bev we might be going for a little ride before dinner."

Woody feels something akin to terror. Life is imitating art in all the wrong ways. At least Cus had a miniature life preserver. Woody grasps for an excuse but can't find one. Joe senses his reluctance.

"Don't worry. We won't be mutilating any fish."

The dock has been swallowed by late-afternoon shade, the sun still illuminating the far side of the calm, cold lake. Joe hops in the forty-foot Cobalt and gestures for Woody to do the same. The throaty twin engines engage. A few minutes later, the boat churns southwest, with twenty-three miles of progressively less populated shoreline ahead. Even after they reach deep water, Joe keeps his speed down so they can talk over the thrum of the inboards. Woody can take the buildup no more and says, "Okay, what's up? You don't like the book?"

A look of great anguish settles on Joe. "I've always admired your writing, Woody."

"But . . ."

"I'm not surprised the book is doing well. It's a good read."

"But you didn't like the fish scene?"

"It's not really about what I like or don't like. Under different circumstances, if we were not connected through your marriage to my daughter, if I did not know who the author was and he did not know who I was, I'd probably love *Fear as Mud.* I mean, yeah, sure, it strays into tropes and some of it doesn't add up, but it's entertaining."

Woody has an impulse to defend the technical merit of the book but keeps quiet.

"I just have one question," Joe continues. "What did I do to piss you off?"

"Piss me off?"

"Because if I did something or said something, whatever it was, I'm sorry. I just wish you'd have said something to me about it. Because whatever I did, I promise it wasn't intentional. I mean, you're fucking family, for God's sake. I love you."

Woody looks over to see a tear running down Joe's face. He expected a bad boat ride but nothing like this. He closes his eyes and envies his alter ego. He would rather be swimming for his life from live rounds fired by Tommy the Torque Wrench than be forced to face the emotional consequences of his online Art.

"I . . . love you, too, Joe," Woody stammers.

He desperately wishes he hadn't posted his latest chapter early that morning:

Al had a knack for finding illegal but profitable pursuits long before he started dumping carcinogens around town. Maybe it was more correct to say those pursuits found him. In his twenties, while working in Southie as a bartender, he'd served a notorious crime boss two double whiskeys one rainy morning and politely declined a $100 tip as excessive.

"You're one in a thousand, maybe one in a million!" the major domo enthused. "I ain't never seen no bartender turn down a freakin' Benjamin." Then he tilted his glass toward Al in a sign of respect. "I like you, kid. Better yet, I trust you. You any good with tools?"

The exchange spawned a lucrative three-year job at a chop shop fronted as a collision repair center. By the time the feds closed it down, Al had moved on after getting a tip about an imminent bust. No record of his employment at Commonwealth Auto Color existed, but he'd been busy and productive, cajoling, coaching, and paying a veritable all-star team of car thieves throughout the Northeast. At twenty-six, with only a high school diploma, he was not a millionaire yet, but now he was the one peeling off Benjamins.

"Hey, I heard you drove that Camaro all the way up from Norfolk," he'd flattered one of his rising stars.

"Yes, sir," the young thief replied.

"What were you doing down there? You found yourself some Confederate pussy?"

"I'm staying with my grandparents for the summer until my dad gets out of the joint."

"You got a way to get back down there?"

"I was just gonna steal another car, I guess."

"Tell ya what," Al proposed. "Steal the car, bring it back here, and I'll fly your ass back to Norfolk and throw in a hundred for incidentals. That work for you, kid?"

From that moment on, Tommaso Vesuvio Nunzio—the future

Tommy the Torque Wrench—was the trusty lapdog of whatever con Al Holmes was running. He'd been shot in the hip in East Boston trying to collect on one of Al's usurious loans. Another time when Al hooked up with a printer to sell counterfeit Bruins tickets, it was Tommy's misfortune that one of their dupes was off his meds—a violation of his parole terms—and had a near-photographic memory for faces. When, two months later, he encountered Tommy by chance in the men's room at the dog track, he stabbed Tommy in the neck and kicked him so hard in the balls that they had to operate to save his left nut. But pain was part of the job. He didn't feel it with the same intensity a normal human does, and he dished out far more than he got. Nothing but bees fazed him. He was allergic to their stings—not enough that a sting or two would kill him but enough for major swelling and pain even Tommy could not ignore.

Al loved to mess with Tommy on the bee thing.

"There's a hornet on you," Al would lie, enjoying the panic on his tough's mottled face.

"Where?" Tommy would ask, motionless.

"On your head."

"What should I do?"

"Don't move."

"Okay."

After a minute, Al would say, "It's gone, I think."

"You think?"

"Yeah, it's gone."

"You positive?"

"Yeah, I'm positive, numbnuts. There was no fucking bee." And Al would dissolve into laughter.

Tommy never knew if Al was bullshitting because sometimes a bee really was hovering near Tommy. Al enjoyed keeping people on their toes.

Yet their partnership endured, almost as if they were father and son, fed by shared savagery, greed, and a near miss in Eastie when someone—they never found out who—forced them off the road and into Chelsea Creek. Tommy never went anywhere without a vehicle escape tool, and this time it saved their lives. He knocked out the back window, and the two hoods made it out moments before the black Ford Taurus turned sideways and sank into the muck.

Many criminal ventures have sprung from the loins of serendipity, and so it was with the toxic dumping racket that came together decades later in Tiberius. While excavating a site for a new medical complex, a work crew encountered Native American remains in a quantity that typically translates into protests, news crews, state regulators, and interminable delays.

"What in God's name am I supposed to do with all this crap?" Carl Cronin, president of the excavation company, had asked Al as they rode to the nineteenth hole at Mont Blanc Country Club.

Al had sketched out an elegant solution on a napkin:

Cronin's boys would be in charge of extracting any large bone fragments and pulverizing them in an industrial grinder. A backhoe would load those remains, plus soil complicated by smaller bits of humanity, into a hopper under which a Cold Harbor truck would sit. The truck's barrel would be partially filled with a ten-inch slump—concrete too wet for most practical applications.

The "Injun dirt," as Al called it, would mix nicely into the sodden concrete, firming it up. The load would then be hauled to the precast yard and turned into two-foot by two-foot by six-foot 3,400-pound "ecology blocks" commonly used in security and traffic barriers and other nonengineered structures. It was a standard disposition of waste concrete. No one would know these particular eco-blocks contained the sacred, not to mention legally protected, remains of Indigenous peoples.

"That work for you, kid?" Al asked Carl with the self-satisfied lilt of a man used to fixing things.

That was classic Al. He wasn't just greedy, he was innovative in his greed. Even as he sketched his drawing, he realized that the sacred slurry did not necessarily need to be turned into all but worthless eco-blocks. It could be delivered as standard product to unknowing customers and turned into swimming pools, patios, and sports courts. Al would get paid on both ends, which was only right, as it was his idea and a brilliant one at that. There was unity of purpose and control of the process. There was also, in Carl Cronin, a well-off co-conspirator as reliably discreet as he was.

Al Holmes allowed himself to look into the future. He liked what he saw. A private jet. A ski chalet in Switzerland. Ten-thousand-dollar-a-night whores. What he never saw was that his then-four-year-old daughter would marry an investigative reporter who in his own methodical way was as sharp as Al and who couldn't be bought. For all his mental agility, Al never understood how anyone could be motivated by principle or a desire to serve the public good. Were such people lacking the balls to game the system, or were they just lazy and unimaginative? Of course, he reasoned, the best scammers hid their dirty work in a shroud of self-righteous bullshit.

A prime example of such duplicity, Al observed, was Sheriff Mike Royce. He used his campaign war chest to fund showy steak dinners for law enforcement buds at Keen's in Midtown Manhattan. He'd also outfitted one of the department's unmarked search and rescue boats with fishing gear, and used more campaign donations to buy diamond jewelry for an Upper West Side mistress twenty-six years his junior.

Al had been invited to one of those steak dinners—a thank you for contributing 10K to successive Royce reelection campaigns. What a blast. He arrived bearing cigar holders in the shape of Cold Harbor mixer trucks with the company name and logo engraved on the side. A $100 Cuban extended from each barrel, which cleverly functioned as an ash tray. They were a talker.

"To Al Holmes," the police chief of Scrontica had toasted. "May your right turns always be slow and uneventful."

The function room exploded in smoky laughter at the inside joke, no one laughing harder than Al. Right turns taken too sharply in a loaded mixer truck were bad news. The fins inside the barrel, rotating clockwise, pushed the mud forward and slightly up on the driver's side. That meant a right turn taken too fast could land a mixer truck on its side in an instant. Most law enforcers in the room had experience with those kinds of wrecks. What made the toast so funny was that the Scrontica chief had helped Al whitewash one such mishap. The accident report had been altered to blame a "spontaneous sinkhole," saving Cold Harbor major fines and headaches. In exchange, the chief's summer place in the Adirondacks got a new rebar-reinforced driveway in environmentally harmonious taupe and stamped in a herringbone pattern. There were limestone, granite, and marble inlays. Gorgeous.

Al delighted at being teased, which reinforced his bond with a dozen well-placed lawmen throughout Cold Harbor territory and beyond.

Woody bobs in the boat with teary Joe. He tries to unravel his thoughts, but there isn't much to unravel. He's pissed that everyone is pissed at him. They're all conspiring to talk him out of finishing his masterpiece. Are Joe's tears even real, or is it part of their campaign? Why, Woody asks himself, has he let them fuck with The Process? Why did he let them badger him into compromises that threaten his Art? Why did he post that chapter this morning?

And now an instant message from Celeste?

"Okay, writer boy, you won back this non-Hispanic fangirl. I was strongly advised to check out your new chapter, so I did. It rocks. Embedding all those chemicals in people's homes, infrastructure, etc.—so effing twisted. I love it!"

"Thanks," Woody messages back without elaboration. He'll keep his exchanges with her as low key as possible even though he yearns for more detailed praise from her.

"Before I lost my brother, he told me something that has stuck with me ever since," Joe continues.

"What's that?" Woody asks.

"He said he didn't want a big funeral; he didn't want any donations in his name to any charities. He said the only thing that mattered to him was his reputation. He said, 'Joe, I want you to make me a promise. Promise me you will protect the Dunn name with your life. I ran this company clean from the ground up from day one. All I ask is, don't ever let that change.'"

Woody feels seasick even though the boat is barely rocking. He fixates on a gray manse atop a verdant rise in the distance and orders himself not to vomit.

"'I won't, Ray—as God is my witness,' I told my brother. I told him, 'You know me better than that. I'd never do anything to besmirch our good name.'"

Besmirch is a good word, Woody thinks. *It's not used enough, which is strange because besmirching has been happening since the dawn of history. If anything, it's on the rise.* He doubts Joe really used that word on Ray, though. Ray wasn't a word guy.

Woody looks up from his minitrance and sees Joe looking at him. He doesn't want Joe to think he isn't paying attention, so he blurts out a generic response even though he's not sure what he's responding to. "That's crazy," he says.

"What's crazy?"

"You know, the whole besmirching thing," Woody flails. "The general situation."

"If you think it's crazy that I wouldn't tell my dying brother I'd keep his company on the level and mean it, I'll knock your ass clean off this boat." Joe grabs the small fire extinguisher from under the steering station and looms over Woody, but Woody doesn't feel threatened. He's horrified he has pushed Joe to this point. He places his hand palm-down to calm Joe and says, "I just misunderstood. I know how honest you are. You don't have to convince me."

Joe puts down the canister. "I'm just a little on edge these days," he says, retaking the wheel.

"Why? What's going on?"

"Ah hell, you may as well know. But don't tell Mandy any of this."

"Don't tell her what?"

"I went in to the doctor a few weeks ago because I had ringing in my ears. I assumed it was from all the demo work over the years. They thought it was tinnitus."

"That's not good," Woody says. "They giving you ear drops or something?"

"They're giving me something, all right."

"Steroids?"

"Jesus, Woody, for a reporter you're not great on picking up clues, are you? They found . . . a mass."

A speed boat roars off their stern, just close enough for Woody to see two bikini-clad hotties hoist beer cans at them. Woody resists an impulse to wave back.

"It's something called an acoustic neuroma," Joe continues. "They think."

"Benign?"

"If that's what it is, yes. But either way it needs to come out."

A rush of concern for Joe, Bev, and Mandy washes over Woody. But it's met by concern for his book. The potential complications to The Process of Joe being seriously ill are difficult to fully appreciate in the moment. But this much Woody gets: It's one thing for people to think a writer is busting on his father-in-law in a barely autobiographical novel. It's another for people to think he's busting on his *terminally ill* father-in-law.

"I'm really sorry, Joe," Woody attempts. "I'm sure you'll be fine."

"Probably. But at my age, nothing's guaranteed."

Woody tries a Hail Mary. "I guess with all you've got going on, it puts my dumb book in perspective. You've got bigger things to worry about, right?"

"You mean the brain tumor?"

"Yeah."

"A brain tumor is never good, obviously, but as brain tumors go, I might luck out. I trust my doctors. I'm hopeful."

"I've always admired that about you—the positivity. Nothing ever seems to get to you. I wish I had more of that."

"Let's cut the bullshit and get to the reason I brought you out here."

"Okay."

"Your online book has become the major source of discomfort and disappointment in my life. If I had to decide between whether your book or my brain tumor has more negatively impacted me every day, your fucking book wins the prize."

A dinner cruise vessel plies past. It's the venerable SS *Anowara*, the Mohawk word for turtle. A line of buzzed celebrants on the upper deck waves heartily at the pair. So much waving on the water. Woody and Joe wave back.

"Maybe it's better if you don't read the new chapter," Woody says.

"I already did."

"What do you want me to do?"

"Two words," Joe says, handing his son-in-law an ominous looking envelope. "Cease and desist. Let's head back in. I'm starving."

That's three words, Woody wants to say, but thinks better of it.

CHAPTER 12
POSITIVE ENTHUSIASM

Later, they sing "Happy Birthday" to Sterling. Woody wonders how many of the grownups know what went down on the boat ride. All of them, maybe. Tanner, who has been pounding Rolling Rocks, adds an extended "and many more" coda to the birthday song. When it has gone on long enough, Cam intervenes.

"Kindly cease and desist," he hollers, adding a smirk. Tanner snort-laughs so forcefully he has to wipe his nose with an Elmo napkin.

"That's funny," Tanner says.

"You're funny!" Sterling opines.

"Are you ready for some cake?" his mother asks.

"Sheesh and dewist," the little boy shouts with delight. "Sheesh and dewist!" The whole room, minus one lonely novelist, shrieks with laughter, provoking Sterling to keep going. "Sheesh and dewist! Sheesh and dewist!"

"See," Cam says in Woody's direction. "Even a two-year-old gets it."

Woody tries to laugh it off between bites of red velvet cake. It's dry and tastes of soap. "Looks like we know who will be heading Dunn-Rite's legal department someday," he jokes, nodding toward Sterling. Then he slinks off to the guest bathroom and calls an Uber.

His initial plan is to leave without telling anyone, but by now

Woody has had a few Rolling Rocks himself. He marches back into the great room, dings his beer bottle with a spoon, and announces, "I'm heading home to make it easier for everyone to talk about me behind my back. Besides, I have some reading to do."

He reaches into his pocket and pulls out the envelope Joe gave him. Then he says, "Thank you for everything. It's been great. Happy birthday, Sterling."

With dramatic flourish, he wheels on the heel of his tritone boat shoe and strides to the front gate, expecting Mandy at least to come running after him. No one does.

This Uber driver turns out to be far less likable than Hamsa was. He's listening to right-wing talk radio and has an assault rifle tat on his forearm captioned "Come and get it."

"This is a beautiful neighborhood," the driver volunteers. "It looks like America is supposed to look."

Woody texts a message to JB: "Need a place to crash. Your offer still good?"

A thumbs-up appears immediately. A minute later, JB sends the passcode for the electronic lock that opens the service entrance in the back. Eventually, the driver understands his passenger isn't up for chatting about how immigrants, minorities, and transgenders have destroyed the country and he stops trying to engage his passenger. Woody opens the letter. It's from Raymond McAlister, founding partner with the law firm that has represented Dunn-Rite for more than thirty years.

Dear Mr. Hackworth,

As you are perhaps aware, I am chief legal counsel for Dunn-Rite Dig and Demolition Inc. of Icarus, New York, and its executive officers, Joseph P. Dunn, Cameron D. Dunn, and Tanner M. Dunn.

My clients assert that a book you are writing and serializing on multiple online platforms, known by the title Fear as Mud, has defamed them, causing severe, irreparable damage to their reputations and emotional well-being.

We hereby insist that you remove all online postings of the book in its present form and refrain from future publication of additional installments, sequels, or versions of the work, including but not limited to television, movie, theatrical, and online video dramatizations.

While we understand that your work is ostensibly fiction, which enjoys significant legal protection, we wish to make clear that fiction does not give license to suggest that an actual business—one you personally know to be honest and responsible—is a criminal enterprise.

Please be advised that if you do not cease and desist from publishing these unwarranted, unprovoked libelous attacks on Dunn-Rite and its officers, we will take appropriate legal action to protect the reputations and financial interests of the injured parties. Such action would include seeking relief in a court of law for monetary damages.

As a courtesy, our firm will, at your request, email you a PDF of this notice to forward to your legal representative. Kindy provide my office with the necessary contact information along with instructions for mailing future correspondence on this matter.

Sincerely yours,

Raymond B. McAlister, Esq.

Woody slumps in the back seat, now barely aware of the blathering from the radio. Seeing the letter in its cold formality hits hard. His mouth feels as dry as the velvet cake, and one of his eyelids twitches. This might be it—the moment he must choose. Life or Art?

Perhaps the letter is making the decision for him. If he capitulates, his so-called life will be a joke. He'll be humiliated, shorn of purpose, a literary Samson left to lament his lost locks of prose. And he won't just be a disappointment to himself and to his thousands of readers. He will have let down the planet. Yes, the planet. What Joe Dunn et al. do not realize is that Woody's book is flirting with a moral center.

He stumbled into it the night he spoke to the small but attentive audience at the NYPIRG meeting.

"Have you considered making your book about forever chemicals?" a retired environmental engineer had asked Woody during the Q and A.

Woody wasn't sure then what "forever chemicals" were, but they sounded bad.

"I don't want to give away the plot," Woody had tap-danced. "But let's just say it's in the pipeline."

As it turns out, something else is in the pipeline—eleven sweet and sour meatballs in a grape jelly "gravy," three jumbo shrimp, gobs of spinach-artichoke dip loaded onto Fritos Scoops!, plus a bratwurst with kraut and a heap of extra creamy mustard potato salad from a recipe handed down by Grandma Morris on Bev's side. It's a family tradition. Also in the pipeline: the Nutella French toast Woody had that morning. Perhaps as his stress levels have mounted, there's been some overeating. But he's too distracted to sense the brewing storm in his innards.

Instead, as Woody's Uber driver turns into his neighborhood, Applegate Heights, he ponders the implications of leaving his Lexus at the lake with Mandy. He could take her BMW and drive to his new home at Cluckin' Clean, but then he'd have to arrange a car swap. It's too much. Instead, he asks the driver to wait while he throws some clothes in a bag.

"Sorry, bro, I already have another pickup," the driver says.

"Allahu Akbar," Woody tells the asshole, throwing in a mock salute.

He heads inside to pack. He'll have to call another Uber. Ella is home from the SAT prep class that served as her excuse to skip the lake. But she's dressed to head out and looks stressed.

"What's wrong, honey?" Woody asks.

"Have you seen my fake ID?"

He shakes his head, trying to strike an air of proper parental disapproval.

"Okay, then maybe you know the answer to this: Are you and Mommy getting a divorce before I go to college, or is the plan to wait until I'm out of here?"

He reaches for his Mister Twister walking stick, a vine-curled curiosity he bought eleven years ago on a fishing trip with Joe and Tanner in North Idaho. It has been propped against one side of the fireplace ever since, but now he leans on it for real, feeling woozy. "Why would you say that?"

She rolls her eyes and fixes him with a stare. "I love you, Dad, but sometimes I have to wonder. Do you think I'm an idiot? You and Mom hardly speak to each other anymore. My friends are constantly giving me shit about your book, so you can imagine what my enemies are saying. Let me give you a sampler: 'My mom says your grandpa gave her dad cancer.' 'Is your dad coming to Career Day to talk about how he wiped bird shit off my mom's Subaru?' 'I just watched *Married to the Mob.* Is that about your dad?' Oh, and someone taped a note to my locker that said, 'Lactation Lounge? Really? Eww.'"

"Are you mad at me?"

"No, Dad," she says, her eyes blazing with the same incandescent fury as her mother's. "You're the best."

"No need to go overboard."

"Oh, that was a good idea to put a window-smashing tool in your book. How'd you come up with that idea?"

She can see his embarrassment. She bores in for the kill. "It's nice to know you care about me as much as you care about Tommy the Torque Wrench."

He doesn't know quite how to answer that. A dog barking in the distance fills the silence. Finally, he says, "It's good we're having this talk." But the door slams, and she's gone. The house goes silent, and he is alone.

Woody fills a large duffle with clothes, a first edition of *For Whom the Bell Tolls*, a jar of cashew butter, a box of Ritz crackers, two apples, a handful of Luna bars, and a liter bottle of orange soda. He also takes a sheet, his sleeping bag, his pillow, his phone charger, his laptop, his spare key to his Lexus, his toiletry kit, and a bar of soap. He takes a long look at his Peloton bike, admiring its sleek, expensive geometry, and whispers, "I'll be back for you, baby. I promise."

He starts to call an Uber but decides to borrow Mandy's BMW after all. He's sick of Ubers.

"Looks like I'm taking you up on your offer," he texts his friend. "It's either Cluckin' Clean or the Homewood Suites for me tonight."

But he's not ready to move in yet; it's too early. He decides to go for a drive. Much as he loves his Lexus, putting Mandy's faster, more responsive Beamer through its paces will clear his head. He cranks Guns N' Roses and heads for the interstate.

Thirty minutes later, he's exited onto Route 71 on the edge of apple country between the hamlets of Gunther and Siba. By then he is mordantly butchering Bon Jovi.

"Whoa, I'm halfway there. Whoa oh, living in a combination laundromat-chicken wing bar."

Woody's groove doesn't last. It collides with a fleeting but impressively urgent need to move his bowels. He tries to remember the last time he passed a gas station or a McDonald's, but all he can recall is the eastbound Thruway plaza ten miles before Exit 19. If there's a corresponding plaza on the westbound side—he's 95 percent certain there is—he can be there in a half hour.

The BMW's tight turning radius is a gift. Rather than keep driving down Route 71 in search of a pullout or driveway, Woody makes an immediate U-turn, the car's tires scrunching on the gravel shoulder. His headlights catch the eyes of something not especially small tearing into the woods—a raccoon, maybe.

The desperate need to void himself returns, but a reassuring lull ensues and he speeds on until he hits a light. The anxiety of just sitting at the empty intersection roils his gut so savagely that he considers running the red, but what if a cop is lurking? He's only fifteen minutes from the rest stop. He's Atwood Effing Hackworth. He's got this.

There's another close call after he merges back onto the Thruway—by now he is sweating heavily—but he pulls it together one last time and counts the miles to the plaza. Six. Five. Four. Three. Two. Then a sign: *Blue Creek Plaza Closed. Next Services 42 Miles.*

Feeling astonishment, horror, and relief, Woody surrenders. He hears the release, but it's a good five seconds before he feels the thermal swell. Then comes an even more voluminous eruption, this one literally levitating him off the Venetian Beige leather seat of his wife's $87,000 automobile.

Atwood "Woody" Hackworth, namesake of a luminary who would go on to win the Booker Prize and international acclaim as a writer, activist, and visionary, has soiled himself.

A minute later, he drives past the shuttered service plaza. It's unlit, and a tall chain-link fence encloses the structure. But he also sees a line of portable toilets available for emergencies.

"Why does the world hate me?" he bellows.

His phone pings. It's JB.

"No Homeboy Suites for you. All exiled writers welcome at Cluckin' Clean."

Woody weighs his options. The good news is that he has plenty of extra clothes. The bad news is that he's perched on a pillow of his own feces, some of which is running down his legs and making its way onto the Beamer's upholstery and carpet. He needs to find a creek or pond and jump in, but then he has another idea.

Fifteen minutes later, he is in a car wash naked. Not Mega-Shine but a do-it-yourself operation farther out on Longhouse Boulevard. Even in a less desperate moment, he'd be embarrassed to be seen at this nonautomated shell of a real car wash. He'd heard horror stories of customers scratching their finishes by absentmindedly using the hubcap brush to soap up a quarter panel and of sessions timing out in the middle of a wax application. No, the cleaning of an automobile exterior requires sophisticated equipment and highly trained professionals such as himself. Still, he's grateful this place exists.

The hair-trigger sprayer complicates the job, but after an unattended blast of clearcoat that narrowly misses his scrotum, Woody's personal hygiene mission is accomplished. He puts on a fresh pair of shorts and a polo shirt and throws his soiled clothes in a trash can.

Now it's time to address the vehicle's interior. He soaps a pair of clean underpants for a rag and almost weeps with relief as the upholstery poo vanishes. The carpeting requires more scrubbing. He works on it with the hubcap brush to get it as light as possible. It's not perfect, but someone would have to be looking for a stain to see anything out of order. He finishes the detail by buying a trio of spearmint-scented air freshener trees and hangs them from the mirror.

As he pulls out of the wash stall with the windows down, he wonders if this episode of incontinence will one day serve his Art. Maybe not directly—it's simply too disgusting to be rendered in a serious work of fiction—but how could it not deepen his understanding of the human condition?

JB's waiting for him in the Cluckin' Clean employee parking lot in the back, a gesture of kindness and, no doubt, curiosity.

"You didn't have to drive out here for my sorry ass," Woody says.

"Isn't this what friends do? And isn't that your wife's car?"

"Long story, but I should have my rig back tomorrow."

Inside, JB pours them both a pint of Longhouse Lager and a shot of Jameson. "To change," he toasts. "May it bring opportunity and wisdom."

As they clink glasses, Woody understands why his new landlord is sitting on a pile of cash (versus a pile of his own shit), boasts a wide network of friends, and looks a decade younger than his forty-three years. It's that dumb phrase Woody's functionally illiterate cousin, Rorke, who has a PhD from Duke in bioengineering, uses: "positive enthusiasm."

Rorke has often advised Woody he needs more of it. "Believe in the power of positive enthusiasm, and anything is possible."

Except negative enthusiasm, Woody used to scoff, but now he

sees that positive enthusiasm is a thing—a thing some people have naturally. Its presence explains why the JBs and the Nick Peters of the species stride purposefully through life transforming problems into opportunities. Its absence explains why Woody will be living above a laundromat, sharing a room with crates of detergent and nonperishable restaurant supplies.

Self-doubt worms into Woody's resolve.

It's not so much that he has chronically lacked enthusiasm. It's more that it comes and goes, like gusts of wind. Moreover, it's too often fueled by the worst kinds of impulses: vengeance, a desire to best rivals, to prove himself to others. External motivators from the dark side. The seeds of his novel were planted in that muck, he thinks. Maybe negative enthusiasm exists after all. It seems to live in him.

Woody's new redoubt is nicely appointed for a supply room. There's a Murphy bed and a metal desk atop which sits a twelve-year-old unplugged printer. Oddly, a small sink stands in one corner. In addition to the laundry soap and janitorial supplies, gallon jugs of wing sauce fill a long shelf. More than likely, the soap and the sauce stored so closely together is cause for a health department citation. But no inspector would come up here.

"I've got an extra TV downstairs we can bring up," JB offers.

"Thanks. I'll pass for now," Woody says, his need for solitude connecting him to many of the Great Writers. "This is perfect. I just need to sleep and write until this all blows over."

"Not really my business, but do you plan to be showering, too?"

"Tomorrow I'll sign up at Planet Fitness by Mega-Shine. They're running a special. Ten bucks a month."

"Good plan."

"It's called street smarts, dude. It's part of the homelessness package."

JB laughs.

"You'll never be homeless as long as I'm around."

Lying alone in the dark in the surprisingly comfortable Murphy bed, Woody thinks about his spite job at Mega-Shine and whether he needs to keep it. The boat ride with Joe, his daughter's harsh words, and the realization that his book is causing real pain to his loved ones make the car wash job feel superfluous. Except he likes it there. Likes the steady but not backbreaking manual labor and the refreshing absence of pretense among his coworkers, most of whom are half his age. He likes the big rain slicker he gets to wear when he's on prerinse. He imagines himself as a noble sea captain braving the high seas of censorship. Even the boss seems cool.

"Just give the word if you want me to put you in for assistant manager," Packy told him the other day. "You'll still have time for your book."

Woody isn't ready to take that step, but it feels good to be part of the Mega-Shine family—his only family apparently.

Sleep comes quickly, but it's interrupted just as quickly by his ring tone, which he changed to "Water Music" when he took the day job. It was supposed to be a reminder that the job was a lark and his destiny lay elsewhere.

Woody sees the call is from Mandy. He doesn't answer, but he checks his text messages.

"Where are you?" reads one from two hours ago. And thirty-three minutes later: "Hello?"

He texts her back. "I'm at Cluckin' Clean. I live here now."

"We should talk," she replies.

"In the morning, okay?"

"I have an 8 o'clock," Mandy informs. "No idea how long it will run."

"Text me after. We'll figure out a time. But if you're just going to remind me that I'm a shitty husband and father, don't worry, I get it."

He braces for the inevitable comeback. Instead, he receives her avatar with a tear pouring from a cartoon eye. It's not cry-me-a-river sarcasm, either.

"No matter what, I love you," Mandy writes.

Woody's noncartoon eyes well up annoyingly. Since when did the

Dunns turn into criers? Now the only ones behaving like assholes are the two brothers, but even that's understandable, even laudable. They're defending their patriarch and only sister. They're akin to the Knights of the Garter, the ancient order of chivalry he learned about in a desperately dull medieval history class at UConn. It's the only fact from the class he remembers besides the baldness of Charles.

"I love you, too," he writes back.

He shuts his phone down and tries for sleep again. Before it comes, his mind drifts to what he can do to repair the fraying, problematic relationship or whether the best solution is to end it. But he's not thinking about his marriage. He's thinking about Cus and Aurora. He sleeps just six hours but awakes refreshed and early enough to write.

A water taxi chartered by Al Holmes arrived on schedule at noon the next day to ferry them back to the mainland.

"Happy anniversary," the pilot, a weathered, sunny blonde in an Evinrude ball cap shouted over the engine. "What a beautiful place to spend it! Water and soda are in the cooler. The head is down the stairs to the right. I'm Captain Cindy, by the way."

"Hi, Captain Cindy," the couple replied together.

"In the unlikely event you need a life jacket, just let me know and I'll order one on Amazon—for myself!" A cackle worthy of Bill Russell burst forth, as if she hadn't made the same joke a thousand times.

They roared swiftly over smooth water with Cus and Jenny seated behind the captain.

"Marriage isn't my thing, but I salute anyone who can make it work," she volunteered. She turned to salute them. So much for eyes on the road.

"You're not married?" Jenny asked.

"I didn't say that," Cindy replied. "I just said it isn't my thing." More outrageous laughter.

Cus thought he might be having a nightmare. Unable to process the greatest journalistic and familial crises of his life, his subconscious was distracting itself by placing him on a boat piloted by a seafaring Joan Rivers wannabe. For one improbable moment, his drive to uncover the dumping story abandoned him. He wanted to be on a giant air mattress, sipping an ice-cold Labatt Blue as the tides carried him to Canada and its eternal promise of refuge.

His phone blinked alive. It was Aurora again.

"1. Let me know when you're back and safe. 2. Sorry about the drunk dial if you got it. That wasn't cool of me. 3. Things getting interesting here. Do they give Pulitzers for exposing your own newspaper?"

Jeepers, Cus thought. His wife's family and now his employer—all in on it?

Perhaps because she wasn't overly attentive to the water, Captain Cindy didn't miss much on the boat, including Cus looking at his phone.

"All this gorgeous scenery, including your lovely bride, and you're looking at your screen?" Then she turned to Jenny and winked. "It could be worse, honey. At least he's not checking out my ass."

Cus was startled by his powerful desire to shove Captain Cindy into the depths.

"Oh, he's capable of doing both," Jenny assured her.

Cus laughed, but it was a worried laugh, the laugh of a man wondering what his wife might know.

"What's that little island over there?" he asked, but he didn't hear Captain Cindy's answer. His mind ran elsewhere, to imagining Al Holmes and the *Daily Informer*'s oily third-generation publisher, B.J. Hayden III, plotting the star reporter's demise.

Aurora had worries of her own. Someone had sent her flowers, too, and what looked like a box of Russell Stover chocolates. The card read "I love you so much" and showed Cus's signature, but the handwriting looked odd. She'd never known him to write in block letters. Carefully, she slid the plastic tray out of the box—and stifled a scream. Medical waste filled the compartments. Brain bits, bowel sections, clotted blood, a nipple, bone fragments, half a big toe, diseased lung tissue, and something else, round and gelatinous. She drew a sharp breath.

"¡Dios mío. Un testículo!"

An hour after posting, Woody reads through a Twitter thread of mostly female readers ripping his latest efforts as misogynistic.

"Jenny starts out as a corrupt bitch on wheels and now drifts into clueless passivity," @peevedgodess66 writes. "Is there a word for committing character development suicide?"

"It's hard to write a believable female character when you despise women," @cynickiley chimes in. "Note how Hackworthless turns a dedicated female journalist into a homewrecker. Same pattern. A*&hole."

"Don't forget the bad woman driver cliché," @buffalotomgirl contributes. "He just used a boat instead of a car. On a positive note, at least I'm not married to this jerkoff in real life."

Woody notes the criticism with detachment. His skin has thickened. As long as they're reading, that's all that matters. Now feeling groggy, he replays the horror at the lake the day before, knowing he has bigger worries than feminist critiques.

"I work 10 to 7 today," he texts Mandy. "I can call you around 8 tonight if that works."

"Yes. How are you?"

He responds with a shrugging emoji, palms upward. Then he checks his emails.

The second one—the one just under a Chipotle Rewards update—makes his heart skip. It's from Livingston Literary of New

York. Woody can't recall having ever contacted the agency.

"We're Interested," the subject heading reads.

Woody detects a slight tremble in his hand as he opens the email.

Dear Mr. Hackworth,

My name is Melvin Stern. I'm an agent with Livingston Literary. I represent approximately thirty-five writers, mostly of fiction, including Tabatha Steel, Jonathan Rathcliff, and Sampath Ranasinge, a runner-up for the Booker Prize.

If you already have literary representation, please disregard this message other than to accept my congratulations and best wishes. However, if you remain unrepresented, we'd love to talk to you.

Woody reads it a second time. He's lightheaded. Although he has never read any of the authors Stern mentioned, he's pretty sure he has heard of the first one, Tabatha Steel. *Didn't she write a book about vegan witches or something?* He wants to call Stern immediately, but he doesn't want to come off as overeager. Instead, he returns the email with an offer to call back at 1 p.m., the start of his lunch break. Stern immediately replies, "Talk to you then."

CHAPTER 13

A MOMENT OF INATTENTION

Woody's so excited he almost runs a red light driving to the hospital to switch cars with Mandy. (A receptionist brokers the key exchange, sparing the newly estranged couple face-to-face contact.)

At the Dunkin' drive-through, back in his Lexus, he buys a medium coffee and a plant-based breakfast sandwich with a twenty and tells the woman at the window to keep the change. Who's a misogynist now?

Positive enthusiasm courses through him as he rotates through various posts on the wash line. He's teetering on fame, not mere local notoriety, the kind of fame he has always craved without fully admitting it. What a rebuke this will be to the rejectors of *Tick Tock, Check Your Sock*, to the newspaper that dumped him for no good reason, to Get-a-Real-Job-Cam and his sneaky prick brother, Tanner.

Fame is the answer. It's something everyone has to respect. But beyond that, it brings healing. Handled with grace and humility, fame can salve the wounds of domestic disharmony. He'll have a podium to tell the whole world that the book is not based on his in-laws, just inspired by aspects of them. He imagines himself on an elevated TV show or podcast, wearing a tweed sport coat (elbow patches?) discussing the birth of his bestseller:

"I was struck by a question, or, a series of questions, if you will—

What if my highly virtuous in-laws, who have supported me through every step of my artistic journey, were corrupt? How would that look? How would that feel? The answer to those questions became the underpinning of the novel."

Back in the real world, he's guiding vehicles onto the conveyor and shouting "NEUTRAL" while brandishing the plastic sign that reinforces the message. It's not particularly dangerous work, but, like many jobs, it can be if you're inattentive—for example, if you're delirious with self-celebration and mulling how you'd adapt your bestselling novel into a screenplay.

As a Chevy Tahoe approaches, Woody checks his phone to see if Nick has weighed in yet with congratulations. It's poor timing as the driver of the Tahoe is responding to a text from his wife. Maybe it wouldn't have mattered if Woody had remembered to display the "NEUTRAL" sign and shout the command as he was trained to do, but that's lost to the realm of conjecture. The Tahoe surges forward, still in drive, slides sideways off the conveyor, and slams into Woody's left thigh. His ankle buckles beneath him.

"Man down!" someone shouts.

Woody feels dizzy, then he feels okay except his leg hurts. His right side aches when he tries to lift his left arm. Someone puts a sack of clean rags under his head for a pillow.

The paramedics believe nothing's broken but want to take him to Mid-State anyway. For several reasons, including that Mandy works there, he waves off their offer in exchange for a promise to get checked at an urgent care.

"You're sure you didn't hit your head?" a paramedic asks.

"My head's fine," Woody insists.

"His head wasn't fine before he got hit," someone kids.

Grudgingly, the Mega-Shine team drifts back to work, concerned for Woody but also disappointed that the distraction has played out. The conveyor restarts. Kaylon is assigned to drive Woody in his Lexus to urgent care. Packy will then retrieve Kaylon so he can resume his shift. One worker short is manageable, but two MIAs screws up the workflow—and workflow is everything at a car wash.

"Lexus, you gonna sue that motherfucker who blasted you?" Kaylon asks once they're underway.

"I didn't hold up the sign," Woody confesses.

"Damn, Lexus," Kaylon says. "Were you thinking about your book?"

"Yes."

"You gotta save that for the library. This is what happens when you lose focus around all these cars and equipment and—"

Woody catches a deep breath and winces. He bruised a rib, hopefully no worse. "It's hard to turn off the switch," he says. "I'm extremely dedicated to my craft. To a fault, it appears."

"Your family is gonna be dedicating a park bench to your ass if you don't pay attention."

The paramedics are right it turns out. X-rays confirm no broken bones, but the left ankle sprain requires a boot. As Woody waits to be fitted, he sees he had a call at 1:20 from Stern, the agent, no doubt wondering why Woody didn't call.

Woody tries to send a text explaining what happened, but there's no cell service in the clinic. He tries the guest Wi-Fi. That doesn't work either. He galumphs out of the examining room and makes his way back to the lobby, past a gauntlet of fellow wretches awaiting their versions of McMergency medicine. He overhears a receptionist saying wearily, "No, sir, we don't perform colonoscopies here."

His urgent care experience hasn't been bad, he reflects, except that his plea for a painkiller stronger than prescription strength Motrin has been rejected. Evidently, the medical establishment views middle-aged guys who work at car washes as high risks for opioid abuse. His thigh aches as he climbs into his SUV. At least he has phone reception again.

"Mr. Stern has left for the day," a receptionist informs him. "Would you like me to take a message, or can I forward you to his voicemail?"

"Can you tell him I'll call him tomorrow? I didn't call today because I was busy being hit by a car."

"Was busy . . . being . . . hit by a car," the receptionist repeats with stenographic indifference. "Got it! Anything else, sir?"

"Nope, that covers it."

Woody drives back to his temporary domicile. The main parking lot of Cluckin' Clean is filling up with happy hour regulars, including Becky, the mom of Ella's teammate Lyla. It takes her three seconds to recognize him as he's extricating himself and his boot from the SUV. She wants details. Woody obliges with a short version of the accident, omitting his contribution to it.

"What'd they give you for pain?" Becky's horrified to hear Woody was deprived of narcotics. "Here, have these," she says, fishing into her purse and handing him a vial. "Tylenol with codeine. I never go anywhere without 'em."

Until now, Woody has been cool on Becky. She's friendly and well-meaning but unbelievably annoying. However, in this moment, she's his favorite person on the planet.

"Are you sure?" he asks.

"Don't give it another thought. I have a whole closet full of T3s."

The coffee-grinder laugh follows. Right there, Woody identifies her as the subliminal inspiration for Captain Cindy. It's magical, he reflects, how a writer at the top of his game draws from his environs.

He falls asleep with his boot on, the codeine liberating him from his sore leg. When he wakes, the ancient LED clock radio on the desk reads 6:52 a.m. A dull light bleeds through a worn window shade. He's not worried about not connecting with Stern. Woody has a valid, sympathy-inducing excuse. Besides, the guy must be used to dealing with flakes. It's the nature of genius.

"All clear here if you want to call," Mandy texts.

Oh, right. That.

Awkward small talk fills the first few minutes. Ella's considering visiting Bowdoin. She thinks she can play lacrosse there. The dry cleaner called. They have eight of Woody's shirts long overdue for pickup. A check engine light came on in Mandy's BMW.

"It just needs an oil change," Woody offers.

"And it smells like something crawled in and died in there. Who knows what that's all about."

Woody says nothing.

She also reminds him—"in case you forgot"—that his mother's pottery exhibition is coming up. "You might want to wish her luck."

Then it gets real.

"You know my dad's sick, right?"

"Yes, he told me."

"He has a brain tumor, Woody." She chokes back a sob.

"I mean, yes, kind of, but it's not, like, a 'brain tumor' brain tumor. It's more of an ear tumor."

"It's a fucking brain tumah, Dr. Oz. A tumah. In his brain. What the hell is wrong with you?"

"Much," Woody replies dully.

He wonders when Mandy found out about Joe's acoustic neuroma. Joe swore him to secrecy on the boat. Why do that if he'd already told her? Or did he tell her after the boat ride—after the birthday party? Maybe the tumor was a hoax, a gambit to guilt him into abandoning his Art. How satisfying would it be to catch Joe in that deception?

"How long have you known?" he ventures.

"Since Cam told me a week ago. He said I should know even though Dad wanted it kept quiet. We figured Dad said something to you on the boat."

Woody's heart sinks. So much for a ruse. "I'm sorry. I'm sure he'll be fine."

"So, you moved out?"

"Yes. I'm sorry about that, too."

"Don't be. We need a break, especially if we're going legal. How does that work anyway? If my family sues you, are they, in effect, suing me, too, because we're married? Anyway, your instincts are spot-on for once. A little separation will be a good thing."

Even through the warm haze of two more T3s, Woody doesn't like the sound of that. His exile to Cluckin' Clean is supposed to be a self-imposed act of literary rebellion and a bold statement of fealty to The Process. Instead, Mandy is telling him to not let the door hit him in the ass, which, he now realizes, is sore as well. He must have landed on his tailbone.

"I got hit by a car," he tells her, long past hoping for sympathy, just desperate to change the subject. Seems he's always desperate to change the subject lately.

"What? Are you okay? Where?"

"I'm fine. Sort of. At Mega-Shine. Nothing broken, but I'm in a boot for a while. A car rolled off the edge of the conveyor and into my leg. Some idiot wasn't paying attention."

"Oh no!"

Recounting the incident has the effect Woody desires. Her curiosity takes over. "Who was the driver?" "What kind of car?" "Did you get his insurance information?" "Which urgent care?" "Who was the doctor?" "Oh, good. He has privileges at Mid-State." "What? The paramedics came? You didn't tell me that." "Which ankle?" "At least you can still drive." And on and on.

Woody strives for non-nonchalant heroic. "I'm a little beat up, but I'll live. It's not like it's a brain tumor." He immediately wishes he hadn't said that, but the comment doesn't get a rise out of Mandy. She's pleased that Woody at least conceded that her father has a brain tumor.

"It's no brain tumor, but getting hit by a car is never good. Sounds like you were lucky. I hope that driver was cited."

"I don't care," he says. "I just need to heal."

"We all do."

They agree to keep things civil for Ella's sake. Woody elects not to tell Mandy about Livingston Literary, in part because there's nothing to tell—not yet—but also because he doesn't want to antagonize her.

"I'm resolving to stay positive," he says. "We can work through this."

"I'm resolving to fix the ceiling fan in the kitchen," she replies.

CHAPTER 14
EUROPEAN CITY PANTS

Aurora and Cus met at Panera on Empire Boulevard, the most generic thoroughfare in Tiberius and its busiest. Cus felt more like himself again, calmer and in control. He was emboldened from surviving the voyages to and from Jupiter Island, each harrowing in its own way, and he was eager to get back to work. He had many balls in the air, but the one that gnawed at him the most was the possibility that his wife was a co-conspirator in a major felony.

Woody looks up from his laptop, annoyed with his verb choice. Balls don't actively gnaw. A ball can be gnawed, but the only ball that can gnaw on its own is a testicle, like his did for weeks after he was kicked in the groin by Fernando, a cranky llama, at a farm sanctuary where they took Ella when she was little. Time to rework that part.

Cus had a lot on the table, including a heaping platter of his own poor judgment—a platter fired in the kiln of denial. Had he really been naive enough to marry into a crime family without knowing it? That did not square with his image of himself as a savvy judge of character. Now, thank God, he could hope his bride, at least, wasn't a slime bucket. Maybe he hadn't booted the biggest decision of his life.

Aurora ran her foot suggestively along Cus's right ankle under the table. "Pay attention to me," she said, pouting, and sipped her matcha iced tea.

"As long as it's about the story," Cus replied. "It's imperative that we get back to just being colleagues—colleagues and friends."

"Cualquier quieras, mi amor," Aurora agreed. Whatever you want, my love. She took no offense to his rejection. She knew Cus was right. The investigation had reached a dangerous and critical stage. The story must come first. But she also knew his resolve had limits.

"So, what was that text all about—the part about winning a Pulitzer?" he asked. His keen eyes spotted a young woman snapping a photo with her phone. For a moment, he feared they were being spied on again, but on closer inspection he saw the girl was merely taking a picture of her Peruvian ceviche and molé-infused sweet potato salad. Still, they probably should stop meeting in public places, he thought.

"Do you recall the name Kyle Staley?" Aurora asked.

"The press guy who was fired for peeing in the parking structure?"

"Yes, your memory is good."

While Cus did, in fact, command impressive powers of recall, he declined to credit them in this instance. "It's hard to unsee public urination in the workplace, even if you weren't there."

"Well, they pissed off the wrong guy."

"Talk to me, kiddo."

"Don't call me kiddo. It's patronizing."

"I'm sorry. I'm just . . ."

Cus wasn't sure what he wanted to say, so Aurora got the last word. "It's okay, kiddo. I love you, too."

Their equilibrium restored, the work lunch resumed, now with a surly pressman as their primary focus.

Kyle Staley had been a cause célèbre for a few days at the

Informer. A twenty-two-year pressroom veteran, he was good at his job and viewed by his colleagues with affection despite his lack of couth—or because of it. His undoing sprang from his small bladder and propensity to drain it outdoors when no one was looking—except this time, someone was looking. A handful of *Daily Informer* cheapskates—ad reps, lower-rung administrative staff, and the like—had a habit of eating lunch in their parked cars. Staley wasn't thinking about that when he ducked behind a support column and, while puffing on a Marlboro, relieved himself in an adjacent planter containing exhausted potting soil and dozens of cigarette butts, most of them his. An overwhelming majority of *Daily Informer* employees, had they witnessed the voiding, would have ignored it or at most sent the offender an embarrassing note asking him to keep it in his pants, to cease and desist, as it were.

Woody pauses, the legal term yanking his mind back to the boat. Back to Joe handing him the letter. And then the flip "Let's head back in. I'm starving." Apparently, Joe's brain tumor came with a hearty appetite. Fascinating. Woody urges himself onward: "Keep writing."

But in this case, the wrong worker, from Staley's perspective, was gumming her egg salad sandwich behind the wheel of a Nissan Sentra. Frances White affected the manner of a gentle Christian woman, but underneath the slightly too-large cross around her neck roiled great reservoirs of judgment and easily triggered indignation. When she looked up from her phone, Staley's exposed member so offended Frances's sensibilities—all she really saw was his guide thumb—that she screamed, "What the fuck?"

But it was a silent scream. Her windows were up, so Staley never heard her. Perhaps that was the only thing that worked in his favor that day. Had he heard her, he might have pissed his navy-blue Dickies, already stained from the messy labors of printing third-rate journalism for a morally bankrupt media company.

Frances slunk down behind the wheel, averted her eyes, and prayed. As soon as Staley left the parking garage and returned to his post, she beelined it to human resources, where an equally devout believer took her statement.

"Thank you so much for bringing this to our attention," the HR lady told Frances, handing her a tissue.

In a less cutthroat work environment, Staley would have been reprimanded and sent home for a day or two without pay, if that. But this was the Age of Dying Newspapers, and Staley's poor potty comportment spelled opportunity for the bean counters. His long run at the *Daily Informer* meant he made too much money, especially with print plant crews shrinking as automation increasingly ran the show.

It was in that context that Staley was fired for "sexual harassment." His union lawyer managed to have it downgraded to "gross misconduct"—winning Staley (if winning was the word) a six-month suspension without pay.

The cost-containing suits assumed he would just move on. To further tilt the odds in their favor, he was required to undergo intensive counseling aimed at curbing his "alarming and inappropriate exhibitionism."

Management underestimated Staley's defiance. He wasn't just stubborn; he lived for revenge. For six months, he scooped the paper off his front porch, toted it into the privacy of his backyard, and pissed on it. On Tuesdays and Fridays, he attended counseling. By the middle of his second session, Staley had convinced the therapist—eighteen years his junior—that his predilection for public urination wasn't born of deviancy, but of laziness and nicotine addiction.

That was true. Whizzing outside allowed him time to smoke two cigarettes on his break instead of just one.

"I thought I was hidden from view," Staley told the mental health professional. "Isn't that the opposite of an exhibitionist?"

The mental health professional agreed in his report to HR. That, plus loud hints by Staley of a wrongful firing suit, led to his reinstatement, conditional on a promise to acquaint himself with the men's room.

Staley was back in the fold of the *Daily Informer* and its fracking-enmeshed parent company, Digital Thermo Inc., with its cryptic slogan "Media and More!" But returning to the pressroom didn't dampen his quest for vengeance. His ritual pissing on his morning newspaper had been symbolic of his desire to desecrate the institution itself.

Staley's moment arrived in the form of a call from one of the few reporters he knew, the cute one, Aurora Connolly, who had written a moving tribute to his neighbor, a barber killed in an armed robbery.

"Staley knows everything about the dumping," Aurora informed Cus after she interviewed the pressman off the record.

"You're sure he's not cooking up some revenge fantasy out of nothing?"

Aurora gave him a cockeyed look as if to say, "Doesn't your skeptical nature ever take a day off?"

"He let me take a photo of this photo," she said, calling it up on her phone.

An image of an unmarked white box truck, backed into the pressroom loading dock, rattled Cus. The truck looked like one of two in the Cold Harbor fleet used to ferry supplies to pour sites and make warehouse runs. For good measure, the photographer, presumably Staley, had captured the license plate.

"I already ran it," Aurora said. "It's a Cold Harbor truck."

Cus should not have been surprised, yet the visual affirmation that two cornerstones of his existence—his employer and his wife's family—were converging in something so sinister rocked him. For a moment he sat there, saying nothing. A single tear ran down his cheek.

"I'm sorry," Aurora whispered.

Cus felt lost. "What are we going to do?" he asked for the first time in his career.

"I was hoping you'd be able to answer that."

"I suppose the first thing we need to do is talk to Staley."

"'We' is complicated," she cautioned.

"You don't want me there?"

"He doesn't want you there. He knows you're married to Cold Harbor. He almost hung up on me when I said I was working with you on the story."

"So, where'd you leave it?"

"I talked him off the ledge," Aurora assured her worried colleague. "I told him you'd been investigating Cold Harbor long before I got involved. I told him I'd trust you with my life, and, if he trusts me, he needs to trust you also."

"He went for that?"

"I think so, but he'd still rather just talk to me, at least initially."

"He just wants to get in your pants."

She waved dismissively. "Who doesn't?"

Something about her flip self-assurance disarmed him. Cus laughed long and hard, which he rarely did, especially these days. "You have a point."

Aurora interviewed Staley the next day. Disproving Cus's suspicions of carnal intent, Staley insisted on meeting Aurora at a bowling alley forty miles north of Tiberius in Crawley County. He was being chivalrous; he wanted her to feel at ease, to focus on his story, not to be half-expecting him to expose himself. Moreover, his pet python, Judas, had a way of freaking out certain people. Best not to make that introduction under these circumstances.

Indeed, Staley had learned a thing or two about discretion since The Brandishing. He believed it wise on several levels not to invite any reporter into his home, least of all an attractive woman twenty-five years his junior.

Cold Harbor had spies everywhere. It wasn't a stretch to think they'd gotten to some of his neighbors, like the Hogues, Bill and Nancy.

Bill, a retired penitentiary guard, found pleasure in firing pellets into dogs and cats that strayed onto his immaculate lawn. Nancy, the meaner of the two, was a retired school nurse and violent quilter whose endless hours of stabbing and yanking were accompanied by murmured mantras of rage against enemies real and imagined.

She'd once threatened to call the police if Staley didn't move his camper van, which he'd parked on Sherwood Drive for a long weekend while having his driveway resurfaced. Nancy cited the city ban on parking in the same spot for more than twenty-four consecutive hours. When Staley tried to plead his case, she'd snapped, "Tell me again why this is my problem? Move your damn van."

Rather than tell her, Staley had shown her. He had set his alarm for 3 a.m. for five straight days, revenge-rousing himself in the dark to repark the van at different locations in front of their obnoxious barn-red ranch house. Each time, he revved the engine a minute or two. A few times, he triggered the antitheft alarm "by accident." He also took photos of his vehicle to establish it had been moved. Nancy had met her match. Staley was good at petty, which was bad news for the *Daily Informer*. Still, he needed to be careful. Much as he yearned to sink his former employer, Cold Harbor goons sinking him to the bottom of Lake Ranswill in a concrete corset was too high a price.

"I'm leaving for Bowl-a-Ram now," Aurora texted Cus. "I'll check in when we're done. Don't worry." A heart emoji followed.

Cus hated that he couldn't be there for the interview. He walked to burn off his restlessness. That didn't work, so he sat in his study rereading the Bill of Rights and sipping a good bourbon. His mind went down dark alleys. What if Staley was in on it? What if Aurora and Staley were in on it? That seemed unlikely, but who knew anymore? The walls were closing in. Could he trust anyone?

Once Stern learns about the car wash accident, he emails Woody to express his concern and his eagerness to meet the new author in person.

"But we can set up a teleconference if you don't feel up for coming down here."

Woody wants no part of a remote meeting. He wants his New York Moment; he wants to be the foundling from the sticks jetting in on their dime to assume his rightful place among the literati.

"We'll have a car waiting for you at La Guardia," Stern says. Woody silently pumps his fist.

Plans were made to fly Woody down the next day. Now, what to wear?

The boot is a complicating factor. It might look silly paired with a suit. He would be wearing a dress loafer on one foot and just a dress sock on the other. Weird. The walking boot demanded a smart, casual look, but how to make it happen?

Rolling a pair of jeans over the device proves impossible, so he tries tucking the pants leg inside. He gives that a test run in the hallway that leads to the Cluckin' Clean freight elevator, but it's uncomfortable. His shin is slightly swollen and scabbing in places. It just wants to be left alone not rubbed by denim crammed into a CAM boot. It's better when he tries it with khakis, but he fears even those, in the course of a long day of travel and meetings, will break a scab. He can't risk bloodstained trousers at Livingston Literary.

Bandaging the shin might fix the problem, but Woody doesn't consider that, or, more accurately, doesn't want to consider it because he is looking for an excuse to call Celeste. A chance to appeal to her sympathy, minimal as that might be, and crow about being summoned to The City is too much to pass up.

He catches her in a silly mood, two-thirds through a bottle of Finger Lakes Gewürztraminer with one of her bridesmaids, Kelly, a TV reporter who was once reprimanded for unwittingly repeating one of Woody's inaccuracies on the air.

"How about a pair of capris?" Celeste offers over speakerphone, causing Kelly to mouth the word "No!" and cover her face with a throw pillow to muffle her laughter.

"What are those?" Woody asks.

"You know, three-quarters-length pants. They'd be perfect."

"Aren't they for women?"

"Oh, Wood Man. You can be such a plebe. When I was in Barcelona last year for the online investigations conference, that's all I saw—men in capris. They're in New York, too. They've gone mainstream."

Kelly, struggling to keep it together, whispers to her friend, "You are such a bitch," and writhes on the sofa with her pillow.

"Hmm," Woody says. "Don't you think they'll call even more attention to the boot?"

"What's wrong with that?" Celeste insists. "Play the sympathy factor. Underscore you suffered a work-related injury in a physical job, that you're not another cloistered writer dork."

Celeste still has a hold on Woody. He loves conspiring with her, even if just on a wardrobe choice. Besides, she makes sense, as she usually does. Woody is all in.

He has no luck finding men's capris for sale in Icarus, but acting on Celeste's suggestion he settles on having a pair of his khakis altered for $45 plus a $25 rush fee. Whatever Asian country the seamstress is from, apparently it's one that places low value on social niceties. Ms. Wendy seems rushed and put out.

"You just want one leg short, right?" she asks, eyeing his boot.

"Both legs."

She cocks her head as if to say, "Really?" and writes the order on a pink pad.

"They're in style in Europe and big cities," Woody offers.

"Cuff or no cuff?"

"No cuff."

"Both legs, that's twenty dollars more," she says, handing him his ticket. "Tomorrow."

Woody realizes he did not make clear the extreme urgency of the matter.

"No, no, I need them today. I'm leaving town tomorrow."

"Today not possible. Too busy."

Woody looks away, but just when all seems lost, good fortune visits. Miss Wendy's young son zooms out of the back room in a toy car. The rack of plastic-wrapped pickup orders hides him, so Woody only sees him at the last second. For the second time in four days, a vehicle crashes into Woody.

Without acknowledging his fault, let alone apologizing, the kid scoots back behind the counter, laughing with demonic glee. Woody lunges backward, pain slicing through his ankle. Miss Wendy notices his distress and yells at the boy in her native language and apologizes to Woody.

"I'm very sorry. He have high energy. You are all right?"

"I'm good."

"Your European city pants done by four o'clock today."

"That's awesome. Thank you."

"You have cuffs, too. No extra charge."

"Sure."

"Cuffs no problem. Easy."

He galumphs out of the shop but with a bounce. It may not always seem that way, but someone must be looking out for Woody Hackworth.

The short business class flight to La Guardia proves uneventful. No one notices or cares about his wardrobe. He sits next to a young woman who looks as if she might be heading back to college—she wears a Columbia sweatshirt. But other than pro forma hellos, they keep to themselves.

At the pickup zone, his driver—an elegant Italian type, lanky, silver-haired, in a dark suit, and in his late fifties or early sixties—stands next to a Lincoln Town Car.

"Welcome to New York, Mr. Hackworth. I'm Dominick."

Heading toward Manhattan and the Maison Parc Lux hotel, a panel van veers in front of them, forcing Dominick to brake slightly. He hits his horn a few beats longer than necessary.

"Can you believe this asshole?"

The van driver rolls down his window and flips them off.

"Fuck you, you piece of shit!" Dominick leans hard on the horn for a good five seconds. He looks back at Woody in the mirror. "I apologize for the language, sir. My wife says I need to take it easy or I'm gonna have a heart attack, you know? I've actually been a lot better lately, but this cocksucker . . . anyway, enough about me. What brings you to town?"

"I'm finishing up a book and meeting with an agent."

"*Salut!* I've always admired people who can write. I'm more of a talker, as you can tell." They chuckle over that.

"You got a title?"

"Fear as Mud."

"Fear as Mud?" Dominick repeats, puzzled.

"Mud is slang for concrete in the sand and gravel industry."

"Yeah, yeah, yeah. I remember now. My cousin Tony did that work for a while. That's right—they were always calling it mud."

"Fear as mud is a play on clear as mud," Woody further assists.

"Yes, sir. I get that."

The Town Car is making good time through Queens, its occupants blissing on that satisfying blend of pity and superiority that comes with cruising unhindered when it's bumper to bumper the other way.

"What's Tony doing now?" Woody asks. He doesn't particularly care, but a reporter's reflexes don't die with the job. He envisions himself as a headless journalism rooster scratching out information kernels he cannot consume. *Good image*, he thinks. *That should be in the book.*

"Don't ask," Dominick says, looking in the mirror and making a slashing gesture to his throat. "That's a rough fucking business is all I gotta say." He crosses himself. "I take it you're writing a crime novel."

"Yes and no. There's a lot of crime in it, but it's much deeper than that."

"Nice," Dominick says, cutting off a tour bus the way the van driver cut him off earlier. The bus driver honks. "Go fuck yourself!" Dominick advises. "They're giving out CDLs to monkeys these days. Anyway, as you were saying?"

"In a nutshell, it's about a newspaper reporter investigating his corrupt in-laws."

"No shit. How'd you come up with that?"

Woody doesn't know the answer or if there is one. Perhaps the answer is buried so deeply in his subconscious among countless insecurities and petty resentments that the journey to understanding will take years. But why go there? Why taint his breakthrough moment with psychological bullshit?

"I'm not really sure. My wife's parents are in construction. That's part of it."

"How long you been married?"

"Eighteen years."

"What's your wife think of the book?"

"She loves it."

"She must be a saint! And your in-laws, they know you're writing this?

"It's all over the internet."

Dominick pops a Nicorette square in his mouth. "I like you, Mr. Hackworth. You got a pair of brass clangers."

"So they say."

"Because you know what my father-in-law—God rest his soul—would have done if I ever wrote a book like that?"

"What?"

"He would've cut off my balls with a rusty tomato knife." Dominick laughs hard, a knowing laugh that could have come from Al Holmes.

"Somehow I doubt your wife would let that happen."

"Let it happen? She'd hand him the fuckin' knife."

Sweat surges under Woody's arms. "That's quite an image. I might use it in my book."

"It's all yours, Mr. Hackworth. I'm here to serve."

At the hotel, Woody struggles out of the limo. It's too early to check in, but he figures he'll drop off his bag and boot-walk the two blocks to the agency for his first meeting.

"You sure you wanna walk in that thing?" Dominick asks. "I can wait here and drive you over if you want. I'm salary, plus tips. No skin off my ass."

"I'm sure," Woody says, handing him a twenty. "I can use the fresh air."

Dominick looks skeptically at the cottony brown sky. "Fresh air in New York City? Let me know when you find some."

To Woody's surprise, his junior suite at Maison Parc Lux is ready even though it's only 9 a.m. It smells gently of lavender. There's a New York taxi-themed gift tote tucked in one corner of the writing desk.

"Welcome to New York from Your Friends at Livingston Literary," the card reads.

Woody sits on the purple duvet that matches the peonies in the slim porcelain vase on a bedstand. He grabs a bag of mini bagel chips from the tote and munches a few. Then he gets up to inspect the bathroom. His bad foot bumps a corner of the wardrobe, briefly snuffing his lux-buzz. But he feels no pain. Woody has a love-hate relationship with his walking boot. It's ugly and cumbersome, yet it bestows upon him the gift of crutchless ambulation and serious impact resistance. He gives silent thanks to the boot's protective plastic shell and proceeds into the bathroom, where a woven artisanal bathmat hangs over a clawfoot tub. He sees that the walk-in shower has front and rear showerheads. "Well played," he murmurs. The office/storage room at Cluckin' Clean feels far away.

CHAPTER 15
STERN

With his ten o'clock with Stern looming, Woody brushes his teeth and heads for the lobby.

"Will you be needing a taxi?" asks a desk clerk.

"I'm good. My meeting's just a few blocks from here."

Except the Park Avenue vanity address does not convey the actual location of the understated entrance, which is on East 36th Street and much closer to Lexington than Park. Woody walks past the entrance twice, oblivious. By the time he arrives at the front desk, he has walked half a mile and galumphed himself into a medium lather. Far worse, he'd overheard a homeless person opining on his capris to another homeless person.

"Check out those goofy-ass pants on that dude."

"Excuse me?" Woody had snapped.

"Nah, you cool, bro," said the more heavyset man, slouched against a wall with a sleeping bag on his legs. The other man had given him a friendly thumbs-up and shouted, "Lookin' sharp!"

Woody had continued as the pair spasmed with laughter. From then on, Woody thought everyone was laughing at his pants.

It's hard enough for a new author to meet the power brokers who control his fate, who can hit levers that could catapult him from obscurity to James Patterson-level acclaim. It's hard enough to strike the right balance of confidence and gratitude, to stay on point while trying to read the room, to size up friendlies from detractors, to be the best possible version of yourself with strangers. But to accomplish all that as you apprehend that your pants incite ridicule even in the homeless population . . . that's a lot to ask of anyone.

A stunning receptionist, possibly Iranian, greets him by name.

"You wouldn't be Mr. Hackworth, would you?" she asks, her smile blasting him like a high beam. She can't be the same officious receptionist who took his information after he was injured.

"That's me," he says, relieved she can't see his pants because he's behind the counter.

"I'll let Mr. Stern know you're here. He's looking forward to meeting you. You can take a seat anywhere you like." She winks at him. "Your book is awesome," she adds.

Woody blushes. Did she really wink at him, this angel of the Euphrates? She's reading his book? Really?

For reasons unknown, his mind turns to an interaction the year before with a receptionist at the gastro doc. That was before he learned that his bloody stools were caused by a foodborne parasite "likely to clear up on its own in a week or two."

Inspecting his medical history form, a sourpuss receptionist had shouted into the lobby in a nasally Downstate whine, "Mr. Hackworth, you missed the box asking if you've ever been diagnosed with colon polyps. Have you ever been diagnosed with colon polyps?" He recalls how the other patients looked at him, awaiting his answer. So much for HIPAA.

And now Stern's secretary just winked at him? He wonders if he's having a stroke.

He desperately wants to say something witty, but all he can manage is to repeat what the young woman just said.

"I can sit anywhere I like."

"Yes, Mr. Hackworth. Anywhere you like."

"Awesome."

Woody silently castigates the stammering moron who hijacked his brain and takes a seat off to the side. She'll be less likely to see his capris there.

He checks his phone to find Nick has taken a moment from his super-reporter schedule to wish him luck. "Let me know how it goes. Welcome to the big time."

JB also texted, "I know you're busy down there, but do you mind running out to Jersey and picking me up a dryer door assembly? Part #44046701."

Always the kidder, that JB.

As Woody is responding to JB, he gets a text from Ella: "They're putting me in goal today if you're coming to the game."

He's thinking about how to craft a response that softens the truth: that he won't be there because, in hopes of drawing an even larger audience to the book that's making her life suck, he's in New York meeting with a publisher. Instead, he texts, "I'm out of town. I'll be there for the next one. Good luck!"

"Author, author!" a voice booms, and into the lobby strides Stern. He's a good three inches taller than his visitor, athletically built, and with a full head of reddish-brown hair. Early sixties, Woody guesses. He's far from the nebbishy caricature Woody envisioned.

Woody rises to shake his hand. He notes Stern's eyes traveling ever so briefly to his exposed shins and the boot.

"Thanks so much for coming down. I know it could not have been an easy trip with that millstone shackled to your foot."

They both look at his boot. Woody braces for a wisecrack about the pants. Instead, Stern needles in another direction.

"I was surprised to learn Icarus has an airport."

"Only until the corn gets yay high," Woody parries.

Stern emits a thunderous laugh and cocks his pointer finger. "Sarcasm. You're good at that. You ever think about making your main character—what's his name?"

"Cus."

"That's right—Cus, sorry about that—a little more edgy that way?"

"Edgy?"

Jeez, Woody thinks. *He's shredding my main character while we're still in the lobby.*

Stern, as if reading Woody's mind—or his face—apologizes. "Sorry, I'm etiquette-challenged. Possibly genetic. We can save this for my office. I'm just excited about your book."

Once they settle in, Stern picks up where he left off. "You've got a helluva yarn going. It's just that ol' Cus, as rendered—let's face it—he's a bit of a Boy Scout."

"Except for the adultery."

"Except for the adultery, that's true, but even with that there's an earnestness there, dare I say a leadenness. Ever thought of lightening him up some?" Stern pantomimes jazz hands.

Woody scans the office, an old reporter's trick, grasping for insights into his interlocutor. A framed diploma from Princeton. Another, from the Iowa Writer's Workshop. A sign behind him with the word "THINK" in block letters. A few photos, presumably of Stern's grown kids. One is a preppy-looking son, the other scraggly and overweight. There's a slender blonde in a tennis dress holding a puppy. He finds a few shots of Stern, including one of him in scuba gear someplace with palm trees. But the one that intrigues Woody most is the photo of Stern in formal attire. He's high-fiving a young woman beaming with joy.

"That's Penelope Blackthorpe," Stern says, reading Woody's gaze, "at the awards for the Waldo Fiction Prize. What a piece of work she is, but one hell of a writer." Stern notices a hint of dejection on Woody's face and adds hastily, "As are you, my friend. As are you."

"Except you want me to reimagine my main character."

Woody likes the sound of the word "reimagine." It's writerly, a sophisticated counterpunch to Stern's patronizing jabs. Much as Woody covets big city recognition, he has come to share Upstate's aversion to Downstate's arrogance and credentialism. He isn't so much bothered by the fact that The City and its Albany accomplices slurp tax dollars from the sticks like drunks on a distillery tour. It's the pretense. The tiresome "If I can make it here, I'll make it anywhere" horseshit.

"Not so much reimagine as a fleshing out," Stern assures. "That's all. A few tweaks. We can talk about it later."

"You think you can win me a Waldo, too?" Woody asks, half serious. He's mainly desperate to discuss anything but rewriting. He's also fishing for a compliment, which he could use after the early takedown of Cus.

"Sorry, my man—you've aged out. What are you, forty-seven, forty-eight?"

"Forty-two."

"Must be the long hours and the stress. You reporters work your asses off, don't you?"

"Most of us, I guess."

"Anyway, you have to be thirty-nine or under at the time of submission to be eligible for the Waldo. Besides, that one's given for literary fiction."

That's it. Woody's had it with this asshole. It's time to call his bluff. "If you don't like my book, why am I here?"

Stern leans forward and peers over his gold wire frames. "Are you kidding me? I love your book. Screw literature. It's overrated. You've got yourself an old-fashioned page turner. Even my ex-wife is reading *Fear as Mud*. Normally, the only thing she reads is the menu at The Cheesecake Factory. He howls again. "Here's the deal, Woodrow. It is Woodrow, right?"

"Woodrow works."

"Listen to me, Woodrow. I genuinely believe we have a bestseller here. Anybody who claims they haven't had a hard-on to avenge their in-laws is lying through their goddamn teeth. And here you are living the fantasy under the guise of fiction. It's brilliant." Stern casts his eyes to the heavens.

"Actually, my real in-laws, they—"

"Let me guess—like the book?" Stern cocks one eyebrow and shrieks with laughter.

Woody tries to continue. "I wouldn't use the term 'like' exactly, but—"

Stern laughs so violently the room shakes. It's contagious. Woody starts laughing, too.

"Ah, fuck 'em," Woody says, his voice cracking in merriment. The two men quake silently in their chairs, wiping their eyes and avoiding each other's glances so as not to reboot the hysterics. Woody can hardly breathe. It might be the first time he has laughed since he started writing *Fear as Mud.*

When they recover, Stern pulls a bottle of bourbon with a mermaid on the cap and asks, "Wanna drink?"

Woody looks at his phone. "It's ten thirty-five a.m."

"What's your point?"

Woody's wariness of Stern crumbles into a powerful bro love. Stern gets him—gets him in a way no one else does. Not only is he the perfect agent for this book, he's the *only* agent for it.

"Sure, what the hell," Woody says.

Stern places two glasses, nice ones, on the table. "Neat?"

"You have ice?"

Stern fixes him with a stare and in mock seriousness declares, "Never, never underestimate a functional alcoholic." With that, he strides toward what Woody initially mistook for a tiny safe. "You'll love this little gadget," Stern says, thrilled to have a new audience. "It's the world's smallest freezer. My daughter Beth gave it to me as a Father's Day gift. I think they call that enabling. What's your pleasure? Cubes, nuggets, crescents, spheres? I've got crushed if you like that."

"One sphere would be great."

"Good man. That's how I like it. I had a feeling I was talking with a fellow professional."

Big laugh. In just a few minutes, they become a fraternity of two.

From the freezer, Stern extracts a pair of round plastic molds. He snaps them apart and delicately drops an oversized ice ball in each glass. Then he splashes generous doses of bourbon over each and nudges a glass toward Woody while raising his own.

"Here's to Woody Hackworth, to *Fear as Mud*, and to a long, prosperous relationship with Livingston Literary." They clink glasses.

Woody feels what must be happiness as the burn fades to a warm glow. "Thank you. I wish they'd given me this at urgent care."

"I bet," Stern says then peers over his wire rims, looking serious. "We need to strategize about this afternoon."

It's a reference to Woody's 2:30 meeting with other key players in the agency. "Great. I'm looking forward to meeting your colleagues."

Stern cocks his head. "Colleagues?" He takes a dramatic sip of whiskey and leans toward Woody as if he's sharing enemy troop movements with a trusted ally. "Try inquisitors. Here's the God's honest truth, my good friend from Utica."

"Icarus."

"Icarus, whatever. The truth is," he says, his voice dropping barely above a whisper, "I work with a bunch of pricks. They'll eat you and your book alive if we let them."

Woody takes a big gulp in hopes of recapturing the warm glow, but there's only the sting of poison. He feels GERDy, yet also hungry. He should have eaten something this morning, but he was too amped. Stern tops off their glasses.

"They're not fans?" Woody asks.

Stern leans into his intercom. "Hold my calls, Jo."

The big, athletic literary agent gets up to close the door and resumes talking at a normal level. "No, they're not fans—of me! You could be coming in here with the next *Bonfire of the Vanities*, but if I was the one representing it, they'd crap all over it."

Woody feels weariness settle in like ground fog. There's no escape from petty office politics like what he endured at the *Blaze*. "Why don't they like you?" he asks, but he knows the answer. He mouths it in his head as Stern speaks.

"Because they're jealous."

"Jealous?"

"You're damn right. I've had more successes than all of them combined, and it pisses them off. You know why?"

"Why?"

"Because every time I do my job, it underscores they're not doing theirs. What's your best play if you can't hook any big-time writers yourself?"

"Shit all over yours," Woody replies.

"Correct. And overplay my *occasional* missteps, which are part of the business. Hey, no one bats a thousand in book deals, not even me."

"Missteps?"

"Minor stuff. We'll save it for another time. Let's just say that maybe a $200,000 guarantee on a book about a boy who befriends an acorn squash wasn't my best decision. I thought it was the next *Baron in the Trees.*"

"Baron in the Squash."

"Essentially, yes. The book was a brilliant allegory, so of course it went nowhere—one of the reasons I'm on a short leash here."

"How short?"

"Short enough to make for a long afternoon but not short enough for them to walk away from a proven online phenomenon. Just keep the faith, my friend. Between your rough genius and my seasoned advocacy, we shall emerge triumphant just as the badly outnumbered English did at Agincourt under Henry V."

Woody's foot itches. Absentmindedly, he reaches down to scratch it but feels only hard plastic and Velcro. "Anything I can do to help?" he asks.

"Just be your affable self. Don't try to come off as smarter than you are. With all due respect, you're not Albert Camus, and that's probably a good thing. Just don't let them lure you into that trap of sounding like a poseur. They'll be like sharks on a wounded walrus. And if any of them have creative ideas, whatever you do, don't get defensive no matter how stupid they sound. Just say something like, 'What a great idea! You guys are already making my book better.' Give them investment. That's how you defang these cocksuckers."

"Got it. Anything else?"

"Yeah, what's the deal with your pants?"

Fuck me, Woody thinks.

He explains enough for Stern to get the gist and wave him off expounding on additional details. "Did you pack any normal trousers?"

"No. Just cargo shorts for the flight home." Woody hopes his face isn't as flushed as it feels.

Stern's sad expression abruptly shifts to the intensity of a TV faith healer. "We can fix this."

"I can pick up some Dockers somewhere," Woody offers.

Stern recoils. "Let's *not* do that. You have to start thinking of yourself as better than Dockers."

"Jeez, they're Dockers, not sweatpants from Goodwill," Woody snaps, the whiskey loosening his reserve. Yet even as he says the words, he thinks used sweats would have been far preferable to capris. He will never forgive Celeste for her sartorial counsel.

"Now, don't get defensive," Stern says. "We're just problem-solving here."

"Okay, what's your plan? You're a haberdasher on the side?"

"Great word. You must be a writer. I'm simpatico with one. Upper East Side, not far from here. I have him on speed dial." Stern pulls out his cellphone. "Lorenzo! Melvin Stern. You're on speaker with a client of mine."

"Marvelous Melvin! *Cómo estás?*"

After some small talk, Stern cuts to the purpose of the call. "I'm with a young man—a sort of famous writer who's about to become more famous. He needs pants pronto."

"Hello, sir, how may I help you today? You spill coffee on yourself or what?"

"It's more complicated than that," Stern interjects, winking at Woody.

"I see," Lorenzo says. "What color pants do you need, sir?"

"Please just call me Woody. I'm wearing a dark-brown sport jacket, so probably any color works."

"And may I ask your waist size in the interest of time, Mr. Woody?"

"I'm a thirty-eight."

"He looks more like a forty to me," Stern interrupts.

"Perhaps too much bread. My doctor say to me, 'Lorenzo, you need to eat less bread and pasta and more whole grains and fresh vegetables.' You know what I tell him?"

"To pleasure himself?" Stern cackles.

"No. I tell him, 'You're absolutely correct, doctor. Good idea. I will do exactly as you say.' Then I went home and ate a half a fucking pizza. I'm sick of doctors and their bullshit."

Stern howls then puts his game face back on. "Okay, Lorenzo, I'm going to stick him in a cab and send him up."

Woody imagines himself as livestock prepped for transport.

"This all goes on my account," Stern adds.

"You don't need to do that," Woody pleads, summoning what's left of his pride.

Stern waves him off.

"I'll see you soon, Mr. Woody," the tailor says.

The pants procurement moves quickly. An hour later, Woody walks out of C.T. Clothier & Co. in a pair of tan Italian stretch chinos. The leg is snug enough for the boot to wrap over it. A soothing mulberry silk knee-high sock—$85 for the pair—completes the fix.

"Don't forget these," Lorenzo says, placing the capris in a bag and scurrying after Woody as he's about to exit.

"I never want to see them again," Woody replies.

"As you wish, sir. We will donate them to a thrift store in the Village. Your wife talked you into wearing these or what?"

"Or what," Woody replies.

Lorenzo smiles and nods. "It's not your fault. Sometimes, they make us to do stupid things."

Woody heads across the street to another Ray's knockoff, Marginally Famous Ray's, and grabs a quick slice. He finally feels ready for combat. Two hours and change until the meeting. Plenty of time to return to the hotel and relax. This time, his Uber driver is from Chad. Woody is getting educated on the political unrest there when he gets a spam call. Rather than simply end it, he absentmindedly turns off his ringer. Twenty minutes later, the writer sprawls on his luxurious king bed, listens to a siren in the distance, and drifts into slumber.

By the second ring of the room phone, he knows he fucked up.

"Where the hell are you?" Stern bellows.

"I'm . . ." Woody's struggle for full consciousness is like his book—a work in progress. "I'm in my room."

"Yes," Stern says with portentous calm, like a volcano before it blows. "I'm aware of that, having been the one who called your room. I mean why are you not at the meeting?"

"I fell asleep."

"Before the biggest meeting of your life? Are you on drugs? Did you pay a visit to a massage parlor for a quick rub 'n tug? Is that what knocked you out? Make me understand."

"No drugs, no rub and tug," Woody protests, aware he sounds like a toddler. "I'm just not used to drinking in the morning."

"What kind of a writer are you, for God's sake?"

"An apologetic one."

"Can you be here in ten minutes?"

"If I jog," Woody says, hoping the subtle CAM boot reference will win him some compassion.

"Then sprint. I need you here in ten. I can hold them until three o'clock, but that's it."

Woody hails a cab outside the hotel, but a lime-green double-parked produce truck blocks their crosstown progress. He settles with the driver then gets out and powerwalks, the best he can, the final quarter mile.

He enters the lobby for the second time, and just like before he's sweating. Unable to exercise since his accident, he feels it in his lungs and legs. Stern stands in the lobby, arms folded, waiting. The beautiful receptionist doesn't look up.

"Nice of you to join us," Stern says mildly. "Aren't we a bit underpublished to play the self-absorbed artist?"

"I wasn't playing anything. I fucked up, okay?"

Stern eyes his watch and gestures down the gleaming hallway to the restrooms. "Go ahead and pretty up if you want. We have a few minutes. I'll tell 'em you're here."

Woody heads to the men's room to dry his face, run a comb through his hair, and loosen the Velcro straps of his boot. The race walk from the hotel has his ankle aching anew, and his ass feels sweaty in his new wool trousers. Wisely, he'd grabbed an extra mint from the dish at the menswear shop. He pops it in his mouth and grinds it into peppermint pea gravel to speed-freshen his cottony mouth. Then he swallows most of the bits and spits the stragglers onto a soggy nest of used paper towels in a waste basket. Game time.

The Good Stern is back. He throws an avuncular arm over Woody's shoulder and walks him to the elevator. "Let me take care of this, Woodrow," he says. "We'll be fine."

Woody gulps hard. This is the moment to confess his true identity. "Just one other thing in case it comes up, which I doubt it will. My legal name is Atwood Hackworth. My parents named me after Margaret."

Stern shrugs. "Well, that explains the lady pants."

They get off on the third floor, walk past three empty offices, and enter the conference room. Woody counts nine editor types in business casual, most of them noodling their phones. Some offer weak smiles, others look more genuinely surprised to meet the viral social media sensation. Woody offers a smile of his own and a sheepish wave.

Stern announces, "Ladies and gentlemen, I present to you Woody Hackworth of Ithaca, New York, the man whose first novel is breaking the internet."

Polite applause.

"Icarus," Woody corrects.

"Icarus—my mistake."

"No problem. It's basically all the same up there anyway."

Group laughter.

"I don't know how anyone can live in those places," a craggy-faced man with a big head of silver hair says. "It takes a special breed. I spent two weeks at a writers' retreat in the nineties in—what's it called . . . Catatonica? . . . and I've never been so cold in my life. And it was May!"

More laughter.

"Catania, I think you mean."

"That's it," the craggy man exudes. "Beautiful country, I'll say that."

Stern interjects, "Look, before we begin, I want to apologize for making Woody late. He was kind enough to fly down early this morning to be with us, despite being in an accident a few days ago. I suggested a few hours ago that we share a little drink to toast to his success—not to mention the fact he wasn't killed. I didn't stop to consider that Mr. Hackworth might be on some pain medication."

Woody is struck by Stern's elegant bullshit. He took two oxycodones in the hours after his accident but has had only Tylenol and ibuprofen since. Not that he's going to correct the record. He senses the irritation in the room giving way to compassion, especially among the women. The one who looks like the queen bee furrows her brow, exuding motherly concern as Stern continues.

"He went back to his hotel room to relax and—"

"I passed out," Woody attests. "I'm really sorry."

"You're fine, Mr. Hackworth," the queen bee assures him. "We're delighted you can join us. Before we do introductions, would you care for some water or coffee, a soft drink?"

Woody is desperate for a cup of coffee or a Red Bull, but the way his day is going he fears a spill, so he declines. They go around the table, Woody doing his best to keep the names straight.

Nora Pearson, legal affairs.

Betsy Romano, cover art and illustrations.

Seth Zimmerman, senior editor.

Anne Kucera, associate editor.

Neil Himes, senior editor, crime fiction.

Bart Sheehan, director of marketing.

Liz Shelby, social media coordinator.

Destiny Tamar, diversity awareness coordinator.

Julio Quan, intern.

"And I'm Audrey Saltonstall," the queen bee reveals. "I'm president and executive director, which I suppose means I'm in charge—at least of everyone except Melvin."

A few chuckles roll through the room.

"Melvin does have quite an eye for talent," she continues. "Now I'm sure everyone has questions for Mr. Hackworth. Would anyone like to get us started?"

"I don't mean to pry, but how were you injured?" asks Anne, a fortyish blonde with tortoise shell frames and a legal pad.

Woody isn't sure how the truth will play with this crowd. He wishes he'd hurt himself falling off a ladder or playing hoops or, better yet, doing something geographically appropriate like slipping on a patch of ice while shoveling the walkway of an elderly neighbor.

"Well, it happened at the car wash. Kind of a freak thing."

The craggy-faced guy, Neil, the crime editor, jumps in to solve the puzzle. "Let me guess," he interjects. "The driver of the car behind you hit the gas instead of the brake and smashed into you from behind."

"Not exactly," Woody says. "But close."

"Woody wasn't a customer," Stern barks out. "He works at the car wash. Some idiot who wasn't paying attention rolled his SUV off the belt and into his leg—is that right, Woody?"

"Correct," Woody says.

"Let me guess, the driver was looking at his phone," Stern says, knowing that was the case.

"He was, indeed."

"People must stop with such silliness and focus on their driving," Audrey decrees.

The room hums in sycophantic agreement.

"Wait a minute," says Bart, the marketing guy. "You work at a car wash? I thought you were a journalist."

"He was, but—"

Woody cuts off Stern. "I was, but I needed more time to write. You know? Real writing."

Audrey nods approvingly.

"I'm liking the sound of this," Bart says. "Car wash novelist. We can sell that."

"The book isn't about a car wash," Stern cautions.

"Who cares?" Bart replies. "J. K. Rowling didn't write about being a single mother on welfare, but her backstory didn't hurt sales."

"Maybe we can find a better comparison than J. K. Rowling and the Chamber of Transphobia," Destiny Tamar, the diversity expert, suggests.

"Bart has a point," Liz, the social media woman, persists. "Didn't Faulkner work at the post office?"

"He did," Audrey confirms, "as did Charles Bukowski—one of my favorites. Have you read him, Mr. Hackworth?"

Stern kicks Woody under the table, unintentionally striking his protective boot. Woody smothers a wince. Message received: Don't overreach.

"I'm sorry, I have not."

"Who reads that dead White guy anymore?" Stern scoffs.

"Bite your tongue, Melvin," Audrey says. She's fond of Stern—Woody can tell. A good sign. He wonders if they've slept together. She turns to Woody.

"Now, Mr. Hackworth, most of us have read at least parts of your work in progress and all of us have read the summary Melvin was kind enough to send out, but can you kindly tell us in your words what your book is about?"

"Sure, but you can call me Woody."

"By the way, legally he's Atwood, named after Margaret," Stern pipes in.

Audrey nods approvingly, which Bart notices.

"That's marketing gold," Bart says. "Just the name Atwood on the cover will generate big interest."

"I do prefer Woody," Woody protests, eliciting another kick from Stern.

Audrey gives him a quizzical look. "But you wouldn't be opposed to using Atwood on the cover, would you?"

Woody, Atwood, or whoever he is smiles weakly. "No."

"Very well then. Please tell us about your book."

"It's about an investigative reporter, a good one. Kind of like I was. He's on a particularly sensitive story." He waits for interest to build. "He's looking for a polluter, someone who is illegally dumping toxic waste, and the trail is leading to his in-laws—and his wife."

Several nod politely.

Seth Zimmerman, a slight man in a white three-piece suit with long gray hair but bald on top, looks unmoved. "I'll be honest, we don't have a great track record representing strictly whodunits," he says. "That's not to say we don't love crime stories—we do. But we're more inclined to represent books with subterranean tiers of meaning, narratives that speak to the larger human condition, characters who aren't tropes. Is that fair, Neil?"

"That's one way to say it," the crime editor says. "My condensed version: *In Cold Blood,* good. *Murder, She Wrote,* less good. At least for us."

"Does your book speak to the larger human condition, Woody?" Audrey asks.

"I'm biased, obviously, but yeah, sure, it's full of human conditional . . . ism. I mean, you've got this newspaper guy who's just trying to do his job, to hold wrongdoers accountable and protect his community. But the more he learns, the more he realizes the answers are close to home. Too close to home. There's metaphor in that. To a degree, we're all prisoners of hidden realities that track back to ourselves and our decisions."

That was good, Woody thinks. Did he really just say that off the cuff? Even Stern looks impressed. For the first time, Woody feels the room shift in his favor.

"We could use that in a blurb," Bart from marketing says. "Something like, 'In his stunning first novel, Hackworth spins an environmental thriller into a hard truth: We're all prisoners of hidden realities.'"

"I like that," Woody says. "Now we just need to get Stephen King to write the blurb for us."

Big laugh. The Wood Man's on fire. The use of "us" was perfect.

"But in all seriousness, that is what we're talking about here," Woody continues. "It's concrete as allegory—toxic waste embedded in concrete, just as the toxicity of our lives is embedded in our relationships."

Stern uncorks another whopper. "When Woody and I first spoke, we talked about how his main character, Cus, is in the tradition of the American individualist."

"Yes, he's isolated," Audrey says. "From his family. From his own newspaper. A loner but not lonely. Like Thoreau?"

"More like Melville's Ahab," Stern corrects. "Cus is on a mission. He's driven to pursue this huge, terrifying white thing, but it's not a whale. It's his family!"

Cue the diversity coordinator. "Speaking of white," Destiny says, "most of your key characters are Anglo. There's nothing wrong with that, per se."

Woody translates that to: She hates his book.

"But I want to ask about the minority characters you *have* managed to introduce," Destiny continues. "How do you feel about them so far?"

After a moment, Woody says, "I like them. They add col—"

Before Stern can kick his boot again, Woody takes corrective action.

"—collectively a moral center to the narrative."

Destiny gives him a bemused look, as if to say, "Nice try." The others look down.

"I'd like to hear more about that," she says.

Woody bumbles his way through a discursive of his decision to make Aurora a Latina. "To me, she represents the descendants of colonized peoples pushing back against the debasement of their land. Same for Cus, actually."

"Remind me," Destiny says, "Cus is half Mohawk?"

"One-fourth."

The fraction hangs in the air like diesel exhaust.

"And your other racial minorities consist of Aurora, who is half Latina, and Deion, who is fully African American?"

"I'm sorry, who's Deion?" Stern blurts.

"Who's *Deion*?!" Destiny mocks. "He's the African American sportswriter. If you check the manuscript, you'll see he's mentioned"—she makes a show of starting to count the fingers on her left hand—"once."

Woody freezes. He had forgotten all about Deion. He added the character months ago in response to Nick's diversity concerns. The quick, extraneous scene consists of Cus shooting baskets with Deion in the *Informer* parking lot and Deion remarking, "You've got good hops for a White dude."

In a deliberate tone, hoping it will pass for thoughtfulness and will conceal his stalling, Woody defends the character. "I don't want to give too much away, but I have big plans for Deion."

Stern's mendacity is contagious.

Destiny moves in for the kill. "What kind of big plans?"

"Honestly, I'm open to suggestions," Woody concedes. "He's underdeveloped, I agree."

Destiny gives Woody a look of pity and brightly suggests, "You could have the Knicks offer him a two-way contract as a backup point guard!"

Someone snickers.

"We don't need to drill down to that level yet," Audrey says. "Destiny, you've made your point, and we thank you."

Audrey wants to move on. Relief briefly washes over Woody. His greatest fear is they'll ask him for the ending. He realizes he led the discussion in that direction by asserting Deion would have a major role in the resolution, but maybe he'll get lucky. Maybe they'll respect The Process and give him space to finish his book.

"So, what's your ending?" Julio, the intern, asks. "Just curious."

Woody detects a smirk on Julio's face—the look of a young wiseass who calls an elder's bluff.

"That will be determined by my process," Woody says opaquely. He wants to flee the meeting, to wave a jaunty goodbye and just leave. He isn't a quitter, but he has a history of removing himself from deteriorating circumstances.

In high school, due to a shortage of linemen, he was cajoled into turning out for the football team despite his ambivalence toward the sport and periodic flashbacks of severely dislocating his elbow in a Pop Warner drill. As two-a-day high school workouts unfolded, he managed to avoid serious physical entanglement with Octavius Percy, a 250-pound junior who would one day make second team All-Big Ten at Michigan State.

Octavius was a sweet, gentle kid who exhibited savantlike talent as a potter. His cobalt-blue swan won first place at a regional art competition. But once the helmet went on, he changed. He played and, unfortunately for his teammates, practiced in a beastly rage.

One hot August afternoon, as the offense scrimmaged against

the defense, Woody was sent in at right guard, directly across from Octavius. He still remembers the fat orb of sweat running down the bridge of his adversary's nose, how the drop remained suspended at the tip—like pooling magma. He remembers the quarterback barking signals, then nothing until the sting of the ammonia capsule.

The doctor called it a mild concussion. Woody called it the end of his football career. After a night of throwing up, he felt much better, in part because he had a viable excuse to bid farewell to the Fighting Falcons.

But there is no escape here. Even Audrey is circling back for another chunk of Woody's hide.

"I notice you refer in your book to a dinghy as an *old girl.* Are we to take it that the vessel is female of a certain age? Or is that just a seafarer's patois?"

The room titters.

"That's a cliché," Woody replies. "I'll take it out."

Destiny nods in approval.

The inquest moves on to the next phase.

Does the novel suffer from a musty premise rooted in the dying business of local print journalism?

"Do community newspapers even *have* investigative journalists anymore?" Neil asks. "I know a few people who did real reporting at local newspapers. They're in PR now, or they went to law school ."

"That's a valid point," Audrey agrees. "Are we building a modern mystery on an antediluvian substrate?"

Woody, with Stern's help, points to the novel's online success as proof that the premise works, but several on the panel caution that online readership does not always translate into book sales.

Bart's dubious. "They're different audiences," the director of marketing explains. "It costs nothing to read your book online. On the other hand, asking someone to pay seventeen dollars for a paperback set in a virtually defunct profession requires a great deal of promotion and audience education."

What about hardcover? Woody wonders. *Have they ruled that out?*

"With all due respect, Bart," Stern replies, "and I know this is your area of expertise and I respect that, but can we give readers just a little credit? Last time I checked, *The Three Musketeers* was a major hit, and that was decades after musketeering disappeared in France."

"Touché," Bart says, letting the inanity of Stern's analogy speak for itself.

Woody's turn. "I'm biased, but I don't see this as a problem. It's part of the tragedy of loss that informs the narrative. Cus is losing his natural environment, his family, and his profession. People will relate to that. He's not the only one whose job has been phased out."

The counterpunch lands. Stern looks approvingly at Woody like a proud father whose kid finally passed his driver's test. The others nod in agreement.

"I see this almost as a period novel," says Betsy, the cover artist, who until now has been silent. "People respond to newspapers as a nostalgic trope. They're just not interested in reading them anymore."

"How would you feel about setting the novel ten or even twenty years earlier?" Seth Zimmerman asks.

Stern nudges Woody's foot.

"That's a really interesting idea," Woody says, his heart sinking as he mulls backdating thousands of details. "It makes a lot of sense."

"Either that or try something fresh," Seth adds. "Get out of yourself, exercise your creative muscles, and bring us something that doesn't sound like Carl Hiaasen wrote it twenty-five years ago. Does the world really need any more toxic waste novels?"

Next, the panel moves on to whether the novel's scientific foundation is sound.

"I know we're doing fiction here, and suspension of belief is in play, but how plausible is it to dispose of toxic waste by embedding it in concrete?" Anne Kucera asks.

"It's completely doable," Woody replies. "In fact, it's a common and accepted practice with radioactive waste."

"But your fictional in-laws aren't handling that type of material, correct?"

"Not explicitly, no."

"Wouldn't they have to be wearing protective suits or something?" someone else demands.

"I suppose so."

"May we assume you have consulted with a chemist and other experts regarding your premise?" Audrey inquires.

"I have not consulted anyone in particular, although I agree that would be a great idea. There's a lot of stuff online though."

Destiny laughs.

Now, Seth circles the wounded animal and moves in for a chunk. He's been waiting for this moment. "Okay, don't ask me why, but I minored in organic chemistry at Harvard."

Woody is aware of his sphincter contracting. "Did you ever think about minoring in something, you know, less hard?" he says, grasping for flattery and humor. "I minored in sociology."

Seth cocks his head, looking confused and contemptuous. "Why would I avoid a subject just because it's hard?"

Woody stares into the abyss. "Fair point."

"Here's my main issue: If the embedded chemicals are leaching out of the concrete into the water supply, then they're leaching into people's homes and yards first, correct?"

"Correct."

"So, you can't have anything volatile, nothing that might degrade into a gas and cause an explosion. That would create more than suspicion. It would cause panic. You can't have people's homes blowing up all over town."

"That would be bad," Woody concurs. "Dramatic, though."

"Well, yes, dramatic—no question there. Exploding homes are dramatic, but isn't that a different book?"

"Very different."

"Anyway, for the same reasons, not wanting to attract attention, you can't have any chemicals with a strong odor or strange color. If my patio is turning fluorescent green, I don't need to be a chemist to know something's wrong."

"Right."

"So, to avoid detection by the homeowner, you can't use organic compounds."

"I guess not."

"You're not sure?"

"I'm not a chemist."

A snarling Stern charges to the rescue. "All right, Seth, we get it—you're a polymath. You know some chemistry. We're all impressed. But can we cut Mr. Hackworth some slack here? He already told us he plans to consult experts to address these concerns."

Woody looks down at the table, playing the victim but giddy with gratitude for Stern.

Seth senses the room turning on him and backs down. "It's a good read. I like what I've seen so far. I just want the science to be plausible."

"The science," Stern assures him, "will be plausible."

"Maybe we should move on and think about wrapping this up soon," Audrey suggests. "Does anyone have any more questions for our emerging author from afar before we adjourn and send him back to beautiful Upstate, New York?"

She makes it sound as if Woody lives in Alaska. Woody prays for no takers.

"I have a few," says the serious-looking redhead in a serious-looking skirt and jacket seated to Audrey's right. It's Nora Pearson, the legal adviser. "I'm concerned about the book's overlap with the author's family or, more accurately, his wife's family, and any possible legal implications. Are your in-laws supportive of your writing?"

Woody's mouth goes dry. "Supportive?" he croaks.

Stern again tries to help. "Woody and I have discussed this at length, and he has assured me that his in-laws have complete respect for Woody's creative autonomy."

Nora looks impatiently at the wall clock, which now reads 3:47. "That's not what I asked," she says.

Woody finds her beautiful but not humanly so. She's sleekly designed and austerely accessorized—like his Peloton. He notices, too, that her jacket is magenta, not exactly the same shade as the university but close enough.

"Supportive in what sense?" he asks.

"In the sense that they're familiar with your book and they want it to be an even bigger success than it already is."

Thin smile.

There's a lot going on inside Woody: hunger, thirst, sleep deprivation, guilt, mental fatigue, adrenaline, and physical pain. His ankle is throbbing again. And then something else. Clarity. *Fuck it,* he thinks. *Fuck 'em all.* Fuck his book. Fuck The Process. Fuck everything.

"Gee willickers," he says, glaring at his nemesis. "Did someone spill the beans and tell you my father-in-law hit me with a cease and desist order?"

"Christ," Stern mutters.

The angular attorney and the aspiring writer look implacably at one another, both satisfied with the exchange for different reasons. Woody concludes that in a different setting he would, after all, enjoy fucking her. She's thinking she's still on track to make her 4 p.m. webinar on copyright infringement.

Far too late to do any good, Woody reaches for common ground with Nora.

"I noticed you're wearing the official color of Icarus University. Did you happen to go to law school there?"

"Yale."

Another pall settles over the room.

"Why don't we shut this down for today?" Audrey says. "And those of you who wish can follow up with Woody by phone or email or with Melvin in person. Sound reasonable?"

After the meeting, Woody and Stern seek solace at a German

beer hall, Prince Heinrich's Stein Garten. Initially, neither speak of the beatdown in the conference room, opting to talk of kids and cars. But shop talk is inevitable. After a twenty-two-ounce doppelbock, Stern breaks the impasse.

"I thought that went great today."

His deadpan is so perfect, Woody's Kolsch goes down wrong, triggering a brief coughing fit.

"Any idea what font they'll use?" Woody asks.

"Yeah, New Roman Bloodbath."

They howl so loudly others turn to look. Failure is funny.

A *fräulein* with boobs spilling from her dirndl arrives to ask if they'd like menus.

"I'll take two of those," Stern says, making a point of not looking at the menus.

"Uh-oh, you two are trouble," she replies with a wink, placing two menus on a spruce tabletop. "I'll give you a few minutes."

She bounces away. Admiringly, Stern hums a few bars of "99 Luftballons."

There's something freeing about being in the presence of Stern, his absence of inhibition, his never-ending cage match with propriety. So freeing that it might have pushed Woody into sabotaging his book. Woody wonders if that's why he did what he did.

"I didn't mean to sandbag you in there," Woody tells Stern. "She just pissed me off."

"Nora?" Stern takes a swig of beer. "She's all right. She was just doing her job, which, by the way, she's very good at. She pulled my ass from the fryer more than a few times."

Stern advises Woody not to read too much into the meeting, that the jury would be deliberating for the next day or two—or ten—and the verdict is far from assured.

"They don't like the book," Woody says.

"We don't know that. The fact they spent so much time with us is a positive sign."

CHAPTER 16
A FALSE CONCESSION

Woody is two-thirds through a medicinal morning beer at La Guardia when he gets a text message from Stern: "Your biplane board yet?"

"Still waiting for them to hand wind the prop."

"I hope you have a good lawyer."

Woody loosens a strap on his boot and gazes out at a Korean Air jet gliding down over a runway.

"A personal injury lawyer?" he texts back.

His phone rings immediately. It's Stern.

"A lawyer to look over the contract we're sending you. It's fairly standard, but it's in your interest to have someone review it. Congratulations, Woody—Livingston wants to take on your book."

Woody's mind goes blank, but he recovers enough for Stern not to notice. *"Are you fucking with me, Melvin?"*

The writer braces for the big garrulous gotcha laugh but instead gets Mister Serious.

"No, I'm not fucking with you." Stern sounds as if he's addressing a slow child. "I'm one *thousand* percent serious. My search-and-rescue operation worked. You're no longer lost in the internet wilderness. I'm making you an honest author."

Woody feels tears run down his face, but he feigns nonchalance.

"Cool. What's next?"

"For one, it wouldn't be the worst idea if you sent Liz Shelby a thank you note."

"Which one was she?"

"The social media coordinator."

"The one who didn't say anything?"

"Precisely. She didn't have to. They all knew she was hot for your book because it was catching so many eyeballs out there in Blog-o Land. Who do you think found you?"

"It wasn't you?"

"Woody, do I strike you as someone who wades into the internet sewer to fish for diamonds? I can barely remember my AOL password."

"*She* told you about me."

"You got it."

"How did she find me?"

"That meme or whatever you did. Is it meme or a gif?"

The meme had been Celeste's idea. She'd pushed to upgrade the *Fear as Mud* mixer truck art logo Woody had uploaded to his site. Her notion was to depict Cus and Aurora trapped from the waist down in wet concrete, reaching futilely toward one another, their fingers inches apart. Woody liked it, so he hired a graphic artist he knew from the paper. She did the concept justice, creating a loop video of a spinning mixer truck barrel, the words "Fear as Mud by Woody Hackworth" visible on the side. A chute pouring body parts into the wallow completed the scene. Longing, menace, and mystery were conveyed in one weirdly compelling image. The artist was proud enough of her work to post it on her Twitter, Instagram, and five other platforms. It had taken off.

A loud announcement that a nearby flight has been delayed gives Woody a moment to process his good fortune. When a semblance of quiet returns to the terminal, he says, "Maybe I should send her flowers."

"That's weird. Just write her a note. Mention you heard about her involvement from me, so she doesn't think you hacked her email."

"Okay."

"I told you it wasn't as bad as it seemed. I wish I could say the same for my hangover."

The mention of the word makes Woody's temple pulse. Somewhere in the terminal, a toddler shrieks. The Jägermeister/vodka bombs last night were not necessary.

"I was sure I killed any chance by telling them about the cease and desist order."

"To the contrary, they appreciated the honesty. Look, Livingston has been around for seventy-five years. You think you're the first author we've represented who has ruffled a few feathers? They just want all the cards on the table. And they wanted assurance that you're amenable to making changes to the book. You were quite good at appearing malleable. You should take pride in that."

Woody takes a healthy draw on his IPA, noting with pleasure the pillow of foam sliding down the inside of the glass. "Moral elasticity has always been one of my strongest traits," he says.

They chortle at the humble brag.

"One catch," Stern adds. "No more advancing the story online. You're done out there."

"Yep, makes sense."

"No publisher will want to buy a book that has already been given away online."

"Of course." Woody hopes he sounds like an old pro in the publishing game—as if he doesn't want to run up and hug that gate agent and grab her mic and belt out, "If I can make it here, I'll make it anywhere!" Instead, he calmly suggests, "Maybe I'll post a note saying the novel has been temporarily suspended pending a potential publishing deal."

"Do whatever you need to do."

"You got it. Oh, and Melvin?"

"Yes."

"Thank you. Seriously."

The words catch in his throat, but Stern seems not to notice.

"Happy to be of service."

Woody wastes no time cutting off his online fans. He logs into fearasmud.com, removes the 75 percent-completed manuscript and drafts a note.

Dear Readers,

For reasons I cannot disclose right now, I'm unable to continue posting more of Fear as Mud. A potentially positive development is behind my decision. I'm sincerely grateful for your support. Please know that my expectation is to complete this project soon and provide fans with other means to access it.

Thank you for your understanding.
Woody Hackworth

He looks over the message and finds it problematic. Hinting at a publishing deal will cause more trouble at home. He settles on something shorter and more obtuse.

Dear Readers,

I've decided to take a break from writing Fear as Mud to pursue other opportunities. Feel free to check here periodically for updates. Thank you for your support.

Sincerely,
Woody Hackworth

He posts the message along with similar versions on his social media accounts. Thirty minutes later, he's looking down at the clouds and celebrating his good fortune by spiking his coffee with tequila. Why not? He has suffered greatly for his Art. He has given up his family, his home, his health, and his dignity to pursue greatness, to make manifest the totality of his talent. Now, endless possibilities stretch out before him. His expansive mood prods him to engage his seatmate.

"What's taking you to Icarus?" he asks the fifty-something woman in a print dress.

"The sewer line's backed up on one of my rental properties. It's a literal shitshow."

"Bummer."

"What about you?"

"I'm a novelist. I just flew down to New York to sign a book deal. I'm heading home until the book tour starts." He sighs with false writerly weariness. "Those are never fun." What's a little fib at 20,000 feet?

"Don't take this personally, but I don't read fiction. I'd rather live my life than read about somebody else, who isn't real, living theirs. Does that make sense?"

"To each their own." Woody goes back to looking at the clouds. He feels taller, slimmer, calmer, smarter, and better looking thanks to Livingston's verbal commitment. He's not about to let a landlord with a plumbing emergency bring him down.

JB picks him up at the airport in his 1960 Pontiac Catalina Safari wagon, which bears the Cluckin' Clean logo—a cartoon rooster drinking a beer atop a washing machine. For JB, life and marketing are one.

Woody starts to give his friend the good news outside the terminal while they're parked at the curb. A pickup driver, who pulls alongside them with a friendly honk, interrupts him.

"Nineteen sixty?" the guy shouts through the passenger window.

"You nailed it!" JB shouts back.

"My old man had one of those. Used to let me and my brother camp out in the back overnight in the driveway. Different times."

Blue lights flash, accompanied by a scratchy siren blast from behind. The cops want them gone.

"Gotta go, man," the driver says before zooming off. "Love your ride, love your wings."

As they head for the Cluckin' Clean mother ship, Woody gets a text from Celeste. She wants to know how New York went. Once again, he feels the shame of the capris. She's not his friend. She's a saboteur. *Just ignore her*, he tells himself.

It's less easy to disregard a message from Mandy, who doesn't know he was in New York: "I'm meeting with the head of the surgical team at 3:30 to talk about my dad. I wouldn't hate it if you could attend. Apparently, this is going to be a much bigger deal than any of us realized. Sorry for short notice."

"Surgical *team,*" Woody says aloud, puzzling JB.

"What's up?" JB says.

"Ah, nothing. My father-in-law has ringing in his ears or some bullshit."

Ninety minutes later, Mandy picks him up outside Cluckin' Clean. By then, she's already relayed Woody more particulars about the upcoming meeting. The main one is that Joe or Bev won't be there. Joe's already met with the surgeon, but he wasn't especially forthcoming to his children about what was discussed other than to joke, "They asked to borrow one of my excavators to scoop out what's left of my brains." However, Joe was fine with Mandy meeting with the surgeon herself. After all, they both work at the same hospital.

Joe had said to his daughter, "Maybe you can make more sense of the guy than I can."

Through her dad's bravado, Mandy sensed he was overwhelmed and scared. She was, too, which is why she'd asked Woody to come along. It's the first time in four days they've seen each other.

"I'm glad you're going with me," she tells him.

"You sure Joe's okay with me being at this?"

"I didn't ask him, but you're on the list."

They pass by a weathered barn and a dead deer in a ditch. Then Burgerville, where Ella had melted down in her stroller with such intensity that they'd switched to takeout and fled the joint as other diners glared and judged. Ever since, the phrase "Let's just eat in the car" has been code to Woody and Mandy for getting out of bad situations and cutting losses—like Woody did with high school football.

"Let's just eat in the car," Woody says absentmindedly, lost in memory, but Mandy takes it the wrong way.

"This isn't the time to talk about divorce, Woody. Can we make this one day about my dad and not about you?" She bursts into tears.

"I was just . . ." He doesn't complete the thought, but he doesn't need to.

"I'm sorry," she says. "I'm just stressed."

"It's okay."

They merge onto the interstate. A Dunn-Rite flatbed hauling a compact track loader is heading in the opposite direction, but neither mentions it.

"You haven't been writing," she says. "At least that's what people tell me."

"I've been busy."

"I can only imagine."

The conversation has reached a critical crossroads. He can shrug and say nothing, probably his best option. He can tell his wife the truth: that he has been busy having special lady pants made for himself and hobbling onto a plane to New York to meet with his new agent. He could concede that he has been more distracted than busy, more enamored by the trappings of authorial attention, especially the alcohol part, than pounding on a keyboard. Instead, he says, "I took it down."

"Took what down?"

"The novel. It's just a stupid internet vanity book. It's fucking up our lives. Screw it."

Mandy says nothing at first. Then, "Are you sure?"

"Positive. It's down."

Her eyes well again. "That's the first good news I've heard in a long time."

Woody tells himself he isn't lying, and technically that's true. It's misdirection by omission, which might be a cousin of lying but is not the same. Through good fortune and guile, he has bought himself time to finish his book in peace, without his family harassing him—or readers, for that matter, who at times have been distracting and insulting.

Speaking of which, he sees that his phone screen is suddenly stacked with notifications. He skims enough of the comments to get the idea: Readers are furious at him and atingle with conspiracy theories:

"Sounds like Ol' Man Joe finally put an end to it. What's the saying? The pen is mightier than the sword, but less mighty than the threat of being buried alive?"

"I wouldn't put it past him or those creepy sons of his."

"You string us along for months and then tell us all to fuck off? Feel free to check in here periodically for updates? Seriously? You suck, Hackworthless."

"Smart move. Book's not worth being killed over."

"Maybe he has a book deal or something."

"So, we wait two years to spend $25 to find out how it ends? Um, no thanks. Moving on. Too many books out there that are actually good."

Woody spies another thread in which readers are collaborating on their own ending:

"What's wrong, Cus?" Aurora asked, hearing the fear in his voice.

"It's my eyes," Cus groaned. "I can't see."

"She gripped his mighty shoulders and yanked repeatedly until his head popped out of his ass."

"Is that better, my darling?" she inquired, wiping his soiled cheeks with a papaya leaf.

"Much," he said. "The darkness of my colon has been replaced by the radiant beauty of your countenance. I shall now kiss you!"

"Later," she demurred. "Much, much later."

Woody can read no more and turns off his phone, hoping his embarrassment isn't registering with Mandy.

She wheels into her reserved space at the medical center.

"Free parking, at least," Woody says.

"Ella was amazing in goal yesterday. She said you were out of town. Where'd you go?"

"Away," Woody answers.

"Fair enough."

As they exit the car, Mandy gestures to the driver's side carpet. "I meant to ask, did you spill coffee or something down here? The color's off in a few places."

"Evidently," Woody hedges. "I thought I got it all. I'll work on it later."

They meet in a conference room with a projection screen. Dr. Pazman Bathory, head of the surgical team, looks disarmingly young, midthirties tops, but exudes confidence and command. He wears a full head of curly back hair, a white coat, jeans, and Skechers.

"Your dad will be my tenth meningioma, and only one of them turned out to be cancerous," he says in his best Hungarian-accented doctor voice. "The good news is most likely no chemo or radiation."

"That sounds promising," Mandy says stiffly. "And the bad news?"

"Wait, wait—there is more good news first," Bathory says with a broad, self-satisfied smile.

"You're getting a new cafeteria vendor?" Woody blurts, instantly wishing he'd stayed silent.

Bathory laughs. "Not that good, unfortunately. Oh, before I forget, my wife is enjoying very much your book." Then he turns to Mandy. "You must be proud of your husband, the famous mystery writer."

Woody's face goes pink with happy-shame.

"Proud doesn't come close," Mandy answers.

"One evening, my wife and I are reading in bed, and she says 'Oh my God, that poor fish,' and I, of course, have no idea what she is talking about, and she says, 'It's that book by Mandy Dunn's husband, the reporter.' She starts reading some of it out loud to me, and usually I don't like to be read to, but this was—how do you say it?—drawing me in, and finally I tell her, 'Stop. Don't spoil it.' Now I want to read it, too."

"But right now you're too busy to read it, aren't you, doctor?" Mandy says.

"That is correct. I'm very busy."

"You're busy trying to save my father's life."

Bathory's hard-on for the local author wilts under her cryo-gaze. "Yes."

"You were saying there is some additional good news about my dad?"

"That's right." Bathory, back in doctor mode, launches a PowerPoint. "The first image we see here is a cross section of the brain. The green little blob near the top is the general location of your father's tumor—not exactly, but pretty close. If your father was unlucky, the tumor would be growing down from the skull, invading brain tissue, but all the scans show his is growing along the inside of the skull, leaving the brain itself undamaged."

Bathory stops there, seemingly waiting for applause.

"So, what's the bad news?" Mandy asks.

"The bad news is surgery is involved. Three surgeries at once is maybe the best way to think of it. It can be, excuse my French, a real bitch."

Woody knows it's concerning anytime a surgeon refers to a procedure as "a real bitch."

"How long does it take?" he asks, eager to rebound from the cafeteria crack and establish himself as a team player.

"It will vary with each patient, but because of Joe's age, we should factor in the possibility of one or two minor complications. If no problems, I'd say twelve hours."

Mandy slams her hands down on the conference table. "Twelve hours for a tumor the size of a garbanzo bean? What are you using to take it out, a lobster claw?"

Woody tries to pull her back. "It's brain surgery. Better they take their time and do it right."

She sighs and says, "At least he'll be asleep."

Bathory tilts his head sideways into an imaginary pillow formed by his cupped hands. The weirdness of the pantomime surprises Woody, and for an awful instant he fears he might laugh.

The surgeon dims the lights for a PowerPoint and begins. Something about his voice sounds familiar—not the accent but the cadence and intonations. In less than a minute, Woody solves the puzzle: Bathory sounds like the guy at the service desk at the Lexus dealership. He might as well be saying Joe's brake pads are down to 20 percent and there's a recall on his electronic ignition switch.

"What the diagram does not show is the enmeshment of the tumor with the front temporal and sinus regions, which is fairly involved because it has been growing for so long," Bathory continues. "We believe the vomer bone has been spared, which would be very good news. We won't know for sure until we get in there."

They ride home in silence as the sun dips behind gray hills. A strange thought flits into Woody's mind. He imagines discovering that Mandy and Bathory are having an affair, allowing Woody to blackmail her. In exchange for Woody's silence and forgiveness, Mandy will agree to support his book and stand up to her family's efforts to block its publication.

The daydream bothers Woody. It makes him wish he had normal thoughts. Has his Art driven him mad? That can happen with geniuses—Vincent van Gogh and Sylvia Plath, for example. What was that book of hers he never read, *The Mason Jar*? Maybe Woody is experiencing the same cruel cycle they did, the Art feeding the madness, the madness feeding the Art.

Mandy's voice snaps Woody out of his trance. "They're cutting out part of his thigh muscle."

"Why are they doing that again?"

"To rebuild his goddamn face, Woody. Weren't you listening?"

"Jesus," Woody says.

She apologizes. "It was a lot of information to take in," she concedes. "I didn't get it all either."

To Woody's surprise, a single warm tear runs down his face. He turns away so Mandy won't notice and focuses on a white church on a hill. "He's gonna be fine," he says.

Two evenings later, the Dunn-Hackworths convene at Cam's McMansion. Despite the small talk, cheeseboards, and wine, the mood is serious.

"Before we get into the details of Dad's surgery," Mandy says, "Woody has something he would like to say."

The setup takes Woody by surprise. He found it curious Mandy even invited him to Cam's, but now he understands. She wants him to be on the record, in front of them all, especially Joe, with his pledge to terminate the book. If her dad is going to die on the operating table, she wants him to go knowing the reputation he spent a lifetime building won't be posthumously trashed by her husband's not-quite-fictional-enough conceit.

"Well, um, this has been a rough patch for the family, especially Joe. And although I know he's going to be fine, I'd like to try to make things, you know, a little easier."

A muscle car roars in the distance. A dog woofs in response.

"I've taken the book down. It's done enough damage." Woody discreetly crosses his fingers.

"What does that mean—taken it down?" Bev asks.

"It means people can no longer see the book on their phone or computer," Mandy explains. "The nightmare is over."

Bev gasps and clasps her hands to her heart in a silent thank you. "It's better that way," she says.

Cam claps slowly and sarcastically. "Better late than never," he says and drains his glass.

"Better late than never," Woody concurs, affecting humility.

"Maybe you can write a different book," Bev suggests.

"A cookbook," Woody offers with a sardonic huff while thinking, *Yeah, a sequel.*

He has, in fact, been mulling a *Fear as Mud, Part II*, which would explore Cold Harbor's illegal disposal of laboratory test animals. He even has a subtitle: *Barrel of Monkey Parts*. But he mustn't get ahead of himself. He still needs to finish the current book to Livingston's liking. A contract needs to be negotiated. A publisher will have to be wooed and secured, although Woody doesn't see that as a big concern. A bidding war is more like it. He looks over at Joe, who winks back.

"I can't wait to see your recipe for humble pie," Joe kids. Everyone laughs. Even Mandy is amused as she scolds, "Dad!"

Woody shrugs as if to say, "You got me again, big guy." *Joe loves to win, so let him think he won. Let him get wheeled into the operating theater thinking his legal strong-arm tactics worked. It's the humane thing to do.* Woody appreciates his compassionate nature even if others overlook it. That's how karma works. You put kindness into the world, and it comes back to you. He'll be able to finish his bestseller in peace.

"Just busting your chops, Woody," Joe says. "You done a good thing. It takes a big man to admit he screwed up."

"Yes, it does!"

The Dunns laugh.

"And I'll tell you something else," Joe says.

Woody braces for a dig. "Okay. What?"

"You're a helluva writer. If that book had been about pig farmers or plastic surgeons or those goddamn crooks in Albany robbing us blind—anything but construction—we'd all be behind you one hundred percent."

The others assent vigorously.

"Totally," Cam says.

Joe sighs deeply and looks close to welling up. Maybe the tumor is turning him into a crier. "We're all going to see brighter days," he says. "I'm going to kick this neuroma horseshit in the ass, and you, Mr. Hackworth, will take all the lessons you've learned from this test run and produce an amazing book. I really believe that."

Everyone claps. Someone says, "Hear, hear!"

"Thanks, Joe," Woody says, his self-righteousness dissipating. He feels almost barfy with guilt.

"And just so you know," Joe continues, "I'll be buying the first hundred copies."

Big applause. Tanner claps Woody on the back. Joe rises to shake Woody's hand.

"You're a good man, Woody," Joe adds. "I never doubted that. You just got carried away. It happens."

Woody struggles to rally his ire. He tells himself that their magnanimity cannot obscure the reality that they've put him through hell. Even Mandy, setting him up like this in front of her family to give a big concession speech—that was uncalled for. It should have happened at a time of his choosing, not hers, after he could prepare.

Tanner looks up from his phone. "He's not bullshitting us," he says. "The site's down. Thanks, man. I mean that. We all realize you had a lot of time invested in your—"

"Hatchet job," Cam finishes. Everyone laughs except Woody.

"Well, whatever it was, it's over," Tanner says. "Welcome back to the family, Woody."

More raising of glasses.

Mandy gives Woody a peck on the head and whispers, "I love you."

The family meeting moves to the main topic: Joe's surgery. Woody tries his best to focus, but his thoughts keep turning to recent research he's been doing on perfluorinates, "forever chemicals."

Perfluorinates aren't found in nature, Woody has learned. They don't break down in the biosphere. Firefighting foam is full of them. Wherever firefighters train, you've got forever contamination. Fast-food containers use them, too, so the grease won't soak in and make them soggy.

The wannabe chemist at Livingston scared him. Woody needs the science to be right. Maybe, he thinks, he should work a corrupt fire chief into the plot.

The meeting adjourns, and with little fanfare Woody moves back home, back to his Peloton and his Famous Writers clock and the life he had before *Fear as Mud* went live. When anyone asks him what became of the book, he says he's just taking a break. But, in fact, he's more productive than ever. As soon as Mandy leaves for work, he bolts a second cup of coffee and clatters toward a Livingston-worthy draft.

To prevent himself from posting new chapters for readers begging for more, Woody has overpaid for an antique but still functional Royal Quiet Deluxe, similar to the typewriter Papa used. The decision has been a masterstroke, keeping him offline and quieting his insatiable need for external gratification. For one of the few times in his life, he is content to just be, to exist in the world of letters—minus the lowercase "m," which often sticks.

His new work model has opened new creative pathways. Most critically, he has conceived of having Carl Cronin emerge as the secondary hero of the story after Cus. As Woody envisions it, Carl, founder of the fictional excavation company that needed Al's help disposing of Native American remains, feels bad about the desecration gaffe. It was just poor judgment born of panic, and he wants to make amends. Discreetly but sincerely, Carl has taken ownership of his cultural insensitivity and through the years made anonymous donations to a range of Native American causes. He's a devoutish Catholic who believes in Heaven and Hell and who does not want to experience the latter on account of a few dozen dump trucks loaded with ancestral bones. Of course, Cus will still be the moral center of the book, but Carl will be in the mix, a faint glowy echo of the main protagonist's steadfast goodness. After all, Woody rationalizes on behalf of Carl, it isn't like anybody died in the disposal of those remains. They were already dead.

Carl's moral awakening on the Native American matter will prepare readers for his even bigger crisis of conscience. He knows Al and Cold Harbor are spreading poison around the city through a system Al devised at Carl's behest. If Carl risks Hell by mistreating a burial ground full of heathens, what's the price of staying silent about whole parishes being contaminated? Thus, it makes perfect sense for Carl to be Cus's 'Deep Throat.' The fact that Heroic Carl happens to have an excavation business, just like Joe, will bring peace to Woody's nonfictional world.

"I've got good news and more good news," he imagines telling Joe after his surgery. "My book will be published in the spring. The other good news is that the excavation guy saves the day and the town. You're my muse, big guy."

Finally, Woody can relax. It's going to be a cakewalk from here.

CHAPTER 17
THE WISDOM OF KAYLON

Back at Mega-Shine, Woody lays out his plan in the break room to a dubious Kaylon.

"So, your family thinks you're done with the book?"

"Correct."

"But you're not done with the book."

"Correct."

"And your plan is to make a minor character who happens to have a company like your father-in-law a good dude but keep the villain who everyone thinks is your father-in-law the same?"

"Yeah, I guess that's right."

Kaylon scoops up some hummus with a carrot stick, chomps it, and sits back in his chair. Woody suspects he won't like what's coming.

"Come on, Lexus. He ain't gonna fall for that. Nobody gets to be that rich by getting played."

Sweat prickles on Woody's brow.

"And if he isn't falling for it, you think your wife will?" Kaylon laughs and shakes his head. "All that creativity and not a drop of common sense. You know what happens when you start thinking other people are stupid?"

"Please share."

"You're the one who looks stupid."

They say nothing for a minute.

"You think I'm a fool, Kaylon?"

"I didn't say that. If I thought you were a fool I wouldn't be talking to you."

"What do you think I am then?"

Again, they sit in silence.

"So, what should I do? Make Al Holmes an investment banker? A veterinarian? You tell me."

Kaylon spears a pitted olive with a plastic fork and waggles it in front of his mouth.

"You played football, right?"

"A little."

"You know how when you win a game it's, like, the best feeling in the world?"

Woody considers admitting that his football experiment was brief and unsuccessful, but he decides to save that humiliation for another time. Instead, he just says, "Okay?"

"But when you lose . . ." Kaylon's voice trails off.

"It's the opposite feeling?"

"Wrong." Kaylon ingests the olive. "It's worse than opposite. Way worse."

"Worse than the opposite?"

"It hurts more to lose than it feels good to win, especially if it's your fault you lost."

"And your point is?"

"I fumbled at the two-yard line with a minute left in the state championship against Haverstown."

A car alarm activates, as if to underscore the point. When the racket stops, Woody erupts, "That was *you?* Holy shit! I remember that! I was in the newsroom that night. Big fire at the Covington Mattress plant. That must have been ten years ago."

"Twelve," Kaylon says.

There's awkwardness in hearing a grown man suggest he's still tormented by a mishap in a high school football game more than a decade earlier, but Woody gets it. The mind has a way of holding on to pain.

"It was a big hit, right? The guy just made a great play."

"I slowed down to look at my girlfriend, Serenity, in the stands. I got stripped from behind by the fattest motherfucker on their team, Mark Mezzaroni. I'll never forget that name."

Woody feels embarrassed for his new friend. "Hey, you did it for love. That's always a valid excuse for being a dumbass."

Kaylon snorts in tepid agreement. Woody hopes his new friend is done wallowing.

"Love? Seriously? The bitch broke up with me the next day."

They laugh the laugh of guys in the know. Rejection by the inscrutable "other" is universal, transcending race and class.

"Hard to blame her," Woody jests. "I'd have broken up with you, too."

"She did me a favor. Told me what she was all about. But it didn't feel that way at the time."

"Things ran their course. Remind me, why are we talking about this?"

"Your book, Lexus. You get this book of yours published, you're gonna feel like I felt right before I got stripped. Ecstatic, right?"

"Definitely."

"Like you won the game!"

"Absolutely."

"No fumble at the two-yard line for you."

"Nope."

"So, tell me, Lexus, how long you gonna have that feeling? Six months? Longer?"

Woody gets up to buy a Snickers from a vending machine. "To have my Art validated by the literati and simultaneously embraced by a discerning commercial audience? After all the shit I've been through both at my old job and at home over the years? To know that my struggle has borne fruit? I'll be stoked for more than six months, Kaylon."

"Your struggle, Lexus?"

Woody feels his cheeks heat up. "I mean, for a rich White dude," Woody demurs.

"Now *that's* showing some self-awareness. Let's build on that. What I'm hearing is that I underestimated how much external validation means to you. Should we say it will take two years for you to come back to Earth?"

Woody sits back down and takes a bite of his bar.

"You shouldn't be eating that garbage."

"I always eat when I'm being life-coached." Woody chews deliberately and swallows the peanuty poison. "Two years might be a little much," he finally answers. "Maybe I'm over it by a year and a half. But there's going to be an afterglow that will last forever, not to mention the creative opportunities this will open up. Dude, I could be famous. I already *am* famous, sort of."

"Me too—I was all-state."

"Impressive."

"I was offered a free ride at three schools: Youngstown State, Central Michigan, and Maine, despite the fumble."

"Where'd you end up?"

"At home. Taking care of my baby sister while my mom recovered from a drive-by."

Woody hangs his head, panged by White guilt. For him, violence is merely abstraction grist for his Art, the sand in his sandbox. Entertainment. "I'm sorry that happened," he says. "How'd things turn out for your mom?

"She's okay. A little paralysis on one side of her face, but you know. She's alive. She was gonna make meatloaf and mashed potatoes for supper that night. She says to all of us, 'These breadcrumbs are stale. I'm gonna pop down to Majule's to get a fresh can.' That's the verb she used: pop. Like a gun. I offered to go instead, but she said not to bother, she had some other things to pick up. Ten minutes later, I heard the sirens. I didn't think anything of it. Sirens in my neighborhood are not unusual."

Woody thinks about his mom puttering in her art studio in Sedona. Different set of concerns. "You got a bad break."

"My mom got a bad break. For me, it wasn't all bad."

"How so?"

"We came together as a family. I got to know my sister, Rashanda. She's ten years younger than me, but now we're inseparable. I even started dropping in to see my dad now and again."

"He's local?"

"About an hour from here. A little bedroom community called Mid-State Correctional. A lot of aspirational Black folks are moving there."

Woody tries for a rough equity. "My uncle's stepson did some time at Fossburgh."

Kaylon guffaws. "Club Med on the Susquehanna."

Woody tries to nudge the chat back to football.

"So, you never played college ball?"

"Nope."

"You must have regrets about that."

"Regrets? For doing what's right for my family? Sometimes, you do what you gotta do."

Woody senses where this is going —another family first lecture– and yearns to be back on the wash line, hosing down the parade of vehicular vanity. He especially loves turning the spray at full power on luxury wheels, how the encrusted mud flies off the spokes and center caps revealing anodized glints of the more lustrous vehicle to come.

"You can have both, family and accomplishment," Woody counters.

"Sometimes. And sometimes you have to choose."

"It sounds like you made the right choice. For you."

"I did. You know how I know that?"

Woody signals his readiness to receive the hard-won wisdom of the 'hood.

"Because of that damn fumble. Two types of people in the world, Lexus—people who love you for who you are and people who love you for what you do. I learned that from Serenity."

Woody isn't impressed. "That's just how the world is. We all exploit each other."

"Correct. And there's nothing wrong with that—as long as you know who's who. Like your new friend in New York—what's his name? Melvin? Which category do you think he falls in?"

"Both."

"So, Mr. Melvin, he'll be going to your daughter's high school graduation even if your book never makes a dime for them?"

Woody doesn't answer, so Kaylon keeps going. "After I fumbled, I was feeling like shit, obviously. Didn't want to talk to anyone. Just sitting in my room and smoking weed. Skipping classes. My mom says to me, 'Kaylon, you messed up, but that doesn't make you different from anybody else. We all make mistakes. Some people let their mistakes destroy them. Other people learn from them and get stronger. Which one you gonna be?' I said, 'I don't know, Mom.' She said, 'I know. You're my son. You're no quitter, and you're no idiot. You will learn from this, and it will make you a better player and a better person.' 'Maybe,' I said. She says, 'No, not maybe. Next time you're about to score, how many hands are you going to have on the ball?'"

Woody reaches for the napkin dispenser and makes a small show of tucking it securely to his side with both hands.

"That was my answer," Kaylon affirms. "Two. And she said, 'And if Jesus himself were to descend and stand on the fifty-yard line, how many hands would you have on that ball?' 'Two,' I said. 'And would you stop and turn around to look at Jesus?' 'Probably,' I said. 'If it was really Jesus.' And for the first time in a week, I laughed."

Woody puts down the napkin dispenser and sits with his arms folded against his chest. He's defiant but also fascinated by a mother-son bond he will never know. He loves his artsy mom, but he feels no great rapport with her. Truth is, she's often over the top, some narcissism in there. Maybe that's their bond. Anyway, things work best for the two of them when exposures are limited.

"You think I should give up the book for good?" Woody asks.

"That's on you. I don't know your family. Or your wife's family. All I know is Mom was there for me at my lowest moment, so there was never a question I'd be there for hers. Sometimes I think, what if I had been on a scholarship and I'd been the one who got capped going to the store? Couldn't ball no more. Who would have my back? Take me to PT, pay my hospital bills, make my meals, fight with those insurance fuckers? The university or my mom?"

"Your mom."

"Damn straight."

"Your mom sounds amazing."

"You don't know the half of it."

Break time is over. At Mega-Shine, even a sort of famous writer can't goldbrick.

"I'll take what you have said under advisement," Woody says stiffly. "You make a lot of sense."

But Woody isn't ready to sign off on Kaylon's unifying theory of family virtue as a counterweight to institutional indifference. Admittedly, he's living proof Kaylon's not completely wrong. His former newspaper, for all the team-building seminars and gold stars for stories well done, dumped him at the first hint of a possible indiscretion. Yet examples abound of corporate entities rallying around a fallen soldier. Didn't he just read something about the Red Sox still staying in touch with one of their players whose career was cut short by a brain tumor? He heads toward the door but stops and looks back at Kaylon.

"Just out of curiosity, Kaylon, did your mom ever serve you with a cease and desist order?" Woody turns back around and heads for the tunnel.

That evening, he lies again to his wife.

"What are you working on?" Mandy asks, prompting Woody to curse himself for not shutting the door to his study.

"Just my self-eval for Mega-Shine," he says with calibrated nonchalance despite a quickening heart. "It can wait."

"I hope you're giving yourself all five stars," she says, wrapping her arms around him.

Lately, things have been much better between them. That would no longer be the case if she'd been able to read the paragraphs he'd just finished typing.

Jenny had put on weight. The stress of having a husband hellbent on destroying her father and a father hellbent on destroying her husband was getting to her. To his credit, Cus remained attracted to his wife despite the extra pounds. He understood that beauty was only skin deep. But even Cus had limits. He was tired of the empty pastry boxes on the counter, put off by her moony looks of rapture when she bit into a fresh bear claw or lemon poppyseed muffin.

Beyond that, there was no denying that the stench of criminality that wafted about Jenny like toxic dust had crimped his ardor. When they made love, an infrequent occurrence, Cus imagined he was with Aurora.

"You feel like going for a walk?" Woody asks his wife.

"I'll take a rain check," Mandy says. "I'm watching *Step Right Up!* with Ella."

Woody is dimly familiar with the reality show that delves into the romantic, professional, and pharmaceutical entanglements of carnival workers. He has some expertise on the topic. Icarus enjoys the distinction of hosting the annual Great Northern Expo, a sprawling miasma of craft booths, chainsaw art, legacy rock bands, imprisoned livestock, and culinary explorations such as deep-fried nacho tubes and locally sourced winesicles. Covering the expo is top priority at the *Blaze*. Even Woody, generally protected from intern-level chores by his enterprise reporter status, had not been exempt. Like most of his colleagues, he'd loathed the "Great Northern Shitshow," as it was disparaged in the newsroom.

Yet he had a thing for the carnies. Like many journalists, the fringe intrigued him. The carnies were a rough bunch, with their homemade tats, smokers' coughs, and dental impairments. It took a level of estrangement from society to trick kids into throwing dull darts at half-filled balloons. But that's part of what made carnies interesting. Woody found them even more compelling after he'd won their confidence and heard their secrets. Once, he wrote a story about the lack of health care benefits for carnival workers and their nascent efforts to unionize. That story had been a tough sell to the top editors, whose commitment to comforting the afflicted rarely matched their commitment to remaining employed. The *Blaze*'s corporate parent and its figurehead publisher, E.J. Haley II, were fiercely antiunion. It was no accident that Woody had chosen a similar sounding name, B.J. Hayden III, for the publisher of the fictional *Tiberius Daily Informer.*

"Mind if I watch, too?" Woody asks.

"Sure," Mandy says, "but some of it won't make sense unless you've been following along."

He settles in on the sofa and is soon immersed in a three-way spat between a carnie named Duane, his carnie girlfriend, Lizzie, and Duane's wife, Mallory, a former carnie who separated from Duane four months ago. Duane desperately wants to recover his ATV from Mallory's garage, but she has a restraining order against him. He's not supposed to call or text, either. But there's a loophole: Lizzie has no restraining order against Mallory, and she's happy to serve as Duane's emissary against "that bitch." Her love for Duane is a complicated love, but one aspect of it is simple enough. He is her primary source of Wild Turkey, weed, and Vicodin. They plan to marry as soon as he divorces Mallory, which could take a while because Duane might still have feelings for her.

"What's the restraining order all about?" Woody asks.

"Shh," Mandy and Ella admonish.

"That's not your Arctic Cat, you (bleep)," Lizzie hollers through Mallory's screen door.

"Is that what he told you?" Mallory shouts back. "You dumb bitch, did he also tell you he's not fucking Stacey in the pirate ship?" Mallory doubles over laughing.

During a commercial, Ella explains, "Duane punched Mallory in her boobs after she hit him in the nuts with a gallon of milk. The cops took her side. She's disgusting."

"These people make a compelling case for finishing high school," Woody opines.

"Ella didn't tell you?" Mandy teases. "She's joining the circus."

"No need," Ella says. "I already live in one."

Mandy and Woody exchange a look.

"Oh, come on," Mandy scolds. "All families have disagreements, but have you ever seen your father or your mother resort to violence?"

"Emotional violence is still violence, Mom."

Mandy gets up and resettles herself between Woody and Ella. "I want us to be a family again, like before," she says.

Woody experiences a twinge of nostalgia. He squeezes her hand. "We never stopped being a family," he assures her and gives her a quick kiss followed by an overly robust one that causes Mandy to playfully slap him on the head.

"Gross," Ella says. "Our species cannot heal until society frees itself of male sexual aggression. Hey, the show's back on."

Woody checks his phone. There's a text from Nick Peters, who has been scarce lately.

"Call me," the message reads.

Must be another promotion. The arc of Nick's career unfailingly bends up.

Woody is curious to hear the news, but he's enjoying the family time. He knows he's missed a lot of moments like this. Work got in the way, of course, but that wasn't the whole of it. Woody always found the ferocity of the mother-daughter bond intimidating. It was like infiltrating a secret society only to be discovered and escorted off the premises. But tonight, Mandy and Ella seem happy to have him here. Maybe it's the novelty of him being back in the house or their gratitude that he took the book down or both. Whatever the cause, they're having one of those pleasant domestic interludes that shows up more in TV ads than in reality. Another stab of guilt pierces Woody. Whatever his rationalizations, *Fear as Mud* has inflicted injustice on his daughter. He should be making her life better, not worse. Isn't that the whole point of being a parent?

He pushes those thoughts away—maybe getting teased about the book will make Ella tougher, he tells himself—and lets Nick dangle. He wants to see clips from the next episode, which include a scene of Duane arguing with a park ranger as his Arctic Cat is impounded.

"She's messing with you, too!" Duane bellows. "You should be citing her for kidnapping a motor vehicle."

Fifteen minutes later, Woody's on the phone with Nick. First, he assumes the grave tone on the other end is Nick being silly, but soon it's evident his misery is no put-on. *The Apocalyptic* is making changes—again—meaning it has entered another cost-containment spiral. (Its publisher prefers the term "reimagining.") Nick is worried they might be trying to nudge him out. His main offense: His articles are too measured and fair. His award-winning coverage of the defense industry moves the needle among policymakers, but it isn't generating enough online hits to justify his six-figure salary.

"My stories are not apocalyptic enough," Nick laments. He sounds hoarse.

CHAPTER 18
THE APOCALYPTIC

At first, Woody can't believe his successful friend's number finally came up, but as he thinks it through, it makes some sense. To the extent Woody reads *The Apocalyptic* anymore, he has noticed Nick's work has a certain dissonance with the highbrow magazine's ever-more alarmist tone. Nick would write about, say, an M1 Abrams subcontractor drawing the attention of whistleblowers for cutting corners on the turret ring. His colleagues, meanwhile, would be cranking out stories with headlines like, "Flabies: Will Flu and Rabies Merge to Make Us Miss Covid?" and "Your Furniture is Killing You."

One of the more insipid features in the magazine is "Remember to Breathe," a mental wellness column intended to "quiet the anxiety and fear of living on a planet in mortal peril." Nick had once read a poem from the column aloud to Woody, causing both to laugh so hard Nick slightly strained one of his intercostal muscles.

For pauper, prince and in between
There's a refuge
Cool and clean
A calming burst
Upon the tongue
Why must mints be

So unsung?
Let fascists march
As foul winds blow
Enjoy a mint
And feel the glow
Of hope returning
With each breath
Each mint a mighty
Rebuke of death

But Nick is not laughing today.

"I've given up everything for these people," he bemoans. "I left BBC.com to come to *The Apocalyptic*."

It's not like Nick to feel sorry for himself, but Woody gets it. Nick has sacrificed to an extreme for his job. The toll includes two ex-wives, missed birthdays and holidays with three kids from those marriages, and countless vacations not taken or cut short when duty called. He has allowed himself only two hobbies, although even that's a stretch because there's obvious overlap with work. He collects signed first-edition books about the military-industrial complex. His archive includes the book he penned on the survivability of the airborne communication system for the nation's nuclear submarine fleet. He also collects Department of Defense items flagged as taxpayers rip-offs—a $1,200 wrench, a $2,000 mosquito net, a $750 coffeemaker, and so on—all purchased for a pittance at military surplus stores years after they made headlines. One wall of his home displays nine of the notorious $640 airplane toilet seats. "The world's largest collection," he boasts.

It's a comment on the peculiar world of DC media that Nick has lured more than a few attractive, tipsy female reporters to his condo with offers to show them his montage of overpriced thrones.

Headier days.

Now, Nick sounds borderline drunk and despondent. Woody offers to fly to DC for a visit, but Nick has another idea. He's planning to take some time off to process the nightmare and rethink his career. How about if they meet in New Orleans? It's been twenty years since they road tripped to JazzFest. Both remember it fondly. They still laugh about a titty bar where they were so consumed exchanging career notes they barely noticed the stripper suspended six feet above their heads. At subsequent stops, there had been more engagement with the talent. At one club, Nick had wandered with a mint julep through the back passages to find Woody casually spraying down a nude dancer with a garden hose.

"Why are you doing that?" Nick asked.

"Because I can," Woody replied.

Alas, three was a crowd.

"No looky-loos—get the fuck out of here," the stripper admonished Nick in an alarmingly masculine voice. The two journalists fled, later resolving to stay off Bourbon Street and pursue more elevated interests such as cigars and the Voodoo Museum.

Those memories leave Woody warming to the idea of a reconquest of NOLA. "Let's do it this weekend. I just need to check with The Boss."

As it turns out, The Boss isn't thrilled with the bro trip plan. She's been planning a surprise getaway for her and Woody that same weekend.

Mandy holds back on mentioning that, but Woody senses his wife's displeasure and takes appropriate action.

"I might just tell him I forgot we have plans Saturday or whatever," he says. "Why do I want to go all the way to New Orleans to be around a guy who's miserable?"

"Your friend, your call," she says.

Soon, Nick is added to the list of people Woody is bullshitting. Woody doesn't want him to think he's controlled by his wife to the point he'd spike New Orleans for her, so instead of fabricating a garden-variety blame-my-spouse excuse, over the phone he tells his friend that he "forgot" he has a conflict; his new agent, Melvin Stern, is coming to town and they're going to the Magenta's football home opener.

Now, it's Nick's turn to be disappointed, and not just because New Orleans has fallen through. Despite his troubles, he's excited for Woody and his book and emotionally invested in *Fear as Mud.* The pot of Woody's Art has been stirred by many chefs, too many, perhaps, but Nick doesn't know that. He believes he's Woody's primary muse, his de facto editor, and he's miffed that someone else will run the show from here.

They pledge to return to New Orleans soon, when they both have more to celebrate; but by that point in the phone conversation, Nick has mentally moved on.

"Hey, you caught me in the middle of reading *The Economist,*" he says. Woody knows the code. Professing to be reading *The Economist* is Nick's way of saying playtime is over. It's a curt reminder that Nick inhabits a world of great urgency and gravitas.

Mandy's mood, on the other hand, brightens upon hearing her husband has dumped New Orleans. In the afterglow of renewed relations, she tells him about the planned getaway. Woody feigns elation but ponders the complications. Not only has he given up a weekend of frozen daiquiris overlooking the Mississippi and beignets at Café Du Monde, but now he will be trapped in a Lake Placid rental with Mandy and his own deception about the book.

Despite all that, the couple enjoy a pleasant, picturesque drive into the Adirondacks, chatting about normal stuff, stopping for Swedish pancakes at a venerable diner with a commanding view of the high peaks, and arriving at their luxury log cabin in time for a reviving three-mile hike.

It's all lovely except that Nick isn't out of the picture after all. The morning of the game, he calls Woody to talk through possible career moves. Should he dig in at *The Apocalyptic* and force them to try to fire him? Should he try to rehabilitate himself by writing more clickbait? The conversation drags deep into midmorning, pissing off Mandy, who finally goes for a walk in the woods by herself. Only then does Nick change the subject.

"Oh, shit, you have to get going to the game," he says. "Where are your seats?"

Woody eyes the leather recliner in front of the big screen. He's two hundred miles from Lee Gumpman Ferrous Recycling Stadium, named after the region's publicity-crazed scrap metal king.

"They're farther back than I'd like but still a great view of the field."

"Awesome! Go Magenta! Shoot me a photo of your seats."

"Sure," Woody chokes.

By the time Mandy returns from her walk, Woody has settled into the recliner with a beer and a ham sandwich.

"Aren't we going to brunch?" she says, standing in the foyer with her coat on.

"We were, but now we can't."

The TV camera is fixated on Gumpman, seated in the luxury box between his latest trophy bro, John McEnroe, and his latest trophy wife, Melody, a weather presenter for the local Fox affiliate.

"We have twelve thirty reservations," Mandy reminds him.

"I understand that," he says, not looking up.

"I'll go by myself."

"Look, I fucked up. I have to stay here and watch the game. This is my fault. Again."

"I don't understand."

"I told Nick I was going to the game. He thinks I'm there now."

"Why did you tell him that?"

"I didn't want him to think I was blowing off the New Orleans trip for—" He stops himself too late.

"Your wife? God forbid."

Woody's pissed off at himself for the clusterfuck he created. But she gets the brunt of his anger.

"Doesn't self-righteous ever get old?" he asks.

"Enjoy your sandwich," she says and walks out.

For the next two hours, Woody exchanges texts with Nick under the pretense that he's at the game. A few of his friends are there, so Woody has them text him photos of the court from their vantage—just in case. But Nick never repeats his request for a seat view. The Magenta win by six in a double-overtime dramatic upset. Fans spill onto the field.

"What a game!" Nick texts. "I would have felt bad if you'd missed it because of me."

Woody's relieved he pulled off the deception, but that's not to be confused with being proud. He glumly thinks, *This is a crappy thing to do to a friend who only a few months ago rescued me from an international incident.*

Woody had decided to drive to the Canadian side of the Thousand Islands to research the chapters set there. When he pulled up to the booth, he realized he'd forgotten his passport.

"No passport necessary if you have an enhanced driver's license," the agent assured him. But that flustered him even more. Why hadn't he remembered he didn't need a passport?

"Oh, right, yeah, good," he'd stammered, his voice breaking into a pubescent squeak. "My lucky day. I knew that. I actually did, but, hey, senior moment. I like your earrings."

"Have you been drinking, sir?"

"No."

"Are you ill? You're sweating quite a lot."

"No, my AC needs servicing, I think. Warm day."

"It's seventeen degrees, sir."

"But that's Celsius, right?"

"Do you have any firearms or explosives in the vehicle?"

"I'm just a writer," he'd replied, hoping to defang and distract. Women liked to read more than men. Maybe that would help him here.

"I need you to answer my question: yes or no?"

"Sure . . . I forgot the question."

"I need you to pull over to the right side of that building, sir," she said, pointing toward a grim single-story structure that hinted of trouble.

Woody had no way of knowing that while he was bantering, Canadian authorities in another office hidden from view were sifting through criminal databases and coming to the belief that Atwood Wilson Hackworth was Atwater Watson Hackworth, an ex-con with an impressively violent history who had lived in Massachusetts at roughly the same time Woody had.

Ten minutes later, Woody found himself in a small conference room. A man in a blue sport coat with a badge popped in and without introducing himself asked, "Was MCI-Walpole one of your Massachusetts addresses?"

"No, sir."

In the end, his well-connected DC reporter friend saved Woody. As soon as Nick received Woody's panicky, typo-filled text message, he called in a few chits with the junior senator from New York and a media relations specialist for Canada's defense ministry. Within the hour, Woody was released with an apology "for the mix-up." He even received a complimentary Welcome to Canada kit: a maple leaf refrigerator magnet, a mini-packet of Canadian bacon jerky bites, and a coupon for 15 percent off at any participating Tim Hortons.

Nick had done Woody a big-time solid, and *this* was how he repaid him?

Woody does his best to smooth things out with his wife once she's back from brunch.

He reverse-engineers his lie, telling her, truthfully, that he needed a premium excuse to pass on New Orleans so as not to further demoralize a friend in crisis. He adds that if he had known earlier that Mandy was planning the getaway, he would have told Nick that instead.

Mandy is eager to move on and salvage the weekend, so she accepts his explanation. They switch on the gas fireplace and uncork the complimentary cab left by the Airbnb host. Things seem well on the way to makeup sex when Woody's phone rings. It's Nick.

"Is this an okay time to talk?" Nick asks. He sounds worse than the last time they were on the phone.

"Uh, yeah, I guess so, sure."

"I don't want to take time away from you and your friend."

"Friend?"

"Marvin Stern. Isn't that his name?"

"Close. It's Melvin." Woody squeezes shut his eyes. Why does lying have to be so complicated? "He's not my friend," he replies within earshot of Mandy. "He's already heading back to New York."

"So, I'm thinking of coming up there for a few days. I need to get out of Washington."

"Great," Woody says, drifting into the sunroom for privacy. "When are you thinking of coming up?"

"Tomorrow. I'm thinking maybe we get some dinner to talk through my situation in person. I don't need to stay with you guys. I'll just get a hotel."

Woody sheepishly returns to Mandy with an update. Nick will be in Icarus tomorrow. He wants to have dinner—not just with him but with her, too.

"Fun!" she replies sarcastically. "Who's Melvin?"

"Eavesdropper!" he snaps.

"It's not eavesdropping if someone is speaking ten feet from you."

"Okay, fine. Looks like I've been caught in another lie. When I lied to Nick that I was going to the game, I told him I was taking a cousin, Melvin, who was coming up from the city. It was a value-added lie on top of the larger lie."

"You don't have a cousin Melvin."

"Correct."

Woody beholds himself with wonder and disgust. He can't stop lying even when he's trying to tell the truth. This is how otherwise smart people end up in prison.

Mandy shuts down the fireplace and gives her husband a *Who are you?* look. She takes the wine—her glass and the bottle—and her book up to the bedroom. Woody hears the door latch behind her.

The next morning, they wordlessly pack up the car.

"You couldn't just not take his damn call, could you?" she says, savagely shoving the cottage key into the mail drop. The hand-carved moose fob catches an edge. Woody yanks it free, but the keychain breaks, so he has to send the key and fob down the chute separately.

Back home, Mandy takes a pass on dinner with the boys. She has more on her mind than the apocalypse at *The Apocalyptic*—like her dad's upcoming brain surgery. It's one week from tomorrow. The three siblings have details to talk through, including the care and handling of their mother and the business in the event of "complications." The complication they fear most is Joe not surviving the surgery, but no one mentions that.

"To my knowledge, Dad's never had a headache in his life," Woody overhears Mandy tell one of her brothers on the phone. "His overall health should work in his favor despite his age."

Woody waves to Mandy to signal he's heading out for his dinner with Nick. She turns away and keeps talking to her brother.

Nick is unexpectedly upbeat as they settle into a booth at Luther's Chop House. The waiter informs the pair that the duck comes with a macerated cherry reduction.

"If it's macerated, I'm in," Nick jests.

Nick's opening play is that *The Apocalyptic* has done him a wondrous favor, liberating him from a failing, rudderless magazine.

"Some of the best journalists in the world have already jumped ship," he says, draining a Manhattan. "They know the place is a joke. My only mistake was remaining loyal to them."

A starburst of optimism for Nick overtakes Woody. "You'll land on your feet. You were a bad fit for that place because you're a professional."

Woody's use of the past tense snuffs the good vibe. The two clink glasses, but rather than the moment serving as a launching point for celebrating a new beginning, a solemn quiet envelops the former journalist and the foundering one.

"They fucked me," Nick says. "They lied to me. I'm suing those pricks."

For the third time, Nick rehashes how he was assigned to write a story called "Flowing Toward Justice." It was about a Marin County, California, high school club dedicated to "degenderization" of the menstrual cycle.

He'd had no interest or expertise in the subject, and the story had confused him from the start. Weren't girls who identified as boys still girls when it came to reproductive processes?

When his piece finally ran, it was crucified as insensitive and ignorant by LGBTQIA+ advocates, particularly for its "binary bias." The story, critics complained, had neglected to adequately address that people who identify as both male *and* female or neither could have periods, too.

The Apocalyptic's editors used the blowback to initiate an exhaustive performance review to justify more nuanced forms of torture meted out by kowtowing middle managers. Suddenly, management was making Nick rewrite almost every sentence of every story.

"I keep wondering what have I done wrong," he complains to Woody. "And my answer is always the same: nothing. They're the ones who changed, not me."

"It's editorial terrorism," Woody concurs. "I've been there."

As Nick sinks deeper into a cycle of anger and self-doubt, barely touching his duck, Woody hears another voice, Kaylon's: "Two types of people in the world, Lexus—people who love you for who you are and people who love you for what you do."

Someone in the galley drops a tub of silverware.

"What's going on with your book?" Nick asks when even he tires of discussing *The Apocalyptic.*

"It's going," Woody says dully. "Pivoting to more important news, looks like Ella might go to James Madison."

Nick's phone buzzes. Without even glancing to see who it is, he gets up from the table. "Sorry, I need to take this call."

CHAPTER 19
THE CUDGEL

The following morning, Woody starts work on a critical chapter of his book. He never meant for Al and Vivian Holmes and Cold Harbor Concrete to prompt an association with the Dunns. That has been an unfortunate but unavoidable consequence of his vision. But he most certainly *does* want the Tiberius *Daily "MisInformer"* to work as a stand-in for his gutless former employer. The *Blaze* deserves it. Maybe it's asking a lot of readers to uncouple his fictional characters from his actual family while grasping that the fictional newspaper is modeled on the real one. So be it. The book is in charge now. It goes where it must. It's not Woody's fault that his narrative demands an unsparing rendering of the *Blaze*.

To finish the story, however, requires reconciliation of a conundrum. How will Cus's illegal dumping scoop hit the front page of his newspaper if his newspaper is one of the illegal dumpers?

He addresses the problem on the fifth floor of the downtown public library in a nook with a view of the *Blaze* building. Once, the Gothic Revival tower inlaid with a stone frieze of a sun and the Latin *Fiat Lux*—let there be light—nourished Woody's ego. But in the past year, he has averted his eyes from the *Blaze* to spare himself a blood pressure spike. He knows what lies within—backstabbers and cowards hiding behind abolitionist Henry Ward Beecher's quote in the marble lobby: "The newspaper is a greater treasure to the people than uncounted millions of gold."

But today is different. Today, he soaks in the sight to fuel his revenge. The words come easily.

Aurora was shooting photos of contaminated bridge abutments while Cus hammered out a story lede. His workstation sat in a far corner of the newsroom. Some found it strange his desk was positioned so he couldn't see out the windows. But he preferred to see anyone who might be approaching him. He'd learned that trick from a childhood reading of a biography of Wild Bill Hickok, who liked to sit the same way for the same reason. Better to see your enemies coming than have your back to them.

Cus and Aurora were weeks away from being ready to publish. The duo had numerous loose ends to run down and still needed to give Al a chance to comment on their findings. Neither reporter was looking forward to that exchange.

Still, as the bulbous fruits of their labors ripened, the two were itching to work on a first draft of what promised to be the most sensitive story in the 134-year history of the *Informer*. And so Cus wrote in his crisp, clear, award-winning style:

Dangerous chemicals have been embedded in countless public and private structures in Tiberius and beyond through an illicit waste disposal operation run by the region's largest concrete supplier, Cold Harbor Concrete, a *Daily Informer* investigation has discovered.

Documents, independent laboratory analysis, and sources close to the company, whose names are being withheld for their safety, point to Cold Harbor adulterating its concrete with a stew of heavily regulated chemical waste, including radioactive material from Angel of Gethsemane Medical Trauma Hospital and at least three veterinary clinics.

Among the customers linked to the disposal scheme are a

dozen fire departments throughout Catagawa County as well as the *Tiberius Daily Informer* itself. Despite slumping circulation figures, the newspaper generates approximately 20,000 gallons of chemical waste annually, including suspected carcinogens carbon black and titanium dioxide.

Cus surveyed the screen with pride. The clause about circulation was snarky—unusual for him—and he figured they'd probably take it out. But he also knew Aurora would find it delightful, which mattered to him. In hot pursuit of the scoop for the ages and in fear for their lives, an uncomfortable truth bubbled on the backburner of his emotional stovetop. He'd fallen in love with her.

"Working on anything good?" Vern Meekes, one of the paper's six managing editors, intruded.

"Depends on who defines 'good,'" Cus replied. Their eyes locked until the scribe's steely mien forced Meekes to look away.

"Got a minute?" Meekes asked.

Cus nodded and rose from his chair, first taking care to log out. He was changing his password daily these days. They relocated to a small conference room, the Mensa Room, as it was playfully called. Normally, it was used for brainstorming sessions, but increasingly it was doubling as a chamber of rebuke.

"We're hearing you're looking into your in-laws' business," Meekes began.

"Among others," Cus replied.

"We can't have you doing that."

"Why not?"

"You know damn well why not. It's a conflict of interest."

"It's a conflict of interest if I don't investigate them."

During the ensuing silence, Cus observed a blotch of red in the corner of Meekes's left eye and that a lapel button of his cornflower blue gingham shirt was loose.

"No more, Cus. Publisher's orders."

"What gives the publisher the right to interfere with newsroom decisions?"

Meekes shrugged. "The publisher owns the newsroom. He signs our checks."

"Now who has a conflict of interest?"

"Point noted."

"What if my name isn't on the story?" Cus persisted. "Will that fix it?"

"Come on, Cus."

"So, you're submarining our investigation without even seeing a story?"

The middle manager paused. He looked weary of everything, especially Cus. "'Submarining' is a loaded term. Let's just say reassigning."

"Reassigning to who?"

"TBD."

"To nobody."

"Publisher's call."

Now it was Cus's turn to look fed up.

"Sounds like we're done here."

The men rose to their feet. Cus was six inches taller than the managing editor, a physical manifestation of the reality that Cus was the larger of the two in all ways.

"Just one more thing," Meekes said.

Cus waited for more drivel.

"You remain a valued team member, despite—"

"Despite me doing my job?"

Meekes threw out his hands. "Let it go, Cus. Stories are like Doritos. If one falls on the floor, you just grab another chip from the bag."

"Inspiring."

"I just work here."

"To paraphrase Noam Chomsky, should the nation succumb

to dictatorship, the uniformity and obedience of the US media will be a major reason."

"Who's Norm Chomsky?"

"Never mind."

The reporter turned toward the door but stopped to address the marshmallow middle manager whose salary was twice his own.

"You should do something for that eye," Cus advised. "It looks infected."

Back at his workstation, Cus loaded a satchel with important notes and documents and headed to his truck, crafting his resignation letter in his head.

Woody reviews his labors. The red-eye mention was not a random detail. It was a shot at one of the real-life editors at the *Blaze,* a not-so-recovering alcoholic who had whipped up Woody's misidentified source gaffe into a froth of recrimination. Woody giggles when he rereads the eye dig, drawing irritated looks from other library patrons. That only adds to his glee.

He isn't as sure about his artistic decision to affirm Cus is in love with Aurora. The last thing Woody wants is for Celeste to read this and think he's telling her he's in love with her even if that's maybe still a little true. Infatuated is more like it. But he decides to leave it in. Again, the narrative's running the show. Atwood Hackworth is just the medium.

That night, he and Aurora spoke by phone. She was determined to resign in solidarity with him.

"If I stay, I become one of them."

Her resolve rattled Cus. Because of him, she'd be out of work. He didn't want to live with that—or die with it.

"You will never be one of them," he assured her.

"This is so much bigger than us and our jobs," she persisted.

"There must be a way to tell people what is happening."

Cus thought he heard Jenny in the hallway and lowered his voice. "It's not secure here," he whispered. "Let's meet somewhere."

"La cabina," she whispered. The cabin.

After they had made love four times, serenaded by coyote yips and the cries of Common Loons, they talked shop, cobbling together an imperfect but plausible double-barreled strategy.

First, they would turn over what they knew about Cold Harbor to state and federal authorities—the local ones were too corrupt—and hope for justice there. If that didn't work, they would post their story on multiple social media platforms, leave Cold Harbor out of it, and let readers connect the dots.

Both understood the personal risks of publicly implicating Cold Harbor without the protective umbrella of the *Informer*. They'd be exposed in the legal fight of their lives, and that was if all went well. A libel suit could be the least of their worries.

As staff reporters, normally Cus and Aurora had a measure of protection against Al Holmes and his goons. Killing a newspaper reporter was not unheard of but still a big deal in the country and sure to attract national attention. On the other hand, snuffing a couple of rogue online pests was a minor errand for a monster willing to poison an entire city.

Without question, the reporters' self-preservation instincts were justified. Trouble was, writing online stories that left out the major culprit offended their professional sensibilities.

"¿Qué somos? Cobardes?" Aurora challenged. What are we, cowards?

But five minutes later: "I don't want to die," Aurora said, suddenly losing her courage. Tears—just a few, but large ones—ran down her lovely face.

They were a mess.

"Show, don't tell," Woody reminds himself yet again. "Lovely" is too generic. He reworks the sentence.

. . . ran down her olive-colored cheeks, softening the proud visage of a Mayan warrior princess.

"It's not the dying I'm afraid of," Cus countered, attempting black humor. "It's the torture."

She shuddered with dread, so he tried again.

"But maybe I'm conditioned for it. I'm already tortured every second we're apart."

That made her smile. "Don't patronize me, cabrón," she said, giggling, and they ravaged each other again.

Near the end, as he was reaching fruition, she yelled out a name that was not his: "Staley! Staley! Staley!"

Woody does a word search for "fruition." He used it earlier in a similar way. Has he reached fruition on fruition? Best to say it a new way.

Near the end, as the great rockets of his passion ignited and liftoff became imminent, she yelled out a name that was not his: "Staley! Staley! Staley!"

Cus did not take offense. To the contrary, he understood her in context, understood that she, like him, had been contemplating their journalistic predicament even as their loins melded in feverish passion. No, Aurora was not fantasizing she was being taken by the cranky former pressman who reeked of Marlboro smoke and had been fired for exposing his member. She was hatching a better plan, and Cus wondered if she was on the same wavelength as he was. Staley possessed both an insider's knowledge of the pressroom and an abused employee's rancor, the perfect ally to help publish an unauthorized edition of the *Informer*.

"Yes, Staley!" he agreed, pushing himself past the brink. "Oh, God, yes. Staley." And then they were as one.

But not for long.

They'd taken care not to turn on the lights in the cabin, preferring the discreet ambiance of Cus's camp lantern set at 100 lumens. But when they heard tires rolling on pine needles, their woodland tryst was officially finished. Aurora gripped his arm so tightly it left a mark.

"Don't move," he whispered to her.

Cus untangled himself from his cariña and calmly put on his jeans and forest-green lumberjack shirt. Then he reached for his . . .

For his what? the author ponders. *His gun? His knife? Too jejune.* Woody's mind goes to his Mister Twister walking stick, the one he'd bought during that fishing trip in Idaho with Joe and Tanner so many years ago. It was nature's version of a barbershop pole, harvested and hand lacquered to a lasting sheen. It would make a fine cudgel for Cus. *What the hell?* Woody thinks. *Write what you know.*

Then Cus reached for his trusty vine-gnarled walking stick, given to him by a Mohawk chieftain in gratitude for an award-winning series that shamed the state into restoring a trout stream through tribal land. The staff had proven itself a handy cudgel six years ago, when Cus was approached by a poacher displeased with the reporter's recent story about that topic. One blow with the Mister Twister was enough to persuade the poacher to drop his machete. Cus's lightning-quick left hook finished the deal.

But this was no backwoods trapper paying a visit. This was a professional. Cus could see through his night vision binoculars that the masked figure approaching on a fat-tire electric hunting bicycle was Tommy the Torque Wrench. Tommy's neck had been clipped by a .38 slug twenty years ago, and while he'd escaped serious damage, his head was permanently cocked to the left ever so slightly.

Cus watched through a horizontal slit between the window frame and air-conditioning unit as Tommy dismounted the bike and crept toward the porch. He carried a crossbow. A knife was sheathed to his waist.

Cus wasn't one to cede the initiative. He nimbly slipped out the back porch, motioning for Aurora, now fully clothed, to join him.

That's when a steel-tipped arrow grazed his right forearm, flew through the open doorway, and lodged in the kitchen wall.

The couple's instinct was to disappear into the woods and leave Tommy to massacre an empty cabin. But Tommy was onto them. He burst out of the shadows onto the screened-in porch. He had discarded the crossbow, which was useless for hand-to-hand combat, but Cus now saw the deadly Natchez Bowie flashing in Tommy's hand.

Yet even in arming himself with two deadly weapons, Tommy had underestimated his adversary.

During a spring semester in Avignon, Cus had become friends with a Garde nationale colonel who taught him the French martial art of canne de combat. Had Tommy done his research, he would have known never to bring a knife to a stick fight, especially if a newsroom ninja is wielding the stick.

The walking stick found Tommy's throat first. Before he realized he couldn't breathe, another blow buckled his knees and yet another punched the knife from his grasp. Aurora did the rest. She brought down hard on Tommy's wrist an embroidered boot from her mother's home village near Pastores, just as he lunged for his knife. With her other boot, she kicked the dagger into the underbrush behind a picnic table.

"Vete a la mierda, cabrón," she hissed at him. Fuck off, asshole.

Only when the Torque Wrench began to struggle to his feet did Cus finish the job, bringing the stick down hard on the back of the thug's thick skull. He fell to the floor, still alive, but barely. Cus grabbed the crossbow and the five arrows in the quiver. Aurora retrieved the knife, and they started for the woods.

"Wait," Cus directed. "Give me the knife."

"Don't kill him," Aurora pleaded. "I can't bear to think of you that way."

"Give me the knife," he repeated, and she obliged.

He dashed to the e-bike in long, graceful strides and plunged the blade into the tires. Then he dug through the pannier hanging from the rear rack and extracted Tommy's phone.

"Good thinking," she said, and he kissed her. Then he turned off the location tracking on Tommy's phone.

"Let's get out of here," he said. A bullfrog croaked in assent.

They left the crossbow outside the porch, knowing it was useless without arrows, which Cus took with him.

Back in his truck, silence overtook them. They had escaped—but to where? Where could they go?

"It was Jenny," Cus said, stating the obvious. "She had Tommy follow me."

"Are we just going to let him die there?" Aurora asked. "Assuming he isn't dead already."

"It's tempting," Cus replied, wiping a rivulet of blood from his right arm. "Is his cellphone unlocked?"

Aurora reached into the console. "It's not locked."

He pulled into the parking lot of a bait shop, took out his phone, and went to his contacts list. "Use his phone to send a text here," he told her, reading her the number.

She punched it in to Tommy's phone. "Whose number is this?" she asked.

"A park ranger, a source. You don't need the name."

"What should we tell him?"

"It's a her."

Aurora looked embarrassed then suspicious. "Are you fucking her, too?"

"No," Cus said. "She's an invasive plants expert. She's a source."

Aurora hung her head. "I'm sorry. I don't know why I said that."

"Because you're not convinced I love you."

"It might help if you told me."

"I love you, Aurora."

Here Woody remembers he had a plan to demonize Aurora to appease Mandy. He shrugs. Too late now. Pulling the rug out from under her character makes no sense. Even worse, the main female characters, Jenny *and* Aurora, would both be evil, conniving bitches, which would open him to more accusations of misogyny. "Screw it," he says. "Gotta live with it."

She smiled a shy smile he rarely saw from her.

"Yo también te amo," she replied and touched his arm, gently this time, avoiding the wound.

"What do you want me to say to your park ranger friend?"

"Text her, 'This is Tommy Nunzio. I'm a convicted felon. I used a crossbow to try to kill an innocent man in Cabin No. 3 at Deer Run Campground. I only grazed him, and he got the better of me. I'm there now, around back. I'm hurt bad. He took the rest of my arrows and my knife. I'm unarmed, but you should still approach me with extreme caution.'"

She quickly typed the words and read them back.

"Good," he said. "Send it."

It was 2:14 a.m.

"When do you think she'll read it?" she asked.

"It doesn't matter."

"We need to get rid of his phone."

Fearing cameras, they opted against tossing it into a dumpster in the littered side yard of a bait shop. They also considered there might be evidence of interest to authorities on the phone, evidence that might send Tommy, Al, and Jenny where they belonged—prison.

"Let's make this easy," Cus said. He drove a few miles and pulled alongside a USPS drop box outside an ice cream stand fittingly named Super Scoop.

"No cameras here," Cus said.

"I see one right there," Aurora exclaimed, pointing at a corner of the building. Sure enough, a camera was mounted on the overhang.

"It doesn't work," Cus assured her. "It's just a decoy."

"How do you know that?"

"Last summer, vandals used baseball bats to knock down dozens of mailboxes around here. The cops came here to look at security video, but there was none. It's not a real camera."

Again, Aurora was impressed. Was there nothing her dashing defender of Earth and sky didn't know? "Knowledge is power," she said.

"Knowledge is power," Cus agreed as he donned work gloves. "But it can also get you killed."

He used a disinfecting wipe to clear the phone of their fingerprints and placed it in a faded Magenta souvenir string bag. Then he wrote "Police Evidence" on a sheet from his reporter's notepad. He used duct tape to affix the sheet to the bag. He paused to kiss her again, exited the truck, and dropped the bag in the box.

With clean consciences, they drove south into the night, destination unknown.

Hours later, they checked into the Extended Stay America Suites in Netcong, New Jersey. They'd chosen to lodge there as a nod to karma. Netcong had been the postmark on the letter tipping them off to the Spruce Road dump site months earlier.

They slept in so late they missed the free breakfast buffet. As the two crusaders lay entangled in the sheets, elsewhere Jenny and her father were having an unpleasant phone discussion.

"You heard from Tommy yet?" she asked.

"Not a fucking word," Al groused.

"You tried calling him?"

"Of course, I tried calling him, you dumb bi—sweetheart. He isn't picking up. You heard from that asswipe husband of yours?"

"Nothing."

Al fed his daughter back her line. "You tried calling him?"

"He doesn't pick up."

"He's probably screwing that beaner whore as we speak."

"Fuck you, Dad."

"Hard to blame him. You got stock in Ben & Jerry's or what?"

"You sure Mom isn't getting some side action, too? Because I'm pretty sure she is."

"That's my girl. Shit on your own mother to deflect from your caboose. Hey, for what it's worth, I still think you're a hot piece of ass."

"Speaking of fecal matter, your boy Tommy shit the bed," she hissed.

"No, he didn't. He's just lying low, cleaning up maybe. I give Tommy a lot of freedom to handle these assignments. He's earned my trust. It wouldn't surprise me if your betrothed and his little homewrecker are chained to a couple of eco-blocks at the bottom of Lake Ranswill. Or he's pouring them into a tennis court as we speak."

"I don't think so, Dad."

"What do you mean you don't think so?"

"They're in Hamilton, Ontario. Looks like they're headed to Toronto."

"How do you know that?"

"Because I put a GPS tracker on his truck, Daddy Dumbfuck."

That gave them both the giggles.

"You're something else, Jen-Jen," he said. "Maybe you learned a thing or two from your old man, after all."

"Maybe I did!" she said proudly.

"Let's leave 'em alone for now. Just monitor the situation. Hey, you owe me an apology."

"For what?"

"Wherever Tommy is, he put the fear of God in Cus and that nosy twat."

"True enough, Dad. Something tells me they won't be back anytime soon sniffing around."

"They're Canucks now. Hope they like gravy on their fries."

Maybe Al and Jenny should have been smarter than that. Maybe they should have learned never to underestimate the hunky wordsmith Jenny spotted at the gym twenty years ago running rivals ragged on the handball court.

The moment he'd seen Tommy sneaking toward the cabin, he suspected a tracking device might have been placed on his rig. Something about a maniac coming for you with a knife and a crossbow makes you paranoid.

After he and Aurora discarded Tommy's phone, Cus pulled into a self-service car wash—the low-budget kind with low-quality equipment and no onsite professional—and ran his hands under seats, bumpers, and wheel wells.

"What are you looking for?" Aurora snipped, exhausted and irritated.

"For this," he told her, emerging from under the truck with a black disc showing a faintly glowing green light.

She knew what it was. "Let's just leave it here," she said.

"I have a better idea."

Forty-five minutes later, Aurora, now at the wheel, dropped him off at the Nero, New York, Amtrak station. Ten minutes after that, he boarded the northbound train to Toronto. Twenty-two minutes after that, he got off in Archimedes, where Aurora was waiting for him in his truck. Along the way he'd used his trusty duct tape to affix the tracking disc under the unoccupied passenger seat in front of him. He'd also ignored several calls from Jenny, who would no doubt play concerned spouse with him if he answered but was surely hoping his not answering was a promising sign he was dead.

It was a good motivator for Cus to return his phone to factory settings, disable it, and toss it in the trash, although not before emailing himself his precious source list to his supersecret Gonzo account. It was time for Cus Stanton to disappear.

Now, as they roused from their slumber in their extended stay suite, Cus and Aurora had reason to hope they'd thrown his murderous wife and in-laws off their trail.

"Let's go out and get a real breakfast," he said. "We're going to need it. We have a story to write."

Over eggs and pancakes soaked in lingonberry syrup that reminded Cus of the blood from his now-throbbing crossbow wound, they discussed how best to ask a favor of Staley. Would he parlay his pressroom know-how to print their story, on page one, in an unauthorized edition of the *Informer*?

Woody stops typing and reflects on one of his favorite aphorisms, "Revenge is a dish best served cold." Before deep layoffs made parking spaces at the *Blaze* bountiful, he was forever at odds with the more zealous security officers prowling the premises. He'd lost his blue parking pass and, on principle, refused to pay the $10 replacement fee. Replacement passes for a far-flung red lot were free. Why not the blue ones?

"There's no logic except you're punishing me for losing a worthless piece of plastic," he'd insisted to the director of security, a world-weary Marine veteran whose duties included caring for a housebound wife with lupus.

"The logic is we want you to be more careful with your pass," the director had explained. "We have two hundred twelve spaces in that garage. If we have two hundred fifty blue passes floating around, we have a problem."

Woody had taken offense at the inference that his pass wasn't really lost and he'd sold it to someone else, so he'd doubled down on his self-righteousness and parked in the blue lot anyway.

"They think I'm trafficking employee parking passes on the black market," he'd fumed to Mandy, who ignored the rant.

The citations added up until one day, Woody's Audi Quattro was towed. His outrage was so total that the executive editor quietly paid half the impound charge from the newsroom holiday party fund on the condition Woody never mention it. Thus mollified, Woody paid the $10 for a new blue pass. Fond memories. His book would not be complete without a fictional avenging of those newsroom security doofs.

CHAPTER 20
THE FINISH LINE

That afternoon, they labored in the hotel room over a sidebar explaining which chemicals could be most easily mixed into concrete without detection and which would stain or carry suspicious odors. Suddenly, Cus grew despondent.

"What is it, cariño," Aurora asked, rubbing his shoulders.

"Meekes is right," Cus said. "It's a conflict of interest. I can't do this story."

She threw up her palms in frustration. Sometimes his pronouncements, which she knew were born of deep reflection, could nonetheless seem grandiose and out of the blue.

"We're doing the story," she said.

"It can't have my byline. It will undercut all our work. It's distracting." He slumped miserably in his chair. "I'm like a headless journalism rooster scratching out information kernels I can't consume."

She turned on the kettle in the austere kitchen to make a cup of tea.

"Okay, fine. No story. It's not worth it. Let's just kill ourselves before they do."

Adrenaline could only carry Cus so far. He needed sleep, not Aurora's melodrama.

"I never said no story. I just said it can't have my byline."

"My byline only?"

"Your byline only."

"That's not fair—to either of us."

"Life's not fair. Besides, you're going to be doing the hard part."

"What do you mean?"

"You need to talk to Al for comment, not me."

The kettle whistled.

"Thanks a lot, asshole," she said, and they laughed. Then they sat in furtive silence as she sipped on her mug of hibiscus orange blossom.

"We need to talk to Staley to find out what's possible," he said finally.

"Can we order room service first?" she asked.

"It's Extended Stay America. There is no room service."

Cus went down to the lobby store and bought Hot Pockets and chili in a pull-top can.

"Nice to have our own kitchen," he said.

"Que suerte!" she sarcastically replied.

After they ate, she called Staley.

His tone was gruff and wary.

"Hi, Kyle. This is Aurora."

"I can hear that."

"Is it okay if I have you on speakerphone with Cus?"

"Just Cus?"

"Just Cus."

"Hello, Kyle," Cus interjected.

"What do you want?"

Aurora laid out the predicament, including that Tommy the Torque Wrench attacked them.

"What were you doing in the cabin in the first place?"

Cus and Aurora said nothing. Finally, Aurora spoke up. "We were fucking, Kyle, okay? Do you want details?"

Cus noticed she pronounced "details" with a slightly Spanish accent, with the stress on the second syllable.

Staley laughed throatily. "I appreciate the honest answer," he said. "I suppose I can trust you two libertines."

"Can you trust us enough to help us print an extra special edition of the *Informer*?" Cus asked.

The line went quiet. Finally, Staley spoke. "What do you have in mind?"

Staley walked them through their options, starting on a promising note. Oversight at the print plant was minimal. The half-dozen pressmen still on the job never read the paper for content except during breaks. They scrutinized the pages for proper ink transference and straight columns. If a folio line was a few millimeters off, they were all over it. If there was ghosting, out came the worried looks and the wrenches. Back-trap mottle—a print defect caused by unevenly transferred ink—triggered hurried ink sequencing adjustments and scrutiny of roller contact points. But the stories themselves, they could be about anything, from a terrorist attack to gardening tips. The pressmen looked for smudges and bleeds, not content, not during press runs when time was money.

Another plus: Company attitudes about print products ranged from indifference to contempt, and the mindset filtered down to the pressroom. Skilled workers who once took pride in their contribution to democracy now kept their heads down waiting for the next round of layoffs. Digital ruled. Even if a lone pressman were to notice a routine story had been swapped for a blockbuster, the chances he'd mention it to his supervisor, let alone to an editor or anyone in the publisher's office, were beyond nil. It was, after all, only print.

But Cus was old school. The tactile, tangible quality of a real newspaper made a story real. There was permanence, and permanence mattered. Once a story was in print, it could never be undone. A digital version could be quickly discovered, taken down, and, in the event anyone saw it, dismissed as a hack. Cus and Aurora could end up with just a screenshot of their exposé. Better than nothing, but the impact would be much diminished. No, it had to be in print.

Staley offered that it would be relatively easy to sneak into the old offset pressroom adjacent to the new modern plant and produce an unauthorized extra. The old press was still in use, cranking out circulars and shoppers and a few smaller papers, including the moribund alternative weekly, the *Tiberius Serendipitous*.

"I bet the *Serendipitous* would run your story," Staley suggested. "They'd love to stick it to the *Informer*."

But Cus was having none of that. "It's our story," he insisted. "It needs to run in the daily."

Cus had lost what little respect he had for the tabloid and its ads that blared "Totally Nude Dancers." In better days, the *Serendipitous* had been a healthy beast, talking truth to power, including to the *Informer*. But it had been purchased five years ago by a former fast-food industry consultant, Dale Smart, whose expert advice had failed to save Waffle Burger, Chicklicious, Bowl Boy, and several other marginal chains.

As his reputation in fast-food circles dipped below E. coli, Smart parachuted into a new zone of ignorance—newspapers. The *Serendipitous* was doomed the day he took it over. It would be taken off life support twenty months later, and that was the end of its fifty-two-year run.

But for now, the weekly was still publishing as Smart looked for a buyer dumber than he was.

Aurora agreed with Cus. "The *Serendipitous* is a joke. It's just fluff and entertainment. No one will take us seriously."

Staley had another thought. "You could do it as an insert in the old plant, and we can drop it into the regular press run at the new plant. Except . . ."

"Except what?" Aurora asked.

"Except it will look slick, like a shopper. And in full color. Or like one of those little giveaway papers we do for the Jews and the Blacks."

Cus and Aurora winced but let it go. Staley was coarse and cantankerous, but he was all they had.

"My concern with an insert is it will come off as sneaky," Cus said, "like we're hiding a massive public health story. It wouldn't be the first time the *Informer* buried my best work."

"Or mine," Aurora said.

"Jeez, picky aren't we."

"Is there a Plan C?" Aurora asked.

"Yeah, we sub your story into the Holston County edition. We have to replate anyway."

"How do we do that?" Cus asked.

"We don't do anything," Staley snapped. "I do it. Just like I've done everything else. Would you like me to hold your dick for you in the little boys' room, too?"

Cus absorbed the insult without comment, tempted as he was to remind Staley that penis handling wasn't one of the pressman's strengths.

"We appreciate your contribution to this important investigation," Cus replied.

"Remember that when they put me in the can for industrial sabotage."

Aurora squeezed Cus's thigh and pointed to herself to signal she'd take it from here. "You're not going to the can, Kyle," she said. "You're going to be a hero."

"Wonderful. That and eighteen bucks will get me a pint of Jack."

Outside their door, children sprinted up and down the hallway. A couple argued in the parking lot below.

"You spend more than that on booze in a week." a man hollered.

The woman's reply was too pitched and rapid fire to be understood from the second floor.

Then it was strangely quiet, and the trio went back to work. No one needed to state the obvious—that the Holston County edition existed in name only. The bureau had been shut down for years. Reporters were no longer assigned to the economically depressed, winter-whipped hinterland. The Holston County edition was distinguishable from the home edition by the nameplate below the masthead and by a few local high school sports scores if the games ended early enough. But beyond that, it was a sham—a ghost edition.

In other words, it was perfect.

"When do you guys want to do this?" Staley asked.

"You tell us," Aurora replied. "We'll be ready."

Staley thought a moment. "Saturday nights are good," he said. "There's never any real news in the Sunday paper. Mainly just repurposed bullshit from Tiberius.com from the previous week. If you're looking for a day when the don't-give-a-fuck factor is off the charts, Saturday's it."

"That's in three days," Cus thought aloud.

"The man can count!" Staley jeered.

The next twenty minutes was mostly Staley talking while Cus and Aurora took notes. Their exposé would run on the heaviest circulation day of the week. In one forgotten outpost of *Daily Informer* country, Sunday would bring "real news" of the highest order. From there, it would spread as far and wide as Al Holmes's toxic mud and beyond.

Cus and Aurora craved fresh air. They grabbed sweaters to ward off the evening chill and strolled through the small town flanked by a calm lake. For the first mile they said little, but when they reached an outdoor fitness park, Cus brought up an important point.

"We can't run the story without getting comments from the

principles," Cus said as he whipped through a set of chin-ups.

"I know. You told me you want me to talk to your father-in-law."

"Hayden, too."

Aurora pouted adorably. "Interviewing the publisher—that's always fun."

"Use your charm."

"Here's what I don't get. How are we supposed to—"

Cus understood where she was headed and interrupted. "I know. As soon as we ask them for comment, they'll know we're planning to publish the story and they'll try to stop it."

"It will never run."

"It will if we're smart about it."

Cus ripped off a few more chin-ups and gracefully dismounted the bar. "The window between asking for comment and starting the presses has to be tight," he said.

"How tight?"

"Minutes. No more than ten."

"¡Dios mio!"

They walked back to town in the gloaming.

"Maybe we're being unfair," Cus brooded. "They should have more time to figure out what they want to say. These are serious allegations."

Aurora's Latina temper spiked. "Give them more time to lie?"

Woody fretted. Was "Latina temper" a stereotype? He wasn't sure. No one ever seemed to take offense at "Irish temper." But best to play it safe anyway.

"Give them more time to lie?" Aurora nearly shouted, her fury flaring like Guatemala's Volcán de Fuego.

Cus looked around to make sure they weren't being followed. "We'll do the best we can," he said.

"What does that mean?"

"I'm not sure anymore." He stopped to gaze at the lake. "It's a beautiful world," he said.

"It's a complicated world."

"Not everything is complicated." He kissed her.

"Is that the best you can do?" she teased, and they kissed again, this time their passions roiling and colliding like whitecaps on a windswept bay.

They ventured to a nearby Italian place and asked for a table in the back, away from the bar. Over candlelit chicken liver crostini and bistecca alla fiorentina, they agreed not to name every business implicated in the scandal but would target a few for comment and mention only those. Then, despite the wine, they went back to their room to thrash out one of the more unusual passages in the history of American journalism. Cus typed while Aurora looked over his shoulder.

He began, "Due to the far-reaching nature of the allegations—"

"Don't say 'allegations,'" she corrected. "We're not the police. We're not alleging anything. We're stating fact. Say 'far-reaching nature of the improperly embedded waste.'"

He made the change. "Due to the far-reaching nature of the improperly embedded waste, it was not possible to contact every business and individual participant for comment."

Cus stopped. "Now, we're basically saying they did it. We're not even alleging. We're convicting."

"We're convicting the people we're not naming? How is that even possible?"

Cus shrugged in semiagreement. What did it matter, anyway? A libel suit from Cold Harbor or their own employer was the least of their concerns.

"Maybe we can spare B.J. some stress," he said with a wry smile.

"Spare him some stress? What are you talking about?"

"Let's try this," he said, and resumed writing. "Dozens of businesses are involved. The publisher of the *Informer*, B.J. Hayden III, was not immediately granted an opportunity to respond to evidence of this newspaper's patronage of Cold Harbor's clandestine dumping service.

"This extraordinary breach of journalistic protocol was made in the interest of public health and safety and informed by the reality that Hayden has unlimited access to this publication to respond as he wishes.

"Alerting management that a story was imminent risked censorship."

"¡Maraviloso!" Aurora erupted and placed her arms around the writer's neck, her perfect breasts resting heavily on his weary shoulders.

"Yeah, I like it, too."

Woody, now back in his study, joins his fictional creations in approving of the paragraph, but the image of Aurora's breasts resting on Cus's shoulders triggers spatial alarms. The last thing he wants is to turn sleek, sexy Aurora into a plus-size with droopy D-cups. Stern wouldn't approve. Woody rises from his writing station to recreate the scene by stuffing wadded-up pages of the *Blaze* down his polo shirt. He needs to know where smallish breasts would make contact with the six-foot-five seated Cus.

Carefully, he leans over the back of his writing chair, extending his arms in a semicircle to replicate Aurora's embrace. Immediately, he sees that Cus's brawny shoulders would be too wide and possibly too high up. It looks like her breasts would make contact somewhere between his lower scapula and his lats.

"What are you doing, Dad?" Ella asks from the doorway.

Woody bolts upright so quickly that one of his *Blaze* boobs slips out of position and settles over his navel. "Just doing some editing for a friend," he stammers, extracting the wad of newsprint from under his shirt and casually tossing it in a Buffalo Sabres trash can. "He's writing a short story about . . . about a sumo wrestler who falls into a well. It's . . . what do you call it . . . you know, magical realism. You ever read *Love in the Time of Cholera*? I started it, but after thirty pages . . . Anyway, what I'm trying to say is that even in magical realism, I like the facts to add up. That's just how I am. It's the journalism thing. I was just acting out the scene to see if it's possible for a sumo wrestler, even a small one, to fall into a well."

He holds his arms out in a semicircle again to suggest a well.

"Can I have twenty dollars?" Ella asks. "I'm going to Starbucks."

Woody opens his wallet with haste. "Here's forty," he says, handing her two crisp twenties. "Maybe enough for a grande."

"Maybe," she says, sounding both grateful and disappointed.

He hands her another twenty.

"Thanks, Dad," she chirps, then vanishes.

Woody slam-dunks the remaining breast in the trash. *Leave Aurora's tits out of the scene and just move on,* he berates himself. The Extended Stay pitstop has extended too long. It's getting claustrophobic. He needs to get his characters out of there.

Woody checks his email. Stern has checked in.

"Do we have an ending?"

"It's getting there. Talk next week?"

Woody sees that Stern's email was carelessly added to a string Woody wasn't meant to see.

We're not seriously representing this crap, are we?

Not my cup of tea either, but it could sell. Nobody ever went broke underestimating the semiliterate.

Encyclopedia Brown gets laid.

Stop pranking us, Melvin!

No cape for Cus?

Just my impression, but is "Woody" overcompensating? Cus "the larger man in all ways." Hmm.

Woody is tempted to reply to every snarky comment, but he doesn't want to undermine Stern, who was probably loaded when he sent the thread. Stern's opinion is the only one that matters anyway. Screw the rest of 'em. They're interchangeable drones, jealous of a true creator. Woody's energy will be better directed addressing a major loose end: What becomes of Tommy the Torque Wrench, clubbed senseless and left for dead at a New York State rental cabin?

Tommy's life options were few and dim as he struggled to his senses, brought back to life by the first blush of morning and the pitched whistles of wood thrushes. His best choice, had he known, would have been to lie there and wait for rangers and state police to find him. Once they'd determined he was unarmed, they would have summoned an ambulance. It would have been a week, at least, before doctors considered him well enough to be interrogated from his hospital bed. Even then there would have been convenient memory loss. But the best possible outcome, such as it was, was not the outcome Tommy got.

Tommy wrongly assumed that Cus and Aurora had not notified law enforcement about his whereabouts. If they had, he figured, the cops already would have arrested him. In fact, the park ranger Cus and Aurora had texted using Tommy's phone, was just waking up. In another few minutes, after she got some coffee in her, she would check her phone and see the bizarre message explaining Nunzio was outside Cabin No. 3. Had Nunzio stayed put, he'd still be alive, but instead he did what came naturally, what he had done countless times before: He fled a crime scene.

The last thing he wanted was some asshole dog walker or nature-loving pussy spotting him splayed out like a corpse on the back porch and reporting him. Cops crawling up his ass like termites wouldn't be good for him or, most importantly, for his boss. And so, woozy from a severe head wound and dehydrated, Tommy the Torque Wrench pulled himself to his feet and stumbled to the hunting bike only to find the tires flat. Someday, he vowed, he would take the air out of those fuckwad reporters permanently. His resolve doubled when he discovered they'd made off with his phone. He started to scream an F-bomb but stifled it, which made his head hurt even more. It was an amuse-bouche of greater suffering to come.

The autopsy would show Tommy had a fractured skull and a tiny brain bleed but that neither caused his death. He had hiked deeper into the park, away from the main entrance, looking for the remote trail he'd rode in on to avoid detection. Just a half mile into his escape route, he realized he'd made a wrong turn. He kicked a dirt clod into the woods and sat on a log to rest.

That's when he heard the hum. The first sting landed just above his knee, then another pierced his forearm. He ran down the trail but tripped on a hawthorn stump, tumbling into the barbs of adjacent trees. By the time he regained his feet, he'd been stung at least seven more times. He tried again to outrun them, but by now it was pointless. The furious swarm encircled him like a tornado. A jogger heard his screams from nearly a mile away, but she couldn't tell from where. She surmised it was a man, and the jogger wasn't high on men these days. The previous week she'd dumped her verbally abusive shithead boyfriend, and now she was training for the Tiberius Marathon. She felt empowered and free. Men are assholes, she reminded herself. No doubt the screamer was just clowning around with some asshole friends. After a quick look at her Apple Watch, she sped off, away from Tommy, whose screams were turning to moans, then to whimpers.

It's doubtful the EpiPen would have saved Tommy from all that venom even if it had not been five years past its expiration date, but it was a moot point. As he lay on the ground, repeatedly stabbing himself in the thigh, he was acutely aware his trachea was closing. He tried to recall the last time he'd replaced the injector. He couldn't. His last thought was that a hornet was inside his nose.

That night, about the time even Al was becoming concerned about Tommy's whereabouts, Jenny called him with news—Cus and Aurora had crossed back into the United States and were apparently heading toward Tiberius.

"They're taking it slow, staying off the Thruway," Jenny noted. "I wonder what that's all about."

"Maybe they're afraid I got somebody at the Thruway Authority tracking 'em."

Jenny was worried as she sat on her sofa pouring Chablis from a box into a red wine goblet. "They should be pedal to the metal. They gotta deadline to make."

Al had doubts. "There's no way that ass rag of a newspaper will run that story. They're as dirty as I am."

"Maybe someone else is publishing it. You ever think of that?"

"Of course, I thought of it. Hey, are you wiretapped?"

"Blow me, Dad."

"I didn't mean you," he fibbed. "I meant your phone."

"My cellphone? You're a piece of work, Dad. What's it like to not even trust your own flesh and blood?"

Al stifled a comeback and tacked in a new direction. "Looks like it's time to welcome our international lovebirds home in style."

"With no Tommy?"

"We go to war with the army we have."

With Cus and Aurora's return seeming imminent, if weirdly leisurely, Al activated a four-man goon squad. Two of them had proven useful eight years earlier in dampening enthusiasm for a nascent unionization push at Cold Harbor. The other two were selected for their brawn. None were scholars.

He positioned the men—two per unmarked van—on either side of the *Informer*, just in case, and told them to wait for further instructions. Their only job, unless otherwise specified, was to spot Cus's truck, follow it if necessary, and report back.

"Does this rig have satellite radio?" one of the goons whined.

Al unleashed a string of obscenities and hung up. "Where the hell are you, Tommy?" he muttered to himself.

Thirty minutes later, Al got a call from Jenny: "They're somewhere out near the train station."

"Out near the train station—that's the best you can do?"

"Shitty signal. Maybe they're behind a hill or something. Wait! Now they're driving east again, away from here!"

Both vans sped east in pursuit of the ghost truck. More updates from Jenny followed.

"They're in Scrotius."

"Now they're in Venus going along the river."

"They're in Monolithos."

Then, "Looks like they stopped for a break just outside Monolithos."

Al was done with monitoring the chase. "If you see an opportunity, take 'em both out," he ordered.

"You got it, boss," the lead goon replied.

But Al's thirst for vengeance would go unquenched this crisp fall evening.

The Amtrak carrying the tracking disc had stopped on the edge of a cornfield to let a freight train pass.

"I don't see 'em," the driver of the other van reported. "We're in the middle of nowhere. There's a parked Amtrak blocking our view. They must be on the other side of it."

That's when Al knew he'd been punked. He put his hand to his temple. A vein was pulsing furiously. "They're not on the other side of it, you dumbfuck!" he screamed. "They're nowhere near there!"

"Where are they?" came the confused reply.

Al hung up and punched the wall, which was made of concrete, the uncontaminated kind. He didn't scream, but he knew he'd fucked up. The next morning, after a night of throbbing misery, he did something rare for him—he consulted a doctor.

"These metacarpal fractures usually heal up pretty fast if you leave them alone," the hand specialist who looked to be about nineteen cheerfully informed him. "You shouldn't be in that cast more than six weeks."

Al was in a hydrocodone-and-gin haze as Cus and Aurora headed back toward Tiberius on a Greyhound bus. They had left Cus's truck in a long-term lot in Hackensack. Less chance of being followed. Meanwhile, Cus had changed his mind on the use of his byline. He was too responsible to abide by his decision to not have his name on the story. He didn't want her out there by herself, facing the fury of the Tiberius underworld as the lone face of the story. They were in this together.

So, during the bus ride, he had added his byline above hers and a separate section in the story disclosing his intimate relationship with the wrongdoers:

For the Informer*'s senior investigative reporter Custer Stanton, who is cowriting this story, the overwhelming evidence of unlawful toxic waste disposal hits home. Stanton's father-in-law is Al Holmes, president and CEO of Cold Harbor Concrete. Stanton's wife, Jenny Holmes-Stanton, is the company's vice president of operations.*

While conflict-of-interest concerns normally preclude a reporter from investigating family members, exceptions have been made in extreme cases, particularly when the public is at risk.

John Barger, a media ethics professor at Northeastern University in Boston, noted that a journalist who suspects serious crimes have been committed by a relative has several choices: Say nothing, tell the police, funnel the information to another reporter, or pursue the story as if there were no family connection.

"The last option, one could argue, is the most ethical, assuming the journalist discloses his relationship to the public," Barger said. "It all gets back to transparency. Ethicists don't just assess conduct. We assess whether there were efforts to conceal conduct."

Aurora scanned the last paragraph and laughed as the

bus rumbled through another poorly maintained stretch of Pennsylvania highway.

"I love journalism," she said. "You can always find someone to say anything."

"You don't agree with him?" Cus asked.

"I agree with whatever makes you feel good," she said and ran her slender hand up and down his thigh.

"Not here," he said, meaning it, and she pulled back.

"Muy serioso." She pouted. The bus rolled on.

They knew it was too dangerous to stay at Aurora's apartment. Al's henchmen would be all over it. So for the night, they booked Winkel Haus, a B&B in Xenophon with a two and a half star rating. They'd found it on Tripadvisor. The drizzly walk from the Xenophon Greyhound station was less than half a mile.

From the bus station, they took different routes to the lakeside cottage. It improved the chances that at least one of the scribes would survive to shepherd the story into print in the event of an abduction or worse. Aurora grew up hearing terrifying accounts of pedestrians thrown into cars in Guatemala. It could happen here, too.

But they arrived unscathed at the cramped lobby almost simultaneously.

"Who was Xenophon?" Aurora whispered.

Before Cus could answer, a heavy German-accented voice shouted from a back room. "A Greek philosopher! I tell you more in a moment!"

A minute later, a stocky man in his fifties in lederhosen emerged, apologizing for the delay and blaming his wife for calling him at an inconvenient time. He introduced himself as Dieter.

"Wives can be difficult sometimes," Cus dryly concurred.

"Oh, but you must never say such a thing in front of your own wife, especially to this lovely lady," Dieter chided.

They let it go. Who cared what Dieter thought? It was only one night.

The check-in process was slowed by Dieter sharing details about the town and its namesake—the great historian, military leader, and philosopher Xenophon, who promoted civic virtue.

"I gave a lecture about him once at the University of Chicago," Cus informed their host. "Long time ago."

Aurora looked at him in wonder.

Sadly stripped of his incentive to impart more knowledge of Xenophon, Dieter checked them in. "Zee cocktail hour is at four o'clock," he said, handing Cus an enormous antique key. "Vee have several excellent local Rieslings and one from my hometown of Oestrich-Winkel. Maybe I see you for a drink and later in zee hot tub."

"Doubtful," Cus said. "But thanks anyway."

The room was a third the size of the one in Netcong. A four-poster bed took pride of place but also notable was a suffocatingly large collection of decorative pillows. The place gave them the creeps, but it was perfect in its quirky obscurity for two crusading journalists with civic virtue on the agenda.

"I'll pick up the car," Aurora said, referring to their prearranged rental. "Stay here and relax."

They had a busy Saturday night in front of them. After an early dinner and the briefest of naps—even Aurora wasn't in the mood for intimacy, in part because a row of antique child bride dolls was staring down at her—they commenced their final commute to the *Informer* in a black Chevy Malibu.

"The word scoop doesn't even do this story justice," Aurora almost shouted. "It's just so . . . enorme."

"I know," Cus calmly replied. "Let's not think that way, though. We need to stay in the moment."

He dropped Aurora across the street from the *Informer*. She slipped silently into the near-empty newsroom and hunkered down at a terminal well across from her usual workstation. Everything was on schedule. In thirty minutes, the presses would roll with the Holston County edition, which would carry their mega-scoop.

Thanks to her copy editing skills, Aurora had the easier job, assuming she wasn't discovered. It would just be a matter of coding their story, plugging in the material Cus would send via WhatsApp, writing a headline, captioning three photos, and using her cursor to drag the whole package into the spot occupied by the lame lead story: "A-peeling to History: Tiberius Dome to Serve Apple Whiskey." Then it was a matter of hitting the typeset button, and Staley would do the rest downstairs.

Cus found a spot on nearby Poplar Street and took out a notepad and his burner phone. Then he took a deep breath. The most uncomfortable interview of his career was next.

Al answered the phone with his usual charm. "Who's this?"

"Hi, Al. It's Cus. Do you have a few minutes to talk?"

"About what?"

"About toxic waste. I'm working on a story about—"

Al interrupted. "What the fuck! You're interviewing me?"

"Correct. We've been looking into—"

"Where are you?"

"Why does that matter?"

"Jenny says you disappeared. You run away with that little fajita?"

Cus refused to be thrown off track. "We have records, interviews, and photographs showing Cold Harbor has been collecting hazardous waste at multiple locations and mixing it into concrete then pouring it all over town. Do you have any comment?"

Al said nothing, then, "My comment is I don't do phone interviews with assholes."

Cus considered this for a moment. Al didn't get to be Al by being stupid. He was setting a trap. "Under normal circumstances, I'd meet you to talk in person," Cus said, "but I have a crossbow phobia."

"I have no fucking idea what you're talking about."

"I can't talk to you in person, Al."

"Pussy."

"So, what's your comment?"

"Fuck you."

"Double fuck you, pencil dick!" he heard Jenny yell from the background. The line went dead.

Cus hadn't known his wife was on speakerphone, but in this case it was helpful. He pulled up WhatsApp and sent a single sentence to Aurora: "Al Holmes and Jenny Holmes-Stanton both declined comment."

Much cleaner that way.

Aurora's fear, not shared by Cus, was that Al would launch into a long-winded denial/explanation that would blow their deadline. That was in theory a flaw in their scheme—the chance, however unlikely, that Al would handle the interview calmly and at length. But Cus knew Al better than Al knew Al. As a trained observer of the human condition, Cus understood that the rich and powerful tend to overinvest in the traits that made them rich and powerful. In Al's case, intimidation and bullying had made him rich, so that's where he reflexively went now, a self-destructive human tornado of hubris, rage, and narcotics.

"I'm going to kill that son of a bitch myself if he prints that story," Al screamed at his daughter.

"There's not going to be a story," Jenny said with resolve. "Everything's going to be all right, Dad. I promise."

Meanwhile, things were going swimmingly for Aurora. She'd sent the new lead page and the jump page down to Staley in the composing room.

"We're good," he'd texted her.

She was just about to tell Cus to pick her up in the visitor parking lot when she caught a flash of white heading toward her usual desk, now unoccupied. Someone had alerted security. She couldn't tell if it was two or three officers, and she didn't stick around to find out.

She tried calling Staley from the stairwell, but by now the presses were running with their story. He couldn't hear his phone. She sent him a text and copied it to Cus: "Security hunting me. Hiding in stairwell."

Cus froze. Should he go in and rescue her or wait for further instructions?

"Just stay there for now," she texted him. "Te amo."

Staley checked in. "Can you get to the pressroom?" he texted Aurora.

"I'll try," she replied.

"Heading to the pressroom," she texted Cus.

As Cus agonized in the Malibu, Aurora made her way to the pressroom, where Staley was waiting for her. Her instinct was to duck out of sight, but Staley motioned not to bother. "Nobody down here gives a shit," he said.

Aurora saw another pressman in the distance and possibly a third on the other side of the hulking offset press. But that was it. This place was even deader than the newsroom.

It was Al, of course, who had touched off the search by calling the publisher to ask why he was being interviewed by the "Daily Dick Smoker, my son-in-law, no less." "If I go down, you go down, too, B.J.!" he screamed at Hayden, who was enjoying a soak in his Jacuzzi and initially had no idea what Al was talking about.

Eventually, Hayden understood that two of his reporters were working on the very story he'd ordered his quislings to quash.

"You needn't worry, Al," Hayden said with implacable patrician cool. "I'll put an end to this. No one's going to prison."

"You better hope not," Al menaced. "Because I will be right there in the shower with you, auctioning off your pasty Brahmin ass to the highest bidder. Count on it."

Al hung up, and Hayden restarted the spa jets, which covered his own profanities. "Those mother-fucking motherfuckers," the privileged grandson of a Rhode Island media tycoon squealed.

Despite their fury, neither co-conspirator considered the story imminent. Hayden's first thought after Al dressed him down was to phone Meekes, the managing editor he had enlisted to dissuade Cus from pursuing the story. Meekes was home but passed out in his recliner with a half-drained bottle of Dewar's. He never heard his phone ringing because he'd left it upstairs in the bathroom. Not until the next morning would he check his voice messages and hear Hayden's rant.

Hayden climbed out of the tub and put on his robe. Then he called the newspaper's director of IT, Asa Montclair, who answered on the first ring.

"We've got trouble," Hayden said.

"What kind of trouble?"

"Rogue reporter trouble."

"Let me guess: Cus Stanton and Aurora Connolly."

"Correct. I need you to block them from the system immediately."

"Do you want me to disable their email accounts, too?"

"Leave those. I doubt they're using our email anymore, but we can see what's coming in."

"Good thinking. Uh-oh."

"Talk to me."

"Looks like Connolly logged in recently."

"Remotely?"

"Hold on."

Two minutes later, Montclair returned to the phone to tell Hayden it was taking longer than expected. "I've never done this remotely before," he said.

Hayden poured himself two fingers of Scotch and downed it in one gulp. When Montclair resurfaced, his voice had an edge.

"She logged on in the newsroom forty-seven minutes ago."

"Concerning." Hayden said. "Make sure it's the last time."

He hung up and ordered security to hunt down Aurora, but like everything else at the *Informer*, that operation had been downsized as well. There was only so much ground the not-so-dynamic security duo could cover. With flagging interest and labored breathing, the two hitched up their Dockers and hiked the perimeter of the complex, flashlights probing shrubs and shadows. Nothing. Meanwhile, out went the trucks, dozens of them, not just to Holston County, but now to the inner suburbs and into Tiberius itself. The blockbuster seventy-two-point headline rivaled in size the one used for the attack on Pearl Harbor.

TOXIC CONCRETE

Embedded waste a health threat, experts warn

Illegal Operation used by hundreds of businesses, including *Informer*

Staley popped a green hardhat on Aurora's head.

"OSHA rules," he said. "Follow me."

As casually as if he were strolling out for a smoke break, Staley walked Aurora out to the loading platform and to the driver's side of the rumbling circulation truck.

"Hey, Archie, you're heading to the outlets, right?" Staley shouted up to the driver. The West Village Outlets mall was a major staging area where contractors lined up to grab bundles of papers, which were promptly or not so promptly delivered to convenience marts and homes.

"Same ol', same ol'," Archie replied.

"This is Aurora Connolly from the newsroom. You mind running her out there? She has car trouble. Her boyfriend's picking her up there."

"Not a problem," he said, surveying Aurora approvingly. "I've read your stuff. You're good. If I was your boyfriend, I'd drive here to get you."

"He's working," she said, with a little frost.

As Aurora was about to hop into the cab of the truck, Staley said to her under his breath, "Just have Cus meet you out there. Tell him they're having a sale on ladies' underthings."

"Cus is a stud," she said, then she stood up on her toes and kissed Staley on the cheek. "And so are you."

"I hope I'll be getting one of those, too," Archie tried, and they were off.

Aurora slunk down to avoid being seen, but there was no one around. She took out her phone and texted Cus. "All good here. In a delivery truck. Meet me at the outlet mall. Our story looks great. We did it!"

Cus wasn't in any position to check his phone. Nothing in his makeup made it possible to sit passively in a rental car on a side street while the only woman he ever truly loved was in danger. He bolted from the car and jogged to the back of the plant and up the stairs of the parking garage, crouching behind pillars and passing the same planter Staley had fatefully used as an outdoor toilet.

When Cus stepped inside the building and passed the elevators, he saw a familiar face, Andy Torgelson, the assistant photo editor, heading for his car. Cus had never warmed to Torgelson, who wore his blond hair in a bun and had a reputation as a player. Cus could smell a cad from a mile away.

"Working the late shift?" Torgelson offered as they passed.

"Or the early shift," Cus rejoined, and something clicked. The photographer who had snapped compromising photos of Cus and Aurora in the lactation lounge—it had been Torgelson. Cus couldn't prove it, but he knew it in his gut and his gut rarely betrayed him.

He also realized that Torgelson might know security was chasing Aurora. If true, the photographer would be alerting them to Cus's whereabouts, which is exactly how it played out. Three glorified mall cops—there was a third, after all—were waiting for him on the second-floor landing of the same stairwell where Aurora had briefly hidden. His route down to the pressroom was blocked.

Cus pivoted with the quickness of a running back and dashed back up the stairs three at a time. He reentered the newsroom and blocked the fire door with a desk that had been vacant since the book critic was laid off in 2004. He knew they'd be coming for him from a different direction, but now he had time to check his phone. He smiled. Aurora and their scoop had made it out safely.

"See you at the outlets," he texted her back, omitting his current predicament so she wouldn't worry. "Yo también te amo."

Now the sweaty, panting security team rushed him. All three flatfoots had their batons out. Nothing in their four-week training program prepared them for what came next.

A regulation canne de combat fighting stick is ninety-five centimeters long—just over a yard—and made of chestnut. The sport became popular in the nineteenth century among the French upper class. It resembles a combination of fencing and Taekwando as fighters jump, spin, and thrust to gain advantage.

A pica pole, meanwhile, is a specialized ruler used in newspaper layout before computers took over. An antique brass one hung on the wall near the city desk, a nod to publishing days ofeyore.

Cus snatched it off its hook. Although it was two feet shorter than the fighting stick he had trained with as a younger man, it would do nicely.

He went for the fat one first, knocking him off his feet with a sideways blow. Then he jumped up on a desk that had sat empty since the higher education reporter was laid off in 2007. The extra elevation was almost too much of an advantage for the rangy reporter. He had to bend at the waist to take on the shortest of the three assailants. He deftly jumped over a baton headed for his shins, stepping on it, and rained blows on the guard's head. The rent-a-cop released his grip. Cus followed with a lightning-fast kick to the man's chest—a violation of the sport's rules, but so be it—and sent him sprawling backward.

Cus claimed the baton for himself. Now, armed with two weapons, he launched himself onto the desk that had sat empty since the courts reporter quit to go to law school in 2009. He hopped down and flew at the final officer with cyclonic fury, the baton and the pica pole whipping the air like turboprops. That guard was the smartest of the three. He dropped his baton and ran.

Cus ran, too—back down the stairs and into the empty main lobby. He burst out of the *Informer*. Two minutes later, he was back in the Malibu. "On my way," he texted Aurora.

He zoomed down Poplar and turned right on Arsenal Way, heading west in the general direction of the outlets and, coincidentally, Cold Harbor Concrete. He saw one of their trucks on the road, odd for this hour. As it roared past him in the opposite direction, and way too fast, Cus recognized the driver. It was Jenny. He also observed that the pusher axle was engaged, indicating the barrel was at least partially full—but with what? Cold Harbor wasn't a round-the-clock operation. Whatever was in there wasn't concrete.

Soon enough, the contents would be known to all. Her load was 10,000 pounds of infectious hospital waste —pus, blood, urine, nasal swabs, blood, tumors, tissue, bone, feces. All of it was to be mixed into a four-inch slump the next morning and poured into the foundation of a new varsity training center at Tiberius University. But Jenny had a different repurposing in mind. Consumed by rage, jealousy, and fealty to her deranged father, she sped toward the print plant. What did she have to lose? Disgrace, financial ruin, and prison?

Cus made a U-turn and pulled alongside her, honking and

gesturing for her to pull over. "Jenny!" he screamed through the open passenger window. "Don't!"

His wife looked him in the eye. The deadness of her face lifted and quickly turned to fury. She yanked the steering wheel to the left, a dangerous move in a mixer truck at any speed. Jenny didn't care. She just wanted Cus dead.

The Malibu careened onto the sidewalk and into a hedge. By the time Cus got the car back on the road, Jenny was two blocks ahead running a red light. He saw her turn toward the plant.

By then, Staley was enjoying the sight of the unauthorized edition running off the press. The run was almost complete, all 65,000 copies—down from two-and-a-half times that twenty years ago. To celebrate, Staley did Staley. He grabbed a copy hot off the press, moved to a more discreet location, unzipped his greasy work pants, and urinated on the transfer cylinder housing of the great roaring beast. As he relieved himself, he held Cus and Aurora's story aloft with his free hand and noticed a bit of tinting in one of the halftones probably attributable to calcium buildup on the rollers.

Cus heard the impact from a quarter mile away. The 35,000-pound bio-bomb barreled through the glass and steel print plant, smashed into the feeder housing, and rolled over on the driver's side just as Staley was zipping himself. He never knew what hit him.

Cus gunned the Malibu toward the smoking, hissing wreckage. Somehow, the press was still laboring to print newspapers, but the newsprint was backing up and gumming the works. Hammering and screeching filled the air, but more ominously, a foul-smelling, green liquid oozed from the mixer truck. Ziplock bags containing everything from biopsied lung tissue to gall bladders were strewn about. Nearby, a stream of cyan, one of the four ink tones used in printing along with black, yellow, and magenta, pooled under the truck. Cus saw that Jenny was regaining consciousness in the cab. Staley was beyond dead. There was no need to check for a pulse.

"You better Uber back to the Winkel Haus," Cus texted Aurora. "There's been an incident. RIP Kyle Staley and the Golden Age of Print."

Woody finally stops writing. It's 5:52 a.m. on the Great Writers wall clock on whatever day it is. He doesn't care.

"Holy shit, this is really good," he congratulates himself.

CHAPTER 21
THE LEDGE

All he needs now is an epilogue and some self-rationalization. He has kept his promise to himself. He has written a great novel, or at least a very, very good one. Yet in doing so, he has broken his promise to Mandy. He hasn't rehabilitated Al Holmes, let alone his daughter, Jenny. They're more evil and unhinged than earlier in the book. He tells himself it won't matter when the book is a national bestseller. All will be forgiven. Even Kaylon will get it. His advice, however well intended and wise, skipped lightly past one of life's great truths: Meaningful achievement only happens with sacrifice.

Woody reminds himself he is merely the vessel for an imaginary world so skillfully rendered that it runs itself. He's just a typist now, a mere conduit to a power only a chosen few can access. The key is to finish the thing and accept the consequences, good and bad.

Two days later, he's in his library carrel overlooking the *Blaze*.

"Book is done," he texts Nick, who texts back immediately, rare for him.

"Awesome. Can you read me the ending?"

Having an audience again excites Woody. He locks himself in the restroom so he can read without drawing the ire of the two homeless people at a nearby desk.

"You did this to me," Jenny said, spreading her arms to put his focus on her orange prison suit. "Everyone here hates me."

As they should, Cus thought.

"As they should," Jenny acknowledged, as if reading his mind.

A guard interrupted a conversation at the adjacent table. "Ma'am, I need you to hand over your phone. They're prohibited, as the sign says."

The woman stared icily at the guard but complied. Cus wondered what she was up to with her phone much as he had been wary of the girl foodcasting her lunch at Panera. Phones were handheld spying devices, and they were everywhere. He wondered if the prisoner the woman was visiting might be a collaborator of Jenny's, with Al listening in on his conversation.

Al had not been charged with killing anybody—yet. He remained free on bail but had been indicted on eighteen state and federal charges. He was in deep trouble, which made him more dangerous.

"I never testified against you," Cus told his wife.

"You testified against my father!" Jenny spat. "Same difference."

"That's not fair, Jenny. How was I supposed to know your dad would turn state's witness against his own daughter?"

His words sounded false even to him. After all, Al Holmes was the kind of man who had no moral qualms about tempting his future son-in-law with a hooker.

"Seriously?" she asked, sipping water from a paper cup. "You're a fucking idiot if you didn't see that coming. Or a liar. Is that what you really are, sweetie, for all your self-righteous, tree-hugger bullshit? A fucking liar?"

He barely recognized her voice. It had turned hard and husky. The guard intervened again. "Watch the language over there. We have minors in the room."

Jenny dropped her voice to a hiss. "You could have just divorced me and been done with it. But that's not how the Boy Scouts roll, is it?" She raised her right hand and gave him the three-fingered

Scout salute. "Be prepared, Cus," she said with menace. "No, really."

Cus sighed, suddenly feeling much older than his years. Some gray had come in at the temples, making him look even more handsome if that were possible—but gray is still gray.

"I did what's right for the community at large and for future generations," he said.

"Congratulations, Saint Asshole."

"I never meant for you to be here."

She glared at him. "It's not all bad. The girls in E Block have tongues harder than your cock."

"I should go."

"Good idea. Maybe we can get a drink and catch up in twelve years, three months, and eighteen days."

"I'd like that," Cus lied.

She laughed the husky laugh of a moll who had her father's thirst for vengeance. "You're not dumb enough to think you'll still be alive then, do you?"

Cus felt a pinprick of fear but just as quickly it disappeared, replaced by a satisfying calm.

The Pulitzer Prize he shared with Aurora had brought him professional peace without complacency. Cus appreciated the recognition, but it wasn't nearly as meaningful as what he had seen while driving out to the prison: work crews replacing contaminated Cold Harbor concrete on a pedestrian bridge spanning wetlands frequented by herons and bald eagles. That's all the recognition Custer Stanton needed.

"I'll never regret having loved the person I thought you were, Jenny," he said. "Take care of yourself."

He nodded to the guard and exited the visitation room, a quiet hero striding confidently into the unknown. Difficult as it was, he had done his job. His father-in-law would be incarcerated as well, joining the publisher and Bill Wilde, the previous director of press operations. The new director, Shane Sheldon, had spared himself the trouble and hanged himself in the pressroom decontamination shower. Tommy the Torque Wrench and Kyle Staley were dead, the latter a martyr, having given his life for democracy, press freedom, and a greener planet.

There would be more stories and more prizes for Cus and Aurora until the *Informer* was sold to a new corporate owner, Hamlin-Archer Enterprises, newspaper disembowelment specialists. H-A did not need a runaway mixer truck to blow up the *Informer*. Flipping the property to a condo developer accomplished the same thing. But by then Cus and Aurora had already launched a journalism foundation in Guatemala and were finalizing plans to move there and get married.

Outside the prison, Cus imagined his future bride in her wedding dress and smiled. But only for a moment. Daydreaming was not his forte. In this crazy, upside-down world, all that mattered was moving forward, action, the now.

Now was 5:08 p.m.

Cus reached instinctively for his notebook. He was still employed by the *Daily Informer*. The newspaper, although disgraced by horrific scandal, had been paradoxically redeemed by its most fearless reporter, who had declined a generous buyout.

He checked his phone and saw that the two stories he'd filed earlier were still leading Tiberius.com. A rabid raccoon had bitten a pair of Jehovah's Witnesses, and powdery mildew was attacking local apple orchards.

Both stories needed updates. He took a cleansing breath and walked purposefully to his truck. As he drove, he rolled down the windows. The prison scent of body odor and ammonia lingering in his nostrils gave way to honeysuckle and woodsmoke. This was Custer's last stand in Tiberius, but it was not the end. As long as his byline remained in the *Daily Informer*, light would be no stranger to truth.

Custer Stanton had work to do.

"That's really good," Nick critiques. "Are you in a submarine? There's an echo."

"Let me take you off speakerphone," Woody says. "You liked it?"

"It's great. One question: Did they win the Pulitzer for Public Service or Investigative?"

"Why does it matter?" Woody asks.

"I was just curious. My package on the Apache helicopter was a finalist for Public Service. The numbnuts at *The Apocalyptic* should have entered it in Investigative, but they didn't."

Woody isn't pleased. Just this once, he wants Nick's undivided attention on the book.

"In a sense, my book turned out to be a paean to a dead industry," Woody tries. "It's not about my in-laws after all."

"Correct," Nick says. "You pulled it off. Hey, I gotta take a call. Talk later?"

Woody's irritation with Nick's signoff doesn't last. By the time he's home that afternoon, his pique has given way to pride in himself beyond measure. He's done it. He's finished the son of a bitch. He settles in on his back porch with a whiskey and one of his occasional Cohibas saved for special moments like these. The cold, dry air invigorates him. He feels alive but also alone. For obvious reasons, he can't share the moment with the other occupants of the house.

JB's probably best not disturbed either. He's vacationing with his wife in Thailand, cavorting with elephants and taking outdoor cooking classes. Plus, there's the twelve-hour time difference—it's 4 a.m. there. Woody texts him anyway. "Hope you're having a blast in the Land of Smiles. All smiles here. I finished the book."

No response.

Briefly, he considers texting Celeste.

No.

Maybe?

No. Maybe once it's published. Nope, not even then. Let her discover his book at Book 'n' Bean, her pretentious hangout. What an awful person. Sexy and beautiful and really good at her job. And funny, too. But so damaged.

That leaves Melvin Stern.

"I finished it," he messages Stern.

"Holy shit!" Stern replies. "That didn't take long."

"Mind if I give you a call and read you the ending?"

"Luv to hear but I'm w my kids," Stern types back. "It's my birthday. I'll read it Monday when I'm back in the office."

Woody feels needy and childish. "Didn't mean to intrude," he replies. "Happy birthday."

A wind from the north kicks up just enough to make the patio uncomfortable. Woody snuffs his victory cigar, swigs the rest of his whiskey, and heads back inside.

"Why were you smoking a cigar?" Mandy asks.

"No reason. Just felt like it," he answers. His self-congratulatory buzz recedes, replaced by humanity's oldest question: Is this all there is? He tries not to let it bother him as he carves a hunk of banana bread Ella made. A little letdown is understandable, just the creative mind rebooting—a healthy byproduct of The Process. That's how the journey is for serious writers. Lonely.

Although, on second thought, plenty of serious writers partied their asses off: Fitzgerald, Capote, his boy Hemingway. He does a quick search on his phone and is soon skimming a long list of literary revelers that includes Oscar Wilde, Dylan Thomas, and Zora Neale Hurston.

If anything, the writer-as-recluse thing is a trope, more romanticism than reality. Yes, some writers walk alone—Thoreau, for instance. But that guy was weird, out there in his shack in the woods. Surely the children of Concord were forbidden to go within five hundred yards of that creepy hidey-hole. Woody isn't like that. He isn't a hermit. He's just a regular guy with elite writing talent.

He flashes back to the 10K runs for the Cure that the *Blaze* sponsored before the suits killed that, too.

That day, his overlapping goals were to raise five hundred dollars to fight breast cancer and to stay within visual range of Celeste in her pink shorts. Woody feels a twinge of nostalgia laced with bitterness. The place spit him out just like *The Apocalyptic* is spitting out Nick. This is what the world does. Maybe Kaylon's right.

"Great banana bread," Woody shouts to Ella. "So moist."

"Dad, it's way better with whipped cream," she replies from the TV room.

Woody's hit with a lot the following week. Gratifying news comes six agonizing days after Stern promised to read Woody's ending.

"You nailed it, bro!" Stern exhorts. "Yes, it's overwritten, but that's your style. We can always rein it in. But I dare anyone to start reading this and put it down. No. Fucking. Way. It's a cyclone. You get swept up in it, and you're not coming down."

Stern's especially pleased by how Woody has firmed up the chemistry of the embedded hazardous materials. "You shoved it right up Seth Zimmerman's ass, although you realize that isn't how he's going to see it. He's going to take credit for saving the book. Let him. If that's what makes his wee-wee hard, fine."

Huge laugh, and this time it's not just Stern.

There's a coda to the good news. Stern's "not at liberty to name names," but a "respected publisher" of mystery and crime fiction is "extremely interested" in *Fear as Mud*.

"Don't let it go to your head, but you are on the threshold of accomplishing something that doesn't happen anymore. No new author sells a book practically over the transom these days to one of the Big Five. Frankly, it didn't happen much in the best of times. This is special stuff."

"It wouldn't be happening without you," Woody says, feeling strangely distant.

Booming laugh.

"No shit, Sherlock. You can make it up to me by spending the next eighteen months whoring your book at every Barnes & Noble on the continent and thanking me by name. How do you feel about Spokane in February?"

More laughter.

Then a terrifying development—a text message from his father-in-law.

"Let's have lunch," the message says. "Just us. I'll buy."

They meet at The Ledge, a woodsy honky-tonk overlooking three-tiered Haniger Falls. Unless there's a band playing, the area sees little traffic aside from an occasional dog walker. Woody didn't even know The Ledge served lunch.

During the two days prior, he works himself into a paranoid fever. Somehow, Joe knows—knows the book is still out there, knows about his deception. Of course, he knows. Joe has people everywhere.

Woody recalls once stopping at an ice cream stand in tiny Caleb thirty miles north of Icarus. He saw Joe a few days later at the Double A Tubers game.

"Maple nut ice cream with pineapple topping?" Joe had remarked. "Sounds disgusting."

Before Woody could process the comment, Joe gave him an "I see you" sign that seemed like joking at the time. But was it?

Now, Woody's scared. It's a trap—life imitating art. The writer ruminates on Tommy bludgeoning that fish. Is Joe scheming a similar fate for Woody? Woody fixates on Joe's director of security, Rubin "Big Ruby" Laughton, an arthritic but-still-menacing former defensive lineman for the Magenta. Woody's on good terms with Big Ruby, but so what? He hardly knows the brute beyond a vivid sense of his thirst for violence.

Years earlier, when Ella was little, Big Ruby made Woody an unsolicited promise to "destroy anyone who even thinks of trying to dick with you or your family."

"Appreciate it," Woody had meekly replied.

Rumor had it that Big Ruby had used an ice knife to dispatch an unbalanced employee who hinted at shooting up the warehouse when he was let go for failing a pee test.

Woody's fear inspires him to ask his friend for a favor. "Can you follow me to The Ledge and wait in your car?" he beseeches JB. "Just to keep an eye on things. Make sure nobody throws me in a van or something."

JB looks up from the motorcycle carburetor he's rebuilding. He's weary of Woody's dramatics.

"Sorry, dude, I can't do that."

"Why not?"

"One, I'm busy. I have a job. Two, from everything I've heard from you and others, your father-in-law has as much Don Corleone in him as Joni Mitchell does. Three, if I'm wrong, is it really in my interest to be the guy in the parking lot who might have seen something? Have a nice lunch."

Woody backs off. As usual, JB makes sense. Even so, Woody makes the thirty-minute drive to The Ledge in a fear sweat. About halfway there, he notices a gray sedan following him. Two left turns and a right turn later, the sedan still trails him as he wheels onto Route 8 and crosses the county line. By the time Woody reaches the homemade wooden sign for the joint, he's near panic, clutching his phone and praying the sedan won't follow him down the dead-end dirt road. The sedan cruises past. Woody can see it's driven by a woman probably in her eighties.

"Grow a pair!" Woody admonishes himself.

"Pears are fruits produced and consumed around the world, growing on a tree and harvested in late summer into mid-autumn," Siri replies.

The private drive is narrower and longer than Woody remembers. A few slender branches rake his windshield. He slows through the potholes and passes a fenced-in substation. "KEEP OUT: High Voltage Inside May Cause Injury or Death," the sign reads.

Woody recalls the scene from *Batman* where Jack Nicholson's Joker electrocutes a rival with a joy buzzer, giddily informing the smoking corpse, "I'm glad you're dead! I'm glad you're dead!"

A turkey vulture pecks at a raccoon carcass in the road.

"Enough with the foreshadowing, already," Woody mutters.

He was last at The Ledge three years ago with a casual friend, Mike Albanese, an orthopedic surgeon. Local sexpot electric cellist Alison Chaudre was playing. Albanese was fixated on her. His other fixation, it turned out, was slapping the bare buttocks of anesthetized patients. It had been another Celeste Henry A1 scoop, one that had embarrassed Woody. It's never a good look for a reporter to have a friend in the news for the wrong reasons and to get scooped on the story by a colleague, no less.

Woody spots Joe's F-250 in the lot and finds him at a table in the back sipping a bottle of Miller.

"Thanks for coming out here," Joe says, half-rising to say hello but not extending a hand. "I'm not supposed to drink for a week prior to the surgery, but screw it. If it's my time, it's my time."

Woody doesn't want beer. He wants a ginger ale to settle his stomach. On the other hand, a nonalcoholic choice might come off as timid and distancing. "I'll have one of those," he says, gesturing at Joe's bottle.

"Excellent choice," the waitress says, and Joe winks at her.

Once she leaves, Joe says, "I wish we got together more often, just the two of us, you know."

"This isn't just lunch, is it?" Woody replies.

"No. I have an enormous favor to ask of you."

Woody's face hardens. Here it comes.

"How would you feel about taking Digger off our hands while I'm recovering?"

"Digger?"

"I know. It's a lot to ask, but . . ." Joe shrugs and lowers his eyes, a rare expression of humility.

"You want me to watch your dog?"

"For a month, maybe two. Until I can get around better. Bev has that bad hip. Thanks to my horseshit, she had to postpone getting it replaced, and he needs so much damn exercise. Ever since you took him on that eight-mile hike up to Lake Wetherby, you've been on his A-list, so I thought of you first."

"Of course, of course," Woody says. He doesn't know whether to cry or laugh. His beer arrives. He drinks half in one swig. Joe orders a cheeseburger. Woody settles on a turkey club.

"I'm all in on Digger," he assures his father-in-law. "You didn't have to bring me all the way out here to ask me that."

"I just wanted a little privacy. Trying to keep my health stuff close to the vest. Icarus is a small town."

"So, that's it—this is a pet-sitting request?"

"Like I said, it's a lot to ask."

"To the contrary, it will be a privilege and an honor."

They clink bottles.

"Another round, please," Joe says to the waitress when she arrives with their food.

"So, what else is going on?" Woody asks.

"Besides brain surgery, not much. I have been thinking about your book, by the way."

Blood rushes to Woody's face. This was all a setup, after all.

"I've been looking back on my life lately, no big surprise given the circumstances. What do you call it, introspection?"

"Retrospection, maybe. Either's fine."

"Well, as you probably know, I don't waste a lot of time with either. Life should be lived in drive, not in reverse, but there's a time for everything."

A hungry highway crew wearing high-vis vests enters the restaurant, talking loudly and filling a nearby table. Joe drops his voice a notch. "I don't have many regrets. I've lived a good life, an honest life, and I've been lucky as hell to make a lot of money doing it."

"You've worked hard for what you have," Woody says.

"Yes, I've worked hard *and* I've been lucky. The two go together."

"Your luck will continue on Tuesday," Woody says, referring to the surgery.

"Maybe. Then again, this could be our last meal together. I hope not, but it could be."

"Then you better pick up the tab."

Joe laughs. "I'll make a deal—I'll buy if you accept my apology."

"Apology for what?"

Joe swallows and briefly looks to the ceiling. "I never should have bullied you into dropping that book. That was wrong of me."

Woody's too stupefied to speak.

"I'm perfectly fine with you finishing the book, getting it published, and selling a million copies if that's in the cards. I was a schmuck for getting in the way."

Woody is now acutely aware of his own schmuckyness. His throat feels dry. "You don't have to apologize for anything," he croaks. "I'm sorry I made you guys look bad. That was never my intent."

"Look, if my reputation can't survive a potboiler about a guy who's the opposite of me in every sense, my reputation isn't worth a racoon turd anyway."

Woody looks at the highway workers who he initially feared might be Joe's death squad. The waitress says something to the workers, and they erupt in laughter.

"I mean, it's more than a potboiler," Woody protests. "It's a literary potboiler."

"Okay, fine, but, it ain't *Moby Dick.* All the more reason I shouldn't have made a big deal of it. Like I told you before, it's a fun read. Finish it. Publish it. I'm on board. Next subject: Did you see the Magenta landed that four-star kid from Fresno? Mamadou Gadiaga. A six-nine guard who can shoot."

Woody feels both relieved and lost. He had donned the cloak of persecuted literary figure and found it fit nicely. Now, in the space of a club sandwich and a couple of beers, it's gone. He's just another guy who wrote a book. Who cares?

"In Gadiaga we trust," Woody says.

"That's funny. Get the copyright," Joe says.

He signals to the waitress for the check. Mandy sends Woody a text with crummy news.

"Ella has strep," Woody reports.

"That's not good," Joe says. "Give her a hug from Grandpa."

Woody checks his phone again. "I'm supposed to pick up her antibiotics on the way home."

"You better go."

Woody starts to get up but sits down again. "The rest of the family thinks I'm a hero for dropping the book. I can't just tell them it's back on because you're now okay with it."

Joe sighs. "I thought of that. I'll talk to the gang. They'll be fine."

"You don't need to do that, Joe."

"I want to."

"That's not what I mean. I mean it doesn't matter. I don't have an ending. Without an ending, there is no book."

The lie tumbles easily from Woody, but this time it's not purely self-serving. He wants to distance Joe from the book's fate. Joe shouldn't be the heavy who bullies Woody into self-censorship or the good guy who gives Woody "permission" to publish his book. Joe should just go back to being Joe. He deserves that.

For a moment, Joe looks annoyed. "You want me to give you a fucking ending, too? That's not my department. I dig holes and blow shit up."

One of the highway workers looks their way. "I'm not asking you for an ending," Woody says.

Joe softens. "You'll figure it out."

A deep calm washes over Woody like the water spilling over Haniger Falls. He feels reborn as a man making his own choices, charting his own course. He doesn't need Nick, Celeste, Stern, Mandy, or anybody else to hold his hand. What he says next isn't forced. It's freeing. "The problems with the ending are intractable," he says, looking

Joe in the eye. "There's no solution. There never will be a solution."

"There's always a fix," says Joe, still not getting it. "Isn't that what writers do, work shit out?"

"This can't be worked out."

"You're giving up?"

"I didn't say that. I'm saying the ending will never be resolved."

Suddenly, it's clear that Joe understands Woody has an ending. But it will never see daylight. "You're the boss," he says, signing the credit card receipt and getting up. "Keep me posted on Ella."

Woody sits alone for a few minutes, absorbing the enormity of his sacrifice. He has abandoned his Art, and that should be a terrible thing, but instead it feels clean and liberating. He rises and strides through the parking lot to his Lexus.

A shout comes from a pickup nearby. Woody startles, but it's just JB.

"Everything good, Wood Man?"

Woody quickly appreciates that his friend had a change of heart.

"It's all good. Thanks for coming out."

"Pure self-interest. I realized if you were murdered, it might be bad for business."

"It might be good for business."

They bump fists.

"You're a good dude, JB."

"You'd do the same for me, right?"

"Nope."

Summer edges toward fall, and Woody remains at peace with his choice to cancel his book. His home life has never been happier. Ella is hanging out with him more, laughing at his jokes, asking for his advice. He's reading a ton and working on some freelance magazine pieces. He and Mandy get season tickets for Icarus In-the-Round.

By the time Ella heads to James Madison on a lacrosse scholarship the next year, she and her dad are buds. She held her grudge as long as she could, and one day it was gone. Yes, her dad screwed her over big time, but not on purpose. She's sharp enough to understand that it wasn't easy for Woody to quit his book, and that he did it, in part, for her.

All of this goes unspoken until the night before Woody and Mandy move Ella into her dorm. Woody pulls Ella aside and apologizes for the trouble his book caused her, leaving out the part that he kept working on it after he claimed he'd stopped.

"Dad, that was a million years ago," she admonishes him. "Let it go. We're good."

They hug and he tells her he loves her and she does the same.

Mandy descends into a fierce bout of empty nester blues. After weeks of near despondency, she shakes it off and proposes that she and Woody take a Thai cooking class. Woody's interest is near zero. There are eight good Thai joints within five miles of their home.

"Sounds like a blast," he enthuses.

The air dries out, and the leaves hint of colors to come. Husband and wife find themselves driving out to the Adirondacks to hike the forested peaks and kayak the cobalt lakes just as Custer Stanton would have. Just as they did before Ella. Only now, Digger trots ahead or rides regally in the kayak, sporting his orange *chaleco salvavidas*.

Joe comes back nicely from the draconian surgery. After three months, the doctors took him off the antiseizure meds, and his brain fog cleared. He's taking Tylenol for occasional headaches, but he's back at work, reasserting himself as Dunn-Rite's alpha. Mandy credits her husband's decision to spike the book for speeding her father's recovery.

"The stress would have killed him," she tells Woody.

Woody basks in Mandy's gratitude. Most days, he congratulates himself for making the right decision, the noble decision. He and Joe have resumed as before, their exchanges flecked by good-natured banter. In what for Joe constitutes the ultimate display of love, gratitude, and forgiveness, he lets Woody detonate a controlled implosion of a crumbling municipal parking garage. They never discuss *Fear as Mud* again.

But in other moments, he wonders if *Fear as Mud* was a test of his writerly dedication—a test he failed. He googles a Faulkner quote, prints it out, and push-pins it to the bulletin board in his office: "The writer's only responsibility is to his art. He will be completely ruthless if he is a good one. He has a dream. It anguishes him so much he must get rid of it. He has no peace until then. Everything goes by the board: honor, pride, decency, security, happiness, all, to get the book written. If a writer has to rob his mother, he wil not hesitate. The 'Ode on a Grecian Urn' is worth any number of old ladies."

Every time he sees the quote, he's tempted to call Stern to find out if he's still interested, but he talks himself out of it. After all, he has gotten "rid of it." He did write the book. What difference does it make if no one reads it? He'll just write another book. Who was it who said, "Stories are like Doritos. If one falls on the floor, you just grab another chip from the bag?" He can still use that line. He can harvest a lot of lines from *Fear as Mud*. His book will not be lost. It will serve as source waters for a mighty river of great works to come.

Breaking the news to Stern had been hard.

"Come on, Woody," Stern pleaded over the phone. "Don't do this. What can I say to get you to change your mind?"

"I'm sorry, Melvin. Nothing."

"Look, I wasn't going to say anything, but I've got connections out in Hollywood. How'd you like to see *Fear as Mud* up on the silver screen? Now, be prepared. I'm sure they'd want to extend the big crash scene to at least ten minutes, you know, have Jenny take out a school bus on her way to the print plant, crap like that."

"A school bus?"

"Maybe just tip the thing over without any kids getting hurt, or maybe Jenny doesn't clear a railroad crossing in time and a freight train grazes the rear-end of her mixer truck and derails and smashes into a fireworks stand. Kaboom! How fun would that be?"

"It's not the manifestation of my Art that I envisioned. But either way—"

"A musical then?" Stern was so desperate he tried to jolly Woody with an Ethel Merman imitation. "There's no business like mud business, like no business I know."

Woody laughed but he was dug in. "No."

Finally, Stern backed off. "I get it. I was always worried it might come to this. Family first, blah, blah, blah."

"Thanks, Melvin. I knew you'd understand. This isn't easy for me, either."

Stern graciously promised to look at anything Woody might write in the future. "Maybe in your next one you can develop your characters a bit more, especially the women, not that I'm any expert in that."

One last big laugh.

"Sure. Thanks."

"And if you could make the main character more marginalized, you know, anything but another White guy, that would help a lot. Just a tip."

"But I made Cus one-fourth Mohawk."

"It felt weak for the modern marketplace. Had we moved on to the next stage of editing, I would have asked you to make him half, probably on his mother's side."

"Why the mother?"

"Mother Earth. Nurturing. He inherits her sensitivity to the land. That kind of crap."

Nick had been another loose end. He had moved on from *The Apocalyptic* and was now vice president of a new think tank, Sage Group. He was freelancing weighty foreign policy articles and working on a short history of submarine warfare.

At first, he wasn't pleased to hear Woody had given up on *Fear as Mud.*

"Other than you, no one has put more intellectual energy into your book than I have. What a waste."

But they talked it through. The debacle at *The Apocalyptic* had tempered Nick's careerist impulses. He saw that even he wasn't immune to the vicissitudes of a cutthroat industry. That made him better able to grasp Woody's conclusion that the personal price of his book was too high. Woody, meanwhile, found himself less envious of Nick. Kaylon's family-over-all sermon had landed just as Woody's friend was being cast off by a publication that had lost its soul. None of this was an excuse to give up the chase, but it was cause to reassess priorities.

"I was just excited for you," Nick told Woody. "I had senior-grade officers in the Pentagon hooked on your book."

"There will be another book," Woody vowed.

So Woody sketches out a new novel. He will steer clear of even a passing inference to the family business and work doubly hard not to lean on personal experiences and relationships. But if there's some overlap, so be it. Ultimately, one's fiction is the sum of oneself. That's just how The Process works.

Tentatively at first, but then with growing confidence, he types out the first few lines of *Heart Beat*, the story of a brave reporter who stumbles onto an uncomfortable truth.

Salivating with fury, the Doberman charged past the police tape toward Choochai, a veteran reporter with the *Northern California Independent*. Choochai's affable disposition and rugged good looks could not help him now.

The dog's teeth sank into his left buttock—a painful bite that reminded him of when Thai security police chased him onto a beach, provoking a troop of violent monkeys. That night, the scribe's wife, Alana, pleaded with Choochai to seek medical care even though the bite wound hadn't seemed serious at first. As regional sales director for Ayerdorf-Pulsometrics, a leading pacemaker manufacturer, Alana was a worrier and a problem solver.

She was also, unbeknownst to Choochai, America's most prolific active serial killer.

Woody leans back and inspects the effort. He approves. The

Great Writers clock shows eight minutes past Herman Melville. Had it been up to Woody, he might have replaced Melville with another writer. He's not a fan. He wouldn't go around saying it to just anyone, but Melville's overrated.

Woody's fingers return to the keyboard.

"*Moby Dick,*" he murmurs, "can kiss my ass."

ACKNOWLEDGMENTS

So many people have donated so much time to help me finish this book that I wonder if I should have been a volunteer coordinator instead of a writer.

Long-time pal Michael Balchunas, a retired copy editor, ventured the first full read. Although he was struggling with a personal tragedy, the draft made him laugh. He made me believe that *Mud Season* could attract a quality publisher, and he was right. Koehler Books has been professional, flexible, and kind every step of the way.

It fell to other friends and former newspaper colleagues to slog through subsequent versions of *Mud Season*. Critical catches and critiques were provided by Clea Benson, Gigi Gilman, Andy Himes, Tonnie Katz, Ken and Helena Hartnett, Ana Menendez, Kristin Richardson, Terri Sforza, C. P. Smith, and Robert S. Williams.

Freelance editor Sherry Clark line-edited multiple drafts, and her formatting expertise was invaluable in readying the manuscript for submission.

Special thanks also to Steve Elders, for helping me get the details right on newspaper production, and to my friend Brian Harber, a real-life concrete mixer truck driver in Seattle who logged overtime as my technical adviser.

It was Brian's suggestion that I consult a chemist to make the story more plausible. I consulted two: Adjunct Professor Bill Carroll of Indiana University and industrial chemist Mark E. Jones. If I got something wrong with the alchemy in *Mud Season*, it's not their fault. It just means chemistry is hard. Allow me to hide behind poetic license.

I'd be a major jerk if I didn't thank my family. My wife, Leigh, has been with me for every word and every authorial expletive. Without her, there'd be no *Mud Season*. Our daughters, Miranda and Lily, weren't required to read the manuscript, but they did anyway, and they made it better.

Finally, a belated thank-you to my late, lovably gruff father-in-law, Bob Neumann, who ran his successful building materials company with impeccable integrity. It takes a larger-than-life presence to inspire not one but two fictional fathers-in-law, but that was Bob. I have only one regret about *Mud Season*—that he's not here to read it.

www.ingramcontent.com/pod-product-compliance
Lightning Source LLC
LaVergne TN
LVHW041749060526
838201LV00046B/952
* 9 7 9 8 8 8 8 2 4 6 4 9 8 *